Praise for the novels

"Sexy, smart, and sizzling w[...]
The Friendship Study is a delight. Jess[...]

—Ashley Herring Blake, author of *Delilah Green Doesn't Care*
and *Astrid Parker Doesn't Fail*

"Soft, sensual, and refreshingly bittersweet. Ruby Barrett expertly
portrays the visceral experience of being human—the way we crave,
the way we ache, and the way we heal—sometimes slowly, almost never
in a straight line. This is the rare book that can both singe off
your eyebrows and soothe a jagged piece of your soul."

—Rosie Danan, author of *The Roommate*, on *The Friendship Study*

"Reading a Ruby Barrett book is always like spending time with the
dearest friend. In *The Friendship Study*, Barrett so perfectly depicts
two lonely people who carefully, deliberately make their way to each
other. But when they can't keep their hands to themselves, will it
elevate their friendship or destroy everything? I was so invested in
Jesse and Lulu's journeys both together and as individuals."

—Alicia Thompson, bestselling author of *Love in the Time of Serial Killers*

"The feelings in this one are dialed up so high you almost can't look
at them directly: It would be like staring into the sun...
Like Rosie Danan or Kate Clayborn, Barrett has a way of
making palpable the full journey of a relationship."

—*New York Times* on *The Romance Recipe*

"Simply put, *The Romance Recipe* is a treat."

—*USA TODAY*

"In her debut, Ruby Barrett wrote one of my favorite romance heroes
of all time, but it's her heroines who shine in *The Romance Recipe*.
A prickly restaurant owner butts heads with her new chef in this
steamy f/f romance, which will be the perfect way to
celebrate Pride when it publishes this June."

—Meryl Wilsner, for *Entertainment Weekly*

"Sensual feasts abound, both in luscious culinary creations
and detailed sex scenes, as Barrett masterfully portrays
the sensation of infatuation growing into true love."

—*BookPage* on *The Romance Recipe*

"A down-to-earth queer romance."

—*Publishers Weekly* on *The Romance Recipe*

"Sexy, smart, and fiercely feminist."

—Helen Hoang, author of *The Kiss Quotient* and *The Bride Test*, on *Hot Copy*

Also available from Ruby Barrett

Hot Copy
The Romance Recipe

THE
FRIENDSHIP
STUDY

RUBY BARRETT

carina press®

ISBN-13: 978-1-335-47603-6

The Friendship Study

Copyright © 2024 by Ruby Barrett

For questions and comments about the quality of this book, please contact us at CustomerService@Harlequin.com.

® is a trademark of Harlequin Enterprises ULC.

Carina Press
22 Adelaide St. West, 41st Floor
Toronto, Ontario M5H 4E3, Canada
www.CarinaPress.com

Printed in U.S.A.

For all of us who have been told we're too much.

And for the ones who love us, who took one look and thought, if that's too much, I want more.

Chapter One

Jesse

Between the music and my pulse thrumming in my ears, I think the pounding on my front door is thunder. The sky outside my window is slate gray, the clouds full to bursting.

But the pounding comes again, along with the ring of my doorbell, the two-tone sound distinctly un-storm-like. I turn my music down as I drag a balled-up T-shirt over my sweaty chest. My heartbeat is still coming down from the last set of back squats and my thigh aches from when the leg was in traction. A phantom pain that the doctors have hummed about skeptically in the two years since.

The doorbell rings again, three times in quick succession. "I'm coming," I yell.

A broad-shouldered, stocky person stands on the other side of the glazed glass door. "George?" I ask as I yank it open, already knowing the answer. I'd recognize the shape of him anywhere.

He narrows his eyes and gives me a once-over, his lip curled in disgust. For a panicked moment, I wrack my brain for some event I've missed. One that I agreed to attend with him and forgot to cancel.

"You need a shower."

I look down at myself. He has a point. My sweat has acted like glue, sticking dirt and dust to my skin. I need a shower and clearly my home gym needs one, too.

"I was working out," I say stupidly.

He walks past me, careful to avoid skin-to-skin contact. George never liked to join me at the gym when we were together. We'd hit the yoga studio or spin class but he "declined to participate" in the toxic bro culture of most weight rooms. The result is that George has stacked, lean muscle and some of the best cardiovascular stamina of anyone I know. Since my accident he's tried to get me to come with him to yoga again, and I've even acquiesced a few times, but I'm positive I didn't agree to that today.

George stands in my entryway, his head swiveling between the living room and the kitchen.

"Not that it's not nice to see you but…what are you doing here?" I ask.

He nods once and, seeming to make a decision, moves into the kitchen, placing a tote bag I hadn't noticed on the counter and opening the fridge. Bottles and jars clink as he moves stuff around, placing a six-pack of beer inside.

This is officially weird.

The last time George drank beer, we'd stolen it from my grandfather's beer fridge in the garage.

A fly buzzes past me and my still-hot skin puckers against the cool air. I've left the door open. I pull it closed and follow him into the kitchen. "Did we have plans?" I finally ask.

The answer is no. I know that it's no. Not for his lack of trying. I've just been a terrible friend—ex—whatever, this past year…maybe even longer.

"Why don't you go shower, Logan. You stink." He places a bag of tortilla chips, a brick of cheese, sour cream, salsa, and avocadoes on my counter. He opens the cupboard at his feet. Shuts it.

"Where'd you put your casserole dish?" He sounds livid. Like rearranging my kitchen was a personal attack. But I'm still stuck on his use of my last name. He hasn't called me Logan since we were in high school. Since we were both dragging ourselves through comphet in public, while giving each other hand jobs in his parents' basement in private.

He came out first. By baking a cake and piping *I'm gay* in rainbow icing on top, serving it to his parents after dinner. They were happy for him. His mom cried—out of happiness that he'd shared such an important part of himself with them, not out of any sense of disappointment. George came out and came into himself.

I came out more slowly. First, just to him.

I * don't * just like girls, I'd typed into our private chat. Words I had written and deleted what felt like hundreds of times. The backspace button was practically smoking.

I know 😊, he'd responded. He'd promptly asked me on a date.

Then I came out to our friends, but since most of my friends were George's friends, other outcast kids he'd collected over the years, mostly queer theater kids, telling them felt less like coming out and more like landing in a loud, fluffy pillow of love and acceptance.

I came out to the fire station, too, but only after a few years on the job. After I made sure they saw my contributions as invaluable, and after a few of the old-guard vets, who used "gay" as an insult, had retired. For the most part, they were chill. A few blank faces that I'm sure were working hard not to show disgust, some confusion since bisexuality continues to be one of the most perplexing of all the sexualities known to straights. After I dropped a few "hose" jokes at my own expense, everyone calmed down. Since having sex in the firehouse, regardless of the gender of your partner, is expressly and certifiably prohibited, I didn't have to hide much. But I was always worried that someone—one of my older coworkers who kept in touch or a rookie who'd idolized him—would out me to Pop.

Even when we were dating, to Pop, George was always just a friend. My best friend, but *just* a friend. Back then, we'd used all of the same tools that straight boys used to emotionally distance themselves, including calling each other by our last names.

I probably don't have the right to the feeling, but *Logan* makes me angry. Pop isn't here and to George, I'm Jesse. Jess. I'd even accept *Juicy*, the name he called me only when he wanted to make me blush. A name I'd asked him to stop using once we stopped being boyfriends.

I let that anger dictate the next words out of my mouth. "Listen, you can't just barge in on a Saturday afternoon, *uninvited*, and start making lunch. What the hell are you doing here?"

"No, *you* listen." He points a finger at me. George has always been able to give as good as he gets. "I tried giving you space. We all did. You've got yourself some new job you didn't even tell me about, which is…whatever. You haven't been dating and I get why you might not want to share that with me, anyway. Hell, you're a private guy, Jesse. OK? I get it. But you are also my best friend." His words end on a sigh, losing all of their bluster.

He slides his hand across the countertop, the tips of our fingers touching. My heart squeezes and I hope it doesn't show up like it feels, a crack down the center of my face.

"You're my best friend, too." My voice is shaky, and I swallow the other words down, that he's the person I'm closest to in this world, other than Pop.

George doesn't let me off the hook, though. "You haven't been texting anyone back for months. You don't pick up the

phone. You didn't join the softball team this year. I'm trying
to be understanding, but I miss you."

After over a decade of knowing each other, George is used to
my silences. Still, I can't help but feel self-conscious about them.
I stare down at the old Formica countertop, trace my finger over
the faint brown crescent moon burned into it, marking the spot
where Grandma had once put a hot pot down without a trivet.

"So, you're going to shower," George says, softer. "And I'm
going to make this new nacho dip I found, and you're going
to drink beer, and we will watch some rugby match on whatever channel you pay too much money for. And we're going
to start again."

"Start again?"

"Our friendship," he says, quieter still. "We're going to re-
start it without the baggage of being exes and the decade that
we've already accumulated between us. We're just going to be
two queer dudes, hanging out. Being friends." He clears his
throat and clenches his jaw, a little embarrassed.

"The casserole dish is above the stove," I say after a moment.

The shower is too hot, then too cold. Never an in-between.
I dress still a little wet, my shirt sticking to my back. I putter
around my weight room, what used to be my bedroom until I
moved everything into the master bedroom last year, after Pop
moved into the assisted-care home. I wipe down the floor mats
I installed, and the bench, the bar and the plates, the mirror on
the wall, with an all-purpose cleaner.

Pre-match commentary blares as I enter the living room
and I join George on the couch, a bowl of chips and the casserole dish—now filled with some sour-cream-salsa-cheese
concoction—between us. "I also ordered a pizza," George
says, his eyes on the TV screen as if he's actually interested in
what two old white Welsh men have to say about these random teams' prospects this season.

I shrug and dip a chip. "It's good," I say with a full mouth.

He preens. George has a separate Instagram account dedicated to his cooking and baking projects. I assume he's already uploaded photos of this dish to the account. Meanwhile, I have an Instagram account I have forgotten the password to.

I sip my beer; it's still warm after too few minutes in the fridge. A rugby player drop-kicks the ball from the middle of the field. George scrolls his phone. Despite his claims that we are starting fresh, he's as comfortable here as I am. He's as familiar as the furniture that's been here for twenty years at least, the school pictures and my grandparents' wedding photos hanging over the fireplace; nothing's been changed since my grandmother was alive. The only new things in this house are the television and the close-cropped haircut I got last week.

Eventually, the boredom gets the best of him, and George regales me with the drama at his job. He's the administrator for the psychology department at the University of Wilvale, the school that's the only reason this town is on a map at all. George is also, slowly, getting his PhD part-time. He doesn't want to be a psychologist, he says. He just wants to be able to psychoanalyze our friends. Since this is the exact level of meddling I expect from him, I've never said anything about how he's spending a shit-ton of money to be able to dole out the best advice in our friend group.

"OK," George says, breaking the comfortable silence that has settled between us. "There's more to this intervention than just starting fresh." His voice is pitched high. He catches his lip between his teeth.

I freeze with the beer bottle halfway to my mouth. This is what his nerves are about.

"Don't be mad," he pleads.

I place my bottle on the coaster and resist the urge to say I'm not mad, I'm just disappointed. Because George does this. He's the king of not-always-welcome surprises. Most of the time I'm quiet because I don't know what to say but this time, I let the silence hang thick between us.

The doorbell rings. George winces at the door and back at me. "That's the food."

George's eyes are bigger than my stomach. I'm already full.

He says quickly, "You're going on a date tonight." Then gets up to answer the door.

"A what?" I ask when he comes back carrying a pizza box. Normally, I'd reach for my wallet, but he can cover this one. "A *date*?"

I'm not disappointed. I'm definitely mad. But underneath that anger is the gripping fear that makes it hard to speak, to breathe.

"Why?" I ask, then before he can answer, "With who? When? George, *why*?"

He slides the box onto the coffee table. "Just listen."

"No." I stand up. Sit down. It's been two years since my accident but in this weather—unseasonably cold, damp, the air heavy with rain that hasn't fallen yet—my leg stiffens, aches. I press my fist against it, as if the pressure on the muscle will distract my nerves from the metal in my bones, the muscles that were torn and shredded.

"No. I'm not going on a date with anybody. You can't do this to me, George."

"There's this woman who works at the university." He plows ahead as if I haven't already said an adamant and resounding absolutely the fuck not. "And we've become lunch buddies and we've been talking and she's really lonely—but gorgeous—and she hasn't been on a successful date in forever—I don't know why, she's lovely—and she reminded me of you."

He walks into the kitchen, the floorboards creaking under his feet. The sound of cupboards opening and closing drifts in over the quiet hum of thickly accented rugby match commentary. As if this is just a casual conversation and not George meddling in my personal life. Again.

"She reminds you of me because…we're both lonely and can't get dates?" I ask. "Do you know how rude that sounds?" I don't get angry often. Even now the feeling is burning up, leaving something empty and airless in its place. But my voice still trembles.

He comes back with two plates and starts doling out slices. "And I told her about you, and she said you sounded great and how about this Saturday, and I said I'd set it up and now…" he says, breathless. "It's Saturday."

"What if I had plans already?" I ask, as he shoves a plate into my hands.

He snorts.

"I didn't say I *did* have plans, just *what if*," I grumble.

"Maybe if you'd answer your phone or text me back once in a while," he hisses, his hand still gripping my plate. "We wouldn't be finding ourselves in this predicament."

George leans back, holding his plate up at his chest to avoid crumbs falling everywhere. He takes a huge bite of his pizza, grumbling around greasy pepperoni. I dump my plate onto the coffee table. My stomach has soured to the thought of food, and instead I worry; about how terribly my last date went, with a man I'd met through an app, who turned out to only want sex but definitely not sex with me; at how I used to be strong, capable, a firefighter, a man who trusted his body, and how now I'm not strong or capable of much at all, how I'm not a firefighter, how I've lost that trust.

I know, somewhere deep down, that this is probably anxiety. I know that I should probably do something about that but losing my job didn't just affect my identity. It affected my access to things like therapy at anything close to an affordable rate.

Mostly, I worry about George's supreme ability to meddle.

And my inability to say no to him. Because he does meddle, but George also loves me, and he worries, too. And if he's done this, knowing how I'd react, I've made him worry. A lot.

"I need to visit Pop," I say, a little helplessly. A last-ditch effort at no.

"Lulu said you should meet her at The Pump at seven. You have lots of time."

"Lulu?"

He shoots me a look. "Yes. Lulu."

"Sounds like a cartoon character," I mumble.

He shoves me, his shoulder to mine. With the difference in our size, I don't move. "It's short for Eloise. Don't be rude."

"I'm not," I say. "I'm sorry." I feel sheepish. "This is just… a lot."

The match plays on, the Welsh accents on the announcers so thick I can only pick out every third word or so. But I don't want to hear them talk. I watch since it's better than not watching. If I can't play anymore, at least I have this.

"Jess," he says, softly. "I really am sorry for meddling." George nibbles his pizza.

"I know you are." The invisible fist wrapped around my chest loosens. Everything feels a little bit better now that I'm Jess again.

"It's just cuz I want—"

"What's best for me. I know." I sigh. And I do know. I love him enough not to care…too much. "Next time could you just set up a dating profile without my permission instead, though?"

George throws his head back as he laughs, his dark curls flopping on his forehead, and it's not until hearing it that I realize how much I've missed it. Laughter: his, Pop's, my own.

"So, you'll go?" he asks.

I sigh. "What's she like?"

George lights up. He knows he's winning and I hate it. "She's smart and funny and a little quirky. Here." He pulls out his phone and navigates to an Instagram account for someone named @luluvsyou.

And she may not be a cartoon character of the Saturday morning TV variety. More like my thirteen-year-old Sailor Moon obsession. Her eyes are big and blue, framed by winged eyeliner, her lips a shiny bubble gum pink. Her hair is a purple cloud around her head.

"She doesn't have that hair anymore," he says. "She just doesn't update her social media a lot."

So, we're both lonely, bad at getting dates, and terrible at content creation. At least we'll have something to talk about. "George, she's…"

He won't let me get away with saying she's too pretty for me. But he can't stop me from *thinking* it. And not even in an "I'm ugly" way. I know what I look like. But there's more to a relationship than attraction and I'm not sure I can bring the rest.

"If you really, really don't want to, I'll text her right now and cancel but… I really do think you'll like her. And at the very least, you could be friends." His gray eyes are big and pleading. He's got his palms pressed together like he might beg.

"It's weird," I say. "That my ex is setting me up on dates."

"The straights could never," he says and this time I laugh.

"Yeah. I'll go," I say, even though it makes my chest feel tight, a date that might end like the last one. Or a person who might expect me to fit within their life when I can barely fit into my own. "On one condition," I say.

"Anything."

I can tell he means it.

"You stop meddling."

George is quiet, staring blankly at the TV screen. Like he has to think about it and he's weighing his options, as if it might be worth canceling on this "Lulu" for the right to keep sticking his nose in my business.

"George."

He sighs. "Fine."

I sit back against the couch and focus on the match. This feels like a win, even if it isn't really.

Chapter Two

Lulu

Wilvale University boasts fewer than ten thousand students on one hundred and fifty acres of land and yet I always seem to run into the same people. I expected the history department to be quiet today since the Phillies have a better chance of winning the World Series than an academic has of dragging themselves to campus on a Saturday, but the bathroom door swings open just as I'm ready to flush and I freeze in my stall.

I try to catch a glimpse of the shoes that enter the stall next to mine but they're not the heels that Miranda wears or the orthopedic sneakers that the semiretired Dr. Hoff wears. They're flats, but fancy, the kind with a pointed toe. They tell me all I need to know about who this is. My bathroom companion finishes their business as I stand stock-still and it doesn't occur to me that they a) probably know I'm in here, too and b) think it's weird that I'm just standing here listening to them pee?

Get it together, Lu.

And yet. I wait until the door opens and closes on their retreating footsteps before I unlock the door. I lean against the sink after I wash my hands. The summer semester started last week and I find myself teaching the same first-level course that I've taught since I started here in the fall: Introduction to Western History, which is really just a sterile way of saying, we're going to teach you about a bunch of old dead, white guys from the fall of Rome until the First World War. And let's face it, that's already a pretty sterile topic.

"Imagine," I say to my reflection. "The horrific finality of being remembered only for the worst thing you've never done."

I make a face like *blech*. It's a bit dramatic and over the top, but it's gripping. It's exactly the way I'd want to start my gender and witchcraft course, if I could ever get out from underneath this first-year survey course the department has saddled me with.

As I finish washing my hands, I recite more of the lecture that I've lain in bed crafting, that I've spent hours working on when I should have been reading a new article about gender theory or grading exams or working on a proposal for a book.

"Between the fifteenth and eighteenth centuries, thousands of people—mostly women—were murdered because they were believed to be witches..." I swing the door open with too much force, the handle hitting the wall with a loud bang. I cringe and poke my head out into the history department hallway but whoever was in the bathroom with me doesn't seem to be around now.

A lot of academics see teaching as a speed bump, something that gets in the way of research and writing, but I grew up watching my dad take hours to prepare his lectures. He'd practice in the mirror and rehearse for mom at the dinner table. He cares so much about his students, about giving them the chance to love history as much as he does. I didn't have any other choice but to feel the same way.

"Other than their alleged crimes, historians don't know much about them. Sometimes names were recorded, sometimes ages. But their lives before they were 'witches' are lost." I pause, patting my pockets down for my phone. I open the notes app, ignoring the red notification from my lunch buddy, George, and type: "Anonymous. Erased. Their history was burned up along with them, on flaming pyres."

Damn. I'm good. That's good, right?

Behind me, someone giggles, sharp and high. In this hallway, with the tiled floor and cement brick walls painted white, the sound echoes, matching the stark and impersonal feeling of the history department. I hunch my shoulders up to my ears, a defensive position before I've even turned around. Dr. Audrey Robbs and Dr. Frank Hill peer out from the now open doorway of Dr. Miranda Jackson's office.

"Who are you talking to?" Audrey asks. Her tone makes it clear she knows I was talking to myself and she thinks that's a little bit weird.

"No one," I say quickly. "I was…" I clear my throat, trying to buy myself time to come up with an excuse, but I've always been a terrible liar. "Practicing."

"Practicing for what, Dr. Banks?" Miranda smiles, welcoming and warm where Audrey and Frank are skeptical, sharing a look.

"Um." I clear my throat again. They're going to think I'm getting sick if I keep this up. "A lecture."

"For Intro to Western History?" Audrey asks. Audrey's style resembles Miranda's more than the grad student chic that I still sport, despite receiving my doctorate two years ago, which consists of any available clean clothes that match my Keds. Which means really any type of clothing at all. Everything matches Keds.

Audrey wears a pair of pointy-toed flats, made to resemble animal hide, a skirt in the graphite-est of grays, and a blouse that buttons to the collar. She'd never be caught dead in sneakers, or talking to herself. Frank already looks bored and disdainful, offended by my presence, though he doesn't reserve that for just me. He thinks he's God's gift to the study of eleventh-to-thirteenth-century monastic orders and manuscript illumination.

"For a..." I wasn't planning to pitch this idea until the planning meeting later this summer, but Miranda's here now, I guess. It would be good to get her input. I look from Audrey to Frank, gauging the level of judgment on their faces.

Ever since my own survey course in European history in high school, I've wanted to understand the women I study, to speak their names into the history books. Those too old, or poor, or angry, or independent, deemed not good enough by men who were too scared and powerful to see them for what they were: mothers and sisters and daughters, neighbors and friends. Healers. Humans. I want give my students the chance to love history as much as I do.

But right now, staring down Audrey and Frank, I wouldn't mind a little bit of my witches' anonymity.

An anemic oscillating fan whirrs in the corner of Miranda's office, gently lifting papers and blowing Audrey's hair against the back of her neck. Sunlight hits the window behind the desk at just the right spot this time of day, reflecting off the picture frames on Miranda's bookshelf and the shiny lacquer of her desk, blinding me if I glance in her direction. At least, I tell myself it's the sun and not the hero worship I feel at the sight of *the* Dr. Miranda Jackson, the only Black woman in the department, a tenured historian of Africa and the Caribbean, race, gender, and power, and African diasporic religions, waiting for me to explain what the hell I'm muttering about in the hallway on a weekend.

"Actually, it's for a class I'd like the opportunity to pitch at our next planning meeting," I say.

There's a half-empty tub of hummus on Miranda's desk, and laptops in Audrey's and Frank's laps. I've interrupted a meeting, something friendly and personal. Something I wasn't invited to.

"Let's hear it." Audrey's smile is as sharp as her tone.

"You don't have to, Dr. Banks," Miranda says quickly. I want to think that she's uncomfortable but truth be told, I don't know Miranda all that well. Dad always speaks so highly of her. I'll swallow my tongue before I back down in front of her.

I wave my hand like it's nothing despite the ice in my veins. "It's a history of gender and witchcraft course. Something we could offer to second- or third-year students after they've taken the survey course." The one that I'm teaching. "As a popular grassroots movement that was informed by the geopolitical issues on the European continent, I think there are connections between this cultural hysteria and—"

Audrey makes a humming noise, her face scrunched up in an apology that she doesn't mean. "Sounds a bit…derivative."

"Well, you haven't heard anything about it yet—"

"And I'm not sure we have the budget for a new course," Audrey continues, turning back to Miranda, as if she knows anything about the department's budgets. As if she's not a contract instructor holding on to employment by her fingernails, just like me. "Right, Miranda?"

I shouldn't be embarrassed, I know. It's just a pitch, just an idea. That's what I tell myself, over and over again even as my face flushes, the heat of embarrassment scalding like a wash of hot water.

"Well." Miranda winces. "We do have to review the budget, yes…"

"See." Audrey shrugs like that settles it, her face contorted in what I think is supposed to be sympathy.

I don't know what I'm more embarrassed by: the fact that I was fool enough to pitch it at all, to share something that feels so precious; or how, despite her obvious dislike for me, I'm desperate to be Audrey Robbs's friend. Frank I could take or leave.

"Plus, we're offering my new course next, History of Magic."

Audrey sets her jaw, squares her shoulders like she's challenging me to respond. But I won't. I never will.

Sometimes I wonder if I wouldn't be better off back in the UK, trying to make it work. Sure, my history prof boyfriend, Dr. Brian Mason, cheated on me with my best friend and colleague, Dr. Nora Carpenter, effectively blowing up my entire professional and personal life and making every migration to the department's shared kitchen a walk of shame, but at least when I taught at the University of Lancaster, my dad hadn't had to get me the job after all my other academic leads had dried up. News of Brian and Nora's twin betrayal reached my coworkers here at Wilvale University before I did since academia is basically a gossip magazine with tweed elbow patches. So, now not only am I that fishy nepotism hire, I can feel their stares when they wonder what kind of social deficit I had, like a witch's mark, that pushed my bestie into my boyfriend's bed.

I've only been teaching here since last September but I've spent every minute trying to prove that I didn't just get this job because of my dad—that I am actually good at this. It's why I volunteered for the intro course this semester.

Frank huffs, turning his back to me. His body shakes. He's *laughing* at me.

Maybe it's to check if she's noticed—as if she could somehow not notice—or maybe I'm just a glutton for punishment, but I can't read the expression on Miranda's face other than to know I don't want to see more of it.

"Right. Well. I'd better…" I jerk my thumb behind me, turning on my heel fast enough my sneakers squeak. A sound, like a snort that's been contained, then Audrey's quiet shushing, follows me out of Miranda's office.

I love my work, when it's just me and books and words. Me, standing at a lectern teaching; sometimes people want to be there, they've chosen that course because they're interested, but sometimes they have to be there to fulfill a history credit before they graduate. Those ones are my favorite. I love persuading them that history is more than just a requirement.

History is fun, but *this* isn't fun. Sometimes it feels like every academic got a rulebook, one that counsels competition over partnership, to step on the throats of anyone who might be in front of you on the tenure track. One that champions working to burnout, past burnout, as the best indicator of success. It expects you to work for free and give feedback even if you won't get any. It teaches you how to posture, to demean. And everyone got a copy of this rulebook except me. I'm sure of it.

I manage to close my office door behind me with a soft snick instead of a slam. But just barely. I'm sweaty, my heart thumping like a punk band's drum. I left Lancaster to get out from under the shadow of a man only to find myself so desperately in need of a job that now I'm stuck under the shadow of my father. And while I now have a job, I've alienated the very people I was once so excited to work with.

My phone buzzes in my pocket, another reminder of the text message I still haven't opened from George.

Jesse said he's SO excited to see you tonight. He wants to meet at the Pump @ 7. I told him that would work for you, right? J

Crumbs. I slump down into my chair, the wheels rolling me back into my desk.

Can't wait!!!

I type back with the kind of false bravado that is only capable through text message. I won't ever admit this to George because I'm pretty sure he'd freak out but I definitely forgot I agreed to go on a date with this Jesse.

★ ★ ★

Gravel pings on the undercarriage of my new—to me—car as I pull into The Pump's parking lot. Little Texas, the restaurant next door to The Pump, has leaned so far into their rustic theme that despite being located in a college town in Pennsylvania they cover their floors with sawdust and kept the parking lot unpaved. The lights in Little Texas are still dark; it's too early in the evening for them to bother opening yet. But a warm glow comes from The Pump, with its decidedly more steakhouse vibe.

I don't know why I even agreed to The Pump. I'd be more comfortable at Little Texas, with its neon signage and combination of pop and country music. Although, now that I think about it, a loud combo of pop and country probably doesn't make Little T's a good "date" location, and if I've somehow gotten myself talked into a date with George's friend—maybe ex? The way he talked about him, I thought he could be—I should at least be able to hear him.

"You could cancel," I whisper to myself, the desire like the small, sputtering flame of a Bic lighter. After the afternoon I've just had, all I want to do is go home, sit on bed in my underwear, and scroll social media for satisfying cleaning videos.

"No, you absolutely cannot cancel," I hiss back. "You're supposed to meet him, like, *now.*"

The door to The Pump swings open and two women walk out, laughing. "Must be nice," I grumble at them, then immediately feel bad about it. It's not their fault they're normal, adult humans who can make friends.

I shouldn't have agreed to this. Not when the burn of Nora's betrayal aches like a phantom limb. Not when the thought of meeting someone new, of trying to convince them that I'm worth the time, makes me feel sick and exhausted. I was just so excited to be making a friend in George. The first time he spoke to me I assumed he was talking to someone behind me and kept walking until he waved his hands in the air.

And now we're...friends...almost. We're at the very least semi-consistent lunch dates. Our conversations don't get into very personal territory, mostly sticking to work, my teaching position at the university and his work running the psych department. And at a time when my desperation for human connection outside of my parents borders on rank, it's so stinky, I didn't want to say no to him about his friend Jesse.

I bare my teeth into the rearview mirror and pat down my hair. I hike up my jeans and adjust the crop top that seemed like a good idea when I tried it on but now seems too cutesy and far too underdressed in the fading evening light. I review my list of acceptable conversation topics: my work/his work; the Phillies/whatever sports team he likes (though if he doesn't at least tolerate the Phillies, I'm not sure what more we could say to each other); recent travel; summer holiday plans.

Safe, normal topics of conversation.

Pausing at the front door, I pull my spring jacket on, despite knowing I'll have to take it off in a few moments anyway. The air is cool enough that my nipples are pressing through the fabric of my shirt. I'll never apologize for having nipples that react to the temperature, but I just know I won't be able to keep my mouth shut about them, if I walk in there like this. I'll make some joke about my breasts and then his gaze will fall to them because where else would they go and he'll either be horrified or think it's a desperate come-on.

Unacceptable conversation topics: the aforementioned nipples; if he has a favorite tree; the top ten stupidest ways early modern men attempted to identify witches; why the 1983 Phillies' uniforms are the best uniforms, which is really less of a topic of conversation and more of a slide deck.

"Just a drink with a nice guy," I mumble. "George wouldn't set you up with a serial killer."

Although, how well do I know George, really? What if George is a serial killer? What if they're a serial-killing duo?

"Go inside, Lulu," I growl.

The hostess who stands at the front is a young Black woman with a bubbly smile. "Do you have a reservation?"

I search the restaurant, but the few men all have a dining partner already. At the back of the room, where a dark bar fills the space between the "in and out" doors to the kitchen, one broad-shouldered, white man in a navy blue pullover sweater sits perfectly centered. Part of me is tickled by the symmetry of it all. The girl who takes pleasure in this kind of movie-scene kismet wants to frame him between my thumbs and forefingers and take a mental snapshot. But I can't get hot for kismet anymore.

I try to channel a little bit of the kismet-loving, happy-go-lucky girl I used to be as I let the hostess know I'm all good, stride between the tables, and hop onto the stool next to him. Letting my hair fall over one shoulder, I smile, following a template for flirtation. Fake it till you make it or whatever.

"Hi, Jesse Logan? I'm Lulu." I stick out my hand to shake.

Jesse turns toward me, his mouth flat. Not the reaction I expected. Maybe since this is technically a date we shouldn't shake? Maybe we should hug? Should we kiss? A double-cheek peck? Surely, we shouldn't. Now that I've thought the word "kiss," my brain must immediately collect data about the kiss-ability of this man, and my eyes drop to his mouth.

Double crumbs, he definitely saw that, and what if now he thinks I want to kiss him?

"Can I get you anything?" the bartender asks, saving me from this spiral. He has that classic style, a white cloth folded over his shoulder, a perfectly crooked smile aimed at me, suspenders and a slick haircut. He looks like he can call a woman "doll" and it doesn't even come off that patronizing. I feel Jesse's eyes on my face while I order a beer and the bartender asks for my ID, confirming that the crop top was definitely the wrong choice. His stare feels heavier as I flush, rummaging through my bag, which is one-third purse, one-third work tote, one-third gym bag, for my wallet.

Jesse Logan shifts in his chair, sighing, and if I dropped dead right now the coroner would have to put humiliation as the cause of death because heck am I rattled. My eyes are so wide from trying not to suddenly cry, they feel like they could fall out of my head as the bartender studies my license, my face, my license again, and finally nods. As I tuck my ID back into my wallet and ask once more for the closest beer on tap.

He looks at me out of the corner of his eye as I settle beside him. The bartender returns with my beer, refilling Jesse's drink, which is…soda water? Silence descends as the bartender walks away, wiping down the dark wood of the bar. The dining room behind us tinkles quietly with the sounds of utensils on plates and clinking glasses. I have to have arrived at least two minutes ago. That span of time doesn't seem so long in general but in the context of a first date with a man I've never met before, it's an eternity.

My heart doesn't beat any faster, just harder, like each pump is more difficult than the last. My palms sweat. I don't know when this happened, or how. All I know is that I left the UK, where I'd built a healthy, thriving social life, a best friend I trusted, a boyfriend I loved, all to have it blow up in my face. I came back to beg for a job at my hometown university, with the early modern historical equivalent of a rock star in Dr. Miranda Jackson, and found that most of my high school friends had moved away, moved on. I was left with a vacuum, of time, of space. Wake up, teach classes no one seems very interested in despite my efforts, grade mediocre scores, go home, repeat. And now this: sitting here in the kind of silence that grows louder and louder. This must be what it feels like to burn alive, every second longer than the last.

His jaw works, his five-o'clock shadow thick by seven. "Hello, Eloise." His voice is deep, flat.

Eloise?

"How do you know my name?" I ask, my voice prickled with irritation. I *hate* Eloise.

He studies me. "George. He said your name is Eloise." He sounds accusatory, like either I or George has lied. After a beat, he smiles, mouth closed, lips tight.

I turn my chin toward the bar to hide the flush that I can feel creeping up my cheeks. "Right." I make myself laugh, like *ha!* "You're not going to call me Eloise all night, are you?"

I was named after my father's mother's aunt; an oops baby according to me, a delightful surprise according to my mother, when my parents were already well into their careers. I was nameless for the first week of my life before they finally pulled Eloise out of a literal hat. My father still owns the head covering in question and wears it on particularly sunny days in the garden. I met my great-great-aunt Eloise once when I was seven and Dad took us back to his home, a small village in Kent. Eloise loved my father dearly, but she did not even tolerate seven-year-old me. Which didn't offend me too much once I found out that she coughed up phlegm almost constantly. The incident that sealed our resentment was when I watched her eat a piece of her own long hair like a slowly slurped noodle. Even my young seven-year-old self knew that was a bridge my over-active gag reflex could not cross.

I say *none* of this out loud.

Add that to the list of inappropriate conversation topics.

Jesse frowns and it takes putting my hand to my forehead to understand why. I was frowning at him first. I smile instead, a duplicate of his closed-lip version.

He says, "I'll call you whatever you want me to call you."

With his deep voice and the frown still marking up his face like my red pen on an undergraduate's essay, he doesn't sound the least bit accommodating. More sinister. I lean back in my chair.

Who are you, George's friend?

He shifts in his chair, looking immediately uncomfortable. The bartender, who'd stopped in front of us, must feel the awkwardness settling because he turns on his heel and walks away. Jesse drops his gaze to the bar, flushing, and *oh*. I was so busy feeling nervous, not wanting to come, I never considered that he might also be nervous. But as he turns away from me, grabbing a few cocktail napkins and dabbing at the water ring around his glass like he's defusing a bomb, huffing another sigh that upon reflection could be a deep, steadying breath, I'd say yeah. Jesse is just as nervous as I am.

He clears his throat. "What do you prefer?" he asks. "Lulu or Eloise?"

My mother has called me Lu or Lulu since before I can remember. Eloise has never felt like my name. More a label, the wrong one, slapped on a bag to say "these are caramels," when they're Fun Dip or Fizzy Pops or…gosh, anything but caramels.

Brian was the only person who ever called me Eloise. Even before we were anything but colleagues, he'd insisted. Lulu was a child's name, according to Brian. Eloise was distinguished. I let him, desperate for someone like Dr. Brian Mason of Lancaster University to think I was distinguished. Now, every time he called me Eloise feels like a betrayal. Brian trying to fit a square peg into a round hole and the square peg desperately wishing she could wear down her hard edges to fit.

"I like Lulu." Even now, saying it sounds like asking for permission.

"Sure, Lulu."

A bloom, something affectionate and warm, floats in my chest. He flattens his sweater down his torso, navy blue merino wool giving way under his hand, hinting at the muscle definition underneath. In this light, his brown eyes are a perfect contrast. I can't tell if Jesse is the type of man who would pick a sweater that purposely complements his eyes, but I'm tickled by it either way. His forearms fill out the sleeves, his biceps stretch the fabric. As I follow the wool over the wide line of his shoulders, I notice a square of white cardboard sticking out of the back of his collar.

He's left the tag on.

"Were you planning on returning that sweater?" I ask, my hand halfway to his collar.

He eyes that hand like I'm holding a knife. "Uh…no. What?"

I give the tag a tug, snapping it off. *The Gap. $59.99.*

"Tag." I crumple it in my fist.

Jesse makes a mumbled sound like *oh no*, patting at the back of his shirt, his face turning a deeper and deeper shade of purple. This date is a bit of a disaster. I reach for whatever I can to save it.

"George said you were a firefighter?"

He blinks through a moment of pointed silence. "Yes." His tone is flat, flatter than normal. Final. "He said you have a PhD in witchcraft? At the university?" Jesse frowns like that's not right.

I take a big gulp of my beer, now warmer than it should be after sitting.

"I have a PhD in the history of witchcraft. I'm not a witch."

He nods very seriously.

"That would be cool, though."

He keeps nodding.

I can feel the silence threatening to descend again like a funeral shroud ready to declare this evening dead.

"I read that candles are one of the top five causes of house fires," I offer.

Jesse blinks, his brow furrowing. To be fair, I'm not sure what I expected him to do with that information. "I really love scented candles." I laugh like, *what can you do?* "But like what if they…start a fire in my house…" I trail off. It's either that or I physically restrain myself from speaking.

"As long as you leave twelve inches of space around the candle and don't leave it unattended, you should be safe," he says.

"Oh. Great. Thanks." I take another deep pull of my beer. At the very least I can walk away with this important safety tip.

"What do you enjoy about firefighting?" I ask. "Fighting fires? Fire…extinguishing?"

Jesse takes a sip of his water, shaking his head with a quiet "no thank you," like he doesn't want to answer the question. I was not aware that we could just decline to answer questions, but he does it so seamlessly I catalog the interaction away for myself. The next time a colleague tries to ask a leading question about my productivity I will simply do as Jesse does and decline.

"Tell me about your research," he says and either he knows other academics and thus knows we can't shut up about our research, or he's secretly my evil nemesis who somehow knows my one and only kryptonite. So, I spend far too long talking about the history of witches and the Witch Craze, gender and perceptions of witchcraft, especially within the context of early modern Europe, especially, *especially* in England and how, now that I've moved home I'm focusing on witchcraft in the colonial period; witch hunts, the bubonic plague, war, fear-mongering misogyny, and law in the sixteenth to nineteenth centuries. Once I start devolving into torture devices used to coerce confessions and Royal Witch-Hunter King James VI or I and explaining how he was both a sixth and a first at once, I stop myself. I've definitely wandered into unacceptable conversation topic territory. I don't know how long we've been sitting here but my butt is sore from this hard barstool, and I've finished one beer and started halfway into another. *Whoops.*

It's time to pull this back into safe conversation territory, although Jesse doesn't seem too concerned about anything I just said. He sat and listened quietly, maintaining eye contact the whole time, nodding, *hmm*-ing and throwing in a couple well-timed *I see*'s.

"What about you?" I hiccup into my hand before taking another gulp of IPA. "Why'd you get into fighting fires?" I try again.

He fiddles with the hem of his sweater but at least doesn't deflect me this time. "Family business." He says nothing else, and I resist the urge to duck to his level and catch his gaze. It's probably just the beer but something about Jesse's attention feels warm and familiar.

"George mentioned you're not doing that anymore, though?"

Jesse is the All-American type. Like he'd have smiled into the camera of the local TV station on his football field in high school after making the game-winning play, with an *aw shucks*. He fills his chest with air, like he wants to say something, then never does. He catches me staring, admiring the line of his sweater, his straight back, his freshly buzzed hair. I smile—because that's what I always do—and something about him loosens.

"Can I get you anything else?" the bartender asks.

Jesse and I lock eyes for that awkward moment where both of us try to decide who's going to answer. The silence ticks away again, filled only by the few diners left in the restaurant, the sound of the kitchen behind the swinging doors.

"Do you…?" I ask.

"Maybe we should…" he says at the same time.

I smile. His mouth flattens. He looks over his shoulder then back at me. "Just the check, please."

"I can pay for my drink."

His throat bobs. "I'd like to pay for it, if you don't mind," he says quietly.

The bartender slides the slip of paper between us, his eyes bouncing back and forth, like he's placed bets on this standoff. After a moment I reach for it, pulling some bills from my wallet. Jesse nods and I feel like I've disappointed him and care that I've disappointed him, even though I shouldn't care. I barely know him, other than the weight of his gaze on the side of my face and the sound of his companionable silence.

I stumble as I hop off the barstool, staggering a step, the stool next to mine making a loud, scraping noise along the floor when I bump into it. *Perfect.* Now he'll think I'm drunk, when I'm not drunk. I haven't been drunk since England.

Brian's hobby was wine. He'd bring rare and expensive bottles to my flat, with never enough cheese, and make us listen to French singers he knew I couldn't understand.

The urge to tell Jesse about the distaste on Brian's face when I played "Bitch Better Have My Money," dancing in my underwear after too much wine, bubbles like Brain's favorite cava on my tongue. He'd frowned, said *Eloise*, like the word left a bitter taste in his mouth, and left. At the time I was hurt, but looking back, I think he was withholding sex and punishing me for behaving in a way he didn't approve of. Also, he left to have sex with Nora, so.

I rummage through my purse, weaving between the empty tables and out the front door, Jesse trailing quietly behind me. "I'm not trying to find my keys," I say over my shoulder. The sky is blank, the stars covered by storm clouds I can't really see but feel low and ominous nonetheless, like they'll sink lower and lower until Wilvale, Pennsylvania, is nothing but fog. The wind blows my hair into my face, catching on my lips. "I'm trying to find my phone so I can call a ride. I'll get my car tomorrow. My dad can drive me into town."

"Your phone is in your hand, Lulu."

And he's right. I shake it at him, showing him the case with a flower that says "Votes for Women" in the center to distract him from the complete mess I am right now.

He scratches the back of his head, undistracted. "And I can give you a ride."

"It's fine." I wave his words away. "I can get a cab." The lights are on in Little Texas now and music isn't exactly audible but the bass of it reaches my feet on the pavement. Soon there will be a lineup of people outside and a procession of cabs coming in and out of the parking lot as students from the university and nearby technical college arrive to kick off their summer vacation.

He points to a rusty blue truck a few spaces down. "I'd feel better if I dropped you off at your door, but I understand if you're not comfortable." We stand off in the middle of the parking lot, the wind growing stronger. I hiccup and close my eyes; if I can't see him then he can't see how red I'm getting. And it's not that I wouldn't like a ride from him, it's just that I'm still not sure what he even thinks of me. "OK," I hear myself say. "That would be really nice of you."

He opens the door to the old Ford Bronco, the rust most prevalent around the tire wells. It smells like leather and car air freshener and, I imagine if I knew him better, Jesse: peppermint and pine. There's a bench seat and as I climb up my eyes slide over it, the leather soft and cool—and OK, this is definitely the beer talking but—sensual.

I wonder how many people Jesse has had sex with on this bench seat. If I were Jesse, I'd have sex with everyone on this bench seat. He's pulled on a plaid jacket over his sweater, and he fills it out so well, I think I answer my own question: he probably has sex with *a lot* of people on this bench seat.

"Just be cool," I whisper as he walks around the front of the truck. "Be cool, Dr. Banks."

Jesse cranks the engine as he settles in. His hands are big and veiny and a quick, sudden image of how those hands would look on my bare thighs imprints itself on the back of my eyelids, real enough that I can feel his palms, how rough they'd be on my skin. I'm so caught up in wildly inappropriate thoughts it takes me too long to notice that the truck is rumbling, the engine warm, and Jesse is staring at me.

"Turn right on Main," I say too loudly.

We drive through town in silence, except for my quiet directives. In no time, we're in front of my parents' house, which I moved back to last September, heading down their long and bumpy driveway in silence. He cuts the engine and the headlights shut off. A raindrop falls here or there on the windshield then stops.

"Do you, uh, want to see my room?" I ask to break the silence, then immediately wish I could just shut up.

Jesse's mouth is a flat line. A very grumpy face. He says nothing. *Shocking.*

"I just mean that, my parents let me live in the studio apartment that's attached to the house. It has a separate entrance but it's around the back. I don't still sleep in my childhood bedroom. My mom keeps her art supplies in there now." I wonder when—or if—I'll ever stop talking.

He peers out the windshield at the dark pathway that leads to my apartment and opens his door. I shiver at another gust of unseasonably cool air. "I'll walk you," he says.

I rummage through my bag on the short walk around the side of my parents' farmhouse, almost plowing into his back when he stops at my front door. It takes me a second to line the key up with the lock before I can shove it in and open the door to my dark, tiny home. The crisp air has cooled my beer buzz enough that I know what I'm about to say is a bad idea. But the thought of walking into this dark, cold little apartment, alone, makes it so I can't stop myself.

"Do you want to come in?"

I'm not even sure what I want him to do if he came inside. We could sit and watch a reality TV show or a baseball game on my laptop while I scrolled my phone or read student papers, sex the furthest thing from either of our minds. It just seems better than the alternative of being alone with my thoughts. Jesse pokes his head through the door, surveying. His mouth twists into a little pucker. Not grumpy face.

"What's this?" I point to his mouth. "You're not making your Grumpy Face anymore."

He seems skeptical. "What's Grumpy Face?"

"It's like this." I flatten my mouth and do my best to shape my forehead in a way that will create a V between my brows. I jut my jaw. "Hello, Eloise," I say in a barely passable impression. Jesse Logan laughs. He actually laughs. It's quiet, *duh*. But it's a laugh and it transforms his face, lifts a load from his shoulders. It turns a little personal sun on above him, to follow him around until he frowns again. He has one dimple in his flushed cheeks. His jacket stretches across his shoulders. And curses to the beer and the cold and the loneliness, but all of these seem like Very Good Reasons to kiss him.

So, I do.

Jesse Logan, who drinks soda water quietly, and drives for fifteen frickin' minutes quietly, and laughs quietly, does not kiss quietly. A moan rumbles up his chest, against where my nipples are firmly pressed to him. He lets me kiss him for a few more seconds before gently pulling away, his hands wrapped around my biceps.

"I'm sorry," I say, the pads of three fingers pressed to my lips. "Was that OK?" I ask.

"Yeah." He seems surprised by his answer.

"Do you want to do it again?"

He thinks for a moment. "Yes."

Jesse pulls me into him, gently pressing his hands to my lower back. I should feel cold, standing in the open doorway to my house, the wind picking up, the rain about to fall, but heat radiates off him. My body jolts every time my nipples brush against him through my thin jacket, tiny lightning bolts right through my skin.

His lips move softly, almost shyly, and who is this man? So quiet and kissing me, holding me, like I'm something that might break. Honestly, I might, and I hate that. I want to kiss this gorgeous man on my front doorstep without thinking about the ways I am jagged pieces held together by masking tape and sheer force of will.

I slip my tongue past his lips to quiet the tiny implosions in my head. And it works. Jesse squeezes me. A rumble moving through his chest, the sound like melted butter or falling asleep in a sunbeam or the smell of turkey on Christmas morning: good and warm and safe. I sink deeper into him. His hands travel up my body. He cups my face, pulls away just enough to press his thumb to my lower lip.

A joke, maybe another invitation inside, the urge to speak bubbles up—but whatever words I want to fill this silence with, he presses them back into my mouth with gentle pressure. Jesse's brown-eyed gaze travels over my face and I think this might be the first time he's really seen me. That little V returns to his brow, and I smooth it with my fingertips. He inhales, a sound like resolve, and settles lower against the doorframe, pulling me against him, his thigh between my legs. He presses his lips to mine, slipping his tongue into my mouth, and I moan; his leg holding me up, his hands cupping my face, fisting my hair, our mouths, pressing and pulling at each other. I laugh, surprised, into his mouth and it doesn't stop him. He kisses the smile on my face. Tips my head back and works his mouth over my chin, my jaw, my neck.

Cold water hits my shoulder, another drop on my cheek, startling me from where the rest of my body is warm and liquid. I lift my face to the sky and another raindrop lands in my hair. Since this night has been full of me having bad ideas and now the weather has provided the perfect excuse, I ask again, "Do you want to come inside?"

It sounds illicit, combined with how close we're pressed together and my open door. It sounds like I'm asking him something else, and even I can hear the desperation in my voice when I toss each word over the cliff into this cold, quiet evening.

Jesse cools against me. His lips against my jaw slow. He doesn't so much push me away from him as plaster himself against the doorframe. He blinks, frowns, says, "Eloise."

The nebula of lust dissolves and leaves me numb. "Lulu," I say.

"Sorry." And he does sound sorry. "Lulu."

"It's fine," I say quickly, even though it isn't. "I almost bailed on this date," I say loudly and stupidly. Maybe he thinks I'm trying to save face but really I'm just trying to show him that this, stopping, is the right choice. I'm a fucking mess.

He makes a fist, tucking his hand under his arm, mirroring my own stance.

"I've been having a hard time meeting new people."

I want to punch my own mouth.

"Did George tell you?" he asks. "About us?"

"That you two were together?" I ask.

He nods.

"Not in so many words but I assumed…from the way he spoke about you."

He laughs in that way that makes it clear he finds none of this funny. "What way was that."

I shrug. "Like he cared about you. Like he loves you."

"He didn't tell me about this date until earlier today," Jesse says. He winces. "I just mean that he cares maybe too much sometimes."

A familiar sadness blankets me, warm and comforting in a sick sort of way. At least I'm used to the feeling of my colleagues' rejection, compared to this new rejection from an almost stranger. "You're not going to come inside," I say.

When I blink up at him, there's something about the shadow

from the motion-sensor outdoor light, the slope of his shoulders, that makes me think he's wearing a sad blanket, too.

"No. I'm not."

"It was nice to meet you, Jesse." I hold out my hand. He looks at it and, like last time, he doesn't take it. He steps out of the doorway, shoves his hands in his pockets.

"Thank you for the date, Lulu. It was…" He pauses for so long I think he'll let it hang. "Interesting."

I don't know what I wanted Jesse to say. I don't know if he could have said anything that would make me feel not so lonely right now. But whatever I needed him to say, it wasn't that. Silence would have been better. So, I say nothing back, and close the door, and wait in the dark until I hear the crunch of his boots on my gravel walkway. Leaving the lights off in the main room, I wash my face, brush my teeth, and crawl into bed in my underwear, just like I'd planned a few hours earlier. I open my laptop and there, in my inbox, is an email. The subject line reads "I'm Sorry." I delete it without opening it. There's nothing new to be said.

It's still disorienting sleeping here where everything is so quiet. My bed in my UK flat rested beneath a transom window; every night I heard cars from the high street below, and every morning I woke up with the sun on my face. This place doesn't feel like home, even though it's attached to the house I grew up in. Even though I've been home since last September, my entire life jammed into three bags, and the bright-eyed, bushy-tailed hope that academia wouldn't chew me up and spit me out.

The bed is cold and empty. Outside, the rain is falling in earnest, thunder rolls like the sky's steady heartbeat, and the wind isn't loud but the house creaks around me.

Things with Brian were passionate, red hot. Something about his elbow patches and tortoiseshell glasses, juxtaposed against the soft curl of his hair and his crooked front tooth, really did it for me. We couldn't keep our hands off each other. He also couldn't keep his hands off Nora. I'd tell myself that there was no passion with Jesse, not like with Brian, that the familiarity with which I spoke to him, the ease I felt even in my awkwardness was a sign of a dimmed lantern rather than a blazing bonfire. I'd tell myself that, if it wasn't for that kiss. I'd tell myself we're Just Friends but he wasn't interested in even that. Of course, I'd thought he was nervous, too. I was projecting. He wasn't nervous. He wanted nothing to do with me at all. It was all a favor for George, a last-minute hand for his old friend.

"It wasn't going to be anything," I say into the quiet. Since I moved back to Wilvale, I've lived and relived my entire relationship with Nora, from flatmates to coworkers to best friends, trying to identify the moment it went wrong. Searching for what made me disposable. I've googled "how to make friends as an adult." I've bought books, opening the packages once I get them into my apartment, so my mother won't see the titles on her kitchen table. I've listened to podcasts and watched old talk shows. All the advice comes down to this: be yourself and your people will find you.

When am I going to learn that myself will always be a little too much—and somehow not enough?

Chapter Three

Jesse

I make it home just as the sky opens up. In the time it takes for me to run from my driveway to my front door, I'm soaked. I hang my jacket on the hook by the door, throw my keys in the same dish Pop always did, and leave my clothes in a trail behind me as I strip all the way to the bathroom. The shower is lukewarm. I really should get the water tank fixed. Another problem on an unending list of things I need to save up for now that I'm bringing home a security guard's wage rather than a firefighter's salary plus benefits.

The discomfort of my shower's lackluster performance does nothing to calm the erection that started when Lulu pressed herself against me. Despite a double body wash, I can't get the smell of her, lavender and light, out of my nose. The water splashing over the tiles can't drown out the sound of her voice, excited and confident when she talked about witches—*fucking witches*—and gay kings and early modern whatever the fuck; then breathy and hopeful when she asked me to *come inside* like she was auditioning for my next wet dream.

"Fuck," I growl. *"Fuck."*

I stare at the slate gray shower tiles as I wrap my hand around my dick. But all I see are her cheeks, flushed from the beer and the sudden, unseasonable cold. Her lips swollen from *me*. This time when she invites me to come inside, I say yes. We'd shut the door, keep the lights off. She'd push my jacket from my shoulders, and I'd do the same to her. She'd kiss me with my back against the door for what felt like hours. I'd suck her nipples through her shirt, and I hear her cry out, the sound so real it echoes off the tiles. We'd fall on the bed, our clothes gone. I'd touch her everywhere. I'd taste her while her thighs and hands pinned my mouth to her body.

In the fantasy, I'd fuck her for hours.

In reality, I don't get past the part where I thrust into her, her body hot and soft, her fingers in my mouth. I come and the water washes it away. My skin prickles, suddenly too hot in the cooling water.

I dry myself off before the sputtering bathroom fan can even consider defogging the mirror. Lie in bed with the lights off and my phone silenced, George's text—Let me know how it goes!— unanswered. The rain has picked up outside, the wind throwing it like a sheet against the windows. I stare at the random patterns in the stucco ceiling, as the vision of Lulu slowly disappears. Until all that's left is disappointment, mostly in myself.

If she ever saw me again, she'd be able to see it all over me. Not only what I just did to myself in the shower, my lips still hot from her warm exhales. She'd be able to see it all. That I *wanted* to come inside. And not just for sex. That I wanted to sit beside her and listen to her talk about just about anything. George knows one thing, at least: I have a type. They're talkative, where I am not. But what he doesn't know is that getting me out of whatever rut this is can't be cured by one date.

No matter how horny my bi ass might be.

How long will it take her to realize that my silence isn't the kind that wears off with time, that my résumé has two lines:

firefighter and security guard—and that I'm only considered good at the latter because I have experience not falling asleep on overnight shifts and my size makes me "intimidating" even if I feel anything but. How long until she finds out I can't even come out to my grandfather, that I waited so long to tell the man who raised me the truth that now it's too late. How long would it take her to see that I don't fit into her life the way I didn't fit into George's or my grandfather's or my own.

"Stop whining," I tell myself. Because that's a great way to cure myself of self-pity. George will be happy, though. He was right, about Lulu being my type, and that I need to make a change.

I just wish I knew how.

Pop was huge once. He fit into his size, filled rooms with his smile and his laughter, carried others' worries on his shoulders. Mostly mine. I dwarf the man standing in front of the window now, his soft gray T-shirt swallowing him whole.

"Pop." My voice sounds too loud in the quiet hush of his long-term care home. A lot of people complain about the smell. It's not that the nursing home is unclean; there's an astringent bleach smell that permeates every cell. The smell I can get past. Maybe because I've worked with a bunch of smelly firefighters or I've learned, in the many traumas I've been called to, that the human body produces a surprising number of odors.

It's the quiet that's the worst, especially at this time of day. I should have just visited tomorrow, but I wanted to be awake, present, and I knew I wouldn't be after dinner with George, then an overnight shift guarding a construction site. So, I'm here now, my grandfather sundowning or not.

My voice breaks through whatever fog he's lost in, but his anxiety looks high tonight, creasing his quivering lower lip.

"Have you seen your mother?" he asks, his voice raspy.

I've never met my mother, and I can remember only glimpses

of my dad. They're vague enough that I am never quite sure if they're memories or if the many photos my grandparents showed me as a child imprinted on my mind. "I...no, Pop."

His hands shake as he presses his fingers to the glass, the skin on the back of his hand pale and thin, his fingernails bitten short. "It's been over an hour. I'm worried about this blizzard, Joey."

I follow his gaze out the window. The sky is shot through with purple and pink and orange, still dramatic after last night's storm. It brought down trees and blew over my neighbor's trampoline, and it's probably what's got him worrying about the weather. Hearing my grandfather call me by my father's name will never not rip me apart inside. It's the combination of the reminder that Joseph Logan is dead and the hurt—even if it's unintentional—of being invisible to my grandfather. I haven't been Jesse since before my accident.

"She'll be home soon, Pop."

The doctors say that sometimes it's best to go along with him rather than confuse him with a gentle course correction. He thinks I'm my father and he's remembering a time my grandmother was out in a blizzard, but it feels like lying, and I've already spent so much of my life lying to him. Each new lie gets heavier than the last.

He mutters to himself, pacing slowly up and down the length of his room, his brows twitching in silent argument. I drop into the armchair by his window. My quad is sore, the bone aching, as if the plates the doctors screwed into me are rattling to get out. A common occurrence after rain.

"Have to put chains on the tires," he whispers.

After the car accident that effectively ended my firefighting career, George visited Pop while I was recovering in the hospital. He warned me that Pop's lucidity was coming in moments, in glimpses. He'd encouraged me to tell Pop before it was too late. "Now's the time, Jess," he'd said. "I know how badly you've wanted to do this. He'll hear you and understand."

I'd swung into this room a week after my surgery, still trying to navigate the world on crutches, but ready to speak the truth to the man who raised me.

"I'm bi, Pop," I'd wanted to say. But Pop wasn't there. My grandfather hasn't had a lucid conversation since; a switch has flipped in his mind, and the man I knew is gone. At least the version of him I wanted, needed, was gone, ripped out of him by this invisible disease that could, at this very moment, be taking root in my own brain. I felt like, once again, I'd missed my chance at something important, life changing.

I could tell him like this. There's nothing stopping me from saying the words now into this quiet room. His ears still register sound. He just doesn't know who it's coming from.

"There's something I wanted to tell you," I say, testing it out.

"The chains," he whispers. I step in front of him, hoping to catch his attention, but he stares over my shoulder, his mouth working silently.

"Pop, I…" It feels like cheating. Like when he used to ask me where I was going on a Friday night and I'd tell him "the movies," but not who with or why.

He grabs my arm, his grip surprisingly strong despite the near constant shake in his muscles. He looks up at me and his eyes seem so clear, focused in a way I haven't seen in a while. My heartbeat kicks up. This might be it. He might be *here*. Finally.

"Get your coat. We're going out to find her, Joey."

It's silly to be this disappointed. I should have expected it, and it's not his fault anyway. But I've been hiding myself from him for so long, it's starting to suffocate me.

"It's Jesse." I take his hand and press it to my chest. "I'm not Joey, I'm his son, Jesse. And I'm trying to tell you something important."

His cracked lips part in a gasp. The sound of water trickling onto the floor interrupts the silence between us. I look down at the urine soaking into Pop's pants and socks, pooling around his feet.

"Joey?" he asks. "What's happening? I'm so tired."

I close my eyes. Close up the rip in my heart with the reminder that none of this is his fault and the hope that one day he'll see me again. Today's just not his day.

"Let's get you cleaned up," I say, keeping the truth buried firmly inside my chest.

There are many voices coming from behind George's apartment door. When he texted me this morning, demanding that if I'm not going to answer him about the date the least I can do is come over for dinner tonight before work, I stupidly assumed it would be just us.

Already, I can recognize the voices singing along to "Winner Takes It All," with George playing the piano, the same one he learned on at his grandmother's house growing up. I take a deep breath on this side of the door. It's not that I don't want to see them, or that I'm mad at George for not telling me. It's the energy; I'm drained from seeing Pop, I'll drain more once I open this door, hug RJ and Annie and Lacey, if my ears are correct; once George corners me in his galley kitchen and gets the truth out of me. Then there's work tonight, the overnight shift that doesn't require me to talk to a lot of people but does require me to stay awake and alert for none of the reasons that I used to.

So I breathe here, on George's quiet apartment landing, squeeze the loaf of fresh French roll maybe a bit too hard. But it feels good, at least. I open the door just as they hit the second verse and the ABBA is quickly abandoned for squealing and RJ taking my coat and Lacey petting my hand and George slipping the loaf from me and whisking it into the kitchen, where a pot of his mother's spaghetti sauce bubbles. We eat on the couch and living room floor. George insists I am the one to take his new "adult" beanbag chair since it's comfortable and allows me to stretch out my leg, even though it's not bothering me right now. They have pink sparkling wine, celebrating RJ's new part in a Tennessee Williams play at the Walnut Street Theatre. George slices a lemon for my water.

It's nice even if it is tiring. My friends don't expect me to talk much but then they usually don't, and I get by answering only direct questions. Eventually, Lacey curls up on the floor next to me, resting her head on my lap, and the weight of her friendship is familiar and comfortable.

"We're going to go out tonight," she says. There's a sparkling wine and oysters special on Sunday nights at the local queer bar.

"I've got to work. I should leave soon," I say, checking the time on the clock above the empty dinner table.

"Help me clean up first," George says, stacking plates.

Here we go.

I dutifully follow behind him, collecting champagne flutes, and when I enter the kitchen, he turns on me. "You didn't stand her up, did you?" he asks.

I blink, confused for a moment. "No." I thought Lulu would have told him by now what a terrible date I was. "I wouldn't do that."

He starts loading the dishes in the dishwasher and I flip the faucet, letting the sink fill with water. "She didn't…" I start. "You haven't heard from her?"

He leans against the counter beside me, his forehead scrunched in concern. "Did you two make a pact to keep me out? An anti-meddling task force?"

"A…what? No. George. I haven't told you anything because there's nothing to tell." I pull a pot off the stove and dunk it in the sudsy water.

"You didn't like her?" He sounds affronted. He gasps. "She didn't like you?" Now he sounds aghast.

I shrug. The tips of my ears feel too warm under his gaze and I itch to get away from this conversation, but after yesterday's attempt at an intervention, I know I won't get away with that. Whether or not Lulu liked me isn't really the point. "Maybe dating wasn't the right strategy," I say. "For getting me back out there."

"Don't give up yet," he says. "I know a guy I could set you up with. He works in special collections at the library." He pops his brows like "sexy librarian."

"It's not a gender thing. It's a me thing. I just…" I sigh as I scrub at the pot. There's no sauce left on it; at this point I might rub a hole through the metal. "I need you not to rush me, OK?"

"I'm sorry," he says quietly, squeezing my forearm until I stop scrubbing. I turn to him, drying my hands on the dish towel he passes over. "How would you feel…" George asks slowly. "About being a part of a study?"

I check the time on his microwave, cookbooks and little orange bottles filled with his ADHD prescriptions sitting on top. "Do you have another survey for me to fill out?" As part of his research for his PhD, George is always sending us surveys to fill out, usually about the correlation between mental health and queer communities. "I don't know if I'm going to have time. I have to leave for work in half an hour."

George shakes his head and pulls a stack of papers off the kitchen table by the big bay window. George's parents set him up here in his sophomore year and as he's gotten more financially stable he's taken over paying the mortgage. I've had many a breakfast in that little nook, squeezed in next to George and the heater underneath the window, tasting the recipes he's tested over the years.

"I'm running a new study. It's cross-disciplinary, the medical school is involved, sociologists, too." He makes a face like *ugh*; George hates working with sociologists for methodology reasons I've never quite grasped. "Basically, it's a study to find out why adults, specifically millennials, have such a hard time making friends." He holds up the flyer on top of the stack for my perusal.

I laugh, a quiet *ha*. "If I knew the answer to that life would be a lot easier." I know what he's going to say before the words leave his mouth.

"You should apply," he says, like it's that easy. Like the terror invoked by the thought of walking into a room full of strangers isn't one of the reasons I'm like this to begin with.

"Yeah," I say. "Maybe." Sometimes it's easier to just go along.

"I'm serious, Jess. I think it might be good for you to meet new people."

"I thought y'all were pissed I wasn't hanging out with *you* anymore. Now you want me to find new friends?" I'm being petulant, I know, arguing for the sake of it. To get out of whatever new self-improvement project George is trying to assign me.

"First of all, I'm not pissed at you." He pauses. "Anymore. You're a different person than you were before the accident. Maybe you need to meet different people; maybe they're necessary for this different you to flourish."

The living room is silent, our friends clearly eavesdropping on us. I sigh. "Should I join the study?" I ask, projecting my voice to them on the other side of the wall. There's silence, then shuffling, a giggle. A sock puppet with a disturbingly human-shaped mouth peers around the corner and George cackles with laughter.

"We just want you to be happy, Jess," the sock puppet says in RJ's squeakiest voice.

Annie snorts and Lacey bursts into another song, playing the piano badly, and I think, even if I am a different person now, who could ever want for better friends than this?

Eight hours later, the words on the page of my hardcover swim together. Call it confirmation bias or coincidence, but after listening to Lulu's explanation of the history of witchcraft, I'd found a book about the witch craze in a pile of my grandmother's things in the crawl space. Both of my grandparents were big readers and they passed along their love of reading to me, even if I don't have as much time for it anymore. I'd spent a few minutes flipping through it, after giving up my search for the electric hedge clippers I knew Pop had stored somewhere before he moved out. The cover was clearly meant to shock the reader, with the painted image of two women hanging by their necks over a burning pyre, but the information inside is too dry for a night shift on security duty. I readjust the book light clipped to the cover, but it doesn't help. Close my eyes and let the printed words dissolve behind my eyelids. Lulu's explanation was far more compelling than this. I think I might leave the history to her. I scan the parking lot outside the security car's windshield.

A puddle the size of a small house halfway across the empty lot ripples under a faint wind, the last gasps of the storm that blew through last night. I glance at the clock on the dash. Fifteen minutes until I can go home.

I click the light, snap the book shut, stamp my feet on the floor mats to keep the blood in my legs moving. The company that contracts out our security detail to different construction sites around the county said security guards can leave the car on for the A/C to keep cool in the summer but leaving the engine running for eight hours a shift seems like something Cruella de Vil would do. In a way, this is just like firefighting. Hours and hours of nothing, then *boom*. Except I'm positive there will be no boom this time. Unless the sudden urge to pick up this book again counts.

Headlights from another security vehicle move across my windshield. My colleague, early for his shift replacing me, flashes his high beams twice. I flash them back and start the car, pulling out of the lot, the tires squealing unnecessarily on the asphalt. I drive toward the four-story glass building in the middle of an industrial park, five minutes away, where our offices are. As I step inside, the fluorescent lights blind me. Everything looks sleepy at two in the morning. The couch in the breakroom sags. The floors and furniture are washed out in the artificial light. Amir, my boss, isn't at his desk in the expansive and empty office off to the side of the breakroom, but his keys lie on the desk, and a half-eaten tuna sandwich sits on a square of waxed paper.

The A/C kicks on as I clock out on the computer, a process that takes too long since the machine is about fifteen years past its prime. Flyers on the corkboard above the computer flap in the breeze created by the artificial air. The computer fan whirs, the high-pitched whine like the dinky, secondhand dirt bike I got when I was fourteen and promptly wrecked. I input my hours, hitting Enter and waiting again for the processor to catch up, the cursor spinning in a blue circle of death. Finally, the screen shows the landing page, confirming that my hours have been inputted, and I stand to gather my things from my locker. Another gust of air blows from the vent above me and flyers flutter again, this time one falling off the corkboard and landing on the keyboard.

It's a notice for a rec touch rugby league and the grainy, unfocused photocopy of a rugby player in motion is a punch to the gut. That used to be me. Touch leagues, tackle, whatever. I've played since I knew how to toss a ball; instead of playing catch or teaching me how to throw a perfect spiral like all the other parents, Pop had taught me rugby rules in the backyard, while Grandma gardened. He drove me an hour each way to rugby practice two towns over when I was thirteen and showed up to my local league games after graduation. I was never good enough to play in anything more than an amateur league, but I loved it. Loved the sweat and the sometimes blood and the way we could lay all of our aggression out on the field and then crack open a can of soda together after. I loved pushing myself, feeling my lungs burn and my muscles scream. I loved winning.

And maybe George is right, because I don't know who that man is anymore. Even if my doctors hadn't told me I probably shouldn't play again, I don't think I'd play anymore. I want to, though. I miss the guy I was before the accident. I miss me. But the flyer is at least enough to remind me that George shoved a stack of flyers into my hands before I left tonight, asking me to share them at work. I wrench open my locker, flatten one out on the desk, and find a spot for it on the corkboard.

How to Make Friends as Millennial Adults: Psychological and Sociological Challenges in Forming and Retaining Adult Friendships, A Multidisciplinary Study, it says. Other than Amir and me, I don't think there are many millennials here. Mostly Gen Xers and a kid who barely seems legal to work past eight in the evening.

Are you a millennial adult (between the ages of 27 and 37) who:

- *Has difficulty creating new, lasting friendships?*
- *Experiences feelings of depression, anxiety, and/or loneliness?*
- *Feels that factors such as shyness, busyness interfere with forming or retaining platonic relationships?*
- *Believes friendships require too much work?*

Consider applying for the Millennial Effect: Challenges in Making Adult Friendships. This cross-disciplinary exploration of friendship and its effect on our physical, mental, and emotional well-being will take place over six weeks and could pay $1,000 upon completion (per the results of a participant lottery).

It's the $1,000 that gets me. And yeah, OK, I'd answer yes to all of those questions, but with $1,000 I'd have enough for a new water heater. Between Pop's savings and pension, I'll be able to keep him comfortably in the nursing home until his death. Pop and Grandma had put money away for my education but then I never got one. It feels unfair to use that money for home repairs.

I pull the paper back down off the corkboard, stuff it back into my backpack. I won't fill out the application form on this computer. Amir will be back before I can even get the internet browser open. I'll do it at home. Where no one can see me. I'll apply and might get chosen and hopefully I'll make $1,000. And if, in the process, I learn how to get back to the man I was before my accident? Well, that's just gravy, as Pop would say.

Chapter Four

Lulu

The doorbell camera stares at me, an all-seeing eye. I never know where to look. Do I greet it, treat it like the person standing behind it? Ignore it? I ring the bell again, wincing at the sound that echoes back at me through the front door, painted in a green that seems like it's meant to be happy, but is a bit too bright for my eyeballs. Branches and leaves sprinkle the front lawn but the porch managed to remain relatively intact after the storm, laid out like a photo shoot for one of those thick-papered home decor magazines. There's a wreath on the door, not a forgotten holdover from Christmas, the seasonal kind. Eucalyptus leaves and little yellow flowers.

"The door is open, Lulu," the disembodied voice of Calliope Singh, my high school best friend, comes from the doorbell camera. "I'm just putting the baby down. Come on in."

"O-OK," I say, leaning in close to the doorbell camera. This visit seemed like a good idea a few weeks ago when I reached out to her, but after multiple reschedules from both of us and still feeling the aftereffects of The Date, I checked my phone multiple times this morning hoping that Cally would cancel again.

No dice.

So, now my hands are clammy while I obsessively list my predesigned conversation topics: her mother's health; her sister's wedding; her summer plans. I've waffled over what to ask her about new motherhood, afraid that she's had to answer the same questions over and over but not wanting to seem uninterested in the baby. I fell down a rabbit hole this morning and now feel like I could pass the certification exam to become a lactation consultant while researching ways to best support a new mom, but I don't think I should ask her about her nipple soreness. At least not yet. We haven't spoken face-to-face in a while.

From the outside, the house looks big, with a three-car garage and two-story turret and an interlock driveway, but as I step inside I see it's the interior that would get it bumped to Zillow's front page. Cally's house is like something I've seen in a movie, all crisp white furniture and silver appliances, the straightest vacuum lines in the carpet and an entire wall of windows along the back of house, opening up onto a pool. The sun sends reflections off the water to dance on her kitchen ceiling.

It smells nice in here, something crisp and clean, not too floral or overpowering. There's a grand staircase to the left of the foyer but Cally comes out of a stairwell near the back of the house, a baby monitor in her hand. According to social media, Cally's baby is a few months old, still an infant, but Cally doesn't resemble anything close to what I imagine the mother of a new baby looks like; an exhausted mess. She glows. Her dark hair shines and her eyes are conspicuously bagless. She's always been petite, the girl who was perfect for the top of a cheer pyramid, but as she wraps me up in a hug she squeezes me with lean, strong muscle.

"How are you, Lu?" she asks, cupping my face. The shadows

of fading henna wind up her hands and arms. "It's so wonderful to see you."

Cally sits me out on her back patio, in the shade by the pool where she's already prepared a colorful Mediterranean orzo salad, protected underneath a mesh dome food cover. She offers me a glass of white wine, but I'm still feeling a little ashamed at how quickly the alcohol affected me the other night with Jesse, so I drink sparkling water instead. She sets up the baby monitor with the screen facing us, the volume turned all the way up, then she turns to me. I wilt under the weight of her attention, suddenly too aware of the ponytail I threw my hair into this morning when I remembered that I forgot to wash it last night or my short, jagged nails that I spent all of last week tearing at. "So," she says, then pauses so long I'm sure that she doesn't have a clue what to say next. "What have you been up to…for the last twelve years?"

Cally went away to school in California; Stanford. She met her husband there; they eloped in Mexico and lived there while they launched their interior design business. By the time she'd moved back to Pennsylvania, I was already in Lancaster getting my PhD.

"Well." I clear my throat. Cally and I used to smoothly chat for hours on the phone about nothing in particular and also the most important things in our lives, but this conversation already feels like sandpaper. "I decided to shift the focus of my research," I say, neatly skirting *why*—because I couldn't stay in Lancaster another minute with Brian and Nora and their blissful joy. "I'm focusing on depictions of witchcraft and gender in colonial New England."

She hums and nods around a bite of her salad. "Neat."

The bubbles in the sparkling water tickle the inside of my nose and I cringe instead of answering.

"And now you're following in your father's footsteps," she says. "Right? Just like you've always wanted?"

I take a massive bite of salad so I don't have to answer her. Is a nepo-baby contract instructor really "following in her father's footsteps"? By the time my mom and dad were my age, they owned the farmhouse they still live in. Dad was tenure tracked in his mid-thirties and already one of the most celebrated medieval historians in the US, maybe even the world.

And it's not like I can blame my parents' fortuitous fate at being born boomers, right place, right time to be able to afford homes rather than avocado toasts. Look at Cally. She has this huge home, a beautiful home. She's starting a family. She runs a lucrative business. She has her life together while I'm a thirty-year-old woman who still looks for the adult in emergency situations. Who can't afford to live anywhere but in her parents' extra apartment. Whose greatest achievement in the past month was keeping her sneakers clean since she can't afford to buy new ones.

"What about you?" I ask, practicing some of Jesse's well-honed deflection. I need some more time to sit with this uncomfortable emotion before I let it spiral into a full-blown panic attack on my old friend's pool deck. "Do you keep in touch with anyone else from high school?"

Cally is part of a Mommy-and-Me group with other moms and former alumni of our school. "You could come, if you wanted to," she says in that tone that makes the token offer clear. "We have a book club, and, um, a holiday cookie exchange. The husbands get together to watch Steelers' games, although…" She waves her hand in my direction. "That wouldn't be much interest to you, would it?"

Before I can clarify whether she thinks that because I am neither a Steelers fan nor a wife, the baby, Libby, wakes up from her nap. Cally brings her down and I pull out the gift I brought: a picture book I loved as a child, about space and stars. It's made of board and Libby immediately pats it with her chubby, dimpled hand, like one would a dog; I take this as a job well done.

Cally feeds the baby, apologizing at first when she almost flashes her nipple at me, but soon she's talking like there isn't a small person attached to her boob. Due to my recent interest in human lactation, I want desperately to ask her if I can watch but don't know how to do it without sounding invasive. And I certainly won't stare and make her uncomfortable. But it's this, trying not to catch a glimpse of my friend's nipple while simultaneously being curious about the mechanics of breast-feeding and what it feels like in real life and why she decided to breastfeed instead of use formula, that makes me realize how different our lives are.

By the time I'm ready to leave, a glass food storage container filled with leftover salad in hand and vague assurances that we'll "do this again sometime," I'm ready to put my panic spiral to rest. It's not that there's something wrong with me or her. We're just different. At different places in our lives. Like that old saying: some friends stay with you for a season, some for a lifetime. Maybe Cally was a season friend. We have nothing in common anymore, unless she randomly becomes interested in the inner workings of gender and witchcraft or I want to start a design business. And that's OK. I need to find my people. I just wish I knew where they were.

I love campus in the summer. The lush, green lawns where undergrads lounge and throw discs, take lunchtime in the quad surrounded by ivy-covered buildings and a few 1980s replacements. And trees, so many trees, leaves full, some trunks so thick I can't get my arms around them. Trees older than this institution, than this town.

And now so many of them are destroyed.

The storm wrought havoc on my campus. The school's social media department reported that some buildings still don't have power, though I won't know if mine does until I get there. Metal siding was ripped off the library; blasphemous.

And a window broke—luckily no one was hurt—in the med school, which is fine since that building is named after a morally questionable white man and I have to assume the damage was karmic.

The wind tore up Dad's garden, and almost washed out our driveway, which makes it easier to get off the self-pity train I've found myself on since my date with Jesse. It was silly and unfair to hinge my hopes on him, and I was clearly making beer-fluenced decisions. Plus, worrying about storm damage and meeting up with Cally was a great distraction.

I gasp as I turn the corner to the lesser-used back door of the history department's building. "You're OK," I squeal. My canvas knapsack bangs against my back as I run to my tree, my Keds slipping slightly on the still-wet paving stones. "Oh my god, oh my god, oh my god." I'm out of breath from this fifty-foot run but I'll worry about my cardiovascular endurance later.

The tree isn't as tall as the others. But she's hardy and stable and has a perfect climbing nook—not that I've climbed her before. That's where I draw the line. Her leaves reach well above my second-story office window, and I watched them change from green to red this past fall, watched them bud earlier this spring; now she's green again. A few of her branches litter the ground beneath her canopy. I don't know if she's in a well-protected location or if we just got lucky, but my favorite tree has made it through the storm.

Without letting myself think much harder about it, I wrap my arms around her trunk. It's rough and cool against my cheek, my shirt snagging on a whorl in the bark, and although I won't, I feel like I *could* cry with relief that this tree, this one constant, a small piece of joy in my day is still here. I squeeze her a little tighter.

"I'll bring George for lunch this week," I whisper. George is a friend. I think I could call him that. And before I met him, I spent a lot of lunches under this tree, in the fall, before it got too cold to sit on the ground. The tree doesn't answer—thank god—but a breeze rustles the leaves, like a soft sigh, and I decide it's for me.

A sharp laugh, the kind that sounds like it's at someone else's expense, cuts through the small courtyard. I straighten like my tree has been lit on fire. I'd recognize that laugh anywhere. Audrey. Other voices accompany hers. Frank, most likely, and Leo, who share teaching responsibilities for a first-year seminar. The early modernists were already well-established friends when I arrived and apparently, they don't have space in their lives for anyone else. They're the reason I dyed my hair back to blond from purple. According to Leo, I looked too much like a Smurf. Which doesn't even make any sense. Smurfs are blue.

It takes the echo of Audrey's voice between our building and the art history wing for me to realize that they're coming this way, into my courtyard.

And I'm still standing here with my arms around my tree. Like an absolutely unhinged person.

The double doors that lead to the stairwell that always smells like garbage are behind me, but by the sound of their voices I won't make it there before they're here and I absolutely cannot see them today, at least not right now. Not when I'm still tender about this past weekend, and earlier today, and the fate of the campus vegetation.

I look at the tree, at the pathway their footsteps clap down, at the doors behind me. "I hope there aren't any birds in here," I mutter as I hitch my foot as far up the tree as I can and grip two low limbs. I haven't climbed a tree since I was a kid, but it seems to be a lot like riding a bike in that I remember the general mechanics of it but still feel pretty unstable now that I'm up here.

Once I'm safely in the axis of the limbs, I wrap my thighs around the larger one and start scooching my way farther up. There's no way I'm going to let them see my Keds hanging down below the leaf line. I feel like Curious George. I *feel* ridiculous, but I'm in it. I'm a part of this now. I freeze as they round the corner into the courtyard, clinging to the bark, a death grip on one branch and my foot tucked so tightly between another I might not get that shoe back. I cling there as they chat about the upcoming internal conference, a sort of training event for the grad students to cut their teeth on presenting and discussion and critique.

My chest is tight, my hands sweating so much I need to readjust my grip. I feel like I did at Cally's, on the edge of a spiral. If my officemate, Jay, looked out the window right now, he'd be able to see the back of my head. Audrey, Frank, and Leo are below me, following the pathway to the double doors. They slow as Frank kicks a branch out of the way, and I squeeze my thighs and fingertips into the tree. I shut my eyes and imagine I'm as invisible as I've felt in this department since I got here. The bang of the door against the wall scares me, my heart jumping, but then it shuts and the courtyard is quiet.

They're gone. They're blessedly gone, and I did it. I avoided Audrey's suspicious stares and Leo's passive-aggressive digs about my father being a professor emeritus in the department, as if I was only hired because of him. I won't have to endure Frank boasting, again, about the article that was accepted into *Early Modernist Quarterly* while mine was not. I won't have to hear any more digs about my failed pitch for a new class.

I avoided them...

By hiding in a tree.

I, Eloise Alice Banks, Ph fucking D, climbed a maple tree less than forty-eight hours after a thunderstorm just to avoid interaction with colleagues with whom I'd very much like to be friends even if they don't want to be friends with me. I can't catch my breath and maybe I am a little bit allergic to this tree. My skin is hot, so hot and itchy, but I can't release my death grip to relieve it or else I'll fall.

A screeching sound makes me jump out of my skin and for a terrible moment, I brace for the impact of a mother bird's talons in my hair because I've disturbed her nest, even though it sounds more like a window opening than a bird attacking.

"Lulu?" Jay's voice comes from behind me.

Aw, hell. I wish I could go back to this morning, when my biggest problem was how Cally owns her home and I pay bare minimum rent to my mom and dad.

Jay laughs, a little awkwardly, and I turn to smile at him over my shoulder. "Are you OK?" he asks, sounding very certain that I am not.

"I was returning," I say, swallowing down the lump in my throat that could be either my heart or vomit. "An egg," I lie. "It must have fallen out of the tree in the storm."

He cocks his head to the side like maybe he won't believe me but then nods. "OK." Something draws his attention away, and he looks over his shoulder back into our office and this is my chance to get *down* from here, so I shuffle a few inches and reach my toe for the crook in the tree that I used to get up. I reach and as I make contact the flat rubber sole of my shoe, slippery from the residual rainwater covering the surface of everything, makes glancing contact with the slick, damp trunk and before I can scream or wish for a time machine or a leftover lightning bolt to strike me down, I'm falling. The ground comes so much faster than I thought it would, but I get my hands out just in time to land between the roots. Pain shoots through my wrist and Jay yells my name, panicked, and I say out loud to my tree, "You broke my arm."

Jay is at my side incredibly fast for a person who was on the second floor of the building and who is a historian. We are not, *historically*, a fast people. Miranda has followed him out, her phone in her hand.

"Oh god. You dumbass," I mutter to myself.

Jay is talking at me, but I'd prefer not to hear a word he has to say. I recite the monarchs of England since 1066 in my head as a distraction. Even my father has made his way down the stairs on his arthritic knees to watch with the rest of the history department as I pound the final nail into the coffin of my social—and professional—life.

I should have chosen self-pity. If I had canceled on Cally and was still lazing in bed, being sad about Jesse's rejection, none of this would have happened. "In a way, this is Jesse's fault," I say to no one in particular.

Jay frowns at me like he is quite worried for my well-being. "Let's get you to the hospital, Lulu."

"No." Slowly, I make my way to standing. I hop from one foot to the other. Other than the residual pain in my arm nothing else really hurts, but I feel creaky, like my body came out of the tree put together wrong. "See, I'm fine. I'm totally fine."

"You said your arm is broken," Jay says. "I heard you."

"But it's not." I hold it up, wincing as I turn my wrist in a slow circle.

He watches skeptically. "Even if it's not broken, we should still get you checked out." He picks a twig out of my hair and I huff a quiet thank-you.

"You might have a concussion."

I meet Miranda's eyes over his shoulder. She nods encouragingly and I look away only to be confronted by my father's mustache, twitching in confusion.

"Fine." I sigh. "Let's go."

Another code crackles over the intercom but otherwise, the only sound in this teaching hospital is the squeak of the nurses' Crocs on the floor. It's surprisingly quiet for midday, which would usually mean I'd have no distractions from the absurd situation I've put myself in. Except a very nice doctor decided to overmedicate me and give me a prescription painkiller for my wrist pain, as well as a "mild sedative." The panic spiral might have been more evident to others than I previously thought.

But at least the pain is numbed along with every other feeling. I'm not embarrassed, ashamed, or even sad. I'm floating on the golden sunlight drifting through the windows set high in the wall. I'm a dust mote, swirling.

I am very, very high.

High heels tap across the floor, so different from the sound of Crocs that I turn my head to the curtain cutting me off from the rest of the emergency room. Miranda pokes her head in and I don't have the sobriety to hide my wince from her.

"I was hoping you were my dad," I say. "Although, I don't think Dad can make it across the floor in your heels." Even turning my head sends me spinning so I don't look at her shoes, but I point with my free hand, the one not wrapped in a tensor bandage. My injured arm already feels itchy and while I know the bandage is necessary for the swelling, I want to rip it off. I'm lucky, really. I could have—should have—really hurt myself. I could have broken my neck, and for what?

Miranda perches on the edge of the bed. "Dr. Banks and Dr. Miller are taking your car home and then he's coming back here to drive you home." My brain record scratches for a moment on the name Dr. Miller until I realize that Miranda is talking about Jay. Miranda refers to everyone as doctor, which is fair. We've all spent so much time becoming doctors, why shouldn't we use the title?

My head is fuzzy from whatever is in the IV attached to my arm. Each thought feels heavy, turning over like a clunky engine, so it takes a minute before I process what she's saying.

I swallow a couple of times, my mouth full of cotton balls. "I have to teach my first class of the summer semester today."

Miranda doesn't say it but I can hear her *Oh no, honey,* just from the face she makes. "I'll cover the class for you," she says, holding up her hands when I start to shake my head, then wince as the world spins again. "The first class is always the easiest. We'll go over the syllabus." She shrugs. "And you can owe me one." She checks her phone screen. "I'm going to check on your discharge papers and get your dad's ETA."

I must say something. I think I do. Miranda nods, then the pale blue hospital curtain waves in her wake as she leaves. I doze, the drugs making my dreams of falling and falling and falling strange and liquid. When I wake up, Dad still isn't here and Miranda isn't around but my high is wearing off. I no longer feel like I'm in wonderland, and other than a slow throb radiating up my arm into my elbow and down into my knuckles, I don't feel like I just fell out of a tree in front of my employer.

I stand slowly, contemplate pulling the IV out of my hand myself until I remember that once I passed out watching a character get stitches on a prime-time medical drama. I roll my IV along with me as I shuffle slowly around the perimeter of my curtained-off hospital room, just to get some circulation back in my body. With every small throb of pain in my arm comes the echoing shame. No one has asked what exactly I was doing in that tree, but at this point I think it's best to stick with the story I told Jay while I clung to the bark. And that's where the shame comes in. I'm not embarrassed I was found in a tree or that I fell out of it. I'm embarrassed that I felt the need to climb up the tree in the first place.

My pace of shame is interrupted by the chime of my phone and I find it caught up in the sheets of my hospital bed. I think I was sleeping on it.

George: I'm gonna have to cancel our coffee date today. Can I get a rain check?

Me: Yeah np J

I don't bother explaining to him that I would have been a no-show to our usual Monday coffee date since I completely forgot about it until just now.

George: Word of advice: never plan a cross-disciplinary academic study. The only thing worse than working with one department of academics is working with like three other departments of academics.

George has been ranting about the cross-disciplinary study the psych department is spearheading for weeks. *The Millennial Effect: Challenges in Making Adult Friendships, A Multidisciplinary Study* has required George to liaise with professors and post-grads in the sociology department and med school and he insists it's been the worst experience of his life other than the time his middle-school bullies threw poor claustrophobic George into his own locker with his week-old ham and cheese sandwich.

George: No offense :P

"Lulu?" Miranda pushes back the curtain. "Oh good, you're awake."

I pat down my hair. My face feels puffy and like maybe there are pillow creases all over it. It feels entirely too vulnerable to have pillow creases on my face in front of a colleague; a contamination of my professional life with my personal one. Except who am I kidding, I fell out of a tree at work today.

"Yup." I take a deep breath. Best to get this over with. "Listen, Miranda, I'm so sorry about all this. I'm sorry you've had to devote so much of your time to…" I gesture to the mess that is myself. "Me."

Miranda wraps her fingers around my bare wrist, squeezing gently. "Don't apologize. I'm happy to help out a colleague."

She couldn't possibly mean anything by it, but the designation of colleague stings. Even though it's not like she would or could call me anything else. We certainly aren't friends.

"But," she says slowly, taking a step closer. Her earrings, large pearls dangling from a silver chain, swing hypnotically against her cheek. "I was wondering, what were you doing up in that tree?"

This is my chance to tell her the truth, to take control of the narrative even if the narrative makes me look silly. Better to tell her the truth, that my social skills have degraded to the point that I'd rather climb a tree than deal with interpersonal conflict, than the ludicrous lie I told Jay.

"I was…well, you see…"

But if I tell her this, this absolutely unhinged thing about me, she'll never let me lead a new class. I'll be lucky to get my contract renewed, vouching be damned. Inwardly, I cringe at the gleeful looks on Audrey's, Frank's, and Leo's faces when they inevitably hear about this.

"It was for a study," I say, my words jumbled and voice high-pitched.

"A study?"

I nod, as if that will help me sell this story. "I'm…applying to be a part of a new cross-disciplinary study headed by the psychology department."

"And the study required you to climb a tree?"

I swallow past more of this lie. "It was more an exercise in bravery," I say. I wonder how obvious it is that I'm literally making this up as I go. "The study is researching adult friendships and the whole process has been a bit scary. Putting yourself out there, you know?" I keep nodding, hoping to fool her bullshit meter. "So I thought, why not do something else that scares you, Lulu. Climb this tree! And you know, it helped. I climbed the tree and nothing bad happened. Well, nothing too terrible happened. I'm still here, aren't I? Yeah. It's helped. It's really helped."

"Helped what?" she asks slowly.

"It's helped me gather the courage to apply to the study, I mean. If I can climb a tree, I can put myself out there."

She cocks her head to the side. My pulse flutters in my throat.

"Neat," she says. "You'll have to let me know how it goes." Miranda taps away at her phone and my shoulders slump in relief. "Looks like Dr. Miller and your dad are back. Shall we?"

"We shall," I say brightly. She leaves to find a nurse to help with my discharge and I lean against my bed again. "For a smart woman, you're not very smart at all, Lulu," I mutter to myself. Not only did I just *lie* to a colleague and personal hero, but I'm also going to have to apply to George's study.

On the plus side, if I make it in, maybe they can figure out what the hell is wrong with me.

Chapter Five

Jesse

Despite having a map of the University of Wilvale open on my phone, I somehow manage to get lost two minutes before my appointment with the psychology department. I got stuck parking in the overflow lot down by the football field. Then I went to what turned out to be a dorm rather than the psychology building.

And now I'm late.

Fuck.

A text chimes from where my phone is gripped in my sweaty hand.

George: Where are you?

George was ecstatic when I mentioned I had signed up for the "friendship study." He immediately moved the conversation to our group chat, where I was bombarded with exclamation marks and emojis.

Me: I'm coming.

He sends back a clock emoji. He's not mad, I remind my-self. He's nervous. It's the first day of this new study and one of the participants is late. That would drive him nuts even if he didn't know me; the fact that he does know me just makes him more irritated. It doesn't help that since his intervention two weeks ago, Pop's mental state has deteriorated, I've been scheduled on almost constant night shifts, and my leg has been stiff and achy. I'm not trying to be slow as I finally make my way up the steps to the pysch department. My doctor suggested I use the cane they gave me after my surgery, and I have not mastered the rhythm of it.

George is waiting for me as I step out of the elevator, his hair standing on end and a clipboard in his hands. The frown on his face crumples when he sees me. Like he was ready to ream me out for running late until he saw me leaning against the glar-ing reminder of my accident. He'd been white as snow when he'd visited me in the hospital after. Quiet and unsteady in a way I had never seen from him. He's like that now, a moment where his face goes blank, all his breath leaving him in one gust.

"What's wrong?" he asks.

I shrug. "Nothing."

He glares at my leg like he has X-ray glasses, like he's mad at the limb for its structural failure when I slid my SUV into the middle of an intersection on an icy early morning after work. Like the truck that hit my driver's side was at fault instead of a combination of bad weather and my fatigue. I'm pretty mad at my leg sometimes, too; and mad at myself. I almost killed someone with my stupid decision to drive exhausted. I was supposed to be the guy using the Jaws of Life, not the one hav-ing them used on me, watching the recognition roll across my colleagues' faces when they saw through the smashed glass and mangled metal to who was underneath.

"I had to move your intake interview to the end of ses-sion," George says, clicking his pen and writing something on his clipboard. He's all business again. "Remember that I can't guarantee your participation in this study," he says.

"I know. Can I go in?"

He sighs, glancing over his shoulder. "Yes, but…"

"George, I'm fine." And I can't keep the edge out of my voice. It's hard enough to sign up for something like this, to admit that I'm a grown man and I can't do something as basic as meet new people. And now I am walking into this room full of strangers and having them all clock my cane with their preconceived notions about assistive devices and people who use them. I can't manage his emotions right now, too, on top of all the rest.

His jaw clenches. "Fine," he says tightly. And he turns his back.

Shit. "George," I say but he waves me off, turning to the next person coming down the hall. I shuffle into the room, my head down, to contemplate my life choices and avoid eye contact. The sound in the room quiets as the door shuts behind me.

"What are *you* doing here?" a high voice asks.

I stop when a pair of paper-white shoes come into view. I follow the bare legs up to a pair of jean shorts. My stomach sinks. I have never seen those legs, bare, but I know who they belong to. The hair on her thighs looks soft, almost white. Maybe it's their shape or maybe it suddenly makes sense, that George was trying to tell me something, to warn me, out in the hallway. And I'm the dumbass who snapped at him.

She swims in an Oxford shirt that's about two sizes too big, pink and white seersucker. Lulu looks around the small seminar room that's been appropriated for this study, at all the people— other potential participants, I assume—who are now staring at us as we stand off like it's high noon. She pulls her sleeve down over her arm, trying to cover her hand, but I see the bruise around her knuckles. She catches me staring and glances meaningfully at the cane. So, I say nothing. I'm not about to start answering questions in front of strangers.

A range of emotions pass over her face in the span of seconds: confusion, embarrassment, understanding, finally hurt before she shutters it away behind a false smile. It's strange to think that I already know her real smile; it doesn't seem possible after spending only one evening with a person. But I do. Her real smile has the power to blow me over, which makes it hard to accept this forgery.

"What," she says again, quieter, her words controlled. "Are you doing here?"

"I like your hair," I say. *I like your* hair? What the hell is wrong with me?

She rocks back on her sneakers, pressing her hand to the side of her head where her long blond hair is now wavy and shoulder length.

"It looks...shorter?" Panic grips my vocal cords at her continued confused stare. It *is* different, right? What if she hasn't changed it at all?

"I got it cut," she says flatly.

Another person enters the room behind me, and our captive audience divides its attention between the three of us for a moment before deciding that we are definitely the more entertaining ones. I nod to a pair of empty desks and chairs in the corner of the room and she grumbles but sits. I ease into the chair beside her, keeping my leg stretched out under the desk. She is rigid, one hand curled over the other. Now that we are no longer the entertainment, the rest of the participants are scrolling their phones or chatting quietly with each other, sending awkward smiles around the room. No one speaks above a quiet murmur and Lulu matches their volume when she asks, again, "What. Are. You. Doing. Here. Jesse?"

"What do you think?" I answer calmly when I really want to say, I'm sorry and what happened to your hand and I really do mean it your hair looks lovely and I've masturbated to the thought of you more than once I know that makes me disgusting but I can't get the smell of you out of my head. Most importantly, what are *you* doing *here*?

Lulu seems like the type of girl who was friends with everyone in high school, the one who has to decline Friday night plans because she has so many. Lulu is a social butterfly, and I was voted most likely to take a vow of silence in our senior yearbook. I peek at her from the corner of my eye. The more that I think about it, the more it doesn't make any sense that she's here at all.

"George never mentioned it," she mutters.

I shrug. "To me either."

We both glare at the door, where George stands on the other side intaking participants, when it opens and George enters with four other people in varying degrees of academic garb. One in a lab coat, one with elbow patches, another in a blazer, and, finally, a cardigan. George launches into introductions. As the administrator he's been integral to the planning of this and other studies run by the psych department. He complains in private about the workload, dealing with self-important academics, but I can tell that he loves this, the way that none of this could happen without him. Booklets are passed around with scheduling information and waiver forms that essentially state:

> *If chosen, over the next eight weeks, participants will consent to have their blood pressure taken once a week, wear heart rate monitors for the duration of the study, and an MRI scan at the beginning and end of the period so that neuroscientists and cardiologists can collect physical data on the effect relationships and connection can have on us. Participants must also agree to group and individual therapy sessions.*

"Participants must join at least one preplanned group activity a week, but are also free to create their own activities within the study. However, those events must be logged in the tracking app," he says, flipping through the pages of the booklet. "Finally, participants must sign this waiver form." He holds it up for everyone, like we don't have our own copies. "And you must also read the rules clearly," he says, speaking slower. "If you cannot follow the rules outlined within this booklet you might be removed from the study, which would remove you from the lottery for the financial compensation."

A woman at the top of the horseshoe raises her hand.

"Yes." George smiles but he doesn't look pleased with the interruption.

"Sorry. I don't think I've gotten a copy of the rules."

George is skeptical. He would have printed out enough for everyone. "That's OK. Get one from me after we're done here, but the most important thing to know is…" He pauses, waiting for the group's undivided attention. "Participants *cannot* enter into sexual relationships with other participants over the course of the study."

Maybe it's because I've been thinking of her so much. Or because we kissed that one time, one of the hottest kisses of my life. Or maybe I am the most awkward person on the planet, but when George says "sex," I look at Lulu.

And maybe she's thinking about that kiss, too. Lulu looks back at me. Her blue eyes are darker in this bright light, like the deep ocean.

George clears his throat, and we turn away from each other. He's caught us staring and holds our gazes for another moment, blinking between us in a way that reminds me distinctly of getting caught passing notes in middle school. "This is an academic study," he says. "Not a dating app."

We're divided into groups and ushered across the quad to the medical school. A nurse takes my blood, all of us sitting on cushioned recliners with motivational posters for entertainment. "What's the blood for?" I ask.

"Cortisol levels mostly," my nurse answers. She taps my elbow, smiling fondly. "Good veins."

I bury my proud smile beneath a frown. My grandmother was a nurse for thirty-five years. Anything that makes a nurse's life easier makes me happy. "You're all done." She hands me a cookie and her hand to help me up. "They'll book your scan in there." She ushers me to another room, like this is an assembly line of standard medical procedures. After being fitted with wristband heart monitors that we're to wear 24/7, like waterproof watches, we're herded back to the psych department for intake interviews.

My thigh aches. The pain radiates down into my knee, up into my hip and back so that by the time we're seated again, waiting to be called for our interviews, I can't find a comfortable position.

Lulu is one of the first people to go in for her interview. She wrings her hands together as she walks out of the room and I'm stupidly disappointed when she doesn't look back at me. The room is quiet, settled. People pick at their Band-Aids or spin the wristbands, and a few have already grouped off, starting conversations. I don't know what I was expecting; hermits with social anxiety? Basement dwellers who burn in the sun too easily? But everyone seems…normal. Turns out millennials who can't make friends are, literally, just like me.

More people leave for their intake interviews. And come back. But Lulu doesn't. Lulu was a whirlwind, she left me a little breathless. I wonder why she's here at all. If something happened to her that I never bothered asking her about on our date that changed the way she interacted with the world. George had mentioned she was lonely. I thought he meant in a romantic way. Not a life way.

I wonder why all these people are here. Maybe they're not real participants. Maybe they're plants.

I glance around the room, like the plants will reveal themselves to me if I frown at them hard enough. A brown-skinned guy shoots a smile at me across the room. He's handsome. With the sort of wavy hair and friendly, crooked smile that would have charmed me enough to go over to say hello to him a few years ago. Now, it takes me too long to notice I've not smiled back, that I'm scowling. That I could, should, respond. Say hello. *Make a friend.* That is the whole point of this study.

And yet, I do nothing. My mouth stays closed, my face blank, even as internally I feel like I'm screaming—at myself mostly—to do *something.* The guy frowns. Turns away.

Maybe I should leave. Maybe this isn't the path for me.

Stiffly, I stand, my hip throbbing, but as I step away from the desk, my cane tangles with the strap of a canvas knapsack. The top flips open, and a phone falls out, a large pink and green flower with "Votes for Women!" on the case.

The very least I could do is wait for Lulu, explain to her that this was a mistake, that it's not her, it's me. And that it wasn't her before, either. It was me then, too. I slump back into the chair. I'm scrolling a fitness equipment website for stuff I don't need in my home gym and can't afford anyway when Lulu finally walks in a few minutes later. Her eyes are red and puffy, her cheeks blotchy. She sniffles, dabbing her nose with a tissue, and leans forward in her chair, her hair hiding her face. Her body language says *don't talk to me.*

"Your shoes are very white," I say anyway, pointing. Other than a scuff on the toe, her Keds glow like she wipes them down every night. "I like them."

She sniffles again. "Thanks."

"I…" I search for something to say to her other than the worst things, like *what's wrong* or *are you OK?* "I got T-boned on my way home from work." I lift the cane. "That's why I'm not a firefighter anymore. Broke my femur."

She doesn't pay any attention to my leg, or my cane. She

looks in my eyes and asks, "What happened to the person who hit you?"

People make a lot of noise about the accident or want to see scars usually, so I have to recalibrate before I can answer. "She was OK. It was my fault, really. I lost control on a patch of ice and spun out. Apparently, she felt really terrible about it." I shrug. "I was pretty out of it. I didn't talk to her."

"I fell out of a tree," she says. A quiet laugh slips out of her. I pause; coming from almost any other person, I would assume that was a joke, an attempt at sarcasm.

"Wh—How?"

She frowns. "Like, gravity I guess?"

"Why were you in the tree in the first place?" I clarify.

She hums quietly, looking at the people around us from the corner of her eyes, then nods like she's made a decision. "I was avoiding my coworkers." She smiles weakly.

"They…they're part of the reason why I'm here. Well, not them. They're not like responsible for my feelings or whatever…" She stops, starts again. "I just mean, when I was younger, I thought I'd be friends with the people I work with. That's what it's like on sitcoms, right? Everyone is together for eight hours a day so why wouldn't they become friends? But it turns out that sometimes your coworkers are just your coworkers. You don't have to like them. You just have to work with them."

I liked my coworkers. We went out for drinks and had barbecues and they came to visit me in the hospital, in shifts and with cards, gifts, and baked goods. Less often once it became clear that I wouldn't be their coworker anymore, but they keep in touch. Or they try to at least. I've never considered how alienating it would feel to be so lonely at a place I spend so much of my time.

"And you think that if you do this then…what?" I know I sound skeptical, but I'm still processing the effervescent, self-assured Lulu that talked about the past for an hour and a half and asked me to come inside her house with this woman, who felt compelled to sign up for a friendship study. How can she see this group of lonely people and think, *I'll fit here*?

She takes a deep breath, surveying the room like she'll find inspiration there. I follow her gaze, my own stopping on George where he stands in the doorway watching us. "I just need to figure out what's... I need to figure out if it's me. I can't—I don't *want*—to live like this anymore."

"Live like what?" I ask, gruff. I'm prying but I can't seem to stop myself. If I were her, I'd stop me. With a quiet look, a frown. Grump Face or whatever she called it that night.

Lulu faces me head-on like she did on our date, sitting sideways in her chair rather than just turning her head. She gives her attention like she talks about early modern witches, with her whole chest. "Feeling like I don't matter. Feeling alone. Lonely."

"Who makes you feel like you don't matter?" I ask and she blinks at the edge in my tone. "I just mean..." I gesture at her. "I mean, look at you."

Her eyebrow twitches, her nostril flares. "What does my appearance have to do with anything?"

"Shit. No. I'm sorry." I knead my thigh, trying to give myself time to organize exactly what I'm trying to say. "You are successful. And you're quite...pretty." I wince for some reason, despite it being very true. "You've lived in a foreign country and..."

She lives with her parents, at least next door to them. She has friends; George is her friend. Although, George is my friend, too. And here I am.

"I guess I just had it different in my head," I explain. "That people who are lonely, alone, look different—are different—from someone like you."

"You don't look like you'd be lonely either, Jesse," she says quietly.

I nod. She has a point.

"Jesse," George calls. "You're next."

She smiles tightly, her lips pressed together. "Good luck."

I stand slowly, still feeling off-balance in a way that has nothing to do with my leg or cane. "I wasn't going to stay," I say. "In the study, I mean."

"Jesse," George calls again, impatient this time.

My whole life I thought I was going to be a hero like my grandfather. And now I'm…not. But that doesn't mean I can't still be brave, that I can't still do things that scare me. Lulu seems to do them all the time.

"Maybe I should?" I ask with a smile. My face feels green and unpracticed at the movement.

Her answering smile is wide. "You should. I'll be here when you're done."

I swipe my cane and follow George to the intake interview. For the first time in a long time, I find myself looking forward to something.

When I come out of my intake interview, my throat is raw from talking more than I have in a long time. My skin is tight. And I am tired, fucking exhausted. Sometimes when the firehouse got too loud, too full of people—which was always—I'd sit in a truck for a few hours. I'd find something that needed cleaning and take my sweet-ass time. If I could find a quiet place to recalibrate right now, I would, but Lulu stands a few feet down the hall, shifting from foot to foot. Some of the other study participants wait for an elevator farther down the hall.

"There's a bar on campus," she says. "It's called Pete's. I don't even know who Pete is." She winces. "Anyway. Some people from the study were going…"

When I said I wanted to get out of my rut, I'm not sure I meant *right now*.

Someone clears their throat behind me, and I turn to see

George standing inside the room. He shuffles some papers, pointedly ignoring me, but his eyebrows are up in his hairline and he's obviously eavesdropping.

"Yeah," I say, turning back to her. "Sure. Let's do it." I can decompress later, I guess.

We follow at the back of the group of study participants, taking the path between the engineering building that's like a maze and a multistory square building that might be a library. Pete's is located down a quiet hallway in the bustling University Center. It's small and dark and smells a little bit like old dishrags. The decor is decades old and a sign above the bar states that the bar has been "proudly grad student owned" since 1967. Despite the dinginess, the place is packed. I've never seen more academics in one place. Perhaps if I'd actually attended university, this wouldn't be the case.

And they are all, very obviously, academics.

There's a man who looks like Santa Claus except without the red suit. He holds court over a table of skinny white guys with neck beards who hang on every word he says.

"Philosophy postgrads," Lulu says, shrugging in their direction and rolling her eyes like I'm supposed to understand what that means.

"Hmmmm," I say.

People read well-worn paperbacks and thick textbooks and type away at old laptops while they sip beers and bat away fruit flies.

Our group has already commandeered three tables and shoved them together along a back wall with a long booth. A man from the study, Trey—with brown skin and his hair shorn close to his head, he's tall and built, handsome, and *not* the type of person I ever thought would have trouble making friends— starts collecting orders.

"Do you want a curry?" Lulu asks.

I blink. "That's a very specific order."

She frowns, sticking her lips out. She's mirroring me, my face. She wears it better than me. "It's the only thing they make here. If you order nine, you get your tenth curry free."

"Are you getting one?"

She nods. "It's good."

"Then yeah," I say. "Me, too."

She beams and, yeah, I'll risk the heartburn for that smile.

"Hey, big guy," Trey says, clapping a hand on my shoulder. "You want to help me carry some of the drinks back?"

He doesn't mean anything by it, I know, but my shoulders still reach for my ears. I cringe. What about my size says I have the skills to balance a tray of drinks?

"I can help," Lulu chimes.

We both slowly look from her face to her arm bound in a tensor bandage and the purple bloom of bruising on the back of her hand. "It's fine," I say. "I can help."

"I was a server in grad school," she says. "I can carry a tray."

Before I can argue further, she walks past Trey and me to the bar. He shrugs and follows her, and I guess that's that. I find an open spot on the end of the booth to squeeze into. The group chatters around me. About their jobs, their dogs, their favorite video games. And I can feel it, like a creeping fog. It's not just a loss for what to say, a social awkwardness I never grew out of. It's like one of those witch torture devices Lulu told me about the other night; a bridle forcing my mouth shut, filling my tongue with the taste of iron. I could say something, interject, offer a morsel of my life. But it's a skill I've never fully mastered. Maybe it's my size that makes me feel like a Kool-Aid man bursting through the delicately built walls of other people's conversations, but by the time I'm ready to talk, the conversation has always moved on.

Lulu returns, a tray loaded up with pints of foaming beer balanced on one hand, to the applause of the rest of the group. Trey helps her hand out drinks and when they're done, she hovers near the edge of the table, her own drink in her hand. The image of her hand wrapped around the pint of amber liquid reminds me of the night we met, reminds me of kissing her with the toffee taste of the ale on her tongue.

I stand to let her have my seat, and she sits close to the woman next to her, patting the scant inches of booth left for me. I sit for my leg, and not for the chance to feel her thigh pressed up beside mine.

Because, friend. Lulu is a friend. And just a friend. God knows I need one.

Lulu does what I can't. She talks, chatters. The sound of her laugh moves through her into me, a soothing low hum. She turns to me every few moments to ask me a question, to say, "Isn't that silly?", her tongue held between her teeth, the kind of carefree smile people make when they feel truly happy. She looks truly happy.

A server drops off our food, the table laden with steaming plates of yellow curry, potatoes, chicken, and rice, a separate tray of garlic naan. Lulu watches me as I scoop my first bite and blow on the scalding food. She raises her eyebrows. "Well?"

"I think I burned my tongue."

She frowns.

"But it tastes great." And it does. Comforting. Warm. Everyone tucks into their food with the same energy, the table quieting to more stilted conversations.

"Hey," Lulu says, bumping her shoulder to mine. "Thanks for coming."

I swallow too quickly, the burn following down my esophagus. "Yeah."

The bar is dark, the walls wood paneled; the booths are an old, faded rust color. It's populated with people who look, who *are*, far smarter than me.

"Hi, Dr. Banks." She smiles, waving across the bar at a tall, reed-thin white man with white hair and a white beard. He wears suspenders and his pants are a couple inches too short for his legs.

He nods as he sits with a table of other old, white men.

"Aren't you Dr. Banks?" I ask.

"We both are. That's my dad."

They don't look much alike, other than their height. Lulu is pretty tall.

"I get the feeling this isn't really your thing."

"You mean, being around other people?"

She bumps me again. The smell of her lavender shampoo and curry isn't a particularly delicious combination, but I think it will always remind me of this moment. Early aughts pop music playing just loud enough to make everyone have to yell to be heard, laughter, hot food, full stomachs, and teetering on the edge of this booth with Lulu. "You know what I mean."

I shrug. "How else am I supposed to learn?"

"Learn what?"

I look ahead, that suffocating feeling rising up inside me again. Learn how to talk again, how to fit in. Learn how to get out of this rut, what this feeling deep in my gut might be. "How to make friends."

Chapter Six

Lulu

Jesse Logan is giving Grump Face to produce, cantaloupes specifically. I'm surprised they don't shrivel beneath his stare. He doesn't notice me as I pull my cart alongside his and peek inside. There are a lot of leafy greens and enough apples to be considered a bushel.

He hasn't texted me once since our visit to Pete's last week. I haven't seen his name on the list of participants for any of the events the study has shared. My gut reaction is to assume it's me. That he isn't actually interested in friendship, that he was just being nice.

But I haven't texted him, either. I'm too afraid I won't get a response.

As he taps a few melons, I do what any self-respecting woman would when she sees a man who didn't want to sleep with her and would rather be just friends: I pick up two cantaloupes and balance them against my chest.

"What do you think of these ones?"

Jesse startles. His eyes drop to my melons, then quickly back up to my face. He turns red, looking anywhere but at me, until he smiles and finally, slowly, he laughs. The sound vibrates through me; it vibrates in very specific places in my body. Places currently squished by melons.

I put the melons down and stand with my legs and arms crossed, a defensive posture against the particular octave of Jesse's laugh. "Big plans on a Friday night?"

"Yeah, me and these melons have a big date," he says, then looks completely horrified that he said it.

"Do you want to grocery shop with me?" I ask, rubbing my wrist, sore from the awkward grip I had on a melon. I don't need the bandage anymore but I make a mental note to pack one the next time I want to palm produce.

"Sure," he says slowly, and I think, like that night at Pete's, he might not really mean it. Maybe this could count as an event that we can record for the study. We've all downloaded an app that will act as our journal. Every week we have to record the events we attend and our reflections on them. Since I am a lifelong teacher's pet, so far all of my journal entries have been overly long and detailed, with the sole purpose of currying favor with the doctors and psychologists who are studying us. Maybe if they like me more, I'll get an A+ in Friendship.

He pushes his cart alongside mine and together we move toward the meat section. Jesse grabs every animal ever slaughtered for human consumption before turning to me with a whole chicken in each hand. He peers into my meatless grocery cart. "You don't eat meat?"

"I do, but my mom is a vegetarian, and she does most of the cooking at home."

As soon as the words are out, I want to grab each one and cram them back in my mouth. Nothing says *I'm an adult with a PhD* more than *my mommy still cooks dinner for me.*

"That's a lot of food. That can't all be for you?" I say to change the subject.

"All me," he says, clipped. He stares straight ahead as we

make our way to the middle of the store. I make him stop in the health food section and I can feel his gaze on my skin like the softest touch as I read the nutritional information on a box of gluten-free pasta.

"For my dad." I hold up the box but, of course, Jesse says nothing. In the next aisle, Jesse contemplates fabric softeners while I load up on toilet paper made from recycled materials and all-natural all-purpose cleaners.

I'm used to spending time around academics who love to fill silences with their opinions on research and thinly veiled braggadocio. And gossip. Academics love to gossip. I even participated once upon a time, when I thought it would make me friends at work, but then I became the person they gossiped about, and lately my days have been filled with less gossip and more silence. Jesse and I have walked the entire store with only a few words between us.

I don't mind this silence, though.

"Logan," a deep voice calls from across the store. Jesse stops, his shoulders slumping as he closes his eyes. He sighs before he turns around to face the owner of the booming voice. And I almost ask him what he's doing, until I remember his last name and the first rule of bro culture: call everyone by their last names.

A group of men approaches, tall, muscular, and all dressed in the same variation of a casual navy blue uniform. Based entirely on assumptions and stereotypes built from years of watching first responder prime-time dramas, my brain immediately screams FIREFIGHTERS at me.

A Black man with biceps the size of my cantaloupes wraps Jesse in a hug. "Where the hell have you been?" I wince. Jesse is slow on the hug uptake, taking a beat too long to hug his friend back. "And how come you haven't been texting me?" The man gives him a gentle shove, the kind bros give other bros to demonstrate an aggressive sort of affection.

Jesse mumbles something inaudible before he's engulfed in another hug, this time from a middle-aged white man with a red mustache. "Hey, Buck," he says, muffled, into the man's shoulder.

It goes like this, Jesse hugged in turn by the group of laddermen until one notices me. I am tall, at the very least average height, but I feel like the last bungalow on a block that sold out to high-rise condos.

"Who's your friend?" Biceps Man asks.

"I'm Lulu." I wave and my hand is engulfed in his larger one.

"Marcus." His smile dimples his cheeks.

"How'd you meet this joker?" Marcus asks. He puts his arm around Jesse's shoulder and gives him an affectionate shake. Jesse eyes get big like he's trying to communicate something to me telepathically and I send him a message back with my eyebrows. I got this.

"A mutual friend set us up on a date," I say. "But we decided we'd be better as friends."

At the word "date," the affectionate jostling increases, and as a group their volume gets louder.

"Ooohhhhh."

"Logan had his first date?"

"Hope you were home by curfew, bud."

Jesse takes it all in stride, his cheeks pinking up but a small smile on his face. He returns their teasing with some gentle ribbing of his own, slipping into a version of himself I haven't seen yet. He stands with his shoulders back, his feet planted. He grows taller, bigger, instead of shrinking among the rest of these big men. But he's still separate; he's quieter, the low tone and measured cadence of his voice pitched on a frequency that makes him crystal clear despite their laughter and joking. Where they have an almost frenetic energy to them at seeing their old friend, Jesse is calm.

A radio, clipped to the man with a mustache's belt, squawks

and everyone quiets. They listen as a dispatcher says something completely indecipherable, that may be a code or an address or both, but they all seem to understand it. One of them runs back to their carts filled with food to drop off two loaves of bread then sprints out of the store. Marcus squeezes Jesse's shoulder. "Gotta go."

"Yeah." Jesse sounds resigned.

"Hey," Marcus says, walking backward through an empty checkout line. "Pick up the phone the next time I call you."

Jesse nods.

"What just happened?" I ask.

Jesse watches them go. The fire truck streaks past, lights and sirens blaring. I cringe at the sound, my shoulders creeping up to my ears as a shudder moves down my spine. The sound of sirens—or worse, the horn—has always felt like a sensory overload.

"They got a call," he says. He walks over to their carts and pushes them flush along an endcap. "We're—they," he corrects himself. "Are on call 24/7 when they're working. Sometimes they have to leave their groceries. They'll come back if the call doesn't take too long. The staff takes care of anything perishable for them."

"So they were your...battalion?" I ask.

He smiles. "My company. Yeah."

"But you don't talk to them anymore?"

He pushes his cart to a checkout line. "Nope. You ready to go?" he asks, once again declining to answer questions. And I want to ask him, why? And for how long? And if he doesn't speak to all of them or just a few, just Marcus. I want to know if he was out to them and if they weren't good to him.

I want to know if one day someone new in his life will see the two of *us* together and witness the history written between us, if there will be something there in the way we'll talk to each other or touch. From somewhere deep inside me, that's something I want. To be a part of someone's past, to have deserved more than just a footnote in their history.

A desire that's silly when I stare too hard at it. It feels like wanting to belong to him or to own a piece of him for myself.

There's a force field around Jesse and I think it's to protect him, but I think it isolates him, too. The stubborn part of me, the part that stuck with Brian long after it was clear we weren't right together, who stays at U of W even though it feels like dragging my career through a swamp; that part of me wants to get past the force field. I don't want him to be alone over there.

And maybe I want to protect him a little bit, too.

Jesse goes through the cashier line first and bags my food for me after. He pushes his cart to my car and helps me load the trunk. "I can do all this myself, you know," I say as I watch him heft a bag of potatoes.

"It's mostly an excuse to make sure there isn't anyone hiding in your back seat."

"That's a very specific fear to have," I say, peering into the back seat with him.

He shrugs. "I saw it on *Dateline*, and it freaked me out." Jesse closes the trunk with a *thwump*.

In the settling silence, I blurt out, "I can and *do* actually cook but I just have a tiny little kitchen in my apartment so…"

He nods slowly. "I remember."

I flush, at the reminder of that date, of reminding him of the reminder. "I didn't want you to think that my mom cooks for me all the time. Well, she often does but…my parents coddle me."

Jesse's eyes travel over my face. "You should let them," he says and there's no admonishment in his voice, maybe just an understanding of what it feels like not to be coddled. I want to hug him now, though. Jesse deserves to be coddled, too.

"I've been trying to coddle *them* actually," I say. "The storm absolutely annihilated my dad's garden, and I want to help him fix it up but turns out gardening is way more physical than I thought. It's going to take me all summer to finish the job."

"My yard got pretty trashed." He nods. "But I used to help my grandparents with the landscaping so I've been fixing it up."

"Do you think…" I stop myself. It is entirely too rude to ask that.

"Do I think what?" He shifts his weight, like he wants to get away.

"Nothing. Never mind."

Jesse pauses and I feel myself flush under his gaze. A streetlight flickers on, the buzz of electricity harmonizing with the buzz of the night bugs swarming it.

Jesse takes a step back, like he's going to take the out I'm giving him, flipping his keys in his hand. "I had a nice time."

"You did?" Of course, I liked having company while I did one of the most boring chores on the planet but I don't have a translation key for Jesse's face yet. "Me, too," I say quickly.

His eyebrows jump like he's also surprised. "Cool. Well. I better let you go."

I laugh. "Oh yes. I have a busy night of trying to parse meaning from Derrida."

He frowns and maybe that sounded like a humble brag rather than what it really was, a joke at my own expense. "You haven't signed up for any events yet," I say, quickly.

He shrugs. "I've been working nights. It's hard to coordinate sometimes."

"Are you working tonight?" I ask, my voice high. Asking someone to hang out with you is just as nerve-wracking as asking someone on a date.

"No," he says slowly.

"Do you think you could help us?" I ask. "Help me? With my dad's garden."

He sighs but it's not a frustrated sound; in fact, maybe it's not a sigh at all. It might be Jesse's attempt at laughing. "Not tonight," he says.

"No," I say quickly. "Of course not."

"Text me tomorrow. You have my number, right?"

I nod.

Jesse waits until I pull out before he pushes his cart to his truck. "Friends," I say over the pop music playing from the radio, gripping the steering wheel with nervous hands. I watch his retreating form in the rearview mirror. "We're friends." I'm trying to find my place here, and I can't do that if I'm harboring unrequited crushes.

Mom comes out to help me unload the groceries, and after a quick shower I slip back into their house. "Hey, Dad." I knock softly on his office door. He glances up from his book, peering at me through glasses that have fallen low on his nose.

"Hi, Lu."

I let myself in, settling into the wingback chair across from his desk, my own book on my lap. I read once that heaven was your favorite place on earth, and I think this might be my heaven. Dad's office exists in a perpetual golden haze, bathing the books, books, and more books, and my parents' numerous framed degrees in dim light. It smells like leather and coffee and the medicinal scent of my father's gardening hand cream.

My mom putters around the kitchen, humming to herself while she makes a cup of tea. The tinkle of fine bone china and the whistle of the kettle just reach us here in the back of the house. "What are you reading?"

It's a good thirty seconds before he replies. It takes a long time for him to get out of his head. His chair creaks as he leans back, pulls his glasses off his nose, and rubs the spot where the pads left marks. "Just reviewing the sections I've assigned from Bede's *Historia Ecclesiastica* before Monday's class. All these medieval historians stole from each other so much, I can't remember who wrote what anymore." He nods at the book in my lap. "And what are you reading?"

The low timbre of my father's voice is a soothing blanket that I want to wrap myself in; it's the perfect end to what ended up being a really nice evening. I hold up a book Miranda recommended about European witchcraft in Tudor and Stuart England and the Colonies. My dad's eyes travel over my face. "You seem peaceful tonight, Lu."

I press my thumb into the sharp corner of the hardcover. I don't know how he does that, how he knows exactly what I'm feeling underneath everything churning at the surface, but being so known is a warm hug and also makes me want to cry a little bit. The deckled edges of the library book blur as I smile.

One of the worst parts of being a departmental pariah is my father knowing all the details. He heard the gossip about the decline of my relationship with the *illustrious* Dr. Brian Mason in the elevator, the breakup following me all the way across the Atlantic. He can't ignore our colleagues' whispers that *he* is the only reason I am here and they're not wrong. I've conducted groundbreaking research into the social impacts the witch craze had on a small English town between the mid-sixteenth to eighteenth centuries, but I'm still relatively new to the field and to my new area of focus. It's undeniable that my name—our name—has helped me get this job, but there's still nothing that could make me regret being his daughter. Not when my dad still looks at me like I have never done a thing wrong in my entire life.

"I'm excited to teach a seminar over the summer," I say. Summer courses are always an eclectic mix of students who failed a credit during the regular year who have chosen the course they believe to be the easiest makeup and those who truly want to be there.

Dad drops his chin to peer at me over his glasses, his brow arched. "Is the university offering you another contract at the end of this one?" Non-tenured contract instructors are offered a maximum limit of three full credits, so my contract ends at the end of the summer term.

"I don't know," I say. I take a renewed and keen interest in my book. If the school does renew my contract, I'd rather not have Dad be a part of it this time, but there's a pit in my stomach at the thought of telling him that. Like I'll seem ungrateful for all of his past help, for how he still critiques my papers, and gives notes on my lectures, or how I wouldn't be where I am without him, without his name.

He slides a piece of paper across his desk.

"What's this?"

Dad nods at the paper, saying nothing. His mustache twitches as he fights his smile. In epic boomer fashion he has printed out an email rather than just forwarding it or CCing me on it like a normal person. The email is from his friend at Lancaster University, a woman I worked closely with during my undergrad and graduate work.

We'd love to have Dr. Banks (Jr.) back in a more permanent capacity. Our department is deep with military historians and we're hiring new instructors to bring balance to the research on offer. Please share with Lulu to send me an email so we can set up a video chat at her earliest convenience.

Dr. Cecelia Lucas
Department Chair, Lancaster University

Heat rushes up my spine and it takes a moment to identify the hurt. Not only has my dad contacted Dr. Lucas without consulting me, but this means he's seen how miserable I've been and has never acknowledged it.

"You want me to…leave?"

"I want you to be happy," he says, his voice soft and purposefully kind.

My father loves me, and I believe him when he says he wants me to be happy. But I've been home for almost a year now and have yet to hear someone say to me, *I'm happy you're here, Lulu.*

But then it sinks in. Not only does he not want me here, he used his clout to get me another opportunity. "Why did you go behind my back?" I ask. "Why couldn't you have let me try for myself?"

"You had such a hard time finding a new position," he says, and either he doesn't notice my flush or he doesn't care. "I was just trying to help." My face is too hot. A headache blooms in the back of my head, throbbing with every beat of my pulse.

One summer, as a preteen, I became obsessed with word origins after reading some of my father's texts and trying to translate the Latin and Anglo-Saxon. Humiliation comes from the Latin word *humiliat-*, meaning "made humble." This is about as humbling as it gets.

"Lu?" His voice is tremulous, heavy with the concern that he's done something wrong, and I'd rather fix this look on his face than admit this: I am surrounded by people all day and most of the night and yet I feel so very alone.

I smile, big enough my skin feels like it's cracking. If I hold on to the warmth in my chest when I first walked in here, maybe I won't lose it all completely. "I'll think about it. Thanks, Dad."

He watches me until he seems satisfied enough with my answer that he cocks his head to the side, as if listening to a far-off tune. After a moment, I hear it, too. The direction of Mom's humming has changed, now coming from the sunroom where she'll spend as much of her time as possible as the weather gets warmer. His lips twitch in the beginning of another smile. "Why don't we pilfer some of Mummy's cookies?"

Dad stands slowly and walks with a limp while his bad hip

works out its kinks. Sitting on his desk behind him are the untouched gluten-free, sugar-free, vegan cookies Mom gave him
after dinner, citing his cholesterol and general age as the reasons why he can't eat Mom's "special" cookies, which are really just chocolate chip made with lard. Mom charged me with
making sure he drinks more water and takes a ten-minute walk
every hour since we work together now. But she never counted
on the fact that while our love of history is the only thing we
have in common, my father and I will do anything to make
each other happy.

Right now, that's exactly what Dad is trying to do. He's trying to make me happy. So, I smile again. For real this time.
"Yes," I say. "Let's."

Chapter Seven

Jesse

The only person who micromanages yard work more than Lulu is her father, Dr. Banks. Both of them take turns hovering nearby, offering to help dig holes or cut back bushes, despite being told repeatedly by the third Dr. Banks—Lulu's mother—that, a) on the advice of his medical doctors, he should do neither and b) I've told them repeatedly I don't need help. However, rather than offering criticism at my lawn mowing skills, Dr. Banks asks questions about everything from the placement of certain flowers in the garden to how I hold a trowel. He does it in such a gentle, thought-provoking way that half the time I end up doing it the way he would instead. Lulu does the same but most of her questions are about whether or not I have enough sunscreen and if I want to borrow a hat, or asking me to assess my level of dehydration.

If I were at George's house, with his dad—if either of them bothered to care about their garden—I'd have told them both to back off and go inside by now. But it's easier to say nothing and just let Lulu and her dad hover. Plus, I *was* feeling a bit dehydrated earlier and Lulu brought me water and her mom's homemade lemonade. That was nice.

"Dad, maybe you should go inside to cool off." In the last fifteen minutes, as I've started the repair on her mom's raised vegetable garden, Lulu has turned her micromanagement on her father. He is *not* as patient as me.

"I'm fine, Lu," he says firmly. I only met the man two hours ago but even I can tell, after Lulu's third attempt to usher her father inside, that he's fuming. Though she does have a point. Her dad is wearing pants, not shorts, his shirt is buttoned up at his wrists and under his chin. His mismatched Tilley hat is old and frayed on the brim, sweat stained around the temples, and while it keeps the sun off his face, it's clear from the flush in his cheeks that he's overheating.

I get it, though. It's his garden, clearly his pride and joy. He can't leave it in the hands of someone he just met.

"I think I'm going to take a break," I say, setting down the hammer and sitting back on my heels. It's only partly a concession to Lulu's campaign. My leg is getting sore and if I don't take it easy now, I'll have pain radiating into my back and hip soon.

Lulu perks up. "Do you want more lemonade?"

Fuck yes. "That would be nice."

She trots back into the house and after a moment of looking longingly after her, Dr. Banks follows her into the air-conditioned house with a quiet "thank you" and nod.

A few minutes later, Lulu finds me in the side yard, the green garden hose leaking a small ocean onto the paving stones and into the grass. My T-shirt is balled up in my fist, the water nipple-puckeringly cold as it sluices, lethargic, from the nozzle over the back of my neck.

"Oh," is all she says.

I straighten, holding my T-shirt in front of my chest. Lulu looks at me, then away. She stares down into the glass of lemonade she holds in front of her, ice cubes clinking gently.

"Sorry," I say, feeling awkward and exposed.

She shakes her head. "No. It's fine. I'm just…" Her hair whips across her face as she continues to shake her head. "It's hot. Outside, I mean. The temperature is hot. Like, of course. Tarps off. Free the nipple." She lifts her fist in a show of solidarity then laughs, cackles almost.

"Cool." I turn to cut off the water and she hisses my name. I spin on my heel. "What?"

She touches the back of her neck. "What SPF did you say your sunscreen was?"

"I didn't," I say slowly. "I'm not wearing any."

She rolls her eyes. "Come on."

Lulu pulls out a chair for me beneath a vine-covered pergola. "Sit." She snaps her fingers and points at the padded lawn furniture.

I hesitate, my ass halfway into the chair. "What are you going to do to me?"

She holds up a bottle of SPF 50. "Protect you from skin cancer. Sit down."

I do. And not because she told me to in that voice. Well, not just because she used that voice. "I'm all wet," I mumble.

She yanks my T-shirt from my fist and pats it against my back. I cringe, the friction making the sunburned skin there raw and prickly. The lotion is a cold shock, but also soothing, and Lulu's fingertips hesitate for only a moment before she starts to rub it into the back of my neck and down my shoulders. Her touch is ginger and soft, a little awkward. I don't think she's rubbing it in all the way; I'll have streaks for the rest of the day.

It's not until she takes her hand away, the sunscreen still sticky on my back, that I realize I can't remember the last time I was touched by another person like this, skin to skin.

"Thanks," I say, my voice rough.

"Are you sure I can't help?" she asks.

I survey the progress I've made so far, where the sun sits in the sky, estimating how much time I have left in the day. "You could help me weed and mulch."

The way she smiles, I question whether she knows that she's about to spend the next few hours on her knees, the sun baking her neck, her back straining. "Let me go change," she says, running around the corner to her apartment.

Lulu was wearing the kind of yoga pants that seem super soft and make her butt look like a perfect replica of the peach emoji.

Not that I was staring at her ass.

She comes out in a pair of gray linen shorts, a T-shirt, with a mint green dress with large pockets over top. She spins, holding a straw hat with a wide brim to her head, and I see that the mint green thing is not actually a dress at all. "I finally have a chance to wear my gardening apron."

She's barefoot but I guess that's fine, if we're only weeding.

"What?" She points to her own forehead. "You're grumping at me. Do I look silly?"

"No," I say quickly. She looks…adorable, pretty. She looks very much like herself. But that seems like something a not-friend would say. Plus, I still feel guilty. I was definitely staring at her ass.

"You look ready to garden. Pick your poison." I point to the numerous weeding tools her father has in the shed and she comes out with a fishtail weeder. We weed side by side; the only sounds are the birds and insects, the quiet tinkling of music coming from inside her parents' house, and her sporadic frustrated grunts when she can't lift a particularly entrenched weed. The sky is cloudless. The sun at its highest point. As we move along the beds, near the house and under trees, the light catches Lulu in odd ways, making her hair both dark and golden, her skin pink and peachy, her eyes shine.

"So." She wipes the back of her hand against her forehead, leaving a streak of dirt. There's a pair of gardening gloves tucked into one of her gigantic apron pockets but she's let the dirt get under her fingernails, into her fingerprints. "How's work?"

"Like, security?" I ask.

"Yeah." She scoops up a pink worm from the soil, placing it gently in a patch of dirt we've already tilled.

It's hard to condense eight hours' worth of sitting on my ass in a company car into an explanation that doesn't sound mind-numbingly dull. "I read a book during my shift the other night," I say. "About witches."

"No way." She sits back on her heels for the express purpose of shoving me.

"Way."

"And?"

I shrug. "I liked it better when I heard it from you." The words slip out before I think too much about them. They're honest. But maybe too honest. I don't have to look at Lulu to know that she's beaming at me, her smile a little crooked, her lower lip rounder on one side than the other. I clear my throat. "How about your work?" I ask.

I still don't really understand what Lulu does. She teaches, I guess, but the other side of academia is a bit hazy. It seems like Lulu's job is to research the past and then just have…thoughts about it. And write down her thoughts.

It sounds like both the best and worst job ever: getting paid to think; having to share those thoughts with others.

She sighs. "I'm trying to pitch a new class."

"About what?"

"It would take me like, thirty minutes to explain everything. I'm really bad at pitches."

"I've got the time," I say, gesturing to the metric ton of dirt around us.

"I want to teach a class about magic," she says.

I wait.

She smiles.

"I thought you said this was going to take half an hour?"

She rolls her eyes. "I think the witch craze created magic."

Lulu didn't really strike me as the type, but OK. "I see," I say slowly.

"Ugh. No. Not actual magic. There's a historian of religion and spirituality, Audrey Robbs, who teaches a history of magic course in my department."

"That sounds...cool?" I can't tell by her facial expression.

"It *is* cool. That's the problem. She talks about the ways we've conceived of magic throughout the centuries. She'll even re-create some alchemical experiments—the ones that are the least likely to kill you, of course."

I only vaguely understand that reference but nod along as if I know more.

"The history of what we've perceived as magic is cool and sexy, where the history of witchcraft is all burning people at the stake and a rational discussion of the gender-based violence that we are still experiencing to this day."

"Wait. We still burn people alive?" I ask.

She laughs. "Not quite. That's a bit of a misconception. We often associate women burned at the stake with witchcraft but far more women were drowned or hanged than burned."

"Neat?"

She eyes me. "Are you being sarcastic? Am I talking too much?"

"I like listening to you talk," I say. "And I'm almost never being sarcastic."

She still squints at me, suspicious. "Was that sarcasm?"

I laugh. "Lulu."

She digs for a bit before speaking again. "Audrey is doing something groundbreaking. She's found the perfect balance between *Ancient Aliens* and legitimate historical research. Her course makes people excited about history. Whereas I look at the witches, and listen, were some of them actually witches? Probably."

I snort in disbelief and she pauses.

"Real witches?" I chuck a pebble out of the soil and avoid making eye contact with her after the sound I just made.

"Like, not *real*. They're not making covenants with the devil and dancing around topless. At least we don't have evidence of that. Think more like, folk healers and midwives. They weren't magical. But that was the perception. Although, by the eighteenth and nineteenth century there was a theory advanced by a German scholar that there was a cult of witches with pre-Christian origins but that's likely hogwash."

"Lulu," I say, a gentle redirection.

"Sorry. Most were just old, or lonely, or childless, or unmarried, or too loud, or too weird. They were people operating outside of the societal and gender norms of the time. Yes, there was a legitimate and intense fear of the supernatural, or evil and the devil, of magic. But what people were really freaked out about was the concept of people living outside the norm. People created magic, or co-opted it, to use it as an excuse for violence."

"Oh."

"Yeah. Not as sexy." She sighs.

Despite the heat, the buzz of bees, and the chirp of birds in her dad's trees, it's not hard to imagine Lulu behind a podium at the school. Her excitement for the topic is contagious and the soft tones of her voice are a substitute for the music I'd usually play while doing yard work.

"Anyway." She huffs. "I don't think they'd let me teach my class if they already have hers."

"What if you taught it together? Like a combined class."

When she looks at me, her eyes snag on my chest and I decide that I don't care that I'm warm from the work and the fabric will stick to me, I'm putting my shirt back on. It's weird if I'm the only one half-naked.

Lulu waits, watches as I pull my red T-shirt over my head and flatten it against my stomach. Once I'm settled back beside her on the grass, I say, "I don't know how academia works. Maybe that's a stupid idea."

Lulu bites her lip to tamp down her smile. She flushes, her eyes taking on the excited gleam she gets when she talks about historians and gender theory. In the short time I've known her, I have met Lulu in a dark bar and the bright sun, seen her upset, sad, flustered. Horny. Excited. I have yet to find a moment when she isn't beautiful.

Immediately, I look away from her. I stare at the rosebush planted alongside the pergola, follow an ant as it climbs from my glove to my wrist, anywhere but back at Lulu, so she won't have to see the thoughts on my face. Those are not the kinds of thoughts friends should have about each other.

Lulu stares off into the distance over my shoulder. "You're a genius, Jesse Logan."

"Well, I don't know…" I flush outwardly, but inwardly I am warm and liquid.

"Look how much we got done. You should have let me help hours ago."

I sit back on my heels to survey our progress. We only have to finish this flower bed. Lulu stands, brushing her hands off on her apron.

"Yeah." I stand slowly, stretching my back after being curled over the dirt. "We make a pretty good team."

Lulu tips a bag of mulch over onto its side and pulls a wood-handled knife out of another one of her apron pockets.

"Whoa. I can do that," I say, but she waves me away.

"I got it," she says. "You should know that Audrey would probably joyfully beat herself with her own chewed-off arm rather than co-teach a class with me." She smiles down at the bulging plastic bag, the look on her face in total conflict with the absolutely wild claim she's just made. Lulu looks up at me from across the lawn. "But it's a good idea nonetheless."

It happens in slow motion. Or at least it feels that way. She's still smiling at me as she grips the knife in one hand and holds the bag in the other, as she stabs the blade into the corner of the bag farthest from her and pulls.

Her smile stays as I watch the knife slip, the blade carving a deep line into the fleshy part of her palm at the bottom of her thumb, leaving an angry red line. It takes a moment for her mouth to make an O, for the blood to stream from the wound. For me to get across the grass to her side.

"Crumbs," is all she says, staring down at the gash, holding her wrist so tightly with her other hand, her fingers would be white if they weren't already stained with her blood. She leans into me. "I can't… I don't like…blood," she stutters, her face losing all color.

"I'm sorry," I say.

"For what?" she asks, her eyes huge in her face.

"I'm going to get blood on your gardening apron." I wrap her hand in the underside of the apron, where there isn't a streak of garden soil. "Where's your first aid kit?"

"The kitchen…my parents' kitchen."

I pull her with me to the back porch. "Dr. Banks," I call as the screen door bangs open. The hallway is dark, it feels almost pitch-black after the bright sun of outdoors. The floorboards creak under our feet and vaguely I worry about the dirt I'm tracking in from my work boots.

"Lu?" Her dad pokes his head around the corner. His mouth makes the same O shape hers does when he sees us, her blood on her clothes and my hands wrapped around hers. "What happened?"

"First aid kit?" I ask.

I follow him around the corner into their brightly lit kitchen.

Lulu drops into the nearest chair, taking what was clearly her father's spot, where he was enjoying a cup of tea and toast, a thick book laid open flat.

"I'm sorry," she says. "I'm so sorry." The tears streaming down her face are almost like an afterthought, like she doesn't even know she's crying. Other than a slight tremor in her voice, she doesn't sound like she's crying at all.

"What? Why?" I ask, as her dad finally locates their first aid kit—a reused cookie tin—underneath a stack of cookbooks in a shelf over the fridge. He has to stand on a stool to get to it and I am only one man, I cannot deal with two emergencies right now. Luckily, he takes my hand and lets me help him down.

"So stupid." She sniffles.

"What do you need?" Dr. Banks asks.

"Hold her hand up, apply pressure."

"What's all this racket?" Her mother walks in as I assess their abysmal supplies. "Oh Lord. Oh Lulu. Oh no." Her hands flutter around Lulu's head, her voice getting higher and higher pitched.

"Dr. Banks," I say to her. "Can you please get me some warm, soapy water and a clean cloth? Dr. Banks," I say, pivoting to her father. This is going to get confusing. "Check if she has any rings or bracelets on her hand."

The busywork alleviates their panic somewhat, giving me the opportunity to get my supplies situated. I pull up the closest chair and sit with my legs spread, pulling myself as close to her as possible. Settling a towel in my lap, I take her hand from her father's.

"We should go to the hospital," her mom whispers.

"It's not that bad, Mom," Lulu says, but there's a mask on her voice. She's more scared than she's letting on. Sweat gathers at her hairline.

"It hurts?" I ask.

She bites her lip, nodding. "A lot."

"Do you feel any numbness, cold in your hand?" I start dabbing at the wound, as gently as I can. She hisses but doesn't pull away. With the blood cleared, I can let out the breath that's been caught in my throat. The bleeding has stopped. Her fingernails are still pink and when I press on them, color returns to them immediately.

"No," she says. "But I think I'm gonna pass out."

She's staring directly at it, the cut that—if it were any deeper—would have me insisting we go to the hospital for stitches. "Then quit looking at it," I tell her, my voice low. "I'll tell you everything I'm doing, OK?"

She sighs, smiling tight-lipped. "Thank you." She closes her eyes.

"I've cleaned the area," I tell her. "We've confirmed there likely isn't any nerve damage and you haven't nicked an artery. I'm putting iodine on the cut now," I say, as I dab the brown liquid with a cotton ball.

Lulu nods, her eyes squeezed tightly shut.

Their tube of antibiotic ointment is so old I don't think they make this brand anymore, but I apply it anyway. I can pick up more for her and reapply it later. "Now the ointment, then the bandages."

Her mother flutters around the kitchen as I wrap Lulu's hand in gauze. She turns on the kettle, opens the fridge, closes it, wipes the kitchen down with a lemon-scented cleaner. She sighs and *humphs* and asks Lulu repeatedly if she needs anything. Her dad sits on the other side of the table, sliding his tea and toast and book over to him. Lulu watches me while I wrap, her lower lip caught between her teeth, her skin still blotchy from her tears.

Gently, I place her bandaged hand on the table and grab ice from the freezer and two cloths, wetting one with warm water. "Put this over the bandage." I give her the ice wrapped in a cloth. "It will keep any swelling down."

Then, I wipe her face. There's a speckle of dried blood on her chin that could have been mistaken for a freckle, plus it gives me a chance to assess her for shock. It's not that bad. I know it's not. But now that I'm out of the moment, my heart thumps hard enough in my chest I'm sure they can hear it.

"You're good at this," she says quietly. "Taking care of people."

"It scared me," I admit. "Watching it happen to you."

"I'm OK, though. Everything's fine." She smiles and this time it's open and very obviously meant to reassure me.

"You're not stupid," I say, focusing on the path the cloth takes across her skin, watching the flush follow it. I feel exposed, having this conversation in front of her parents, even though neither of us are saying anything radically vulnerable. It feels like having my shirt off again, like letting her rub sunscreen in my back.

"Sometimes I just feel like all I do is…"

"Fall out of trees and cut your hand gardening?"

She snorts.

"Good thing you're friends with a former firefighter slash EMT."

"Good thing," she says softly.

"Jesse." Lulu's mom places a hand on Lulu's shoulder. "You're staying for dinner."

"That's alright, Dr. Banks, I—"

"It's Abigail," she says. "And you're staying. First you fixed our garden. Then you saved our daughter's life."

"*Mom.*"

I check Lulu's expression to see if she really wants me to stay. "Stay," she says.

"I'd love to, Abigail. What are we having?"

"Lentil loaf," she says, and turns away to start dinner.

"Great," I say, my voice wooden.

"Don't worry," Lulu whispers. "Her lentil loaf isn't as dry as it used to be."

★ ★ ★

The sun is low in the sky. Insects chirrup and leaves sway in a gentle breeze as Lulu walks me out to the truck.

"Thanks again." Lulu pulls the sleeves of her dad's cardigan, one she snagged off the back of his chair, over her hands.

I'm drained. Between spending the day in the sun, physical exertion, emotional exhaustion, and socializing, I could sleep for days.

"I'm really grateful you were here. I think my parents were considering calling a helicopter for an air evacuation. You witnessed their aggro coddling." She sounds embarrassed. I wish she wouldn't be. "I meant what I said before: you're really good at taking care of people. Keeping a cool head in a tense situation."

The rational side of my brain knows that not only is she complimenting me, she's right. A cool head is one of the most important qualities an emergency services worker can have, but the compliment doesn't sit right on my skin. It's like old sweat, something I want to slough off as fast as possible. I used to be able to say a quiet thank-you and move on. But looking at Lulu, sometimes it's like staring at the sun; she's so bright. It could blind me.

"I'd better get going." I hook my thumb over my shoulder.

She moves closer, takes a shuddering breath. "Just...thank you. You've been really kind, and generous with your time and..."

"Don't worry about it, Lulu," I say. "Friends help friends, right?"

Her hand is warm on my arm, where she squeezes. "You're a good friend."

I scratch the back of my neck. George probably wouldn't agree with her but it's nice to hear nonetheless. "K. Well."

"Wait," she shouts, even though there's only a foot of space between us. "Sorry." She takes a deep breath. "Hey, I have a question. The study organized a group activity next week. At an animal shelter. Maybe if we can't make friends with people, we can make friends with animals."

She hasn't asked a question yet.

"So, you'll come, then?"

"You want to go together?"

She nods.

I flip my keys in my hand and glance down at the bandage. "You'll need to change that bandage every day. I can bring you new antibiotic ointment. Your parents' tube was…"

"Ancient," she says. "I can get some. Don't worry."

"Yeah."

"You can pick me up," she says, like it's that easy. Like she's that sure. I might not be sure of myself, but she helps.

"I'll pick you up."

Chapter Eight

Lulu

When my mother is stressed, she cleans and cooks. My father had to go into the hospital for a minor surgery when I was in undergrad and the house was spotless, the freezer filled with enough precooked frozen meals to feed them for the rest of the year. When my father is stressed, he shuts himself in his office to work. One of my first memories as a child was coming downstairs for a glass of water and finding him already dressed, reading on the couch at four in the morning, when he was up for tenure.

When I'm stressed I try to commit to their nervous tics, but end up failing at both. Thirteen minutes before Jesse is supposed to pick me up, my bathroom smells faintly of bleach but the shower stall isn't clean and three books sit precariously stacked on the edge of my bed, having been taken down from the shelf but left unread.

Clothes surround me on the floor, piles of shorts and sundresses that I've pulled out of bins under my bed from last summer. When I'm on a date, I just have to impress one person, but when I'm part of a friendship study, suddenly I have to dress to impress any and all potential new pals.

A new email dings as I pace back and forth in my underwear, shaking out my hands. Before I even open my laptop, I just know. Yet, I open it anyway. It's better than panicking half-naked, I guess.

Lu,
I'm starting this letter the same way I've started all the rest. I'm sorry. I'm so sorry. I wish I could come up with something a little less banal and clichéd as "I have made a terrible mistake," but I have.
    As I'm sure you've already heard, we've broken up.

I had, in fact, not heard. "Contrary to your delusions of grandeur, I do *not* keep tabs on the people who broke my heart," I say primly. Which isn't even true. I had to talk my mom through how to block them on all social media platforms for me, so I'd stop stalking them when I was lying in bed at three in the morning in nothing but an undershirt and a fine layer of cheeze-dust.

There are so many things I wish I'd done differently. Especially the way I left things—

Any continued self-flagellation is interrupted by a text message. I send the email to the trash and slam the laptop shut.

Jesse: omw. Be there in like 15 min?

"Crumbs." I look down at my mostly naked self.

Jesse: It's Jesse by the way.

Cute. In the end, I wear none of the clothes I'd laid out for myself, opting for jeans so I can play with dogs who might have jumping habits or claws in need of a trim. I feel nervous in a way I haven't felt in a long time. Nervous but excited; this study is like being graded on friendship. And while I've not been successful at friendship in a while, I've always excelled at being graded.

Want to see lower cortisol levels, Dr. Cardiologist? A+.

Participants should be self-actualized by the end of the study, Dr. Psychologist? Gold star.

And yet, I still convulse in a full-body cringe when I walk down my driveway later and my mother calls, "Lu? Lulu?" She stops on the front steps of their house. "What are you doing, dear?"

I shield my eyes against the sun and yell, "A friend is picking me up. Cally." I haven't spoken to Cally since our lunch. I should probably text her. "She has a sports car so I'm going to meet her at the top of the drive."

I'm thirty and I'm lying to my mom about where I'm going and who I'm with like a teenager about to make a really bad decision. The worst part is, it wouldn't be difficult for my mother to tip over this poorly constructed house of cards. All she'd have to do is get her hair done at Cally's mom's salon in town.

So, I get an F in lying, I guess.

Mom comes down one more step. "Well, let me drive you to the road." A habit we picked up in middle school, when the walk to the bus that stopped at the end of the drive seemed treacherous or just too cold in the middle of winter.

"*No.*" There's no hiding the panic in my voice now. I turn back to the road, taking a few more steps before I answer her again. "She's almost here. It's fine."

Mom beams at me. "I'm so happy you're finding some time to be social." She waves her whole arm over her head. The movement like, *I'm proud of you* this *much.*

I walk away before my mother can find another thing to be overly helpful about. The reminder, in Jesse's voice, to let my parents coddle me hangs low like a storm cloud. It's one thing to tell my parents that my friend Jesse is coming over to help out in the yard. It's another to tell them that I'm in a psych department study and we're going to the animal shelter together in the hopes of making friends with other grown adults. Because who can't make friends?

Me and thirty other adults, apparently.

I stop in the middle of the driveway once I've rounded the sharp corner toward the road, muddy pothole water slowly seeping into my sneaker. "What am I doing?" I mutter.

It's so overwhelming sometimes: the work I have to do, preparing for my next class, writing a proposal for a class that will probably never see the light of day; the petty urge to compose a scathing letter back to my Betrayer in Chief; the desire to meet new people and the warring need to hide under my bed because if I don't try then I can't get hurt; figuring out how to handle the video call with my old colleague at Lancaster, the final sign that maybe I should do what Dad wants me to do. Maybe I should rest on my father's laurels one last time and just leave.

The thought rocks me back on my heels. It's kind of devastating, having to go back to Brian and Nora's Island of Disloyalty—which is what they should rename the British Isles—and not even being able to do *that* without my father's help.

"Hey." Jesse stands at the top of the drive, his truck idling behind him. "Are you alright?"

I blink. Am I? Suddenly I feel like crying, like all of the overwhelm is leaking out of my tear ducts.

He meets me halfway, his hands stuffed into the pockets of jeans tight enough that I shouldn't be thinking about them. Not when we're friends.

I wave my hand at him, the one with a bandage my father has painstakingly wrapped for me every day since I cut my hand open. He squints against the sun. "I could have met you at your door," he says. I'd sent him a text this morning about stopping at the top of the driveway.

"I don't want to sacrifice your undercarriage to our driveway any more than I have already." I gesture to the potholes and divots and tracks made by our cars over many years. "Dad keeps saying he'll fix it himself—what with his boundless knowledge of grading and asphalt and…" I shake my head.

Jesse presses his lips together in a new face. Not a smile, not a Grump Face, but one I put into my mental catalog under "Ways Jesse Communicates."

"Sorry," I say. "I'm not… I don't think my dad remembers how old he is sometimes. He's not in the best shape despite being mentally sharper than me."

Jesse nods. "You want him to take care of himself."

I nod back. I do. My dad is my hero, but his brand of hero-ism is doing more harm than good. Maybe he wasn't trying to help at all, maybe he was trying to tell me the whole time that I shouldn't have come back here, and I was too consumed with my own mortification to listen. Maybe I'm making my-self suffer, through the humiliation of my job, of this study, for nothing.

"Lu?" Jesse frowns. I think that might be the first time he's called me Lu. It's familiar. A name my parents have used forever, a name a friend would use. "You ready to go be friendly?" He says "friendly" like someone might say "roasted" or "impaled."

"Yeah." I smile, for real this time, warmer, like the feeling planted low in my belly at the sound of his voice. I breathe deep, the smell of the mud in my parents' driveway, the smell of Jesse's fabric softener caught on the breeze. Jesse's here, he's doing this. He's a part of this now and so am I. "Let's go."

Chapter Nine

Jesse

The interior of the one-story, long, gray building smells like bleach with an underlying stench of animals and pee. Despite the smell, the floors gleam like they've just been mopped, the windows looking into the kennels are crystal clear, and there isn't a hairball in sight. At the front desk, a brown-skinned woman with a bindi on her forehead and wearing deep purple lipstick sits at a computer. "Can I help you?" She doesn't look up from the screen.

Lulu and I glance at each other. "We're here for the...um... friendship event?" Lulu says, making it sound like we are Care Bears. The woman continues to tap away, her long burnt orange fingernails flying over the keyboard, double-clicks her mouse, then finally glances between us like a tennis match.

"*Oh*. The university thing? Right through this door. Follow me." She grabs a set of keys hanging on the hook behind her and we follow her down an echoing tiled hallway. "Do y'all plan on adopting any dogs today?"

Lulu winces, shrugs. "Is that mandatory?"

She laughs. "No. But you should think about it. Dogs really are people's best friends." The attendant pushes through swinging doors at the end of the hall and we're assaulted with noise. Laughter and talking and yips and barks. A few people I recognize from Pete's bar greet us as we step into the room but most of their attention is—rightfully—on the dogs. Old mutts, well-bred puppies, a fair number of pit bulls, and a lot more small dogs than I expected to see play in an open kennel area or in fenced-off pens. Everyone is down on the floor, rolling around with them and tossing a ball across a long turf-covered dog run. At the other end of the room, a group of three each have a dog on a leash and wait at another set of doors to go outside with them.

I thought we'd get a tour of the place. That they'd let a few people take a dog or two out of its kennel. But not this. This is a dog circus. This is like a dog café but there's no coffee and extra dogs. "This is…" I turn to Lulu, my astonishment at the scale of this event evident in my tone. But she's gone.

"Look! Jesse, look!" Lulu is on the floor a few feet away, a dog the size of a loaf of bread in her lap. "His name is Spot and he *has* a spot. Look at his spot, Jesse." Lulu holds the dog up, a bit awkwardly since the dog obviously does not like levitation and wriggles in her hands, the spot in question around its eye, brown against white fur. She hugs him to her chest, and he licks her chin, forgiven. She giggles and laughs until she has to put his wiggling body down. "Isn't he cute?" she asks it in that way that can accept no other answer but the affirmative.

"He's really cute," I say dutifully.

And so is she. Cute, happy, glowing. I look away. If I don't look away, I'm going to smile. I'm going to smile as big as she smiles. Meet her where she's at. It will be obvious that as much as we are friends, just friends, I think she's fucking beautiful. And smart. And charming. And she makes my stomach feel tight, but not in a bad way, when I look at her.

In a really good way, in fact.

"Not a dog person?" The woman from the front desk leans against the wall next to me. I like dogs. Dogs are fine. I don't have much experience with them. With two elderly grandparents who did shift work, a family dog just wasn't in the cards for me.

"Not enough to adopt one," I say truthfully.

Her gaze lingers for a few unblinking moments. "Come with me." She holds open the swinging doors, waiting for me to follow her. "Before the dogs get out," she says, a touch impatient. I slip out, closing the door tightly behind me, and follow her back down the hall, past her desk, down another hall, past another room where dogs bark and howl. Her keys jangle where she's clipped them to her hip. "You allergic to cats?"

"No." George has cats, Margie and Milford. They've never bothered me.

She opens another door, and the scent of cat pee sizzles off my nose hairs. "Sorry," she says at the face I make. "It won't smell like this if you only have one of them."

"Am I supposed to adopt one of these?"

She shrugs. "Just take a look around."

"What are you guys doing?" Lulu asks behind me, breathless. Her cheeks are pink, still invigorated by Spot's cuddles or because she ran after us, I can't tell.

"He's adopting a cat. I'm Sonia, by the way."

"Lulu."

"I'm…not adopting a cat."

Both women make this face at me like, *sure.* Sonia gestures at the wall of smaller kennels before us. It's quieter in here. Some of the cats meow and paw at their caged doors or blink at me lazily from where they were sleeping. After a moment of her stare down, I walk along the row, trying to breathe through my mouth.

"We don't have a lot of kittens," Sonia says.

"OK."

"It's just that a lot of people want kittens."

"OK."

"Would you like a kitten?"

"I…" I don't even want a cat. "Don't know."

I feel like, somehow, I am adopting a cat wrong. A cat I didn't want. But am now adopting.

There are a lot of black cats. And like she said, no kittens. As I get to the end of the row, I stop in front of a calico cat. The animal sits in the back of the cage. But when I lift my hand toward it, its ears perk forward. "Can I see this one?"

I'm not going to adopt it. I just want to see it.

Sonia opens the cage for me but doesn't take the cat out. "Her name is Betty."

Betty stays in the back of her kennel. She watches me with golden eyes. One of her ears has a chunk out of it. I wonder what kind of life she's had to live to lose a piece of her ear. I lift my hand again, holding it at the threshold of her cage.

I clear my throat before I speak, hoping it comes out a bit softer than normal. "Hi, Betty."

A card in a plastic insert beside her cage tells me that Betty is estimated to be around nine years old and has had at least two litters. Under *Special Notes* are the letters FIV.

"What's that?" I point to the card. "I'm Jesse, by the way."

"It means she has feline immunodeficiency virus. Hi, Jesse."

Lulu makes a tender sound behind us.

"What's that?" I ask over my shoulder.

Sonia launches into an explanation of how it's spread through bites from infected cats. How she's probably spent a lot of her life outside and that's how she would have contracted it. How there's no cure but cats can live long lives if it's well managed.

I don't know the first thing about cats. And I don't need the added responsibility. Except I stupidly want it? If only because Betty's body is giving out on her, and I know what that feels like. I know what it feels like to need tenderness. I don't know anything about cats, but maybe for Betty, I'd be willing to learn.

Betty stares at me with heavy-lidded eyes. Her purr seems to shake the whole room. Slowly, I move my hand closer and when she doesn't shy away, I rub my knuckles over the top of her head. Betty's purr jacks up louder, like she kicked on the kitty subwoofer. Her eyes fall fully closed and she turns her head into my hand. We do this for a while. I pet her and she enjoys it until she eventually stands on all four legs, her belly sagging low to the ground.

"If you adopt Betty, you'll need to make sure she has good nutrition. I can give you a list of the best brands to buy. And your vet will likely recommend something, too," she says, as if I have a vet on retainer. "FIV decreases her immune system's ability to fight infections. So, you've got to keep her healthy and reduce her risk of coming in contact with other diseases or spreading the disease. She'll have to be an indoor cat." Sonia says this last part with a wince, so perhaps this is a fraught topic in the cat community.

Betty leans, resting her forehead on my chest. Her purr moves through me, the vibrations like little earthquakes breaking up the tension in my chest until my heart can beat freely again. "I, uh, work a lot of nights. Shift work."

"Cats aren't on the same schedules as dogs. They're good companions for shift workers, especially if you provide environmental enrichment like scratching posts and food puzzles."

I look over my shoulder at Lulu. She stands with her arm wrapped around her middle, her hand pressed against her lips. She smiles behind her fingers, closed lipped and genuine.

"I'll take her." I say it to Sonia but look at Lulu. I don't know how to identify the surge in my chest when she nods. For now, I'll call it the rush of new cat ownership.

Betty yowls when we coax her into her new pet carrier, a near-constant low-frequency growl that sounds both royally pissed and terrified. Other study participants pass us as we step back into the lobby where Sonia is readying the adoption papers.

"We were going to all meet up later tonight," Trey says as he passes, peering into the growling pet carrier. "At Little Ts."

I didn't adopt a cat to get out of attending more social situations but honestly, I should have thought of this earlier. "I just got this cat." I hold her up as proof.

"Cats are like, easy though, right? You could leave her home for a few hours," Trey cajoles. He's well-meaning, he just doesn't understand that this was about all the socialization I can take today.

"Maybe," I say to get him to drop it. "Put it in the group chat." The one created by the psych department for us to organize spontaneous, external events exactly like this.

I sign where Sonia tells me. She sends me home with a list of the best brands of cat food for Betty as well as enough samples to hold me over for a few days, but I'll have to go shopping for more. She provides me with a list of vets I can choose from when I tell her I don't have one. I turn to Lulu. "I can drop you off at home before I go to the store to pick up cat litter."

Lulu looks between me and the quietly growling pet carrier. "I don't mind hanging for a bit." She shrugs. "I don't really feel like going out to some..." She waves her hand in the direction of the group that has already left. "We could get Betty settled and watch a movie or something?" She shrugs again, nervous. "If you wanted. No pressure."

So, I open the passenger-side door of the Bronco for her. "I want." And when she beams at me as she climbs in, I can't blame that on Betty.

Chapter Ten

Lulu

This all feels so domestic. I stayed in the car with the cat while Jesse ran into the store to get cat litter. He came back fifteen minutes later with cat food, a litter box and litter, a cat bed and two kinds of brushes, special cat shampoo and "healthy treats"—his words, not mine—a mouse that squeaks, another mouse that jingles, a feather teaser shaped like a flamingo, a replica fish that flops when the cat touches it, a baggy full of catnip that looks suspiciously illegal, and a cat tower hanging over his shoulder like a bindle.

He opens the hatchback trunk of the Bronco to neatly arrange everything inside.

"It's OK," he murmurs from the open trunk to the back seat. "We're almost home."

And it's the sound of his voice that finally silences Betty. The rest of the ride home is quiet except for the hush of the tires on the road. She won't leave the carrier once we get back to his house, a mid-twentieth-century one-story home with white clapboard and green planters on the windows and early blooming flowers in the garden. I blatantly snoop at the pictures in frames on the wall, of Jesse and his people, probably his grandparents, maybe his father—for the way he looks exactly like Jesse just with more hair. The urge to ask about his family, why there aren't any photos of his mom, to know these people, is an itch I won't scratch. It's too intimate, too prying, despite wanting to know more about him, everything.

Jesse putters around the house trying to find the best place for the cat litter, while I lounge on his couch and periodically make "pspspsps" sounds at Betty, which she resolutely ignores. He frowns when I suggest he put the cat litter in the hallway bathroom, and to be fair, the half bath *is* a bit small.

"I can't put her in the closet," he whispers, aghast, when I next suggest the small hall closet beside the bathroom, and I guess I can see the optics of asking a queer man to force anyone into—or out of—a closet.

After staring into a room filled with workout equipment for at least five minutes, he settles on the mudroom off the kitchen. But states, to no one in particular, that he'll reassess when winter comes since "it gets cold in there."

At no point do I let any of this affect me—emotionally or physically—Jesse is my friend.

We're friends.

New friends. And it would be inappropriate to think about pushing the large, worried new cat owner who is also *my friend* against a wall to punish and reward him with my mouth for the wrinkle forming between his eyebrows.

Jesse bends over the pet carrier, trying to coax Betty out with a treat, and I have to turn away, back to the photos on the wall. I can't decide what's more distracting, the muscular curve of his ass in those jeans or the leg hair coming out of the bottom of the cuffed hems, his bare feet untanned, also hairy, the toenails painted a shimmering black. It occurs to me that in my whole life I've never met a man who painted his toenails. And on the heels of that thought, what kind of men have I been spending my time with?

The wrong kind.

"Lu?"

I spin around. "What?"

My face is flushed with embarrassment and misplaced lust. Jesse made it very clear that night what he thinks about a physical relationship with me and besides that, we signed a contract explicitly stating there would be no relationship beyond a platonic one.

Friends don't think about friends this way. But friends don't stare at their friends' bare chests, covered in sweat and think, "I wonder what that tastes like," either. And I definitely did that last week.

"What did you say?" I ask, my palm pressed to my throat to hide the pounding there.

"I was going to make something to drink. Did you want anything?"

"Whatever you're having," I say, still too shrill to be normal.

"OK," he says slowly. "Why don't you pick a movie. Maybe if we're sitting down and sitting still she'll come out eventually?"

"Great idea." I lunge for the remote control and start flipping through the menu. "How many streaming services do you have?" I ask as I scroll through the many options on his TV; basically every genre of streaming service is available, from sports to film.

He makes a sound in the kitchen, something that would sound like choking from anyone else but is in actuality Jesse's laugh. "I got a bunch of them when I was recovering from my surgery."

I land on a film by a British director with a proven track record. It seems like one of those movies that has sweeping landscapes and intense close-up shots and a moving soundtrack.

Jesse brings two mugs of peppermint tea from the kitchen. "Is this OK?"

"This is great," I say and immediately, I burn my tongue on the tea.

"Thanks..." he says quietly as the movie starts. "For...you know."

I hold the mug close to me. I'm not cold. The opposite actually. But it gives me something to do with my hands. "That's what friends are for, right?"

He looks at me, his mouth bracketed by the fine lines of a frown. His chest is broad, his back straight, and he leans toward me, the barest inch. My heart does a silly flip, an overreaction, when Betty makes a small chirruping sound from her carrier. We turn to stare at her where she's poked her head out, but our sudden movement scares her, and she ducks back in.

We settle in to watch the movie and it starts like I expect. Long pans of the British countryside, reminding me of the place I called home for so many years; gray skies, a lot of sheep. And then, a sex scene. The sounds of two men having sex hits us in surround sound; I flush and glance quickly over at Jesse, who's leaned back on the couch. He's slouched, his mug of tea untouched on the coffee table, his bare feet up, one crossed over the other. I mirror him. I, too, am unaffected by watching other people experiencing sexual pleasure whilst in the presence of a person I would like to experience sexual pleasure with.

The movie continues without incident. Betty sits, her body half-in, half-out of the carrier. My tea gets cold. There's a hand's-width of space between Jesse and me. The characters on screen argue, but the tension is thick and obvious. There is a romance playing out on the screen and I'm a nervous woman with impulse control issues sitting next to her objectively hot, departmentally mandated new friend. Jesse shifts as the tension ramps up between the actors. An argument outside in the rain that we both know will end in a kiss, in their clothes off, their bodies pressed together. I pull my feet off the table and sit on my hands as shirts are pulled up on screen, pants pulled down only as far as necessary. As music crescendos and two men make love in the British countryside.

Jesse shifts again, pulling his feet off the table as well. I follow his movement, his legs pressed together, his feet firmly on the rug, his hand as it slides up his thigh to cover...

OK.

OK.

I am a historian, not a scientist. But as a historian, I still require evidence to make claims about the past. I value evidence. And right now, the evidence is telling me I might not be the only one turned on. Jesse catches me, and now that I'm looking, I can't look away. He's beautiful, thick and filling out his dark jeans, which leave almost nothing to the imagination. He flushes, color creeping up his neck and into his cheeks, and fifty percent of the reason I do what I do next is because I, too, am horny from a combination of close proximity and film erotica and Jesse is my friend. I don't want him to feel embarrassed or ashamed about what is nothing more than natural. At least, I don't want him to be any more embarrassed than I am.

"Lu," he says, his tone laced in apology, but I stop him with my hand on his thigh.

"It's OK." His thigh, the one with metal plates in it, is rigid. "We're friends, right?"

He closes his eyes, flushing more, and I shake my head. "We're friends and..." I take a deep breath to prepare myself for what I'm about to say and for the embarrassment if he says no. "You're my friend and I'm yours."

He swallows. "Yeah."

"Well." I take his hand from where he's unsuccessfully covered his erection. "Friends help each other out, right?"

He's quiet as I place his hand on my thigh. I thought the

weight of his hand would ground me, but sensation moves like electricity through my body, between my legs.

"Friends do favors for each other," I say, my voice thready and thin. "Right?"

"Yeah." His voice has changed, too, deeper, rougher.

"Maybe we could do each other a favor. As friends," I say quickly. "Just friends." My heart pounds in the back of my throat. I'm not even sure what I'm asking him for. What the favor would be, other than a relief. The ability to sit beside him again and not feel tension pulled tight like a steel cable. "Friends...get each other off? Right?" I whisper.

Jesse stares at his hand on my thigh. He stares at my hand as I run it slowly up his thigh, stopping before I touch him. He stares at me, his face far more serious than how nervous I feel.

"Are you asking to masturbate together?"

"Yes," I say quickly. "Yes. That." And it's perfect. It doesn't technically break the rules of the study; we wouldn't even be touching each other, just ourselves. That's not hooking up. "Friends do that, right?"

He huffs out a soft breath. "My friends do." I don't know exactly what that means but it makes perfect sense. If that's what Jesse's friends do then I should definitely be his friend.

I laugh, too loud and obviously nervous. "So should we like..." I gesture to the button on my jeans, but he stops me, squeezing my thigh. He looks past me at Betty, who sits with her paws crossed delicately one over the other. I have never seen a cat arch an eyebrow but in this moment, I am certain of it; Betty is judging us, for our weak interpretation of the study's rules prohibiting exactly this, our complete lack of self-control, our extreme horniness, or my choice to do it all right here on Jesse's couch.

"Let's go to the bedroom." He turns to me. "Is that OK?"

I nod and then I'm following him, his fingers hooked into mine. His shoulders block out the hallway, and the window in his bedroom is darker back here than at the front of the house, with no streetlights. My heart pounds in my throat in anticipation of relief. It smells more like him here, a concentration of Jesse, warm and already familiar. He turns on the lamp beside his bed. His comforter is a deep, dark blue, the corners tucked in tight and the pillows thick, bursting at the seams of their cases, but as light bathes the room, he seems to lose his sense of what's next.

I sit on his bed, lie back against the pillows. He sits at my hip and I reach for him, like I'm about to kiss him before catching myself. That's not what friends should do. Jesse leans over me, the lamp casting half his face in light and the other in dark.

"Have you done this before?" he asks.

"Masturbated beside someone?"

"Yeah."

"Definitely not." I shake my head for emphasis. "Well, I've gotten myself off after my boyfriend couldn't do it. But he was asleep." I cover my face with my arm.

"That doesn't count," he says, his voice flat. "Do you want me to..." His gaze wanders down my body. "Touch you?"

I bite my lip. Honestly, I do. But there are a set of rules in my brain that I haven't quite worked out yet and all I know is touching each other would be breaking them.

"What if you..." He gestures to my shirt. "And I..." He pulls his off, throwing it to the side and leaning back over me. There's hair on his chest and stomach that was slick, darkened the last time I saw it, from sweat and hose water. Now, the lamp catches threads of gold in his body hair, the light doing moody things to the sharp edges and soft curves of his body. I lift my shirt, not taking my eyes off him. I wait for this to feel weird, to pause at the act of exposing myself to someone new, but my skin feels too warm, flushed, tingling, and even though I said no touching I'm straining for it. To feel the brush of his denim-covered thigh between mine as he readjusts on the bed, the heat from his breath as his chin follows the path his eyes take down my body.

"Can I undo your pants for you?" he asks, and that seems like it would be OK. I nod.

Jesse pops the button, pulls down the zipper. The backs of his fingers brush my belly, sending an answering stroke of heat between my legs.

He clears his throat as he watches my hand slip underneath the peek of pink underwear showing between the V of my open jeans.

"Do you need lube?" he asks.

I think I should be embarrassed by how wet I am, how slick I already feel. I can't even blame the movie. That showed intimacy with an artsy, sepia tint. It's Jesse that makes me feel hot. Jesse and how easy it is to be around him. Jesse and our unfinished business.

"No," I whisper. "I do not need any lube."

He sits back, rummaging through what sounds like a very full drawer, and pulls out a pink bottle of hybrid lube. "Is it OK if I use some?" he asks and I nod furiously. He pops the cap, closes it, as if he's still a bit indecisive about the whole thing. I lift up on my elbow, trying to see what he'll do with that lube. I want to growl at him to just do it, just take it out already.

"Do that again," he says.

"Do what?"

"Your hand. You dragged it across your stomach." He takes my hand, putting it back where it was, under the cup of my bra.

"Like this?" My fingers feel illicit against my own skin, cool where the rest of me is hot.

"Yeah." His voice is just as rough.

"Now what?" I whisper.

He pauses, the lube in one hand, his palm spread wide across his thigh. His shoulders are hunched, his strong back a soft curve.

"Now." His brown eyes are serious in a way that is *more* than usual, since Jesse is always at least a little serious. "You tell me what to do."

My mind is a flipbook of options, of sexual positions, of things he could do to me, himself. "Come here." I spread my legs and he crawls between them. "Let me see you."

Jesse pushes his jeans lower on his hips, and it takes work because he was clearly sewn into them this morning, gripping himself through his boxers. The black cotton stretches over him as he hesitates, then pulls the fabric down. He's cut, a droplet of pre-come glistening at the tip, pink and swollen. He holds out his hand. "Get me wet?" he asks, even though his bottle of lube is right there, wet and cold against my side. It sends a thrill through me, one that starts in my chest and ends between my legs, that he wants to get wet from *me*.

I spit, once, again into his palm and his eyes are big and dark as he watches me.

"If I wasn't here. What would you do?" he asks, his hand hovering over himself.

"This, probably." I stroke my finger over my clit, my jeans stretched uncomfortably around my hand. I pull my bra cup down to glide the pad of my finger over my nipple.

"Would you use a toy?"

"Maybe. Sometimes." I stroke again and he does, too, rubbing himself off every time I do. "Would you?"

"Sometimes."

"Tell me." I push my fingers in and when I pull them out, he can hear it, how wet I am.

He closes his eyes, face flushed. "I thought of you before," he says.

"Yeah?"

He nods, his jaw clenched. "I was ashamed. It felt like a violation. But I still smelled like you after. I could still hear that sound you made when you rubbed against my thigh." He means after our date, after I threw myself at him, and I'm seeing it now in a totally new light, his rejection and my reaction.

"I didn't know I made a sound."

He opens his eyes. "You sounded like you do now."

I smile. "Do the voice," I tease and he bites the inside of his cheek. Maybe he likes to be teased a little bit.

Nodding to me, he says, "Let me see you?" Then, before I can respond: "Can I?" His hand hovering over me. I nod and he pulls my other cup down. My breasts sit high, pushed up and out and on display, my hair feels a mess on the back of my head from how much I've pressed it into his pillow. I don't know what to do with the hand not currently shoved down my pants other than fling it out to the side so my fingers can sift through the comforter on his bed, softer from age than quality. I feel like a mess, but I want to be messier.

He grunts, pushes his pants down farther.

"What did you think about?" I ask. "When you did this thinking of me?"

He flushes and shakes his head, a quick jerk of his chin.

"Tell me," I beg. "Just one thing." I reach for him, my fingers brushing his wrist, the tendons and veins corded and tight from where he grips himself. I move my fingers slowly. I feel so close, like I could trip over the edge by accident, and I don't want to go without him.

"I thought about what I'd do to you."

I feel bold, my chest bared, my thighs on either side of his. I feel responsible for him, for the way his breathing shudders in his chest, the sweat at his temple. "You'd eat my pussy," I say.

He groans, falling forward, all his weight onto one hand. He looms over me, his hand moving faster now. "Are you close?" he asks.

I nod.

"Can I see?" he asks again. He loves watching and although I've never been much of a performer before, I want to show him everything. He makes it easy. Maybe this is what having sex with your friends is like. Easy, comfortable. Safe.

He helps me pulls my pants down farther, then my panties. There's a moment when he turns, pouring lube into his hand, and I catch a glimpse of myself in the mirror over his dresser. I'm naked from collarbone to mid-thigh, my hair is truly a mess, my hand between my legs, my skin golden under the lamp's glow. It's ridiculous, all of it. Us. Two lonely adults who can't make any friends, but we can make each other come, apparently. It's ridiculous and I laugh—at the absurdity, at how good I feel, how comfortable—and I expect the sound to bother him but he watches us in the mirror, too, and I hope he sees how beautiful he is, his body thick and strong, the way his ass curves as he fucks into his hand, one leg planted on the ground, his knee firmly on the bed.

He leans closer, dips his head like he's going to do exactly what he dreamed of—or was it my dream?—and eat my pussy. I almost let him, almost push his head down, but he stops and he says, so softly as I stroke myself, "After you come, will you put your fingers in my mouth?"

He asks for it innocently and like I might say no but now it's all I can think of, all I want. To feel his mouth, warm, his tongue hot around my fingers. To see if he might like the taste, if I'm what he imagined me to be, and all I want is to come for him. My back arches, my heels pressed into the mattress, looking for purchase. I try to find something solid to grab onto but there's nothing, just soft, pliable bedsheet, until his hand is there, his fingers brushing the pads of mine. The only points we're touching are our thighs and those fingers, but I feel him everywhere, like it's his hand inside me, his cock or his tongue as I burst apart. I shout, the loudest moan, my teeth clenched as I come, my whole body orgasming in a way I haven't in forever, maybe never like this. He waits for me, watching, letting me pull it all out before, lazily, I lift my hand, my skin glistening and wet. He opens his mouth for me.

"Come on me?" I ask. Apparently, I ask for stuff like that. I want him to finish this mess of me.

He shuts his eyes as he closes his mouth over my fingers. The sweep of his tongue sends an aftershock up my spine and I moan as his come spills onto me. His first pulse hits my chin, streaks across my breast and nipple, then my stomach, my pubic hair. The only sound is our breathing, like we've been running or fighting. Or fucking, I guess. My fingers are still hooked in his mouth, pulling his jaw down, keeping him open, his teeth leaving indents on my skin. I let them slip out, dragging them across his chin, down his throat.

Jesse sits on his heels; his head falls back on his neck. He pulls his boxers up.

"Lulu," he says. I'm a mess right now, a disaster. In a few minutes I'll be cold, maybe a little embarrassed, probably very worried that we'll be found out and booted from the program, but right now the sound of his voice is enough that if he said "let's run that again," I'd let him do it.

I hum my response instead of risking opening my mouth and letting fly whatever words decide to come out.

He takes a deep breath, filling his chest and belly. The top of his scar peeks out from beneath his boxer shorts, his pants pulled down far enough to see the start of a shiny white line. "You," he says. "Are a very good friend."

I know it would get us kicked out, but when I inevitably write in my study journal about today, I wish I could include this in my notes.

Chapter Eleven

Jesse

The heaviest weight in this waiting room is Lulu's gaze on the back of my neck. The first time I turn around, she quickly drops her gaze. The second time I turn around, she stares back at me, her cheeks pink, her neck pink, her lips pink. For reasons that will remain forever unknown to me, I cross my eyes and poke out my tongue. That makes her smile.

We go in one by one for our blood pressure and stress tests and reflexes or whatever. My nurse, a petite white woman who reminds me so much of Grandma I'm worried she'll have me admitted if she listens to my heartbeat, frowns at the data from my biometric monitor.

I never used to be the type of person who worried that much about my health. I work out. I'm young. I don't smoke or drink to excess. I don't have a lot of risk factors, but I've learned through experience that sometimes you can do everything right and things can still go wrong.

"Everything alright?" I ask.

She glances up at me. "Looks like your sleep hasn't been great."

I shrug. "I do shiftwork."

She nods. She can probably relate.

"You exercise regularly," she says more to herself.

"How can you tell?" I ask.

She flips the report over to show me a collection of line graphs but turns it back before I can make heads or tails of it. "These monitors are basically glorified fitness trackers. I can see the spike in your heart rate around the same time every day. Looks like a routine." She smiles at me. "That's good for your heart and mental health." She pauses as her eyes track the bottom of the page. "Go for a late-night run?" she asks.

I don't like to run. Didn't even before my accident. "No."

It takes until I'm sitting in the waiting room again before I realize what that late-night spike in my heart rate might have been. Even though there's no way she—or any of the doctors and nurses in the study—could know what, or *who*, caused that spike, the back of my neck gets hot. It feels like a sign that says, in flashing neon, "I saw Lulu Banks's nipples last weekend."

Someone calls my name, and my voice is a rough gasp when I say, "Yeah." But it's just George, assigning me to a new group for the "therapy sessions" that feel more like one prolonged icebreaker. People talk, about what they've done to make friends these past two weeks, about how they feel about those things. I try to make myself smaller, quieter, to be unnoticeable. Not only because I don't want to share. I'm not sure how I can talk about anything I've done this past week without talking about Lulu too much to arouse suspicion.

Back in the waiting room again, Lulu sits beside me. Her eyes stare straight ahead, her back is stiff, and her hands grip the armrest like she'll float away without it.

"Hi," I say after an interminably long silence.

"How are you?" she whispers. Her nails are a chipped pink bubble gum color.

"Fine," I say. "How are you?"

"I was wondering," she says, ignoring my question. The light flickers overhead and she jumps.

"Breathe, Lulu," I say, my voice low.

"Sorry." She smiles across the room at another participant. Rather, she bares her teeth. I press my hand into my thigh to keep from reaching for hers. "I just feel like…everyone can tell," she says, exhaling softly.

I close my eyes to avoid smiling like a lunatic, relieved that I'm not the only one. "I'm pretty sure everyone just thinks you've had too many coffees this morning."

The thing about Lulu's smile is that it's limitless. Every time I think it can't get any bigger, it does. It gets so big I could fall inside it. Big enough I want to throw myself over the edge and plummet until I'm swallowed whole. Since I want to keep this look on her face, this bashful, big smile, I keep nodding as she speaks, even as it takes too long for her words to register.

"I think maybe I'm not cut out for this."

My brain is a record scratch. "This?"

She leans forward, bringing the smell of lavender with her. "Breaking the rules," she whispers.

A stone sinks in my stomach; it feels a lot like disappointment. I'm not one to show my emotions on my face but in this moment the realization feels written into my DNA. "Well, we didn't break any rules, right? Cuz we're just friends," I say quickly. "We were just doing each other a favor."

She straightens from her lean. "Right." She shakes her head. "Right, of course. Are you sore?" she asks, gesturing to where my hand grips my thigh.

I let go and shake my hand loose. "I'm fine. How's your hand?"

She holds it up for me. She no longer needs the gauze bandage and three peach-colored Band-Aids cover the cut that is now just an angry red line. "What did you talk about in your group session?"

She switches topics so quickly my brain gets whiplash. I'm still stuck on her maybe not being OK with the friends-with-benefits situation. After we were done that night, I got her a cloth soaked in warm water and wiped her skin clean. She'd laughed, grabbing the washcloth, claiming it tickled. Betty had come in while we sat at the edge of the bed, our clothes finally put right, sweat drying on my skin. She let us pet her, and when I asked Lulu if she needed anything, she'd just shrugged and said, "I'm good."

And then we went back to the couch and finished the movie. Lulu fell asleep on my shoulder, her breathing slow and her body a solid weight against me. She didn't wake up until the credits finished rolling, and when I tried to drive her home she insisted she take a cab and I insisted she text me when she got home. It felt comfortable. Like friends. Or maybe something else. OK, so maybe she has a point.

Also, I didn't talk in group at all.

"What did *you* talk about in group?" I ask instead of answering her question.

She launches into an explanation of how she'd been ruminating on the act of friendship. How when we were children it was as easy as playing next to another kid in the sandbox, of having your parents push the two of you together, and how now it feels like a far more intentional action. She rattles off the names of books she's read, a non-fic about keeping each other close, a romance with a friends-to-lovers trope, *Charlotte's Web*, and a picture book on the subject.

"You read this all in the past week?"

She shrugs, like *yeah, who doesn't read four books in a week?*

I'm still working on the book about the Derrida guy she mentioned, after I gave up on the one about witches. I like to read as much as the next person but not that much.

"It's just interesting," she says finally. "There are all these rules about how we make friends, but we don't really talk about what the rules *are*. And I tried to think about how I got along with people in the UK, and I don't know, I guess I'm a little gun-shy? I've never had a big friend group. I had one or two close friends, plus my parents. And then my best friend at Lancaster, Nora, she cheated on me with my boyfriend. Or well, he cheated on me with her, I guess?" She glances over at me, her mouth a crinkle. "I can't remember if I already told you that."

"That's…" I'm at a loss for words. More than usual. "Terrible."

She shrugs, like *it is what it is*, even though I can tell by the flush in her cheeks, the nervous way she gnaws at her lip, that it is *not* what it is. "His betrayal was bad enough. But hers…" She shakes her head. "Mostly, I try not to think about it too much. Anyway," she says, dragging out the word. "I keep trying to think about what I'm doing differently now. Like how did I become friends with Nora? We worked together and we just…clicked. And it's not like I have a boyfriend for a new friend to cheat on me with."

"Maybe you're not doing anything differently. Maybe the people are different."

"You have to say that," she says quietly. "You're my friend. Maybe I should have stuck it out in the UK," she says, more to herself.

Lulu claims she has difficulty making friends, but she pulled me into her orbit and somehow, I never even noticed. In fact, I think I went quite willingly. "If I wasn't your friend yet, how would you make me one?"

She purses her lips, looking up at the ceiling panels. "I'd ask you questions."

"Ask me a question."

"I had a list of things I wouldn't let myself talk about on our…the first time we met," she admits.

"Why wouldn't you let yourself talk about them?"

She shakes her head. "Second-guessing myself?"

"Like, what?" I ask. "What would you have talked about if you had let yourself?"

"Like…" She sighs. "What's your favorite tree?"

"Favorite type or a specific tree?"

"Either. Both."

Never in my life have I considered what type of tree I might like the most. "A pine tree? I like Christmas. What about you?"

"I have a favorite. You can meet her sometime." She frowns down at her hands. "But don't think I didn't notice you changing the subject. What did you talk about in your group session, Jesse?"

I slump lower in my chair, the plastic creaking under my weight. Sometimes I can go all day without saying a word to anyone. It's scary how easy it is to get by on body language and physical cues. It's not that I have nothing to say, or that I don't want to. Sometimes my chest feels full, so full of words that I can't hold on to them all. There's too much I want to say to too many people: to Lulu, that I don't think I'm good at breaking the rules either but for vastly different reasons; to George, that I miss him; to Pop, that I have a secret.

"My pop and gran raised me; did I tell you that?"

She shakes her head.

"He has dementia."

"I'm sorry."

"I want to tell him about me," I say. "That I'm bi, you know? But now it's like, if I tell him, he won't really hear me. So, what's the point?"

Lulu and I have never really talked about my identity, other than her acknowledgment that George and I were together. Normally, it's not something I'd share so freely. Maybe it's because despite not knowing her for long, we've been more intimate with each other than anyone else in this room, or because Lulu can be as vulnerable as I want to be sometimes, but sharing with her doesn't feel like exposing my jugular. Telling her isn't the same as participating in the group sessions or telling my grandfather, but it's something. My chest doesn't feel so full.

"Maybe it's not about waiting for the perfect time to tell him. Maybe it's about telling him over and over again. Maybe it's about saying it for yourself."

"What do you mean?" I ask.

"You're right that he might not hear you the first time, but if you say it enough times he'll know it. And even if he doesn't, you still get to say it, out loud. There's power in that. In our words."

"Hmmmm," I say. Sometimes Lulu is so earnest I need a moment. "Sounds like a lot of talking, though."

Lulu huffs in mock exasperation, then leans over, her mouth open, and bites me through the sleeve of my shirt. Immediately, I know it won't hurt. She doesn't bite hard and her mark will fade in a few minutes. She makes a growling sound as she does it, her nose wrinkling. She's embarrassed after, she won't meet my eyes, her cheeks pink. I lean into her, drop my voice. "Careful," I say. "I bite back."

I think she sees my pulse thrumming wildly in my throat. I know she must see the way my pupils are blasted wide. I shouldn't have said that, flirted, but her smile gets bigger, her tongue peeking out between her teeth, and mostly I know that if she just wants to be friends, only friends, I can do that.

I get buzzed into the secure floor at Pop's residence and am immediately met by his neighbor, Clarice. "I thought you'd never get here," she says.

Despite her thin skin and her frail frame, her grip is always surprisingly strong on my forearm.

"I'm here to see Pop, Clarice." I gently pry her fingers from my security guard uniform.

"I thought you were taking me out tonight?" Clarice pouts as she swishes in an emerald green dress that looks like it belongs in one of the old black-and-white flicks I'd watch with Pop late on Saturday nights after Grandma went to bed. Her hair is pinned up in an intricate twist. I don't understand how the human brain works, how her mind can remember how to do that hairstyle, but can't remember that I'm not her deceased husband, Tom.

"Next time," I promise. "You look really lovely today, Clarice."

She beams as a nurse collects her and I get to Pop's door without any other cases of mistaken identity. I pause there, straightening my clothes and patting at my hair, even though it's too short to style. I knock and a nurse answers, in the middle of helping Pop with his dinner. "I can do that," I offer, taking his spot beside Pop at the small table by his window.

"Hey, Pop." I offer him another spoonful of peas, but he turns away to stare out the window. Fair. These peas aren't fantastic. I've tried them. "I'm heading into work soon so I can't stay for long."

He chews at his cheek. The sky outside is grapefruit pink, turning his bedspread and tile floor the same vibrant color.

"I, uh, made a new friend." I feel like a little kid again, telling him about my first day of school. "Her name is Lulu. Eloise. But don't call her that."

He looks at me. We have the same eyes, brown, serious.

"She's, um, we, um…" I feel my face turning red. "I think I like her, but she just wants to be friends. It's really important to her to be able to make friends." And that's why I can't let this little crush get out of hand. It wasn't until I saw her today that I realized that I *like* Lulu. Beyond the sex we sort of had or the way she looks. I like sitting next to her while she talks, following the dips and jumps in her voice, and how she approaches everything like she has something to learn. And if I thought there could be a chance of anything between us, maybe I'd just leave the study altogether so no one would be breaking any more rules. But I'd still be where I am now, with nothing and no one. And more importantly, she sees me as her friend, and she wants to make more of us. I don't want to ruin that for her.

I gathered up all the feelings I had for her this morning and shoved them in a box in my head, stuffed them in the closet where my sexuality used to be.

"I know I don't usually talk to you about the people I…like, but…" I take a deep breath and try again with his peas. He opens his mouth this time. "I like—liked—Lulu but I've also liked other people before."

Pop watches me while he chews. A breadcrumb clings to his beard and I wipe it away with the napkin in his lap.

"George, for instance. I liked him, too, Pop."

Pop stops chewing.

"I liked him as more than a friend." I feel light-headed, saying the words out loud to him for the first time. My voice sounds rough. He puts his hand on mine, leaning toward me, his face intent. My heart pounds. Maybe he heard me. Maybe he understands.

"Make sure you take the garbage out tonight, Joey."

I sigh. My pulse still lingering in my ears. "I will, Pop. I will."

Chapter Twelve

Lulu

The thing about medieval European history—or at least the kind of medieval European history that Dad studies—is that it's already been studied for years, for *centuries*. And yet he can always find something new to fascinate him for hours upon hours until it's almost seven in the evening on a Friday night and I'm waiting for him to finish so he can give me a ride home.

I knock at his office door for the second time. "Dad?"

Finally, the whoosh of his chair rolling back comes from the other side of the door, his slow footsteps. "Good evening, Dr. Banks," he says, solemnly.

"Good evening, Dr. Banks." I match his tone. "Ready to hit it?"

He hums and turns back to his desk. From the mess in this office, he is absolutely not ready to hit anything. Books everywhere, a stack of papers balancing haphazardly on the corner of his desk. Two half-empty to-go cups of black tea, as well as a mug. His computer monitor, with the boxy, old cathode-ray tubes, glows blue light over the tumultuous landscape of his desk.

"Sit," he says, pointing at a chair that has a replica of the effigy of Eleanor of Aquitaine's coffin approximately the size of Betty on it. There's nowhere to put Eleanor other than the floor and seeing as Dad has had a mega-crush on her since he was eighteen, I can't do that. She balances in my lap.

"What's up?"

He pushes his glasses up his nose; the lenses are smudged and tape wraps around the bridge. Sometimes, it's easy to forget exactly who my dad is: a rock star in his field, even well into his sixties. A man who changed the way medieval historians thought about the past, who could have gone to much bigger schools, taught in more hallowed halls, but stayed here for me and Mom and our family. He just loves history and teaching and us; his personal sacrifice to Athena.

"Did you set up a call with Dr. Lucas yet?"

"Who?"

He sighs, leaning back in his squeaky, old chair. "Dr. Lucas at Lancaster. She's waiting for you to call so they can set up your position."

"Wait." I shake my head to clear out the cobwebs that accompany still being on campus after dinnertime. "Set up my position? I thought it was an interview for a job?"

He waves his hand like this is all semantics. "I think it's mostly for show."

"Are you kidding me?" I snap back, and my words echo out the door of this small office. In the ringing silence, my face feels hot, my skin too tight. I've never raised my voice to either of my parents before. "Didn't you think of the optics?" I say, quieter this time, calmer. "Of using your name, your reputation, your clout, to get me a job? Again?"

In this moment, Dad is genuinely baffled. His beard droops as he frowns and he won't look directly at me. "This is academia," he mutters. And then, "You've just seemed... I only want to..."

"Do you..." My mouth is dry. I left my water bottle back in

my office. I start again. "Do you think I should go? To Lancaster? That's what you want—for me to leave?"

He harrumphs. "I think," he says slowly. "It would be a good idea to set up a phone call with Dr. Lucas."

He starts gathering his things, stuffing the cardigan on the back of his chair into the soft-shell briefcase at his feet.

I know what it's like to be let down easy, and that's what Dad's trying to do now. He doesn't want me here; he'd rather do a little nepotism as a treat, since to someone like him—a historical superstar—it doesn't really matter. I was running from the UK and my broken relationship with Brian and my broken friendship with Nora, and now I might as well run back.

He's letting me down easy, but the fall still hurts. I've always battled impostor syndrome—it's basically a prerequisite for getting a PhD—but I've never felt like an impostor in my own family, in my own *life*. That's what this is, though. I don't belong anywhere.

"I—um, I need to go grab my stuff," I say. My brain is in a fog as I walk out of his office and almost walk face-first into Audrey.

"Oh." Audrey squeaks, then huffs, turning on her high heels and striding down the hall and around the corner. "Hey," I call, trotting after her. "Audrey, wait. Hey."

I catch up to her just outside my office. "Were you eavesdropping?" I ask, the edge in my tone louder than if I was yelling. Which I want to do, even though none of this is Audrey's fault. She sighs, her shoulders rising to her ears before she turns, any emotion on her face wiped clean. Audrey smiles, slipping one hand into the pocket of her slate gray, wide-legged, wool slacks. I slip past her into my office, hoping she'll follow me so we can have this conversation outside of earshot of any of our gossipy colleagues. She pulls a candy from the small green art deco glass bowl I leave out for students during my office hours.

"You have a job at Lancaster University." She doesn't ask.

She unwraps the candy, popping it into her mouth, the hard candy crunching between her teeth.

"It's not a good idea to chew those candies," I say stiffly. "They get stuck in your teeth and cause cavities."

Shut up, Lulu. Let her get the cavities!

"Your dad got you *another* job."

Taking a deep breath, I say, "I know what it looks like, but I promise you that I have no intention of taking it." My pulse pounds in my throat. She can probably see it. I am a bloody doctor for crap's sake but I've never had such an antagonistic relationship with a colleague, especially one I assumed I'd work closely with when I learned that, for all intents and purposes, we study the same things.

"Oh, you promise?" She rolls her eyes so hard, she'll give herself a headache. "Like that means anything."

"You," I say slowly. "Are being purposefully unkind."

The thing I find most frustrating about Audrey is how much I wish I could be more like her. Where I get flustered and react emotionally, Audrey remains cool and calm. She's a chameleon in our old-school history department, populated by so many old white men. I want to ask her how she does it, how she avoids the label of a *hysterical* woman whenever she has an emotion.

"Why don't you like me?" I ask. I mean to sound nonplussed, to be able to take whatever magical confidence I had a moment ago and inject it into this long-awaited, much-needed confrontation. Instead, I sound exactly how I feel: a little too desperate for her approval. "I mean, it feels like you didn't like me before I even arrived," I say, trying again.

"That's because I didn't."

I wish I could say I'm not surprised, not hurt, but I can't hide it.

"I'm the first person in my family to go to university. Let alone get a PhD. I was so hopeful when I got this job two years ago. Then, everyone started whispering about the *brilliant* Eloise Banks." She spits the word at me. "The preeminent early modernist, the influential gender theorist," she sneers.

"I'm none of those things," I say. At least, I don't see myself that way. At all. "I'm... I'm just... Lulu."

"You're just the daughter of Dr. Peter Banks."

That I can't deny. I am, very much, the daughter of one of the most celebrated historians in the field. My immediate, gut reaction is to be defensive. I can't control who my father is. I've worked hard for everything I've done, especially since my father is who he is. But none of that makes it fair.

"You're right," I say quietly. "It's not fair. I should have... I don't know. I never should have taken this job. I should have recognized the optics sooner. It was obtuse of me."

She crosses her arms over her chest.

"Don't worry," she says with flippancy. "You can just take another one."

Before I can say another word, Audrey is gone again. Dad is probably waiting for me in the lobby. Hopefully, he hasn't forgotten and left without me. He's a bit of a nutty professor sometimes, but at this point I'm not sure I want to share a car ride with him.

She walks, swift and stiff-legged, down the hall, the gentle swishing of her fashionable trousers at odds with the rigid way she holds herself. "Audrey, please," I call, louder when she doesn't stop.

She stops with her hand on the door to her office and finally she looks at me. After a moment, she huffs and opens the door. "What else is there to say?" she asks.

I'm tempted to throw it out there, Jesse's idea that we combine our work, but it feels like asking to partner with the popular kid for group work in high school. An idea that's more likely to receive disbelieving scorn than a positive response. "Can I put your name forward?" I ask. "For them to consider. At Lancaster."

"I don't want your pity."

"It's not pity. It's leveling the playing field."

She rolls her eyes, but finally she nods. "Sure. Whatever."

Chapter Thirteen

Lulu

Group Chat:

Me: Do y'all think that if we organize something separate from the study we can get Jesse to come out?

Trey: lmao yeah i haven't seen that kid since the animal shelter

Nabil: Wait. Who's Jesse?

Trey: 😄

Me: I found a good group ticket price for a baseball game. Anyone interested?

Trey: i'm in!

Nabil: Me too!

Brooke: sure 😊

Text Message:

Jesse to me: Why are you doing this to me?

Me: Because I like to torture you? 😊

Jesse: I think I'd prefer the Witchfinder General

Me: OMG was that a witch joke?

Jesse: Not if you had to ask.

Jesse: What time should I pick you up?

Me: You're going to come?

Jesse: I think I have to now. You called me out in front of the entire group.

Me: 😇

The stadium smells like Philly cheesesteak and beer and popcorn and the kind of desperate hope pheromone that only baseball fans can secrete. The cheesesteak smell somehow turns my stomach and makes it growl at the same time, a Pavlovian response after eating far too many of them in this very stadium in my lifetime. The beer reminds me of the one and only time I saw my father drunk. It was during extra innings the summer before I started high school and he had a second beer rather than his usual one, nursed over the entirety of the four-hour game.

Dad has always been a baseball fan, since the first day he immigrated to Pennsylvania from east London. He wanted to assimilate to his new home and between the choices of baseball and American football, my quiet, book-loving father chose the option that didn't involve traumatic brain injuries. When I told him this morning that I was going to a baseball game—leaving out the not-so-important detail that the event was organized through my friendship study—he'd perked up. Any of the frustration we had held for each other last week burned off in the face of a ballpark.

"Who are you going with?" he'd asked.

"Some friends," I'd lied. Really it's only Jesse who's my friend. Everyone else is a fellow study participant.

A fistful of cash is shoved in front of my face and I lean out of the way as Jesse reaches for it on my other side, passing it to the food vendor, who exchanges it for a bottle of water. The water goes back down the row.

"Thanks for driving me," I say, leaning into him.

"It's no problem." He shifts in his seat, his shoulders hunched.

"Can I buy you a beer to say thanks?"

He shakes his head. "I'm driving."

"Not for another, like, three hours."

He makes Grump Face and I immediately want to wipe it from his facial vernacular.

"Sorry," I say quickly. "For peer pressuring you."

His shoulders relax. "I think it's only peer pressure if I crumble under it," he says. Then, quieter, "Safety is really important to me." He rubs his palm up and down his thigh, an unconscious movement, and duh. Of course he's concerned with safety, especially when he's driving.

"Hey." I grab his hand, squeezing gently. "I really am sorry."

He squeezes back. "It's fine," he says. But is it? This is just like me, the type of gaffe I always make, exactly the kind of foot-in-mouth moment that's the reason I'm here in the middle of an adult friendship study.

More money is hand-passed in front of me in exchange for a lemon-flavored water ice in a soggy paper cup. The Phanatic shakes his belly to a medley of pop songs; the sun beats down on us and the outfield is a gorgeous green, the mower's lines striped in a crisscross pattern, and I feel like I might suffocate. Each breath gets harder and harder to catch. Sweat rolls between my shoulder blades. I close my eyes and try to picture the optimal route to the closest exit, how many people's feet will I have to step on as I stumble for the stairs, how many times will I have to shove my butt in someone's face as I shimmy down this line of tightly packed baseball fans so I can find a public bathroom that is inexplicably damp from top to bottom to cry in until this anxiety passes. Because I have undoubtedly hurt my only friend with my insensitivity.

"Lu." Jesse's hand is a warm and sudden weight on mine. He pulls my hands apart, where I pick at my fingernails until the skin around them is raw and red. "I promise, it's really, really fine."

"OK," I say, my breath shuddering out of me. "Are you..."

"It's fine."

I breathe through my nose, exhale through my mouth, the music and the screams coming back to me. The nerves loosen and unravel like receding tendrils of smoke. He searches my face, his eyes shining in the sunlight.

"You have pretty eyes," I say.

He blushes, looks out over the field as the crowd cheers on a third out. "They're brown."

"They're rich."

"Like dirt."

Gently, I punch his arm. "Take a compliment."

He looks back at me, his eyes still searching. Quietly, he says,

"Thank you." A cheer goes up from our section as the Phanatic points his pneumatic gun in our direction.

"What is happening?" Jesse asks.

"He's going to shoot hot dogs at us," I say.

"Right. Makes sense."

"Wait. Have you never been to a baseball game before?" My voice rises to a pitch that attracts the curious stares of those around us. Jesse's eyes widen at the sudden attention.

"I like rugby," is all he says.

Trey leans forward from the seat behind us. "You like rugby? Me, too." His can of beer tips forward with him, coming perilously close to spilling all over Jesse's faded red T-shirt. I tilt in the other direction to avoid any splash back. Trey pulls Jesse into a conversation about a recent controversial World Cup win.

"He's cute," the girl sitting next to me says.

My eyes feel too big in my face and although I'm slack-jawed, I don't respond. My brain can't decide whether I need to deny that I think Jesse is cute while simultaneously arguing that, of course he is, and also he's *mine*, which he absolutely is not since one can neither own a person nor should they but also because coming on my stomach once does not make anyone mine, although maybe it makes me at the very least a little bit his.

Except then I follow her gaze to Trey's profile. She bites her lip and blushes when she catches me catching her staring.

"Yeah," I agree, nodding quickly like that's who I thought she was talking about this whole time.

"I know we're not supposed to...you know." She waggles her eyebrows. "With other participants but..."

"Maybe after." I shrug and I don't look at Jesse at all.

"Yes." She giggles. "Maybe."

I turn back to the game I haven't been paying enough attention to when it occurs to me that I could, you know, make a friend of her.

"I'm Lulu, by the way."

She smiles wide. "Brooke."

I glance back at Jesse and he seems comfortable, chatting amiably with Trey, who is in fact very cute and animated and entirely wonderful. Jesse is busy making friends. Maybe I should try a little harder to do that, too. That's why we're here, after all. And while it still smarts, like a rubber band snapped on my heart, that my dad is trying to get rid of me, and I still haven't decided whether I should ask Audrey to join forces or not, the thought of not being here, of not having to maintain these friendships, of just having to try, takes a lot of the pressure off.

I turn back to Brooke. "So, what type of trees do you like?"

Chapter Fourteen

Jesse

Lulu is sunburned, despite the sunscreen she applied twice. So am I, if the heat radiating from the back of my neck is any indication. Lulu pets the foam finger she bought for herself. I chose a ball cap, the bill fresh and flat and new. "Are you hungry?" I ask. "Want to stop somewhere? Get something to eat?"

"I'm good," she says. She pulls out her phone when we stop at a red light, frowning at the screen, then frowning harder before she shuts the phone off again and shoves it into her bag.

"Everything alright?" I ask. She nods. Then, before I can suggest ice cream, or a movie, or any excuse to extend our evening, she says, "I talked to Audrey."

I flick on the turn signal, the clicking like a clock. "About what?" I ask, while I try to remember if Audrey is the colleague she admires or the one who'd beat themselves with their sawed-off arm to avoid working with her.

She snorts. "We mostly just sniped at each other," she says quickly. "But I don't know. I guess we ended things on... steadier ground?"

"Oh. That's great. Right? What did she say?"

Lulu is silent.

I glance over at her as I slow down to turn onto her parents' road.

"A lot." She sounds hesitant, a bit nervous. "I don't think she trusts me yet."

I don't know much about academia but it's never struck me as the type of career where you have to actively watch your back. "Why wouldn't she trust you?"

Lulu winces. "My dad helped me get my job," she says. "It's one of the reasons I've been feeling so isolated at work. I'm trying to prove to them that they can trust me after that but Dad can be…overly helpful at times."

"I get that. Between Pop and Dad it was a foregone conclusion I'd be a firefighter, but it was hard at first, for vets and rookies to trust that I had their back. I had opportunities that others didn't."

"But they trusted you in the end, right? Marcus and…" She points to just below her nose. "The guy with the mustache. They genuinely miss you."

"Buck." I laugh. "Yeah. They did. They do. It's different, though. When you're about to go into a fire together all that really matters is knowing that the person beside you has your back."

Marcus has texted once or twice since we saw each other at the grocery store. I wish I could say I've kept my promise to him, but at least I haven't left him on read. I'm avoidant but not *that* avoidant. I've actually been busy. I've been saying yes, to Lulu, to George, to Betty, to Trey.

"Have you finished the history book you were reading?" she asks. "About witches?"

"Yes."

"And?" She's so excited, eager for me to love the things she loves.

"It was easy for me to understand?" I say, perhaps unhelpfully.

"How so?" She sounds hopeful.

"Like…" I pull into her driveway and the shocks on the Bronco don't do their job as we bump toward the farmhouse. "It was boring at first but it made a lot more sense than that Derrida guy."

"I…what?" She shakes her head. "You're reading Derrida?"

I scratch the back of my neck. "That…philosopher guy you mentioned at the grocery store? I thought I'd read his work."

She shoves me. "And?" I underestimated Lulu's potential excitement level, which was my bad.

I shrug and rub my shoulder. The philosopher's theory is… confusing. "I flew through the history of witchcraft book. It was actually, like, interesting."

She hums. "Derrida is interesting."

"I believe you. I know he's supposed to be interesting. I just have to have my dictionary next to me so I can look up every other word. I'm definitely going to have to renew the library book before I'm finished reading it," I admit.

She throws her head back and laughs. The sun is almost down and the light is orange and pink and Lulu is vibrant, her hair a bit wild and her skin glowing and warm. "I have some copies you can borrow. They're in my house." She hops out and doesn't look back. So I follow her. As if there was any other option.

"Have a seat," Lulu says over her shoulder as her front door closes behind us. The only place to sit is the bed. I perch my body on the edge of it before she can notice that I've been staring at it for too many seconds.

Her kitchen is in the corner of the room, small and clean with a tiny apartment stove and mini-fridge. The rest of the space is devoted to her bed—covered in a white bedspread with blue flowers—and books, so many books. Three stacked on the bedside table, piled beneath the small desk pushed up against the wall beside the door. A paperback laid flat on one of her pillows. Some as old as the farmhouse, some with a white tag on the spine from the university library. She already holds two in her hands but keeps browsing the bookshelf across from her bed. "Do you want something to drink?" she asks absently.

I clear my throat, suddenly parched. "No thanks."

She hums a questioning sound as her finger travels down the spine of another book. I shift and the bed creaks. I am too big for this space. Or it's the space that's too small. Lulu's presence, her smell, her things, *her*, take up all the oxygen in the room.

Lulu hands me four books and sits beside me on the bed. She talks about each one like it's an old friend, some of them she loves, others she begrudgingly accepts. Like they've been in her life for so long there's no point in removing them now. She taps the book on top, the one by Jacques Derrida, and explains how the first time she'd ever heard the name she was sitting in on one of her father's graduate seminars during Take Your Daughter to Work Day. A grad student had argued with her dad about the philosopher's theories and she'd been so incensed that they'd dared to offer a counterpoint to her incontrovertible dad, she picked up the book to be able to argue for him. It's so like Lulu to use a book like a white knight uses a sword. She laughs as she talks about trying to understand it at thirteen, picking it up again at fifteen, for a third time at twenty-one, then finally realizing that she actually agreed with the grad student after all at twenty-five.

Like all the other times Lulu has run off on a tangent, she looks a little embarrassed once she's done. I don't know what to say to her to convince her she shouldn't be. Already the sound of her voice is familiar, the cadence comforting. I can predict when she'll pause for laughter or agreement, the husky tone her voice takes on when she's making a particular kind of innuendo, the swoops and valleys of her laughter.

It's dark outside the small window above her kitchen but the room is golden from the bedside lamp. The books in my hands are well-loved. "Thank you. I'll take good care of them." When

I look back at her, I notice how close we're sitting. That she has a scar near her hairline and a thumbprint-sized birth mark behind her ear. "I guess I should get going."

I don't get up.

"Or you could stay?"

"What do you want to do?" I ask. She doesn't have a tele-vision. I'm not much for board games. We need more people to play euchre.

She stares studiously at my shoulder. "Maybe something we can't write about in our friendship journals?"

I tip her chin up to meet my eyes. "I thought you weren't cut out for breaking rules?"

"I think we're technically just bending them."

"Why do you really want to do this, Lulu?" I ask when she won't meet my eyes again. It's not that I don't want to. I just want to make sure it's for the right reasons.

She flops back on the bed. Her baseball T-shirt rides up, re-vealing her soft tummy. I want to press my nose into the skin there, just below her belly button. "When you were in high school did you ever just, like, call up your best friend and pick them up and drive around for hours? Just drive and drive even though gas was expensive and there was nowhere to go and now you feel pretty bad about your contribution to climate change? And you'd listen to music and sing and talk about nothing and solve all the world's problems and by the time you dropped them off, you just felt better? Lighter? Like being seventeen wasn't the worst fucking thing in the world anymore?"

George used to pick me up in his dad's Corvette. I could barely fit and had to push the seat all the way back. He'd take the car out to an empty stretch of road and drive too fast until I begged him to slow down, my knuckles white around the "holy shit" bar. But when he was done scaring the shit out of me, he'd be happier, lighter. Exactly like Lulu describes. "You want a distraction," I say.

"Friends let friends be distracted," she counters, defensive. And she has a point. Or maybe more accurately: this friend is willing to distract her even if what he needs is a distraction from her.

I sigh, like I'm quite put out by the whole thing. "Well, better take your shirt off," I say as I peel off mine. She laughs, struggling with her own, and I help her pull it over her head, her blond hair fanning out over her shoulders and standing on end from static. Lulu wears a plain black cotton bra. Faded from too many washes, it looks devastatingly soft, like I know the skin underneath will be.

We can't touch each other but I can't go another round without doing *something*. I press the heel of my hand against my dick. "Do you have like…?" I gesture at the drawer beside her bed.

She frowns between me and the furniture, her pants half-undone.

"Do you have toys?"

"Under the bed."

"Can I use one?" I ask. "On you?"

She nods quickly. "Yeah."

I waste no time dropping to my knees to pull out what can only be described as a treasure chest of sex toys from beneath her bed. She leans over the bed, biting back her smile. "A woman I worked with in the UK had one of those Ann Summers parties for her hen do," she explains. "It's like a Tupperware party but for sex toys. And the sales rep somehow wrangled me into buying one of everything." She groans at my incredulous face. "I felt bad, OK? No one was buying anything! But now I have all this. You have no idea how much it costs to ship all these sex toys across the ocean. What even is this?"

She picks up a ball gag with her index finger.

"We can work up to that," I say, putting it back into the plastic bin next to a harness that makes me think about things that friends shouldn't and a frankly beautiful pink rose glass plug. "Have you used any of these before?" I ask. "What do you like?"

She points to a silicone vibrator the size of my palm, a color that's probably advertised as raspberry or plum. "That's the only one I've ever used," she says. "It's nice."

One side is flat, the other has a pointed tip. I cup it in my hand, pressing the button to feel the different levels of vibration. It's intimate and unassuming, easily cupped between legs and over bodies. I find a pump bottle of fancy lube. The kind that calls itself a "personal moisturizer." Sitting on the bed next to her, I pour lube over the silicone toy.

"Do you want me to—"

"Should I—"

She seems nervous, her hand a fist between us, her toes curled. She jumps when I turn the vibrator on. "You OK?" I quickly turn it off again, my fingers fumbling from the lube. "We could just talk," I offer. "Or watch a movie. Friends do that."

"I'm pretty sure a movie is what got us into this in the first place."

"Good point."

She takes a deep breath. "I've just never done...sex...this way."

My brain snags on the way she says "this," as if she's ascribed a different meaning to it than I do. Wondering if that difference is good or bad.

"Have you?" she asks and I think from her tone that she's not just asking about my sexual history. She wants to know how I feel about all this, too.

"I've hooked up with friends before," I say. "George and I. We started as friends."

"Is George the only one?" she asks. Her hands move tentatively over my chest, through my chest hair. One finger follows the trail toward my belly button, and I hold my breath to hide that it tickles.

"He...yes." It's not just that it tickles. This might be the first time Lulu has touched me like this, casually but with intent, with care and without purpose. I haven't been touched like this in so long and I lean into it, taking her hand and pressing it to my stomach, the heat of her skin caught between the heat of mine.

"And you're still friends? Right?" she asks, her voice thin and cautious.

"Best friends." I cup her shoulder, rub my thumb beneath the cotton bra strap. "Lulu, we'll still be friends after this," I promise her. "You're still my friend."

It feels more true the more I say it, like I have the power to speak it into existence. We're an Odd Couple. I'm quiet and she hardly ever stops talking. She might be a genius and I'm a bit of a meathead, but she is my friend and I am hers and this silly little crush I have won't change that. We are friends and that will be true long after I've gotten a hold of my feelings. I won't let it ruin anything for Lulu. Not when she's trying so hard to make these changes in her life. "I promise."

We're touching each other in ways that might break the loosely defined rules we've agreed on, but she doesn't seem inclined to stop. So, I don't either. Her eyes travel over my face, stopping on my mouth. "Do you want me to put my fingers in your mouth again?" she asks, casually.

But there's nothing casual about the shiver that moves through me, my skin forming goose bumps at just the memory of her fingers, salty, wet, and warm, before.

Fuck, yes.

"Hold on." I lean over the side of the bed, feeling for the other toy I saw in the bin. I want her fingers in my mouth and on my skin and pulling my chest hair. I want to feel. Everything.

"Here." I draw a hot pink feather tickler along the curve of her body. "How does that feel?"

She shudders. "It tickles."

"Do you want me to keep using it?"

"Yeah." She huffs. "I had no idea what this was. I thought it was a feather duster and I was missing a maid's costume."

I fall back on her double bed to laugh silently. "Of course you did."

Lulu rolls onto her side, trailing the tickler along my side and this time I can't keep it inside. I laugh, my face pressed into the pillow. In retaliation, I turn the vibe back on, reaching around her to run it along the ridges of her spine.

And then it's on. She draws the feathers across my back. I rub the vibe over her stomach. She laughs in my ear, loud, almost a cackle. Her ribs shake against my hands. She goes for my armpit but when I slide the vibrator over her nipple, she stills, her mouth forming a perfect O.

"Yeah?"

She nods.

I pull the cup of her bra down but she shakes her head. "Take it off this time."

Lulu's breasts are bigger than I expect when they're unencumbered by things like clothing and underwire. If we were in the habit of touching each other *like that* she'd fill my hands. But pressing the vibrator around her areola is a fair substitute. She closes her eyes but doesn't stop the slow stroke of her hand at the back of my neck, the feathers from my hip to my shoulder. It doesn't tickle anymore, not in a way that makes me want to laugh; more like every nerve ending in my body migrates to wherever she touches me. At my neck and hip, and the press of her thighs around one of mine.

"OK, OK." She breathes the words. Lulu's fingers play with the dark patch of trimmed hair between her legs. "Touch me here."

She pops the button of my jeans and I push them down. I pause to apply more lube to the toy and when I turn back to her, she's got her hand all the way between her legs and her lip caught between her teeth.

"Hey," I say. Gently, I pull her hand away, kissing the salt on her fingertips. "I've got you, OK?"

As I slip my hand between her legs, she holds my wrist, pressing and pushing where she wants me to go. She moves me back and forth, her hips moving, too. Hooks her leg around my hip, presses her bare chest to mine. We're hot, her apartment isn't air-conditioned and the box fan in the corner is silent. Sweat slides between us, and I rise up on my elbow to brush her hair off her face. My pulse beats with each press of her fingers into my skin. Her mouth is so close, it would be easy to lean in and find out how her kisses taste. I stare at her full lower lip, her tongue. The vibrator isn't loud like one of those wands. Its hum is quiet, and it lets me hear each one of her gasped breaths, the swish of her legs against the sheets. She's blush pink and splashed in gold.

I'm going to think about this for the rest of my life, the way she pulls her hand away from my wrist once she's sure I can use the pressure and speed she needs, how she draws her fingers over my ribs, my hips. The grip she has on the back of my neck that gets tighter and tighter as her hips move faster. The sound of my name, like a question, like she's begging. Lulu goes still against me as she comes. She holds her breath; her eyes flutter closed, her mouth open, teeth pressed gently to my pec. The urge to kiss her is overwhelming. It would be nothing to tip her chin back, to cover her mouth with mine. Nothing. So, I bury my face in her hair. Suffocate myself on the sweet scent of her as she shakes against me.

I roll onto my back, bringing her with me until she's splayed across my chest. Her hair prickles my skin, the ends brushing my nipple. Her breath tickles my chin and neck, cooling everywhere that I'm too hot. My jeans feel tight, so uncomfortable I have to push them farther down my legs, expose more of my thighs and all of my boxers. She slides her finger up the shiny white line of my scar and I shudder, full-bodied and more aroused than I thought possible. A dark spot blooms on the fabric of my underwear.

"Sorry," she whispers, moving her hand away from the scar.

"No." I stop her hand, put it back where it was. "I like it."

"Again?"

"Yeah."

She rubs the tip of her finger down the scar again and again, and a shiver moves through my body, up my spine. She straddles my legs and drags her hand, nails pressed gently into my skin down my thigh.

"Holy." I grab my dick, squeezing once, hard. Her eyes are bright, her skin flushed. She's entirely at ease, her naked body straddled over mine, her nipples peaked and pink. Lulu runs her nails over my legs, my stomach. She rubs her hands through my chest hair, and it could just be the prolonged dry spell I'd had before her or the confusing feelings I have for her or just her, Lulu, herself, but my cock feels everything.

"Use your nails," I gasp as she runs her hands down my stomach again. "On my chest."

She does, softly, then harder. Hard enough that I know there will be marks on my skin long after we're done. I arch up into her, pull my cock out, spreading the come at the tip around the head. Lulu leans over the bed to grab more lube and her hair brushes my stomach. Every new sensation unlocks something new inside me, some new way to feel pleasure. Lulu pours lube over my cock and hands. She scratches her nails down my chest, feathers the tickler under my chin and over my collarbone.

"Blow on me," I beg and she stops, a small frown between her eyes. I purse my lips. "Air, blow air on me."

And without hesitation, she does. She leans over me and

blows over my chest, my stomach. She blows across my cock, the feeling like a touch, and I grip myself harder, fuck my hand harder. My legs saw beneath her. "Baby, please."

She smiles, her breath hot across my cock, my balls, like I am a birthday candle, like I'm made of wishes. And for her, in this moment, I am. I'd give her anything she asked for.

Her hands roam along my thighs, up through my leg hair and close, dangerously close to where my balls are tucked and tight. I come from the thought of it, her hands on me, her breath across my skin. I moan out sounds and curses until I'm sticky and hoarse.

Lulu lies down beside me, her hand under her cheek, watching me as I catch my breath.

"You called me baby," she says a little later.

My face heats. "Sorry about that." But she doesn't seem upset, just curious.

"I didn't mind."

"Did I distract you?"

Her whole face lights up. "You did."

"Are we the type of friends that tell each other about what we need distraction from?" I ask. Even in this soft light, I can see her blush, and not from the pleasure that's still lingering in the balls of my feet, my hips, and the palms of my hands.

"No," she says softly.

Now, it's my turn to blush. "OK."

"It's just…embarrassing. Like, look at my life. Look at how lucky I am." She throws her hand out, as if to say *look at all this*. "What do I have to complain about, you know?"

Where we were hot and sticky before, now my skin is starting to cool. But mostly I need the distraction of movement, of walking the three steps to the bathroom, running the water over my hand until it's warm. Soaking the first washcloth and wringing it out, wiping myself clean. Soaking the second and bringing it to Lulu. She has goose bumps, too, so I pull back the comforter with the little blue flowers and Lulu gets in. I pull on my underwear and she pouts until I lie back on top of the covers.

"When I was a kid I used to feel bad," I say. "For not having parents." I'm still not sure exactly what I want to say until I say it, but she gives me the space and time to get it out. "I didn't have parents, but I had grandparents who stepped up and gave me everything I could ever ask for. I didn't think I was allowed to be sad about my parents when things worked out for me. I could have ended up in the system, with no one. But my grandma liked to remind me that just because someone else had it worse didn't make my feelings any less important."

Crickets chirp outside and my heart aches in this moment for my grandmother. For her quiet, like mine.

Lu sighs. "Do you ever feel like no one wants you around?"

I feel the opposite. Like I could go hours, days, weeks, with no one around. "What do you want?" I ask instead.

Lu's brow furrows like it always does when she thinks really hard about something. "I guess I haven't asked myself that question. What about you?"

I shrug. "I have no clue." A copout. What I want is to feel comfortable in my skin again. To be able to be alone without feeling lonely.

She yawns, trying to hide it in her pillow.

"I really should go," I say. "Betty."

She nods. "She'll be waiting up for you."

I huff. Betty stalks the windows and front door until I come home. Once I'm inside with the door firmly shut behind me, she walks away with her tail in the air and doesn't show up again unless it's to scream at me for more kibble at ass crack o'clock in the morning.

She watches me as I get dressed. Before I leave, I sit down on the edge of her bed again. "Do you want anything? Can I get you a glass of water?"

She squeezes my hand; her eyes heavy, sleepy, sated. "I'm good."

"Hey," I say. "What you said in the group chat. About me never coming out with the group..."

"I was just joking, Jesse. I was giving you a hard time. I'm sorry."

I shake my head. "I can take it," I assure her. "But it did get me thinking." That maybe I am still not as all in on this study as I should be. "What if I...threw a party?"

Lulu sits up, the blanket falling to her waist. "What?!"

I cringe. "Yeah, I don't know. At the game, Trey mentioned we should get the group together like that and I thought, maybe it could be me. Plus, he's pretty persuasive. He was dropping hints that he'd be happy to host but his apartment is..." I look around. "About this size. And I said I had a house and..."

"Oh, Jesse. And you gave me a hard time for buying all those sex toys?"

"I like the sex toys." I really, really do.

She scrunches the comforter in her fist and says into her pillow, "I do, too."

Chapter Fifteen

Jesse

From my spot in the outfield, I have the best view of our team's final-inning defeat, after somehow holding on to a two-two tie since the seventh inning. There's always one team in every rec softball league that takes things way too seriously, and I had to play them on the one night my friends needed me to sub. Since I haven't played softball in years and was never great at it to begin with, they put me at the bottom of the order, and I've only had to strike out once because of it. Then George slapped a glove in my hand and sent me out to stand in between Austin and Annie, the only cis hets in our friend group who also happen to cis het with each other.

"Are you staying for beers after, Jess?" Austin calls over from left field.

"I'll stay," I say. I can commit to the time if not the beverage.

George scowls at us from second base for chatting during game play and we both stand still, staring as the other team's final batter jumps on to home base with a flourish and celebrates with a complicated team handshake. Annie trots over from right field. "Good game, boys."

Austin kisses her and slaps her butt. He kisses me and slaps my butt. We walk to the dugout together, collecting more kisses and butt slaps as we go. From a beat-up red cooler at the end of the bench, George disperses beers and hard seltzers and canned wine. He tosses me a can, too. I almost toss it back to him but then I see it's a Sprite. I hold it up. "Thanks."

George blows me a kiss.

My friends settle around me, teasing each other about some particularly bad plays and doing barely passable imitations. Lacey, the only person on the team who's actually played softball competitively, busts a gut when she describes my batting stance. I laugh, too, when she makes a face that is strikingly similar to Lulu's version of my Grump Face.

The laughter, the affectionate ribbing, the cicadas, and the smell of diesel fuel from the freeway feel like pulling my old plaid jacket on; warm and familiar. Not just for the memories I've already created with this group of friends, but for the hundreds of times I've done something similar with my platoon at station 11. We had a basketball net behind the station and I spent a lot of nights running with them until my lungs burned, missing enough shots to fill a compilation video. And laughing, laughing with my friends.

I stay behind after to help George clean up empty cans and put equipment away.

"That wasn't so bad, was it?" he asks as we walk through the brightly lit parking lot to our cars.

"I never thought it would be." But I am tired now. Sitting on the bench and standing in the grass wasn't physically taxing. It's just a lot, being around people. It's always been *a lot* but after the accident it got to be more.

I check my phone for the time and a text from Lulu; a screenshot of the rules of an overly complicated drinking game for this weekend's party.

"Are you working tonight?" George asks.

"Start at midnight." I have four hours to get home, get a bit of sleep, and get to the construction site, where I'll sit in the company-issued car for eight hours, getting out every hour to do a visual inspection of the property.

"Maybe you could start training new firefighters," he says, throwing his bag into the trunk of his sports car.

"George," I say flatly.

"I'm not meddling. I'm just *suggesting*."

I lean against the driver's side door of my truck. He's not wrong to make "suggestions." Ever since I asked Lulu what she wants, I've been thinking about how I might answer the question myself. I don't know that I have the answer, but I know what I don't want.

"I don't really like the job, it's just…" I gesture at myself.

"Just what?"

I shrug. "Look at me."

George's eyes get big. "Yeah. I'm looking."

I huff. "What else am I good at?"

He slams the trunk and stalks over to me. I would never tell him this but when he's mad George's nostrils flare and it's the cutest thing. His nostrils are flaring. "Jesse Theodore Logan. How dare you say that about yourself. About my friend. What's got you thinking about this?" he asks.

"Lulu."

"Lulu asked what else you're good at?"

"What? No. Lulu needed…" I realize mid-sentence I've backed myself into a corner here. "We were talking," I say in the vaguest of truths. "And she said…" I don't want to reveal too much of what Lulu has told me. Lulu is vulnerable with me. She might be vulnerable with everyone, but that's her choice to decide. "We were talking and the question of what she wants out of life came up. It got me thinking about what I want."

"And…?" George asks, his voice soft. He stands close but doesn't touch, speaks low, like he doesn't want to scare me away.

"And…" I take a deep breath. "I wanted to be a firefighter because I wanted to be like Pop but…" My heart breaks every time I say it. Even though the news is nothing new. "Now I can't be." The ball fields surrounding us are empty. It's just George and me under the bright fluorescent lights, and the crickets. George waits me out.

"Everything I've ever done has been because I'm like him. I'm big. I'm strong. I've got the type of body that can lift heavy things or scare people away."

George opens his mouth, closes it, like he wants to say something but changes his mind.

"I want to do something where people appreciate me for my brain, not just my body," I say quietly, flushing. Vulnerability is still uncomfortable but it's getting easier. Like at the gym, at first a heavy weight feels like too much but the more you lift it the easier it gets.

"OK. How can I help?" George asks.

Before I can think too hard about it, I pull him to me and hug him. He lets out a soft *oof.* "You're a good friend."

"Yeah, yeah, OK. Come on. Tell me how I can help."

I scratch the back of my head even though it's not itchy. "Lulu gave me these books by these historian–philosopher folks. They're really confusing. I don't get most of what they're talking about."

"So, you want to be a historian–philosopher?" George asks with full seriousness.

"Lulu really likes history. Well, obviously. She's a professor. But she's passionate about it and it got me thinking about how if I can't be passionate about firefighting, I need to find something else to be passionate about."

"What are you passionate about?" he asks like he already knows the answer and this is a test.

"Lulu said I'm good under pressure."

He hums, nods.

"Caring for Pop has been hard emotionally but also, re-warding?"

"Hmmmm."

I shrug, kicking at a stone on the pavement, watching a cof-fee cup roll away in the soft breeze. "So I thought—"

"Yes," he says, gripping my shoulders and shaking me sur-prisingly hard for someone I once back squatted as a joke.

"You haven't even heard what I was going to say yet."

"Nursing. You were going to say nursing, right?"

"I…"

He grins, cheeky and clearly pleased with himself.

"How'd you do that?"

"I'm right?"

"Yeah, I guess. I mean. I don't know. It's probably stupid."

George punches me, not hard, and with his fingers wrapped around his thumb. I pull his hand apart to reset his fist. "Jesse," he says while I fiddle with his hand. "It makes absolute sense that with your medical training and grace under pressure you could excel in a field like that."

I sigh. "I feel like I'm having a midlife crisis. Maybe I should just get a convertible."

"We're not old enough for those yet," he says primly. "It's a quarter-life crisis at best. And you were basically forced into this quarter-life crisis because of a traumatic car accident. You're lucky to be alive. You get to learn who you are now, again."

"Yeah. Yeah, OK."

"So, what are you going to do?"

I flip my keys in my hand. "Guess I'll think about it some more," I say, just to annoy him. And it works. "Bye, George," I say as he gets in his car and drives away. He flips me off.

I pull my phone out as I get settled in the car and open my text thread with Marcus.

Me: You off on Friday?

Marcus: Sorry who's this?

I send the middle finger emoji.

Marcus: lol yeah. Why?

Me: I'm having a party.

Marcus: Well, shit kk. I'll bring a couple of the guys.

Marcus: that cute girl gonna be there?

Me: yes Lu will be there

Me: Why? You like her?

I hold my breath as I watch his text bubble pop up and disappear, pop up and disappear. Never have I wanted someone's answer to be a clear and resounding *no* in my whole life.

Marcus: No. But you do.

Well, shit.

Me: Fuck off.

Marcus: See you Friday!!!

Pop was the one who wanted to go into the assisted living residence. If it had been up to me, we'd have hired a live-in nurse. I didn't care how much it would have cost, but Pop didn't want me working extra jobs. He made me promise, though, not to let him end up alone there. That I'd visit as much as I could. It wasn't a promise at all. There was never any other option. Which is why I'm here an hour after my shift ended. My clothes feel dirty. I'd kill for a shower. I'm grimy with exhaustion and guilt. Right now, at this moment, as much as I love him, I just want to go home and go to bed.

Cicadas have already started droning as I pull myself out of the truck. The sliding glass doors whoosh open, sounding like an air lock releasing. I greet the nurses at the desk, in the hall, search for Pop in the dining room, in the rec room, finally in his room. He's still in his pj's, his gray slippers dangling off his feet where he sits on the edge of his bed, facing the window. From this position he would have been able to see me drive in, park, sit in my truck for long minutes. He would have been able to see, if he could recognize me.

"Morning, Pop." I sit beside him, the bed creaking under our combined weight. We sit in silence, a nurse whistles as they walk down the hallway, the pipes in the wall groan. It feels stupid to talk to him when I know that chances are he won't remember. He can't understand where and when he is in his own life.

"I have a new friend named Lulu. I think I told you about her."

Pop looks over at me. I don't see any recognition there. I tell myself it's fine.

"The other day I asked Lulu what she wanted, but it got me thinking about what I want," I say. "I thought I wanted to be a firefighter again, but I don't think I do anymore. I think I'm ready to move on from that. I hope that doesn't upset you."

Someone coughs in a nearby room, one of those loud, wracking, wet coughs that sounds like it hurts. I wince and don't continue until the cougher is finished. "I want Lulu. I like her. I like the way she laughs and how passionate she gets about the things she loves. I love hearing her talk."

Now that I've started, I'm on a roll.

"I know it's probably confusing for you. I told you before that I don't just like girls and then I tell you about a girl—a woman—I like. Or maybe it's not confusing at all. I mean, it's not confusing to me. Well, it was confusing when I was thirteen but not anymore. But that's one of the reasons why I didn't tell you before, I guess. There's this pressure to…" I shake my head searching for the word. "Perform that I'm bi enough. But maybe that was always just pressure I was putting on myself. It's not like you could have put that pressure on me. You didn't know."

I pause to catch my breath and let Pop get a word in. He declines.

"What I'm saying is that I really like Lulu. I liked her from the first day I met her. But being friends is more important. I want a fresh start. I want to feel optimistic. I want you to know me," I say quieter. "And yeah. Yeah, I want Lulu." Pop laughs like I've said something funny.

"Let's keep that between us, though, OK?"

Chapter Sixteen

Lulu

I've done therapy one other time in my life and it was exactly what I needed. My therapist was a tall older woman with glasses and a soft voice. She was a safe person when I felt like everyone was a danger. Like my last therapist, this therapist has a box of tissues on the coffee table in between us, a comfortable sofa, and interesting abstract artwork on the walls. There's a big clock in the corner and a smaller one beside her chair.

She told me her name when I came in for my individual therapy session for the study, but now that we're sitting down, I've already forgotten it.

"So, Eloise, how are you?"

I wince. "Lulu."

"Pardon?"

"I prefer Lulu. Not Eloise."

This therapist seems to be my age, maybe a few years younger. She's Asian-American, with her dark hair pulled back in the standard academic ponytail.

"Sorry." She makes a note in a notebook on her lap. "How are you doing, Lulu?"

"I feel terrible, but I've forgotten your name." There is a swarm of butterflies flapping in my gut right now.

She smiles, tight-lipped. "Leigh. Lulu, how are you doing?"

How I am doing is frustrated. The only friend I've made in the study so far is the guy that I get off with, and I'm not positive but I'm pretty sure that means one or both of us is doing something wrong and that maybe this study isn't working how I hoped it would. Of course, I can't say any of this to her. My ability to give constructive criticism is only available to me within the context of academia. If your interpretation of the causes of the witch hunts is flawed I'll tell you, but if you get my Starbucks order wrong, I'll just say thank you and drink it.

"Great," I say. "Fine." The last one sounds like a question.

Leigh writes something down in her notebook again and I lean forward on the couch to try to see over the edge. The couch, made of some kind of vegan leather, also known as plastic, makes an extremely embarrassing noise and she catches me.

"You don't seem like you're being honest," Leigh says. "Why is that?"

Well, there's a tag along the side seam of my T-shirt that has been bothering me since I got to campus but I can't scratch it without rucking up my whole shirt and exposing my tummy, and Frank corrected me this morning in front of everyone in a departmental meeting about the month in which a supposed witch trial took place in Russia since the empire didn't switch over to the Gregorian calendar until 1918 and so was thirteen days behind the rest of Europe. But mostly, I'm just fed up.

Before I can organize my thoughts, I launch into how I'm really doing. "Fine. To be honest, I thought I'd be farther along by now. I thought I'd have friends. It's not like I expected my social life to change drastically but I've been going to the events and journaling and sharing in our group sessions. I let you all poke and prod me and test my blood and listen to my heartbeat. But I still haven't learned how to make friends with the other people in the study or the people I work with. I left the UK because I felt like I didn't belong there anymore after I got dumped by Brian and Nora—who you don't know but trust me, they're assholes—but I don't feel like I belong here, either. Even my own father doesn't want me here. He thinks I should go back to Lancaster and every attempt he makes at helping me results in me alienating more of my colleagues."

Leigh pushes the box of tissues across the table at me and I pull a few from the stack, loudly blowing my nose and dabbing at my cheeks. Now that they're here the tears don't stop coming and I grab a few more tissues.

"You said you don't feel like you belong here. Let's talk about that."

I focus on the painting above her head, a series of thick, looping black brushstrokes on a white canvas in a gold frame. It's exactly the kind of calming art I'd expect to find here. I follow the brushstrokes over the canvas like a route on a map and slowly my breathing evens out, my blood pressure drops to an acceptable level, and the tears stop.

"My best friend Cally and I were inseparable when we were teenagers. You know that level of obsession that only feels possible when your brain hasn't fully developed yet? And later, Nora was my best friend. My best—" My voice catches and I have to stop. The clock on the wall ticks down our time and my fingers dig into the plush couch cushions. "The thing was I knew I wasn't going to marry Brian. So when he started acting weird, secretive, you know? I wasn't so much sad as, like, pissed. And I started…" I look away, embarrassed. "I followed him," I say quietly. "I know it was wrong. But I *knew* he wasn't going to tell me the truth."

"What did you find?"

"They weren't even trying to hide it. They met at the local pub, the one Brian and I went to every Sunday for Sunday roast. They held hands across the table. They kissed on the sidewalk and walked up the high street to her flat. I asked her the next day what she'd done the night before. She said she'd just had a quiet night in, alone. I knew Brian would lie to me but Nora, Nora was my best friend, my dearest friend, Nora had never lied to me. We promised each other never to lie."

"How'd that make you feel?" Leigh asks.

Her emails aside, I haven't spoken to Nora since I left the UK and I'm ashamed to admit that even after this hurt, I miss her. "Like a fool. It was humiliating. To know that two people who are supposed to care for you the most don't care for you at all? And for everyone else to now know it, too? My whole life I've felt like everyone was in on an inside joke, except for me. It's lonely being left out. I want to know what the joke is, too, and I don't know what I'm doing wrong that no one will tell me."

Leigh nods and jots down another note. "You journal more consistently than any other participant in the study, did you know that?"

I shake my head but internally do a little dance. If they were giving out grades for journaling, I'd probably get a good one.

"And your entries are comprehensive in both what you're thinking and feeling and the next steps you'd like to take. They also feature another participant quite heavily. Jesse Logan."

I pull apart a clean tissue, making a pile of wadded-up cotton on the glass table. "Yes. I guess you could say he's the one success I've had throughout all this."

"One could argue that you have learned to make friends. That Jesse is your friend."

"One could argue that," I say, slowly. One could also argue that the flip in my stomach when I can get him to smile, to laugh, is anything but friendly.

She sighs, sitting back in her wingback chair. "You're an academic, right?"

I look down at myself for a sign that the burnout and impostor syndrome are that obvious.

"Academics tend not to give themselves enough credit. It makes sense. It's basically our job to be graded. We write and then we ask our peers to review our work and tell us what's wrong with it and we do the same to them. At a certain point, it just gets easier to turn that critical eye on ourselves."

"You think I'm being too critical of myself?"

"Well, you talk about belonging. But belonging doesn't just happen. We have to cultivate the places where we find belonging, we must cultivate those relationships and connections."

"Are you telling me to bloom where I'm planted?"

She laughs. "Not quite. The biggest difference between people and plants is we get to choose where we set our roots. You get to choose where you belong, Lulu."

"And you think I'm not trying hard enough to cultivate my belonging here?" That makes sense. Maybe I could join more clubs. Or I could host my own party. Though, I definitely don't have a big enough apartment.

"No." She leans forward. "There's that self-criticism again. I'm saying you already are cultivating belonging, right here. With Jesse. Maybe you do go back to the UK, maybe you don't. But don't ever think that you don't belong when you are clearly working so hard to do exactly that."

The last time I went to therapy I was an empty shell of a girl who had lost her voice and lost her way. Then, my therapist helped me see myself another way, as more than just the sum of my trauma. Leigh must be just as good, because now I see my research into how we make friends, my attempts at conversations, in a new light. I see Jesse in a new light, too, for the way he always checks in with me even if it's just with a gentle hand on my back, for how he sends me good morning texts, and corrects people when they call me Eloise, for the way he'll let me talk and talk and talk and work out whatever I'm feeling onto him like he's a blank canvas and I have a paint gun. If there's one person here that makes me feel like I belong, it's him, even if he's never said he's happy I'm here. But now I also see why the psychologists don't want us hooking up with other participants. How am I supposed to know if I really belong here if I'm falling for my friend?

By the time I leave the session, splash cold water on my face to de-puff my eyes, and get back to my office to collect my things, I'm already running late. I still have to go home, change, prep food, find a bottle of wine I can pilfer from my mom's collection, and get to Jesse's house for his party.

"Dr. Banks, how are you?" Miranda says behind me as I run for the back stairs.

"Miranda. Dr. Jackson. Hi."

"Miranda is fine. How are you?" she asks again.

"Great. Good." Emotionally raw and unprepared for whatever interaction we're about to have. "And you?"

She hikes the strap of her bag higher up on her shoulder. She's dressed in a smart pants suit set, royal blue with a white silk blouse, her lips a cherry red, but her bag is a duffel with a familiar swoosh on the front. "Going to the gym?" I ask.

"Yes. But I'll be back in about an hour and a half. I was wondering if you wanted to grab dinner after, if you don't have any plans."

Crumbs. "I do."

She smiles.

"Have plans, I mean. I'm sorry."

She frowns, a pouty face. It's so outside the realm of experience I've had with Miranda, so unlike the polished idea of Miranda I've always upheld in my head. It reminds me of me. And suddenly I want nothing more than to tell her yes. Yes, I will hang out with her. Yes, let's get dinner, drinks, catch a film. Yes, to cultivating belonging.

Except I have Jesse's party.

"Maybe next week?"

She perks up. "Rock on," she says, throwing up her index and pinkie fingers.

"Great. Cool. Good."

"See you soon," she says, and the minute she rounds the corner to the elevators I bounce up and down, my sneakers squeaking on the linoleum. I have a friend date.

"Yes yes yes yes yes."

"What are you doing?" Audrey asks.

I turn quickly to find her watching me with her eyebrow cocked. Usually her smiles are ready to draw blood, but this one could be generously described as tentatively amused.

"Celebrating," I say. "Miranda and I are going out for dinner next week."

"Ah." She doesn't smile but her dimples make an appearance. "Cool. Well, have a good weekend."

"Do you want to come?" I ask. I feel myself tipping onto my toes, an old twitch from when I was a kid and exceptionally nervous. "Do you want to join Miranda and I for dinner?"

Audrey tucks her hair behind her ear. "OK. Text me when you know the details."

She turns to go and instead of having any chill at all, I yell, "I don't have your number." Which is how I find myself leaving campus with dinner plans and Audrey Robbs's phone number burning up my phone like a hot potato.

"Belonging," I say to myself as I pass my tree, dragging my hand across the rough bark. "I can belong here."

Chapter Seventeen

Lulu

Jesse told me to come anytime but when I turn onto his street, ten minutes past, there's already nowhere to park in his driveway or out front. I have to parallel park four houses down, which is exceptionally difficult when I factor in the fact that I cannot parallel park. Music pumps through the open windows and I check my phone again to make sure I didn't arrive later than I thought, like maybe I drove through a wormhole on my way here and it's actually midnight.

But no. 7:11pm.

I knock but when no one answers, I let myself in. The house is packed. There must be people here who aren't a part of the study.

"Lulu's here," a voice yells and a cheer goes up from the crowd. My face flushes as I wave at the mass of bodies dancing on a makeshift dance floor where Jesse's couch and coffee table used to be. Someone has brought a spinning disco ball with lights and it sits precariously on the edge of his mantel. A Ping-Pong ball sails into the living room, chased by George, who smiles when he sees me.

"You made it!" His face is flushed red and the collar of his white polo shirt is crooked and he has a pink stain on his chest.

"There's so many people here already," I whisper, then repeat myself when he can't hear me.

He laughs. George smells certifiably flammable and it's not even eight o'clock. "What did you expect? A party for millennials has to start early so everyone can go to bed early."

"Do you think Jesse is OK with all these people in his house?" I ask.

George winces but nods as he scans the room. "Don't worry about him. Jess knows how to party."

"Hey," Jesse says, appearing out of the congregation in the kitchen like we summoned him. "Do you want me to put that in the fridge?" He gestures to my bottle of pinot grigio.

"Thanks."

He takes it, then leans in, wrapping his arm around my shoulder. "It's good to see you," he says, his voice deep in my ear. "Thanks for coming."

"Y-yeah. Thanks." I watch him walk away, my hand still raised to where it was wrapped around his biceps. He disappears back into the kitchen and I'm left staring after him, George staring at me. "I'm just going to go mingle," I say, slipping away before he can say anything to me, like why I'm staring at our friend *that* way.

Then, I'm pulled into the throes of the party. I haven't been to one like this since high school, when the laughter was louder than the music, where there's something different to do in every room. In the kitchen is a drinking game that involves a Ping-Pong ball and slapping plastic cups off tables; by the front window is a food table laden with picked-through veggie platters and chip bowls; a group of people sit around on the couch and chairs pushed into the corner debating whether umpires should be replaced with robots; Betty is nowhere to be seen but Jesse reminds people no less than three times to keep the front door closed for the cat.

And George was right. Jesse moves through the party with a drink in his hand, though I never see him take a sip. While he rarely smiles, he does talk to everyone and his face seems lighter, happier than I've seen it in a while. He looks like he's having a good time and that makes me have a better time. It makes me happy.

"Are you here to party or to watch Jesse wear the shit out of that black T-shirt?" Brooke asks, leaning against the snack table next to me.

I choke on my carrot stick. "No," I wheeze as she pounds my back.

She laughs. "Don't worry, I've been hoping to catch glimpses of Trey's calves all night." She points to where he bounces around to a pop song. They're pretty good calves.

"Nice."

"How do you think it's going?" she asks.

"How do I think what's going?" My gaze snags on the back of Jesse's broad shoulders in the middle of the dance floor. He's not dancing, he's more like the maypole everyone orbits around. I'm not exactly sure what the muscles are called that taper toward his waist but they sure are rippley.

"The study. Do you think it's going well? Are they getting lots of good data off us?"

"It feels like summer camp for adults."

"Right?!" Brooke takes a swig of whatever is in her red plastic cup. I'm realizing that Brooke might have had a lot to drink tonight. She shimmies her shoulders and bops her head to the beat. "If I'd known making friends was this easy, I'd have signed up for summer camp ages ago."

"I never actually went to summer camp as a kid," I admit.

She turns to fully face me. "What?"

"My dad was usually off in the summers so we'd just hang

out." I shrug. Dad Summer Camp consisted of library and museum visits and watching baseball either in person or on the old box TV in the sunroom with a never-ending supply of lemonade.

"We have to do summer camp stuff," Brooke shouts. Maybe she's not as drunk as I thought. She's not slurring and her eyes are clear and focused. Brooke just might be an actual extrovert.

"Now?"

She rolls her eyes. "I guess not, but we should do something."

"People go swimming at camp, right?"

She snaps her finger. "Day at the lake?"

"Yeah," I say. "Let's do it." Look at me. I'm doing so much belonging cultivation today.

The playlist rolls from one pop song to the next and Brooke sets her empty cup on the table. "I'm gonna dance. Want to come?"

I shake my head. "Have fun."

I move through the party until I get to the bathroom and close myself inside. I splash water on my face and drink straight from the tap. I try to do something with my hair in the mirror, but it stays fairly straight and a little frizzy from the humidity. I could shoulder my way through the crowd and get myself a drink from the fridge, but I won't. Maybe it's wrong to want but tonight I hope Jesse wants to do…whatever it is we do together and I don't think he'll fuck if either of us are drinking. I make my way back into the party, two minutes in the bathroom offering enough of a reset, and find Jesse standing in a circle of his firefighter buds.

"Lu." Jesse's voice takes on a warm quality whenever he says my name. It feels like the sun coming out behind some clouds or holding my palms up to a campfire. "You remember some of these guys?"

"Firefighters," I say.

He shoots me a finger gun. "You got it." Jesse reintroduces

me to everyone then puts his arm around my shoulder, like he's claiming me. His hand is warm on my bare skin and I give myself permission to look up at him, once, twice and then no more because if I look too much the butterflies might fly right out of my eyeballs. Instead, I sink into the lines of his body, rest my arm on the kitchen counter behind him, my hand lightly gripping his T-shirt.

"Thanks," he says after a moment.

"For what?"

"Being my anchor." He gestures to the party. "It's fun. But it's a lot. I don't remember the last time I had this many people in my house."

I feel dizzy, in the best possible way. That Jesse—steady, stalwart Jesse—needs an anchor, needs me, makes my heart pound and my cheeks ache from smiling. "Happy to be here," I manage. "Any chance I can convince you to dance with me?"

He looks over my head to the group that's already started to settle down and makes a Grump Face. "Maybe next time."

"Promise?" I ask and whoops. I think I'm flirting with Jesse Logan but when he meets my eyes again, he looks like he doesn't mind and that just makes my heart beat faster.

"We'll see."

"What happened to your hand?" one of the firefighters asks.

I hold it up for their inspection. "Cut it gardening." They all wince. "Jesse patched me up, though."

"Tell them what you did to your other arm," he says and if I could name this new face he makes it would be Mischief Face.

I shake my healed arm at them. "Fell out of a tree."

They all nod, like that's a completely reasonable answer for an adult woman to give, but I guess if anyone knows how dangerous trees can be it's the guys who get called to rescue cats from them all the time.

Another yell goes up from the group playing the drinking

game with the Ping-Pong ball. In the living room, Trey is leading the dancers in a rendition of "The Thong Song."

"Hey." Brooke bops up to us, a red cup in her hand, a distinct flush on her cheeks. Jesse introduces her and she immediately takes a shine to a man named Chris with a patchy beard. "Did you know Lulu has never been to summer camp?"

"Me neither." Jesse tightens his arm around my shoulders and I really can't help myself this time. I peek up at him.

"Really?"

"It was too expensive. My grandparents just offset their schedules." He smiles at me like he expects me to chime in with my reasons but I'm too busy cataloging the pressure of each finger pad on my skin, calculating the duration of the squeeze and comparing it with the beats per minute of my heart. I can ask someone in the maths department to come up with an equation for what it all means.

"Yeah," I say, nodding vigorously. "Right."

Jesse scrunches up his nose and if I wasn't locked into his frame I'd fall right over. That is a completely new Jesse Logan face.

The conversation devolves into a competition of sorts: Who can't ride a bike? Brooke. Who never got suspended? Me and Marcus. Who's never left the country? Jesse and Chip. Who was part of 4-H? Chip. Who's never had a surprise party thrown for them? Me.

It's silly to feel giddy over something like this, something as simple and meaningless as collecting random facts about people who aren't strangers and probably aren't yet friends, but the truth is I think I'll remember this forever: laughing until my sides hurt, Sisqó, the counter sticky from spilled drinks, my skin sticky with humidity, and the look on his face as he bends over me, how his brow furrows as he presses his lips together to blow a gentle breeze across my forehead.

"Better?"

I don't even bother to look when I say, "Thanks."

As George predicted, the party winds down early, everyone's energy burned fast and bright, like a dying star. I help organize ride-shares for anyone who can't drive and when all that's left is George, Trey, and me, Jesse opens his bedroom door and Betty comes trotting out, meowing like she's finally able to air her grievances after being locked away for so long.

"Decided she'd be safer in there," Jesse says.

"I've got to go, then," Trey says. "Allergic." He pouts.

George offers to give him a ride and hugs Jesse and me, and then Jesse shuts his front door behind them. He turns the lock and it sounds louder than I know it to be.

"Need help cleaning up?" I ask. We get to work; I sort the garbage from the recycling and he packs up the food. He's switched the music from the synthy, loud pop to quiet folky-country. Jesse moves Betty's litter, food and water dishes out of his bedroom and I load the dishwasher. He vacuums the living room and I sweep the kitchen. I wipe down all the flat surfaces with a homemade cleaner I find underneath the kitchen sink. He turns off the lights in the living room, pulls the curtains in the front window, and meets me in the kitchen, where the only light is the one over the stove.

I lean against the counter, and he stands at the sink. He rolls the sleeves up on his long-sleeved T-shirt and washes his hands, the water and suds sluicing over his blunt fingernails, the veins of his forearms. The night is pitch-black outside the kitchen window, none of the glow from the streetlights reaching between his house and the neighbor's. He's close enough to touch. I could grip the back of his shirt in my fist and pull him to me, which is probably why I shouldn't. He faces me, his hands clenching the counter behind him, and I mirror him, tether myself to this side of the kitchen with the island and the pots hanging from the rack between us.

"Thanks for coming," he says, his voice low and quiet

enough that I lean forward on the pretense of needing to hear him better.

"Thanks for hosting."

My skin goose bumps, my nipples pebble. It's not always like this with him. I can sit next to him on his bench seat in the Bronco, bounce along on shocks that are too old, grab a hot drink before a group session, or sit next to him at dinner and I am fine. I can be normal. But right now, at the end of the night, I don't want to leave. I don't think I can. Not without feeling his heart beating out of his chest, against mine, or hearing the way his breath catches right before he comes. I'm addicted to those sounds, to the sight of him.

From somewhere in the house, Betty caterwauls long and loud and the sound breaks the tension between us, Jesse's shoulders shaking as I laugh. He steps forward, his arms open, and I fall into him, my arms around his waist. He smells different tonight, warmer. His arms wrap around me, his thumb brushing my bare shoulder blades, his fingers drifting under the thin strap of my halter top.

"You look pretty," he says. I feel his voice as much as I hear it.

"Brooke said you're wearing the shit out of this shirt." I pluck at the fabric clinging to his back.

His stomach shakes against mine. "Yeah?"

"You know what you look like," I say. I keep my eyes closed, smile against his chest.

"Yeah?" he says again, and I can hear the smile in his own voice, how it changes the cadence of his words, lightens his tone. He snaps the strap on my halter top.

I bite his pec in retaliation, gentle enough. He grunts and the hug never ends, it just changes. His hands migrate up and down my bare back, our hips press against each other and retreat. His breath is hot in my ear, his thigh thick between my legs. He walks me backward until I'm pressed between him and the counter, shifting so that I'm centered on his thigh, my mid-length skirt hitched up almost to my hips. His hands drop to my waist and he moves me back and forth. I leverage myself up on the counter so I can move with him, my tits pushed out, my legs wide.

"This what you wanted?" he asks.

And yes, I wanted to feel this, my pleasure and his, but also *this*, the way he looks at me, at us. The way his cheeks flush from arousal, the low rumble of his voice when he says "that's it," and "keep going, baby."

"What about you?" I ask, breathless as I roll my hips against him.

He blows against my chest, cooling my sweat. "Don't worry," he says. "After." He rubs the back of his fingers against my breast, sending shock waves through my nipple that border on painful, and I grind down harder on his leg. He hitches me up, but the friction isn't enough. I can't come just from this.

"Can you...?" I ask, pulling my top up and holding my breast like I'm offering it to him.

His rhythm stutters. "What are you asking?"

I whine and blush, embarrassed at having to say it out loud. "I need you to suck me," I whisper.

"Are you sure?" he asks but his hands are already moving up my ribs; he cups my breasts. "What about...?"

"Please." I lean back over the counter, my back arching to give him better access to more of my skin. And that's all it takes to convince him, of what is arguably a bad idea. His mouth is hot, his hair soft under my hand as I guide him over me.

I must look indecent with my tits out and my skirt hiked up my thighs, my back bent at angles only previously achieved by romance novel cover models, grinding against his thigh like I can burn off the rest of our clothes through friction. I am frantic and feral and I do feel wild, for him, to come, but I know I don't have to chase down my pleasure. The gentle strokes of his tongue against my nipple, the steady shift of his thigh between my legs, the way his hands squeeze me, I know I don't have to take my pleasure from him. He'll give it all to me. Of course he will. He's Jesse, my friend, my Jesse. He's the safest man I know.

I take his head in my hands, stroke the soft lobes of his ears. "Look at me," I whisper.

His eyes are hazy, glassy with lust; his lips are wet and so are my pebbled nipples as I roll my hip against him, as he guides me with his hands, as my clit pulses, as my back cramps and I squeeze him between my legs, as I come. He watches me the whole way through, helping me wring all of my pleasure out. I collapse back against the counter, my feet off the floor, body pinned between him and the linoleum. My panties are soaked, my come painting my labia and inner thighs. Every muscle in my body is liquid and Jesse is gentle with me when he gathers me in his arms and turns me around, bending me over the counter, my face pressed to the cool tiles. The sound of his zipper surprises me and I tense but Jesse goes still, putting a gentle hand on my back. "I'm keeping my underwear on," he says. "OK?"

"OK."

The shape of his cock is hard as it presses against the curves of my ass; his movements are short and shaky, his breath coming in harsh gasps, and then he goes rigid, his cock pulsing between my cheeks. I close my eyes, letting the low golden light in the room press at my eyelids. My face is cold against the counter, his front warm against my back. I'm slick and exhausted so when Jesse groans and pulls me down to the floor, our legs tangled together, I let him.

"Sorry," he says, breathless. "I should have asked you first if that was OK?" he says, like he's asking now.

"You checked in," I say. "I liked it."

When he sighs, his chest lifts me with him. "Will you tell

me now?" he asks, his fingers in the ends of my hair. "If there's anything you like or don't like or don't want?"

I open my mouth but for a moment, I am just like Jesse, and I'm silent. There is something I don't like. Of course, it comes up today, when my nerves from my first therapy session are still fresh. It's probably a conversation we should have, not just as two people who have sex together but as friends. If there was someone to tell, it would be Jesse. It's just that it always sucks to say it. There's no eloquent way. It just sucks. My chest shakes as I take a deep breath.

"I had a boyfriend in freshman year. He lived off campus."

My teeth start to chatter and goose bumps form along my arms, suddenly cold, always my inevitable reaction when I talk about Greg; like my body remembers, will always remember.

"He was..." I pause. Often I try to find ways to explain Greg and his behavior to other people, when the only explanation is that he wasn't a good person. "Greg and I were fooling around in my dorm room. I said no and he didn't listen."

Jesse is silent and still for a moment, then he turns me on his lap, leans forward to see my eyes. He doesn't say anything, the only sound is the dishwasher and my chattering teeth. "I don't like to be held down," I say matter-of-factly. "So, if you could not do that."

He clears his throat. "Did you report it?" Immediately, he shakes his head. "I'm sorry. That was the wrong question."

His stubble prickles the pads of my fingers as I rub his jaw. "At first, I didn't even understand that what was happening was wrong. He was my boyfriend and he cared about me and people who care about you don't *hurt* you. At least, they're not supposed to. My brain tried to come up with an explanation, any explanation that wasn't the truth. It wasn't until after that I couldn't stop shaking. I told my resident supervisor and she called the police and went with me to the hospital but in the end, even with the rape kit, I was told it would be a hard case to prove. He said, she said, I wasn't a virgin, and all that. I moved out of res…just bad memories. I went to therapy."

He tucks my hair behind my ear, brushes his thumb across my cheek to collect my tears. His fingers are soft on my lips. "Thank you for telling me. I'm sorry that happened to you. I'm sorry that the people who were supposed to protect you didn't do more."

I shrug. "It's fine," I say even though I'm crying. "I'm fine. It wasn't overly violent or anything. It was just…it hurt. He hurt me. More than just my body, you know? He taught me there are not nice people out there. And that some people are so broken that the only way they can feel whole is to break someone else."

"I don't know how…" He stops and starts again. "I've never met someone who…" His frustration surrounds him like a heat haze hovering over asphalt. "I'm sorry. I know that's not true." This time he speaks slowly, like he's choosing each word carefully. "No one's ever told me before and I want to make sure I do right by you."

He leans closer, tentative and slow, his forehead to mine, his palm over my heart.

"You have," I say. "I'm not sure there is a right thing to say," I amend.

"I promise to always be careful with you. To respect you and listen to you."

"I know. That's why I told you. I trust you. Jesse, you're…" My heart is in my throat. "You're my best friend."

He holds me against his chest, presses his mouth to the top of my head. "You're brave," he says. "I want to be brave like you."

"Oh," I say, eloquent, like a true academic. Is this what adoration feels like? It's one thing to feel brave around Jesse, it is entirely another for a brave person to think I am brave, too. To say it out loud.

"Your teeth aren't chattering anymore."

I didn't notice they'd stopped.

"It scared me," he says.

"I'm sorry," I say like a reflex.

"Don't be. That's a normal response to trauma."

Sometimes what I feel for Jesse, how I feel for him, is almost too big to fit inside my body. Like I'll die if we're not skin to skin, like if he's beside me I can do anything. I'm not sure if this is how friends should feel about each other, and maybe this is exactly why the study doesn't want us to do the thing we just did. I'm filled with so many questions, like how do we know when to stop, or *will* we stop? All I know is that Jesse is worthy of the softest parts of me, the parts that are still growing, pink and thin-skinned and sensitive to light. His strength isn't in his muscles or his size. It's in his heart, in his ability to see me so completely I can't hide the jagged parts of myself, nor do I want to.

That feels like friendship, being our most honest versions of ourselves. It feels a little like love, too.

Chapter Eighteen

Jesse

I convince Lulu to stay. It doesn't take much since once we get off the floor it's long past midnight and we both need showers. She gives me her keys and I have to adjust her seat all the way back, then move her car into my driveway. She sits on my bed, finger combing her wet hair, wearing my sweater and a pair of sweats rolled at the ankles.

"I hope I didn't use up all the hot water," she says.

"Don't worry about it," I say. I'm just eager to get cleaned up. The water is lukewarm but that's good. I'm still running hot on the smell of her hair, her skin in my nose, the feel of her against me. I need to drown out the sound of her moans still echoing in my ears and wash away the way she looked at me. Like I am someone. Like I am precious to her.

Lulu isn't in my room when I get out of the shower. I find her on the couch, curled up with Betty, an afghan my grandmother knitted over her legs. I sit on the edge of the couch, wrap my hand around her ankle. "You take the bed. I'll take the couch."

She shakes her head. "You're too big for this couch. Why'd you buy such a little couch when you're so tall?"

She's sleepy. Bed rumpled on a sofa. I want to see what she looks like in the morning. "We'll share the bed," I say. "Just sleep," I tell her when she tees up another objection on her lips. She waits for me as I double-check the locks on the front and side doors, shut off the lights, check Betty's water.

"Do you have a side?" she asks.

The center.

"You take that side," I say, pointing to the spot she lay the last time she was here.

With her in it, my bed overflows. It makes no sense how one person can take up so much space in a king-size. She rolls toward me and I lie on my back staring up at my popcorn ceiling. The last time I had someone else in my bed, I had a job I loved. I had a body I felt strong in. I don't feel strong enough, worthy to hold the things she's told me. Her words are a baby bird in my hands. I could close my fist and crush them, crush her. But she chose me to hold this with her, and I want to honor that.

"Is there anything you don't like?" she asks.

"What?"

"You asked me if there was anything I didn't want you to do when we're together, so I'm asking you the same."

"Oh. No. I'm good, I guess."

"Is there anything you like?"

"That I like?"

"Yeah. Is there anything you want?"

"I liked when we used the toys," I say, slowly. I can't help but think of the butt plug, the harness and what she could do with it. The darkness, at least, hides my blush.

"That was fun," she agrees. "Do you...have you used toys a lot?" she asks. "You seemed knowledgeable."

I shrug. "Sometimes," I say. "A fair amount."

She snorts. "We should use them, again. If you like them."

I roll toward her. In the dark, I can only see the outline of her. It's beyond past the time when we should have had "the talk." But if I can't see her in the dark, I can't see the myriad of emotions that will undoubtedly cross her face. I'll only have the quiet hitch of her breathing and her feet, cold against my shins.

Lulu is uncharacteristically quiet and still. Like maybe she knows I'm about to say something that will blow up this carefully crafted shell of a relationship we've created. I could ask her *what am I to you?* Maybe I won't get back the answer that I want but more than that, maybe I *will*. Maybe Lulu will tell me exactly how she feels. In fact, I'm sure she would. Lulu always says what she's thinking. But I'm not ready yet. Not ready to be the partner she deserves. I've barely been able to participate in our group sessions. Other than Lulu, I still haven't made many friends in the study. I'm in a dead-end job and my grandfather still doesn't know who I am. She deserves a whole person. Not these pieces I can scrape together.

So instead, I say, "I'd like that."

"We've never really talked about it," she says. Lulu finds my hand in the dark, squeezes. "Other than in the context of your grandfather."

"Talked about what?"

"You," she says. "And George."

"You mean, that I'm bi?"

The blankets rustle as she moves closer. "Yeah. I just want you to know that you can tell me things, too."

I squeeze her hand back. "I know. Thank you." And then, because I can't not ask, "Is that a… It doesn't bother you, does it?"

"Definitely not." Her voice is warm, soothing. Exactly the balm the fluttering in my heart needed. "What kind of friend would I be?"

But that's exactly it. For some friends, girlfriends, it can be a problem. Since George I've dated, had sex with, men and women casually. I've never had a non-binary date but I'd say yes to the right person. Sometimes, it is a problem when even the most progressive of people have some casual biphobia they can't seem to shake.

"What kind of friend would I be, especially when I'm not, like, exactly straight?"

I roll toward her in the dark, thinking I've misheard her. "You're not what?"

I can practically hear her roll her eyes as she snorts a little laugh. "I mean, I haven't… I've never… I just…sometimes when I…" She shimmies in the bed. "I don't just think about guys."

That's how it always starts.

I roll back to stare up at the ceiling. "Cool. Well, thanks for telling me."

"I've never told anyone that before."

"Thanks for letting me be your first." I mean it. I try to inject how much into my words. It means something to me that she feels safe enough to tell me things, anything.

She yawns and switches into Lulu Mode. She tells me about something funny George said tonight, about how cute Betty is. She tells me about an article she's working on, and Audrey and Miranda and how she's going out to dinner with them. Her words get slower, fewer and farther between. She falls asleep, my hand still in hers. As my eyes adjust to the dark, I can see her better. The cool tone of her hair in the dim moonlight, fanning out against my dark blue pillowcase. The curve of her nose. She frowns in her sleep, like she's working hard at it, the way she works hard at everything. When I finally fall asleep, I dream of lavender and laughter and the sound of my grandfather saying my name, instead of my father's.

The air-conditioning in this building borders on arctic. Between the cold and sitting in this cramped waiting room chair, my leg is throbbing, screaming. I take a sip of my lukewarm coffee and tip my head back against the wall behind. Close my eyes and think of anything but the low pulse of pain radiating up my hip and down my knee. The door opens and I crack an eye, just to make sure. It's highly unlikely George or Lulu would come to this administrative building on the corner of their campus, but still. It's good to be prepared. I close my eyes again, smiling this time at how loud they'd both be if they found me sitting here in the registrar's office of their university. The faux anger that I hadn't told them I was going to be here. Their nosiness now that I am here, the demands for lunch, for a coffee, for my time, that would inevitably follow, and how I would acquiesce to them without much of a fight.

Lulu shuffled into my kitchen an hour after I woke up on Saturday morning. Her hair billowed around her in a messy tangle, she squinted at the sun coming through the side door window like it had personally wronged her. She'd grumbled about my NPR being too loud and declined my offer of coffee, tea, and orange juice in exchange for her arms around me, her face pressed into my pectoral. She smelled like my fabric softener and she grinned like a maniac when I gave her shit for being grumpy in the morning.

"Jesse Logan?" A man with a clipboard stands behind the reception desk.

"That's me."

"Come on back."

He's white, tall, and athletic. He smiles wide when we get to his office, inviting me to sit down and taking the chair next to mine instead of sitting at the desk across from me. He has the same energy as a lot of the therapists in our study. Like, we're supposed to be buds already, that I can trust him. It's more than I expected from an academic adviser.

"What brings you in today?" he asks.

"I was thinking of applying to school," I say. "For nursing. I'm researching my options, I guess."

He nods. "Going back to school is a big deal."

"I'm not really going back." I rub at my thigh, following the line of my scar that I don't have to see. "I've never been. To college," I clarify.

He shrugs. "Well, welcome." As if it's that easy. But it turns out it is. His name is Josh, and he walks me through how a mature student applies and how my experience and skills as a firefighter medic will help me and in the span of thirty minutes I have three pamphlets about prep courses and the university and an email address and the instructions to contact my high school for my transcripts.

I walk out of the building in a daze. That was far easier than I thought it would be. It was so easy, I feel stupid for waiting so long. But that's been the theme these last few weeks. Everything is far easier than I thought: talking to Pop, to Lulu, falling for her. The only thing standing in my way has always been myself.

If I told George any of this, he'd smack me upside the head and say *duh*.

Chapter Nineteen

Lulu

My office partner, Jay, who is never here on Friday, is suddenly and inexplicably here.

"Crumbs," I mutter under my breath, gathering my laptop and headphones and a notepad and two pens, in case one dies. He waves obliviously as I leave. There are a thousand places to get work done on a university campus but there are not a lot of places to have a private interview with a professor from another university about job prospects. Between this interview and my plans later today, I am an anxious mess.

I tap on Dad's door. "Any chance you have a class in fifteen minutes?" I ask.

He pauses, his index fingers poised over the keyboard since he types only with them. "Why?" His mustache twitches.

I look up and down the hall for eavesdroppers and step inside anyway, just to be safe. "I have a video call with Cecelia," I whisper.

His eyes get big behind his glasses. "Oh." Dad doesn't move, just sits behind his desk, looking shocked.

"Jay is in the office today and I need some place I can speak to her privately," I say.

"Right. Yes, yes. Of course." He stands, patting his pants pockets for his glasses.

"They're on your face, Dad."

He touches the thin wire rims with gentle fingers, making another astonished sound. "An interview with Cecelia from Lancaster?" His volume is far too loud. If his neighbors' doors are open they'll definitely hear, not to mention anyone walking down the hall.

I push the door closed and step farther into the office. "Dad," I whisper-hiss. "Yes. Remember the interview that *you* pushed me to do? I'm talking to her today and I need a place to do it. Quietly."

Dad spends another minute gathering up books and a stack of viewfoils since the man still uses the last overhead projector on campus during his lectures. "Well," he says, standing at the door. "Good luck."

"Thanks, Dad." I don't tell him that I won't be needing it.

He lingers like he might say more, but then he leaves and I set up my laptop, play with the lighting, and lay out my notepad, pen, and bottle of water. I have just sat down in Dad's creaky old chair that must be the source of his chronic back pain when the call comes through on the screen. I haven't had time to feel nervous. Until right now. Now, I might puke.

"Hi, Dr. Lucas," I say brightly as Cecelia's face appears on screen. She's an older white woman with short white hair and glasses, and a thick Manchester accent that took a while for me to get used to.

"Dr. Banks," she exclaims, crowding in close to her computer's camera. "It is so wonderful to see you."

We get through pleasantries and the usual commentary and analysis on recent publications before she finally sits back in her chair, seemingly satisfied that I can, in fact, see and hear her just fine. "I don't think it needs to be said, but we'd love to have you back, Dr. Banks."

It doesn't need to be said, but gosh it is nice to hear all the same. She starts to lay out the needs of the department, apologizing for how it's still "just" a contract instructor position, when I cut her off. "I'm so sorry, Cecelia, but I don't think I can take the job."

She leans in close again, tipping her ear toward the speaker like she's misheard me. "I'm sorry?"

I take a deep breath. "I so appreciate that you were willing to set up this meeting, but I just don't think it would be appropriate for me to take this job right now. However, I do have a colleague I would like to recommend. If you're interested I could put the two of you in touch?"

Cecelia pauses for a moment and I hope I haven't screwed this up, made her feel like she's wasted her time on a call that could have been an email.

"She's an excellent historian and I thought she'd be a great fit so I asked if I could include her in our conversation and she already gave her permission." A dubious claim but Dr. Lucas doesn't need to know that. "I wouldn't mention her unless I thought she would be a benefit for Lancaster."

"Alright. Tell me more."

I launch into an explanation of Audrey's work and how it would be the right fit for Lancaster, just as much as mine would. By the end of the call, Dr. Lucas seems interested, very interested. "So I can give Audrey your email?" I ask.

"Please do," she says. Mentally, I fist-bump myself. "Tell me why you don't want this position though first, Lulu."

"Things were difficult when I first got back here. It was hard to find a job in academia in small-town Pennsylvania."

She snorts. "It's hard to find a job in academia everywhere."

"To be completely honest, my dad got me this job. And while

I appreciate it more than I can say because it's allowed me to get back on my feet, I don't want to take any more handouts."

"Lulu, we wouldn't have considered having you back if this was just a handout."

"No, I know." I nod quickly. "I want to do things on my own, though."

Except that's only part of the truth. Everything Audrey said was right. I have more opportunities than her, things have been easier for me. But deciding to stay isn't some sacrifice to the cosmic balance of things. In the depths of my grief when I decided to move back to the States, I held on to the things I could look forward to, like my mom's buckwheat pancakes and the smell of the back roads in the fall and yelling my order across the Little T's bar until my throat was sore the next day.

When I think of moving back to Lancaster, I just think of having to see Brian and Nora again, and only being able to talk to my parents at the weekends since between time zones and evening classes we could never seem to get on the same schedule. Lancaster has a great program, but it doesn't have my father and it doesn't have my tree and it doesn't have Miranda, who turns out is as funny as she is smart and who has excellent taste in cheeseburgers as evidenced by her choice of restaurant for our meal later this week.

Lancaster has witches and Pendle Hill but it doesn't have the unique hysteria of the colonial witch craze and it doesn't have Jesse, the smell of leather cleaner in the cab of his truck, Betty's hair stuck to the butt of my pants, his quiet laugh, which is more of a single forced exhale and a smile. And I know that we're not supposed to think this way about each other. I know that we're friends, just friends. Departmentally mandated friends. But there's a learning curve to having a friend with benefits, especially one who made it clear the first time you met that he wasn't interested in much more than friendship with you, but isn't that what friendship is? Choosing the people you love, even if sometimes the line blurs between love and *in love.*

Dr. Lucas smiles. "I can appreciate that. How about this? We'll consider you both. Have Audrey contact me. The department can make the decision once we've reviewed both of your applications."

A plethora of worst-case scenarios roll through my head. One where they still offer me the job and Audrey will think it was all a lie. One where they don't offer me the position and it hurts more than I think it will. One where they give me an offer that's too good to refuse, one that will take me away from here, from home, from Jesse.

"I guess that could work," I say slowly.

"Excellent. I look forward to meeting Dr. Robbs."

Jesse picks me up a few hours later with two steaming to-go cups and a paper bag. "Tea," he says instead of hello when I climb into the truck, nodding at the cup holder closest to me.

"And a honey cruller," I say, peeking into the bag. We've gotten coffee and tea and doughnuts exactly one time, on the way to a group therapy session. "You remembered my order."

He shrugs. Jesse's way of brushing off my astonishment. "What are friends for?" he says, over his blind spot as he merges into traffic.

My chest sinks, something that feels distinctly like disappointment, but maybe if I don't acknowledge it, it will just go away. Like a wasp.

"You don't have plans after this, right?" he says, staring hard out the windshield. "I thought we could grab dinner after the match."

Jesse wanted to watch his old rugby team play today and asked that I come as his emotional support person. I wiggle in my seat and say a garbled "no plans" due to the honey cruller in my mouth; honestly, I had no frame of reference for how long rugby matches take. They could be over in a flash or be days long, like cricket. He smirks over at me and turns the radio up, NPR, and rolls the window down.

He parks in a dusty gravel parking lot, turning off the truck and tipping his head back onto the headrest. A referee's whistle and the crowd's cheering filters through the open windows. He seems tense.

"Do you want to stay here for a minute?" I ask. Dark blue smudges shadow his eyes. "Did you work last night?"

He nods, stifling a yawn. "Yeah. And no, I'm OK." But he still doesn't move.

The parking lot isn't busy. It's small, surrounded on three sides by trees and landscaped bushes. Cicadas drone nearby. "There's still twenty minutes before the match starts, right? Want to nap? I can be quiet." I crumple my empty bag to extinguish any chance it will make noise while he's resting.

"Can you just talk to me?" he asks. "Tell me about your day?"

"Sure," I say slowly. I want to tell Jesse about the interview, about how it felt to know I'm wanted but not wanting to go and I want him to tell me something simple and sweet to help me decide, if I get the position, whether I should go or not. So, I tell him about my dad and how he suggested I go back to Lancaster; I watch his face as I say the words, as I describe the call with Cecelia and how I put Audrey's name forward instead of my own. I wax poetic about what Lancaster is like, but explain how my ex-boyfriend—Brian—and ex-best friend—Nora— are still there. Together. Happy. In true Jesse fashion, his face doesn't change. He could be fast asleep if it wasn't for the way he opens and closes his fist. I reach for him, putting my hand in his, and he squeezes. The longer he is quiet, the more I second-guess myself. Maybe I should have been selfish and just taken the job. Maybe I should have told him my second, secret reason for wanting to stay: him.

"Do you think I did the right thing?" I ask.

He's quiet, so quiet. I look at the clock on the dashboard; we could miss the match completely waiting for his answer. Finally, he says, "What do you want, Lulu?" He sounds tired.

I want to stop having to decide what I want, just for once. I want to feel wanted, right here with the people I love. I reach for his ear, where some past hit has made the skin puffy and pale. I think about Lancaster, but I can't see myself there. I see myself here, in this town, in this truck, with this person.

Chapter Twenty

Jesse

Usually, Lulu is the fidgeter. She'll shake her knee, pick her nails. Tuck her hair behind her ear again and again. I'll grab her free hand until whatever compulsion to move she's experiencing passes. Today, I'm the one who's a bundle of nerves.

There were never a lot of people in the stands when I played, and it's no different now. We stick out like sore thumbs, at the top of the bleachers. A couple players from earlier matches and their families lounge closer to the field.

The metal shakes beneath us as I bounce my leg. There's no reason for it—there's no cloud cover, it's not cold, I'm not overworked or overtired—but my leg aches. I thought I'd be immune from this far away, that the smell of the mud and sweat wouldn't reach us here. That the sounds of bodies hitting bodies, the resounding smack that comes from a well-placed hit, the quiet *oof* that accompanies a shoulder to a gut, would get filtered out. Maybe my brain just can't help but associate this place with those smells, those sounds. Maybe these are phantom senses.

Lulu squeezes my thigh, not in a sexual way, comforting, anchoring.

"Tell me about this game," she says, and I recognize it for what it is: a distraction, something I can focus on that isn't this game that I've loved that I can't play anymore. "I don't know anything about it."

My team, my old team, takes the pitch. "It's like American football in that the point of the game is to get the ball behind your opponent's try line, but players throw the ball backward instead of forward. And the team with the most points at the end wins."

She squints against the sun. She left her sunglasses in the truck. "And no one wears pads or helmets. Nothing."

"Nothing."

"Did you ever break anything when you played?"

"Nope. Not playing rugby, at least." A whistle blows; one of my old teammates touched the sideline, stopping play. "I fell off the roof once helping Pop clean the gutters, broke my ankle."

She makes a speculative sound as play resumes. I don't want to talk about my broken bones when I was a kid. Coming here was nerve-wracking enough, but I feel like I've been sideswiped by that SUV all over again. If anything, the depth of my shock, that she is even considering leaving Wilvale, is just a sign of how far gone I am for her.

Friends should be supportive. Even if I don't want her to leave. Even if her leaving would put me right back where I was before: alone.

"Jess."

I might be imagining the hopeful expression on her face, inserting my own hopes into its meaning. But we're interrupted by another voice calling my name. A young Black woman takes the bleacher steps by twos, her braids pulled back in a low ponytail, her Crocs squeaking on the metal.

"April. Hey." April has a wide smile that matches her cousin Marcus's.

"Where have you been, Logan?" She wraps me up in a hug. I keep waiting for the moment that seeing someone from my past life won't feel a little bit weird. Today, it's still weird. But it's bearable. We get through the niceties, the how are you's and how are things, and when she asks me what's new I introduce her to Lulu.

"I'm Marcus's cousin," April explains. "He mentioned he met you the other night."

"How come you didn't come to the party?" I ask.

She shrugs. "Had to work."

"April is also a firefighter," I tell Lulu.

"Cousin firefighters?"

"And both our dads are, too." April beams with pride.

She sits with us to watch the rest of the match and she and Lulu chatter over me like I'm not even here. Which I don't mind.

I thought coming here would be good for me, that seeing my old team and friends would be hard but worth it. And it is hard. And it is worth it. I just miss Pop. He loved to watch me play, to unscrew a cold water bottle and pour it on my head after a match. He would roar when I scored a try. When I was a kid it felt like he could crack the earth with how loud he'd get, how he'd stomp the ground and tell everyone "that's my boy."

I wore that title prouder than my jersey.

Lulu laughs her cackle of a laugh and it pulls me out of my slow spiral into memory. April is waving as she takes the bleacher steps down the field. The match is over. My old team lost.

"Want to go say hi?" she asks.

I clear my throat. The team is covered in mud and sweat and smiles despite their loss. And I ache to be down there with them, a dirty, happy loser. "Sure," I say.

Lulu scoots past me, leading the way down the bleachers. She waves to Marcus, who cups his hands around his mouth and yells, "Logan, get drinks with us tonight."

Lulu turns to look at me over her shoulder. She smiles in a way that makes me think she wants me to go, us to go. I search for Marcus over her head to give him the universal signal for "quit it," so unlike the last time, I don't see it happen. Instead, I only hear the squeak of her shoes on the metal, feel the gentle breeze as the fan of her hair blows past my hand. I hear her quiet whimper right before she falls, and then the thud.

"Lulu." Marcus yells for her.

Her body bounces, like a toy, down the stairs to the bottom. My heart is in my throat. I almost choke as I run down after her, my hands outstretched like I can somehow pull her back up, pull time back.

She lands in a heap at the bottom of the steps.

"Lu, are you OK?" I drop to my knees at her side.

"I'm sorry," is the first thing she says.

I want to gather her to me, but until we can assess her level of injury I don't move her. "Why are you always apologizing for hurting yourself?" I check her pulse at the wrist.

"Should we get the spinal board?" Marcus asks me.

"I'm fine," Lulu says.

"Maybe?" I press gentle fingers over her head, testing her skull.

She bats my hands away and tries to sit up. "I'm fine. I'm OK."

Lulu is flushed, but as her eyes dart around and she avoids eye contact, I think it's out of embarrassment more than confusion, hopefully ruling out a head injury. "Do you know what day it is?"

This time she's successful in sitting up. "I'm *fine*," she insists, frustration lacing her voice.

Whatever crowd that gathered because of her fall is starting to dissipate. Someone with a cooler full of drinks hovers, ready to offer ice. She's right, she probably is just fine. Lulu knows her body better than anyone else. "I know the team's PT. She has medical supplies. Can I have her take a look at you, to make sure?"

Lulu scoots up onto the closest bleacher bench. "OK." She sighs and Marcus runs off for the team physio. While we're just a bunch of amateurs, it's a competitive league and rugby is a rough enough sport that we always need someone on hand to tape muscles, set bones, and assess for concussions.

The physio shows up a few moments later, behind Marcus. "Hi, I'm Mai," she says. "Is it OK if I do a quick assessment?"

Lulu grumbles her yes.

Mai does the usual tests, having Lulu follow her finger, shining a light in her eyes. She checks her radial pulse, feels up and down her arms and legs for any injuries. "I feel so stupid," Lulu whispers.

"Don't. There are people out there who play football." She leans in closer to Lulu. "And rugby."

"Hey," Marcus says, affronted.

Miraculously, other than a few scrapes and contusions that will undoubtedly turn a nasty shade of purple in the next few days, Lulu is unhurt.

"I'd take some ibuprofen when you get home," Mai says, packing up her stuff after applying anti-bacterial and bandages to Lulu's shins and knees. Lulu stands and I follow her. Mai smiles at us. "I think you gave your boyfriend quite a scare."

Lulu opens her mouth, probably to deny that I am her boyfriend.

"Nah. She's stronger than she looks," I say. I tell myself it's because I don't want to have to endure the awkwardness of that conversation. Mostly I just like the sound of the title.

Lulu blushes.

"So?" Marcus looks at us expectantly. "Let's do something tonight."

I glare at him.

"OK. OK. Never mind."

As we leave, Lulu flexes her fist, staring at the scratches on the heel of her palm, tracing the creases.

"Where are we going?" Lulu asks once we're settled in the truck.

I check the time on the dashboard. There's still way too many hours between now and her surprise. "I was going to suggest the bookstore but…do you want to just go back to my place for a bit?" I ask.

"No way. Absolutely I want to go to the bookstore," she says.

Lulu suggests a stack of nonfiction, historical books written by some of her faves and some of her friends. We end up leaving the store with a handful of books each and still a few hours to spare before we have anywhere to be. I bring her home with me. She sits on the couch, reading while I get a workout in. She brings me a water and prepares a snack. When I get out of the shower she's listening to Rihanna and cuddling with Betty. She's found a rugby match and has it on mute while she peels off the Band-Aids Mai gave her earlier. "I don't need them," she says at my frown. "They're not that bad." She rolls the bandages up into a ball and stuffs them in her pocket.

The couch groans as I sit beside her. Her legs have a constellation of bruises; some are fresh from her fall, just starting to turn purple, but some are older and yellow. "Lulu, what did you do?" I brush the back of my hand over her skin.

"What?"

"How'd you get all these?"

She pulls at a string dangling from her denim cutoffs, snorting as she laughs. "I have no idea. I don't know if you've noticed but I'm a little clumsy." She says it with a tone, like she's embarrassed.

"Maybe it's a platelet problem?" I fish my phone out of my back pocket.

She snorts. "It's an accident-prone problem."

I ignore her for Google.

"Are you googling it?"

I grunt. It's not that I'm *scared*. I don't think she has a rare form of blood cancer or something. I just want to make sure she's OK.

"Don't doctors always say *not* to google it?"

"I get a pass," I say, gruff.

She tangles her feet with mine. "How do you figure?"

"Emergency medical training."

She laughs until I start reading out the symptoms of idiopathic thrombocytopenic purpura. "I don't have that," she says, stony-faced. "I have whatever the medical term for clumsiness is."

So, I google that. "It's called poor proprioception."

Lulu drops her head onto the arm of the couch behind her. "And I'm the nerd in this relationship," she mutters.

"You're not a nerd," I say, still scrolling a page about what causes poor proprioception. "Huh…"

"Is that a good huh or a bad huh?"

I pull her foot into my lap. She cracks her toe knuckles. "Have you ever thought…" I say as I press my thumb up the arch of her foot. "That you might be neurodivergent?"

"I…" She cocks her head to the side, squinting. "Well. No."

My phone screen glares up at me from my lap. The list of other symptoms, including poor proprioception, like a condemnation; I should have seen it before. Or maybe not. According to the article, ADHD in women presents different than in men.

George was diagnosed with ADHD when we were teenagers. His parents noticed that he never grew out of the hyperactive kid stage, he could barely sit through a movie, let alone math class. He'd been angry at first; it was just another thing that made him feel different when that's the last thing a teen wants to be. Now he sees it as a superpower.

Her fidgeting, restlessness, and busyness; how much she talks, and with her hands; how she doesn't notice that she gets louder the more excited or comfortable she is; she's easily distracted; her deep thinking that looks like daydreaming. There are other signs, ones that I don't want to bring up, like the anxiety and the low self-esteem, the perfectionism. "How would you feel?" I ask. "If you were?"

"I don't know. I don't know much about it, honestly."

She's quiet for a moment, the frown crease that means she's thinking appearing on her forehead. "I wonder how many people throughout history were persecuted or institutionalized for being neurodivergent?"

Of course Lulu would think about it in the context of history.

"You could ask George," I suggest. "He's been medicated for ADHD since we were fifteen."

She won't quite meet my eyes. Instead, she sticks her big toe into my belly. "How did it feel today?" she asks. "Watching your old team?"

I accept her blatant change of topic to allow her some time to digest it all. "Honestly, it just made me miss Pop."

She hums, a tender sound. "Do you think you'd want to play again?"

I lift my leg up onto the couch so that we're mirror images of each other, one leg in the other's lap. "Doctors said I shouldn't."

She shrugs. "When was the last time you went to see your doctor? Maybe things would be different if they knew how much strength training you've been doing."

I flex my leg, like I'll be able to assess my strength and stability from this couch, both of us avoiding important conversations.

"Do you want to?" she asks.

"Yeah," I whisper. "Yeah, I do."

She squeezes my foot. "Then you should," she says simply. "If you can, if they say it's alright, you should. You deserve to do the things you love again."

She notices my chipped toenail polish and we take turns painting each other's toes. I choose a bright blue with a subtle shine. She laments the lack of sparkles in my nail polish collection, then chooses a color called Black Hole.

"My mom took me and my best friend Cally for my first pedicure for my thirteenth birthday," Lulu says. "I treat myself every year."

"Mhmm," is all I can say because in her next breath she purses her lips, leans forward, and blows gently across my toes. My whole body tenses to avoid moving, the muscles in my leg so rigid I could probably break my own femur, again. I clamp my jaw, hard enough I might need dental work, as the memory of the last time she did that to me plays like the greatest film ever made in my mind. Forget porn, give me Lulu's lips, her warm breath across my skin, and a bottle of lube. She has to be fucking with me. I dip the brush back into the polish bottle and apply another coat to her pinkie toe. Then I blow gently across her toes. Goose bumps lift along her shin and she shifts on the couch. *Ha.* She's smiling, her tongue peeking between her teeth.

"I've never had a pedicure before," I say.

"I'll take you," she says. "On my birthday." Then after a pause, "Can I tell you a secret?"

I nod.

"My birthday is next week."

I know.

After she admitted that she'd never had a surprise party, I asked George if he knew her birthday. It took him all of five seconds to find the information on her social media, which got me shit for not knowing how Facebook works.

"Happy birthday next week."

We put our feet up on the coffee table to let the polish dry and Lulu asks me more questions about the rugby match. The later it gets, the more texts I get from other study participants, friends including Marcus, confirming our plans. She tries to read my screen over my shoulder, but I stick my palm in her face. It's intimate, domestic. The special kind of being alone together that I've only experienced with George, as boyfriends and friends, or with my grandparents. Being with her is peaceful, even though she talks most of the time, about the books we bought, where we should go for pedicures, what we should do for dinner. But it's not the uncomfortable chatter people use to fill uncomfortable silences. It feels different, like the chatter someone allows themselves when they feel safe enough to say whatever is on their mind. Finally, when the sun is starting to set, I tell her to get in the truck. Lulu, being Lulu, doesn't ask questions. She pats Betty on the head and grabs her bag and is out the door before I can lock up. Fifteen minutes later, Lulu says, "You're taking me to Little T's?"

I expected her to sound skeptical. But she's excited, laughing. And it strikes me that if she ends up leaving for Lancaster, I won't get to see this smile, except maybe sometimes over a video chat. I won't get to hear her laughter. I won't get to have another day like today.

She fits into my life like she fits under my arm, snugly, warm. Like we were made for each other.

And I might lose that. Lose her. To England and an ex-boyfriend and an ex-best friend who sounds like a piece of shit, to be frank.

"Let's go inside," I say out loud. Instead of, don't go, come back home with me, come to bed with me. Put your hands on me and in me and let me show you what I cannot say.

That I want you here.

You are wanted here.

"It's not open yet," she says, pointing to the windows that are still dark.

I shrug, my car door opening with a loud screech. My phone buzzes in my pocket, another confirmation text from Trey. Lulu looks surprised when she's able to pull the front door open, like she was expecting it to be locked. She peers into the darkness inside, then back at me. "I'm not going in there," she says. "I watch *Dateline*, too. Are you trying to have me murdered, Jesse Logan?" she asks but with a smirk.

"I don't have the stomach for murder," I say and finally she walks in. The door shuts behind us, the only light from the fading sunset outside.

"It doesn't smell as much like puke when it's not filled with a bunch of drunk teenagers," Lulu says, so that when the lights flash on a moment later, study participants and friends jumping out from behind tables, the bar, the DJ booth, yelling surprise, I am laughing.

She turns to me. "Happy birthday?"

"This is for you," I say, pulling her into a hug.

"For me?" she says, muffled against my neck.

"Early birthday party. You said you'd never had a surprise party before."

She looks back at the group with new eyes. "You planned all this?"

"Brooke and Trey, too," I say, before she's whisked off by Brooke to the bar. The staff open the doors for the rest of the paying public soon after and slowly people stream in, filling up the tables and dance floor. The bass pumps in my chest, beating my heart to a new rhythm. Strobe lights flash and a fog machine pumps lethargic white smoke onto the dance floor. With each step, I have to peel my shoe off the floor. The DJ performs as if this is a Vegas nightclub, bobbing his head and throwing his arms up to our small crowd. I'm sure if I were a newly minted twenty-one-year-old, I'd think Little T's was an exciting stop on the Wilvale night scene. But since I was about twenty-five, I've thought this place was too loud, too dark.

Or maybe I'm just getting old.

Lulu finds her way back to me, looking around at it all; her blond hair flashes green then purple as lasers strobe around the room. She turns to me, shouting. The music and the growing crowd drown her out but I watch her lips move. "Thank you."

I scratch the back of my neck, nod.

"Shots?" Trey yells, popping up between us like the friendliest whack-a-mole. He holds four shot glasses of amber liquid in his hands.

I shake my head. "I'm driving."

He nods, handing one off to Lulu and to Brooke, beside him. They clink their glasses. "To Lulu," Trey announces.

They throw back their shots and George appears, kisses Lulu's cheeks, shakes Trey's and Brooke's hands. He takes the leftover shot glass from Trey, tipping it back and wincing. A cheer goes up from the crowd as a song that I've never heard before beats deep in my bones.

"Let's dance," Brooke shouts in Lulu's direction. Lulu nods and sets her shot glass on the bar behind me. Her arm brushes mine, her fingers trail over my elbow. She smiles, small. Pauses like she might say something, maybe ask me to dance. I don't want to dance at all but I want her to ask me more than I want to take my next breath. I want the excuse of the dance floor to feel her against me. I watch her as she bounces all the way to the center of the crowd. My stomach pulls itself apart.

I learned to break wooden boards in the dojo across the street from this bar. In the moments before my test, my stomach was in knots. My fear was so paralyzing I almost couldn't move when it was my turn. Pop asked me on the drive home, my parka wrapped tight around my dobok, sweat freezing in my hair, if I was afraid of getting hurt.

It hadn't even occurred to me that it could hurt. It was just the fear; of trying something new, of failing. I joined this study to change myself but it's hard to be a new me when the old me is always right here.

The music beats in my head, my chest, my internal organs. Trey lifts one arm, one leg, jumping up and down in a dance move I've only ever seen on the internet. "This is my fucking song, Jesse."

He bounces over to Brooke and Lulu. Brooke's high-pitched giggle rises above the deep bass of the music. I repress my smile as he reaches them, spinning Brooke. Lulu and Brooke bounce too, off beat and uncaring. At the bar, a kid who most likely has a moderately passable fake ID jostles me for space. My instinct is to plant my feet, not let him push me out, and stay as far away from the dance floor as possible. But Lulu faces me, bouncing on her toes, swaying her hips. Her smile is a cliff's edge, telling me to jump.

I catch George's eye where he stands watching me. Smile and nod.

I let myself be pushed.

I'm swallowed up into the sea of people. Lulu's fingers around my wrist, the smell of her shampoo and sweat, are my life raft. One song bleeds into another. Lulu's face is pink from exertion, dancing, the silent shouts she lobs at Brooke. She's green, blue, red, purple, a multicolor of music. Our fingers intertwine on the dance floor.

Trey moves behind Brooke, his arms linked loosely around her hips. They both glow, sweaty, their teeth flashing in the strobe light. The room moves as one mass to one beat but with limitless arms, twisting, spinning, curving around each other. My shoes stick more than ever on fresh spills. Lulu's hair sticks to my arm.

I'm dancing. Just shoulders and hips, a bend in the knees, but I don't want to stop. We move to the next song, and the next until we're a collection of tired muscles, stomachs sore from laughter, cheeks aching from smiling, throats hoarse from muted words swallowed up by music. Until I can't remember what color everyone's clothes are. They are only whatever color the lights are at this moment. I'm breathless and yet when Lulu tips her head back to laugh, she takes my breath away. Her ponytail is lopsided, her shoulders square as her mouth forms my name. I can't believe there was a time, any time, not just the minutes or hours ago, that I was afraid of this. Of touching her, being near her, dancing. I was so afraid of fucking it up, failing, it never occurred to me that I might have fun again.

The whole time, Lulu never lets go of my hand.

After more songs than I could ever know, Brooke motions to Lulu, her pinkie finger lifted, thumb tipped to her mouth. Lulu nods vigorously. They drag us off the dance floor and find a sliver of space open at the bar.

"Do you like to dance?" she asks, turning to me with a bottle of water.

I nod before I let myself think about it. I haven't danced since George and I were together, when he would drag me onto the dance floor of a Philly gay bar, our friends plying me with shots until I was loose enough to move.

"You're good at it," she says.

I close my eyes, hopeful I'll find the right words in the dark.

"I need to use the restroom."

Those were the wrong words.

Before she can respond, I shove the water bottle at her and walk blindly until I see a door with the outline of a person on it. I squint against the bathroom light. I don't actually have to pee. I just need a moment to think without music and synthetic smoke and Lulu pressed against me. The water from the tap doesn't have a temperature above freezing but it's good on my overheated skin, and besides, I'm used to cold showers. I wash my hands and splash water on my face. The dirty mirror reflects a distorted version of myself back.

"Hey, man." A guy walks in, sporting a patchy red beard and a rumpled band T-shirt. His feet zigzag on the way to the urinal. "I saw you out there with that blond girl," he says, all of his words pushed together. He rests his forehead on his arm against the wall. "Is she your girlfriend?"

Back when I was still a firefighter, sometimes we'd get calls to medical emergencies involving drunks. Usually, it meant ensuring they were hydrated and not a danger to themselves or others. Drunks were always the worst to deal with. Not all of them are belligerent but even when they're friendly, they're so completely self-absorbed that conversation is pointless.

"No," I say to the mirror. My cheeks are flushed, my eyes too big. The only thing that's familiar is my too-short hair.

"Good. Good." He nods like this was all part of some plan. "I think she taught me some history course last semester. Something about...feminism or witches or some shit." He zips up and staggers to the bathroom counter. He uses water, but no soap. "She's not your girlfriend, right?" he asks again.

I think the reflection I see in the mirror is what Lulu would call Grump Face. "No."

"Lucky me."

I frown at him in the mirror. My skin itches to get back to her. To answer her next smile with my lips on her skin. What is there to be scared of? Only this. The possibility that she could leave here. Anyone else thinking they have a right to Lulu's time when they can't even be bothered to know: it was feminism *and* witches.

"I'll see you out there." He lifts his dripping wet hand like he's about to pat my shoulder.

"Please don't touch me."

He goes bug-eyed and he wipes his hand on his pants. I follow him out, my feet take me back to Lulu as if they have a GPS. She's back on the dance floor, bopping with Brooke and Trey.

"Will you leave with me tonight?" I ask. "Together."

She blinks. "OK," she says, frowning, confused.

I lean in closer. "Will you leave with me," I say in her ear so that only she will hear me clearly. "As more than friends?"

I pull back. Her lower lip is caught between her teeth, her forehead creases. I glance over her shoulder to make sure Trey and Brooke haven't caught us doing anything that could be labeled as something "just friends" don't do.

Now that it's done, now that she knows exactly what I want and how I feel, there's nothing left but to breathe, to catch my breath in the space between us. Her hand trails down my arm. Tapping Brooke on the shoulder, she whispers in her ear, waves to Trey. I mouth goodbye to them. We throw smiles at people we know. She hugs George one-armed and as he squints at me over her shoulder, his expression is unreadable, blank. "Tired," I say. "Text you tomorrow."

He nods.

Lulu pulls me toward the door and we don't speak to each other until we get outside. "Your place?" she asks.

"Y-yes."

The wind carries me to the Bronco. The humming of the tires on the asphalt is our radio. I pull out of the parking lot and suddenly I'm turning into my driveway, autopilot having taken over. Even out here, away from the lights of Main Street, the sky isn't fully black. It's a deep blue blanket pulled over us, a few silver stars breaking through the canopy.

She leans across the bench seat, presses her lips against the corner of my mouth. I feel her everywhere. In the tips of my fingers, warming my chest, at the base of my spine. In my cock.

"On our date," she says. That feels like a million years ago. I'm a different person now. She feels different to me, too. "I wondered how many people you'd fucked in this truck," she whispers. She looks excited by my answering blush.

"I want you," I say.

"What does that mean?"

"It means I don't want to be just friends anymore."

"What about...?"

"I don't care about the study. I care about you, Lulu. And if you don't want...this." I gesture between us. "I get it. That's OK. But I need you to know that I'm falling for you."

Lulu is still for a moment, her gaze bouncing back and forth between my eyes and my mouth.

"Say something," I whisper, because I can't catch my breath.

She lunges, swinging her leg over my lap, taking my face in her hands. She kisses me, and we haven't kissed in so long. Not since our first kiss. She laughs into my mouth, and I swallow the sound, get full on it. "What are you doing, baby?" I ask as her hands roam under my shirt.

"Trying to get you to fuck me in your truck."

I pull back. "The first time we fuck like that, it's going to be in my bed." I wipe at my mouth as I flip through all the things I want to do to her and ask her to do to me, now that we can touch without pretense or rules.

She nips at my lower lip. "Let's go, then."

"Yeah?"

She pops open the door in response, hops down onto the gravel path to my front steps. I take a second to readjust myself. I haven't had much sex since my accident, a few dates and hookups with men and women who wanted me to talk too much or share more. Not with someone who knows me the way Lulu does, who will be here in the morning.

"For the record," I say as I put my key into my front door lock. "I want to take your clothes off and my clothes off and I want to wear a condom. I want to fuck you," I say. "With my dick. I don't want to just watch. I don't want those old rules. Not this time."

She holds me by the back of my shirt as she follows me inside. I keep the lights off. Betty makes a quiet *prrwow* from somewhere in the living room.

"Yes," she says. "That's what I want, too."

"OK." Then we stare at each other in my entryway. Apparently, I'm all talk because now I don't know what to do with her. But Lulu does, she always knows.

She pushes me against the wall, lifting up on her toes to kiss me again, her tongue a soft brush against mine. My hands ache to be filled with her and I realize, slowly, that they can be. I start in her hair, feeling the long strands between my fingertips. Her back is strong, her shoulders broad. Her blouse soft, the skin underneath softer. She huffs into my mouth, her kiss turning into a smile, all teeth as my fingers run down her rib cage. Finally, my hands land on her ass. Her cutoff jeans, the same ones she wore the first day of the study, make it easy to grip her. To pull her up into me, cup her ass. My hands on her border on frantic. I'm still not sure this is real, that she is real, and I want to hold on to her so that she doesn't float away. Her lips taste smoky and sweet like the whiskey she shot earlier. I want to know what she tastes like everywhere else.

I pull away from her lips. "Bedroom?"

She nods, pulling me with her, kicking off her Keds, letting go of my hand to unbutton her shirt. I turn the light on in the bedroom so that she's cast in the warmest, golden glow. I almost can't hear from the blood rushing through my ears. My skin is numb and sensitive at the same time. The tips of my fingers tingle. My dick throbs, painfully so.

I've never felt better. I'm thinking too slowly but everything happens so fast. My shirt is off, my skin pebbling in the cold. She's pulling my shirt over my head, popping the button on my jeans, sliding between clothing and skin.

I press my mouth to her collarbone, her chest, as her fingers tense around my length, follow the lace of her bra over the swell of her breast. I want to remember this, the freckle she has on her right breast, the sound she made when I brushed my thumb over her panties, her hair spread around her like a haze. "Can I..."

"Can you what?" she asks, her tongue between her teeth. Her lashes seem to grow longer with each purposeful blink.

"Are you...are you trying to make me say it?"

"If you want to do the crime you have to do the time, Jesse Logan."

"I don't think that's how that saying goes."

She laughs and I want to remember *this*. The way she tips her chin up, her smile spilling over her face, her back arching, the sound of her happiness as it sends goose bumps along my skin. If I remember nothing else from this night, I want to remember Lulu's laugh. The way it fills me up so that if we stopped right here, I'd be happier than I've ever been. I kneel at the edge of the bed, pressing her thighs apart. "Lulu?"

"Yes?" Her voice giggly and golden.

"Can I eat you out?"

She stops laughing, a small tragedy except for the slow curve of her mouth, the way her eyes get big.

"Yeah."

"Yeah?"

She bites her lip, lifting her hips so I can pull her panties down. Her skin is slick, hot, pink and her hair golden brown. I blow across her skin.

"Jesse," she growls. Her cheeks are flushed, her eyes wide as she props herself up on her elbows.

"What do you like?"

"Just touch me."

I press my palm to the inside of her thigh.

She flops back on the bed, throwing her arm over her eyes.

"I don't think you want it bad enough yet," I say, close to her so she can feel the rumble of my voice. She responds by petting herself with her middle finger and holy fuck, I think I love her. I love that she is sweet and nerdy, the sound of her voice, the way her hair clings to me. I love that she is braver and stronger than she knows. I love that she is smarter than me. She makes me feel like myself again.

I reward her boldness and kiss around her finger, slide my tongue against it and she moans, lifts her hips off the mattress. She grabs at my head as my tongue moves over her. Her heels dig into my shoulder blades, pulling me closer until my nose is squished against her. It's fine. I don't need to breathe. I just need to taste more of her salt and sweat, hear her as she says my name, makes those soft sounds, her gasps.

"Don't stop," she says.

This doesn't feel like the first time. I know these sounds, her taste. I know that as her hips lift, her legs saw, she's getting closer. It's just a continuation of every time, of the first time when she kissed me against her door and every time after. She pulls me closer, her fingers gentle on my ears but her heels hard against my back. I wish I had hair so she could pull it. She's so wet, squeezing me so tight. Then everything releases. She pulses against my tongue. Her breath catches again and again. Her fingers slowly let go. Everything is suddenly quiet, except for my pulse. I hear it everywhere.

"Come here," she mumbles, weakly pulling at my arms. I take off the rest of my clothes, find a condom in the drawer beside the bed. She watches me roll it on with heavy-lidded eyes, her fingers playing at her nipple and between her legs.

"I think this is the first time I've seen you completely naked," she says.

"What do you think?" I ask. It sounds more vulnerable than I intend. Lulu sits up slowly, her legs hanging off the bed. She bypasses my cock, jutting out almost comically. She massages her thumbs along my hips, following the undefined lines on either side downward. She runs her palms around my body and cups my ass. I adjust my stance, spreading my feet wider.

"Is this OK?" she asks, dragging her hand up my inner thigh.

It feels like stars are bursting under my skin.

"It's OK," I say, since I can't make myself say that.

She kisses me. Her lips leave a sticky imprint from where I haven't kissed off all of her lip gloss yet.

"I think you're beautiful, Jesse. I've always thought that." She holds up her hands, framing me between her thumbs and forefingers, closing one eye like she's squinting through a camera's viewfinder.

"What are you doing?"

"Remembering this forever," she says, like it's obvious.

I love her for this, too. Not just because I am the object of her affection but because somewhere along the way I forgot to enjoy the small things. I forgot to capture perfect moments or have a favorite tree and I wonder how much better my life would be if I had never forgotten.

I'm grateful for the chance to learn, again.

She lies back and I lie beside her. I run my palm over her heated skin, her breasts that I can freely touch, the soft curve of her stomach. I kiss her shoulder, the scrape on her wrist from her fall earlier today, her hairline. Her hands move over me, scratching down my chest, her nails dragging along the seam of my ass. My cock pulses with my heartbeat. I can feel my arousal in the back of my teeth, my balls, my lower back. There's just so much I want to do with her, I don't know where to start. Finally, she makes the decision for me.

Lulu rolls onto her side away from me, bringing my arm with her so that I'm wrapped around her, her back to my front. From this angle, it's easy to bend her knee, to slide my cock between her lips, slick and wet. To pump into her with short strokes. To be engulfed in her heat, the warm fist of her pussy. I lever up on my other arm to watch the blush roll across her skin as we move and I slide my leg between hers to open her up so I can pet and stroke her clit with the same leisurely rhythm.

I want this to last forever but it will probably end sooner than I hope. We fit together too well. Like a matched set.

"Touch me here," she whispers. She moves my hand up her body. We cup her breast together. She squeezes, shows me how hard she wants it—harder than I expected. She reaches behind her to guide my mouth down to the long column of her exposed neck. Her pulse beats against my tongue.

"Can I leave marks?" I ask, my lips ghosting over her skin.

"Yeah."

I suck, hard enough she cries out. "OK?" I rub my thumb over the spot that's already turning deep red.

She nods. "Again."

I suck again; she cries out. I press into her, her ass in my lap, her pussy soaking my thighs. Her hand moves between her legs and I suck her harder, watching. Her orgasm surprises us both. Her spine is rigid, her head thrown back and all I can do is watch, take a mental picture, remember *this* forever, Lulu coming around my cock, her tit in my hand, my marks on her skin. She lifts her hand, her fingers glistening, and they taste like her come and a little bit like the lube on the condom but I don't care enough to do anything but come, too, forever until we're both sweaty and sticky and clinging to the mattress.

Chapter Twenty-One

Jesse

There's a knock on the door that I mistake for thunder again. I'm half in and out of consciousness and the sound bleeds into the dream that usually ends with my truck crumpled on the side of the road, my blood, pain. I wake up sweating, the sheets tangled in my legs. Lulu lies on her stomach, the wide expanse of her back bare and beautiful, her head turned away. I'm tempted to wake her and tell her the dream in the hopes that we could make enough memories for a different kind. But the knocking comes again, echoing through the house. Betty meows at the bedroom door, like she's pissed I haven't answered yet.

I sit up, swing my legs over the side of the bed. My lower back is sore. My thigh aches, the bone-deep kind that needs an Epsom salt bath and massage and rest. Last night was worth every moment of pain this morning.

Lulu had helped me change the sheets. Then we'd showered together, touching more but not coming. Her stomach growled so we got dressed in my clothes and I made her eggs while she sat on the couch watching a recap of the rugby match that had happened earlier in the day, explaining the game back to me and asking me to rehash the 50:22 law. We slept. Woke up in the dark. She climbed on top of me, and most of what I remember of that is the way the hair on her thighs felt softer than silk, how I could only see her silhouette in the dark, how warm she was, the sounds she made.

I heave myself out of bed, pull on underwear and a T-shirt. Betty follows me as I limp down the hall, talking at me the whole way. Right as I reach the door, the person on the other side rings the doorbell and I cringe that it will wake Lulu.

"OK, I'm coming," I grumble as I open the door. And I should have known, by the way that his never-ending knock sounds like inclement weather, by his silhouette in the window. But I was so caught up in the memories of last night that now George is standing on my doorstep and Lulu is in my bed.

"Hey."

George tries to peer over my shoulder. He's already stepped in close like he's expecting me to open the door and let him in.

"Hi," he says slowly. "Are you going to let me in?" He puts his hand on the door.

I've never been a great liar but right now my brain is a dustbowl, there are no excuses in there. "Uhhhhh…"

He arches an eyebrow. "Listen, I really need to talk to you."

The heat feels heavy and thick already; being my grandfather's grandson, I feel a strong urge to hurry George in and shut the door to save the air conditioner.

My heart beats in my throat. I'll close the door, tell Lulu, come back, let him in. I won't let him come past the entryway.

George is frowning at me. "You look like this decision is really paining you, Jess."

What am I doing? Lying to my best friend.

"George," I say. But I'm not sure what comes next.

"Who is it?" Lulu asks behind me, her voice unmistakable. I expect a myriad of emotions to cross George's face: surprise, intrigue, confusion, then maybe—*maybe*—recognition. But he just seems disappointed.

"I need to talk to both of you," he says.

Shit.

George pushes at the door but I keep my shoulder against it. I may not be as strong as I used to be but I'm still strong enough to keep George out.

He rolls his eyes. "Lulu," he calls and she gasps behind me. "Tell him to open the door."

"It's not what you think," I say. Except when I turn around, there she is standing behind me with Betty in her arms, wearing one of my old WFD shirts. In my distraction, George gets his foot in the door.

"Right," he says, eyeing the long expanse of leg on Lulu. "I'm not going to lie, this is pretty much exactly what I was thinking."

"What?" Lulu and I look from him to each other.

"How'd you know?" she asks.

He huffs and walks around the living room, picking up a throw pillow, putting it down like he's inspecting the space for evidence. "It was pretty obvious."

I feel sick. Lulu looks the same. She sets Betty on the recliner to wrap her arms around her middle. I should go to her, but with George here I feel like I can't. "We didn't think..."

He waves his hand like it's not that big a deal. "Oh, don't worry. I think everyone else just assumes you're close. Good friends. But..." He shrugs, sighs. "I know what he looks like when he's in love," he tells Lulu.

Double shit.

The little wrinkle in Lulu's forehead gets deeper.

"In love?"

It might be the dream still clinging to the edges of my mind, this moment that is as embarrassing as it is sudden, but I feel like crying. In the last few years, I've cried more than I ever have before. Usually alone, usually about Pop, or my leg, or my pain, or my job.

Maybe Lulu can see it on my face. She says, "I think when we have this conversation we should all be wearing pants." And she leaves. Presumably to get pants.

"George, what the fuck," I hiss at him the second she's out of eyesight. There's no way she didn't hear me.

"Have you made coffee yet?" he asks, peering into the kitchen.

"You came to my house to throw a bomb into my personal life and didn't even bother to bring coffee." I grunt as he hits me with a half-hearted punch on my way past him.

"I'm not mad," he says as I measure out grounds and set out cups.

Well, that's funny, because I'm mad.

"I'm just disappointed."

"Cute," I say.

Lulu comes back with the clothes she was wearing last night and her hair in a messy bun. Her eyes still have that puffy, sleepy look. Her lips are puffy from something else. I wish we weren't doing this right now and that we were still cuddled together in bed. I'd open the curtains and the window to let in fresh air. Betty would chase our feet under the comforter.

We all watch the coffee as it percolates. Stand in silence as I fill up the mugs.

Finally, George takes a deep breath, but Lulu cuts him off.

"It just sort of…happened," she says. She stares down into the depths of her black coffee. "We were hanging as friends, like we were supposed to, but." She looks to me. "I guess we're kind of horny for each other," she says with a half smile.

I snort into my coffee. "Yeah," I say. "Something like that."

"And now," she says. "It feels like more."

"How long exactly have you two been having sex?" George asks.

Lulu looks up at the ceiling. "Well, do you mean like fully penetrative or…"

He holds his hand up and I laugh again. I might be able to get out of this situation without saying a single word. Let Lulu and George work this out for us.

"We've been hooking up. For lack of a better term. As friends. Just friends."

"Friends. With benefits," he says.

She nods. "We had rules. I won't get into the details," she says when George pulls a face that screams *no thank you*. "We weren't touching each other exactly. It was more like adjacent platonic pleasure."

He frowns at me. "Are you telling me you watched porn together and jerked off?"

"We never watched porn," she says. "That could be fun, though."

"Lulu," I say quietly. Not the time.

"Sorry," she whispers.

But she's right. It could be fun.

George sets down his mug and runs his hands through his hair. He'd kill me if I told him this but he looks just like his dad the time he caught us making out in his car. We'd had to sit through a terribly awkward conversation about sexual safety and George had ended the conversation when his dad brought out a zucchini and a condom for proper prophylactic application practice.

"I hate to be a cock block. Or a clit block," he says in an apologetic voice to Lulu. This actually might be worse than the time his dad caught us. "But it's not up to me. This can't continue. You need to choose. To be honest, I didn't think it had gone this far. I thought maybe Jesse was in his feelings."

"Thanks, George," I mutter.

"What?!" he says, defensive. "You have a lot of feelings."

I huff but don't deny it.

He huffs back. "I came today to talk to you about that, but if things have gone this far, I'm sorry, Jess. You guys can't continue to participate in the study if you're engaging in a physical relationship together." He does sound apologetic, too.

"I don't want to speak for Jesse, but…" Lulu tucks her hair behind her ear. She looks anywhere but at me. She wants me to finish her sentence. To speak. She wants me to affirm the feelings that George labeled me with earlier. And the thing is, George isn't wrong.

I love her.

Lulu finally looks at me and for the first time maybe ever, I wish she wouldn't. I'm too ashamed, terrified she'll see it on my face. That I'm selfish, the worst type of person.

That I'm scared.

Of what she's about to say and the weight of it. Suddenly, the weight of everything, her stare, her feelings for me, my feelings for her, and what it all means; it's too heavy. I could buckle beneath it, the same way my bone buckled when confronted with an unstoppable force and an immovable object. Because that's what Lulu is, she's unstoppable and I don't know how moveable I am. Not anymore.

I watch her swallow, see the flush creep up her neck. "Jesse, I think we should leave the study," she says but there's that inflection at the end. She's asking. She's not sure anymore. Because of me.

"What about…" My voice is ragged, unrecognizable. I sound like I don't belong here, in this place I've lived my whole life. "The money?" I blurt out the first thing that comes to mind. Money I haven't thought about once since I first signed up.

And doesn't that make me the biggest piece of shit.

That the first words out of my mouth aren't about declaring my love for this woman. This unbelievable, brave, smart, funny, strange woman. It's fleeting, just a random excuse that acts like a drop of acid in a bucket full of love for Lulu, but now it's out there. Now it's other things, more drops in that bucket; I haven't told her that I was thinking of becoming a nurse and does that silence mean something? Because I can't get my brain and my mouth to work in tandem. I love her but does she really feel the same? Or am I going to be alone again at the end of this, left for someone or somewhere else? This is happening faster than I thought it would.

Fast. Like a car crash.

I can't explain that it's not as simple as just leaving the study and being together. I don't know why last night I thought it was. That was stupid, naive. It was the sway of the lights in the bar and the crush of people and the music so loud I could feel it in my throat. Last night I was dreaming, this morning is reality.

At the end of all of this, if things don't work out not only will I lose her love, I'll lose her friendship. I'll be alone again.

"Jesse?"

"What about Lancaster?" I say. The words scratch my throat.

She blinks, not confused. Shocked, maybe? "I already recommended Audrey for the job."

"But they could still offer it to you, right?"

Her eyes shine. "They could, I guess. But I wouldn't go. I don't even know if they're going to. I don't want them to, Jesse," she says, like she's trying to convince me.

"But if they did, you'd decline a job? For me?" In the span of a few words, my heart rate kicks up. I need to sit down, my leg throbbing with the beat of my pulse. I pull out a chair from under the kitchen table. The wooden legs screech against the linoleum floor. The table is as old as I am, the floor probably is, too. I don't remember a time it wasn't beneath my feet. This place is old and I am the old, broken thing that belongs here.

Lulu is like sunlight, fresh air, flower petals. She's too new for this place, for me. She's too *good* for a guy who has a dead-end job, who's broken, who's nobody.

"You can't do that," I hear myself say. "You can't let an opportunity like that go."

"It's *not* an opportunity," she says, frustrated. "And I can let go of anything I want to, by the way." The words are angry but she seems deflated. Her cheeks go bright red. "Especially," she says quietly. "If you asked me to. If you asked me to, I would do that. It's *my* choice to make."

I say nothing, pressing my thumbnail into the skin beside my scar.

"What about last night?" If I looked up right now, I think I'd see her crying, so I make myself look. Her jaw is tense, her lips pressed together. "Last night you said…"

"I know what I said."

"Jesse," George says, his tone quiet, admonishing.

I can't look at him. I feel sick. Breathing hurts. Somewhere in my brain, a calm, logical voice tells me I might be having an anxiety attack. It urges me to breathe, to communicate, to lean on the two people in this room who know me better than anyone else on the planet.

Not that long ago, I was the guy people leaned on. I was strong. I was capable. Dependable. I was a fucking hero. I had friends who loved me and a grandfather who knew who I was. Now I'm weak. I'm not even Jesse to my grandfather anymore. I'm no one.

I'm ashamed.

"What are you saying now?" Lulu asks. Still, she hasn't cried and I hope she's not holding back the tears for me because I don't deserve that gentleness.

"Jesse?"

Chapter Twenty-Two

Lulu

"What are you saying now?" I ask again. I have certain voices for specific situations. When I'm teaching it's the Enthusiastic Voice, but at staff meetings it's the Competent Voice. If I have to deal with students who have been a behavioral or academic problem in my classes, like if they've plagiarized or been disrespectful, I use the Hard Voice.

I've never used the Hard Voice on Jesse. I hate it but it's the only thing keeping me from crying right now. And I will not cry, not in front of the people who humiliate me, who make me feel ashamed. Not anymore.

"Because last night you were saying something completely different."

George makes a sound, a sort of saddened, disgusted *tsk*. "Jesse," he says, disappointed, and I appreciate the solidarity, I do, but it's just more humiliation. Layers and layers like strata waiting to be excavated, piled on top of each other, a cross-section of the moments in my life that I have been made the butt of the joke, the story people tell about the girl who fell out of a tree, who fell down the stairs, a loser, alone. Jesse's rejection is just another vein in the bedrock, more proof that I do not belong here. I do not belong to anyone.

"I'm going to get my things," I say quietly, brushing past Jesse and George before the latter can say anything. I won't hold my breath for word from the former.

My purse's contents are scattered across the bed from where I'd rummaged for a hairbrush and tie. As I throw everything back in and pull my socks on, the two men speak in hushed tones, barely audible from the bedroom. "Please don't come in here," I whisper as I hear footsteps moving through the house. "Please just let me leave in peace."

He stops in the doorway.

I sit on the edge of the bed. I can't look at him. I can't move.

"Lu."

"Don't call me that," I snarl.

He rears back like my words are a gale-force wind, then takes a step forward.

"I wish I could explain to you…" he says. He touches his chest, like there are more words in there and he just can't catch them all and put them in the right order. The fool in me sympathizes, the fool in me loves him. "I wish I could…" He swallows and if I didn't know any better I'd think that Jesse, solid, strong, brick wall of a man Jesse Logan, was about to cry.

"So, explain," I say. "Explain," I demand again when still he says nothing. *"Say something,"* I yell. The house is dead silent. I know that's what Jesse is used to. An empty house, him rattling around this mid-century bungalow like a ghost in an old Victorian. I know that like me, Jesse is alone, but I'm too hurt and I'm too tired of being hurt to give him another inch of leeway.

"It's not you," he says and he closes his eyes, shaking his head before the words have even finished leaving his mouth, probably because he can see the rage bubbling inside me, spilling out of my mouth and eyes and ears like foam.

"Let me guess," I laugh. "It's not me, it's you."

He shakes his head. "It's just too much."

My whole life people have told me that I'm too loud. I'm too emotional. I'm too single-minded or too scatter-brained. I'm too silly or too obsessive. I'm too competitive. I'm too whimsical and naive. My whole life I've been too much, so why do I always feel like I'm not enough?

I'm not enough for the people I love, for the department and the field of study I so desperately want to be a part of. For Brian, for my dad. For Nora.

"Maybe I'm not too much," I say. Tears leave hot streaks on my cheeks, but these aren't sad, embarrassed tears. I am fucking angry.

"Maybe you're not enough." I hold my bag in front of me, a physical barrier between us. "Go find less, Jesse."

George is waiting for me in his car when I get outside. He opens the passenger door but has to get out of the car and convince me before I'll get in. I don't want him to see me, see this, but he's kind and quiet, speaking only to confirm directions until he stops in front of my house.

"Do you want me to come in with you?" he asks.

"God no."

But I can't seem to open the door.

"I'm going to text you later," he says. "You're going to text me back, OK?"

I sniffle. "I'm not…you don't have to worry about me," I say.

"That's not what I meant," he says. He squeezes my hand. "I want to make sure my friend is OK, Lulu."

My smile is watery but sincere. "Thank you."

He leans across the seat as I'm getting out. "I'm not trying to make excuses for him," he says quickly. George winces. "You deserve an apology and an explanation but I've known Jesse for a long time and I'm just saying…" He shakes his head. "Ever since the accident, he's had to relearn who he is. Or rather, learn

who he is for the first time. He's always had all these other la-
bels defining him and now he doesn't have them anymore. And
you know he's not the most verbose person."

I snort. "No."

"I know that he hurt you and I'm mad at him for that, but
I also know that what happened back there? Whatever Jesse
said to you in the bedroom? That's not what he meant. When
you're ready—if you're ever ready—I just know he'd want a
chance to do that all over again."

I'm too numb to do anything other than nod and close the
door.

Dad stands on the front porch as I walk to my apartment. I
keep my face turned away from him, pathetically hopeful he's
just getting some fresh air and not wanting a chat.

"Lu?"

Crumbs.

"Yeah." I shade my face with my hand even though it's over-
cast, anything to ensure he can't see me.

"Do you think your friend Jesse would be up for some more
yard work this weekend?" He's got his gardening gloves on,
the knee pads Mom bought him last year for when he spends
long days kneeling on the ground.

"I…um, I don't…uh. No? I can help you."

Which is how I end up in a pair of old overalls and sneakers, my bloodstained gardening apron, shimmying the trunk of
a dwarf lilac tree across the yard. I don't know what's heavier,
this tree or my broken heart.

"Try lifting it, Lu," Dad says, bending his knees and holding
his arms in a bear hug to mimic exactly what he wants me to do.

"I'm trying," I huff. "It's heavy." A branch smacks me in
the face.

"Maybe you can see if Jesse can come over some night this
week. I'll pay him."

"No," I snap. "I don't need him. I can do it myself."

"Did…something happen between the two of you?"

I should have just pretended I didn't hear him when he was on the porch in the first place.

"Nope." I wrestle the tree into the hole dug into the ground and sit back on the mound of dirt beside it.

Dad watches me, his gaze assessing. I've never been able to hide things from my father and I've never cared to until now. "Ah. I see," he says.

I hope to god he does not.

Dad readjusts his Tilley hat and pushes his glasses back up his nose. "You haven't come for dinners at the house in a bit," he says.

I busy myself with the shovel.

"Mummy noticed."

"I'll drop in for tea." I chuck a shovel load of dirt on top of the tree's roots.

"I overstepped with you a while back," he says.

I stop with the shovel in the dirt pile, my heart thudding. It can't take another rejection, especially not from my father.

"It's fine, Dad."

He touches my elbow, the gloves rough and warm. "I'm sorry, Lu. I…" He swallows. "You remind me so much of me. I've watched you struggle your whole life, trying to figure out how to fit in, and it's just like me when I was your age. Now I just can't muster up the energy to care but for you? I still feel the need to fix it."

"I didn't know that," I say quietly.

"I threw my weight around and made everything worse for you. So I thought I could fix that, too, by getting you the interview with Dr. Lucas. But I made it worse." He sighs. "What you don't see, is how very loved you are. You have people, your people, here, in Lancaster. Or wherever you end up. Jesse is one of those people."

"Daddy," I say. My throat feels too tight, painfully so.

"I never should have made that call to Dr. Lucas. I'm so sorry, Lu. You didn't deserve any more accusations of nepotism."

"It's fine," I mumble. "They were technically correct."

Dad turns me so we face each other fully. He puts his hands on my shoulders, leaning down so we're eye to eye, like he used to do when he was coaching my softball team. "It's been obvious to us that you're not your happiest here. I want you to find the place where you belong."

"I want that, too." My voice cracks. "So much."

"But wherever you end up, I want you to know how much of a blessing it's been to have you back with us, Lu. Mom and I love you so much. We're so proud of you. We don't tell you that enough."

How does he *know*?

"What's that, darling?" he asks, pulling me into a sweaty, snotty hug.

"How do you know?"

"Know what, dear?"

I squeeze him. He's thinner than he was a year ago. It's not obvious, there aren't bones protruding from his body at all angles. It's a lack of softness. His sweater is baggy, plus there's the fact that he's wearing a sweater at all when it's almost July and I'm sweaty and flushed.

"It's my job to know, darling." He pats my back, the feeling as familiar as this farmhouse, the smell of the laundry hanging on the line, the sound of Mom's musical cast recordings coming through the screen door. "It's my job."

I finish in the garden, shower, and eat a bag of popcorn for dinner. I watch a random reality TV show on my laptop. After a while, a few hours, I'm distracted enough that it doesn't hurt so much. I'm more invested than I've ever been in rich people buying overpriced and oversize mansions. The alternative is to think about Jesse, about the emotional whiplash I just experienced, about the pained expression on his face. That pain was the worst part because it makes it easier to lie to myself. To believe that he didn't *want* to end things.

A knock comes at my door in three short raps. I freeze on the bed, like whoever is on the other side won't be able to see me as long as I stay still.

"Lu?" he says, and the sound of my name in his voice *hurts*. He knocks again.

I sit up on the bed, pulling my T-shirt down farther over my thighs to cover my underwear.

"Lu, please?" Jesse calls, his voice muffled and muted through the door. "I'm sorry. I wanted… Can I explain?"

I stand, walk the few steps to the door, put my hand on the lock; it's cold. I could open this door and let him say his piece. Maybe he didn't mean it, maybe it was a mistake. But even if it was, even if he does love me.

He humiliated me.

He took the love that I offered and said a cold and resounding "no thank you."

It's not fair, I know, to lay all of the other humiliations at his feet. Brian's humiliations, Nora's, my parents', even Audrey's, especially my own. He wasn't responsible for them, except he knew, he knows how very much I just want to belong.

Suddenly my anger fills me, fills this tiny apartment. My hand shakes on the lock as I flip it. I swing open the door, my heart pounding. I cry, immediate and hard when I see him. The gut-wracking kind of sob that makes it hard to speak. That makes it so I can get only this out: "No. I don't want to talk to you. Ever again."

Jesse is blank. Way beyond Grump Face. He's blank as he steps back, turns his back, walks away. But then he turns around and part of me, a very stupid part of me, is so relieved. He's coming back.

"You're not being fair," he says, and his face is blank but his voice is hard. It's something I've never heard from him before; at least, not directed at me. "Don't I get a fucking say in this?"

"You got your say. You said nothing."

"I'm not like you, Lulu. I can't just jump headfirst into something and hope for the best."

"I don't do that." I cross my arms over my chest. Do I?

"I'm not saying it's a bad thing. I'm just saying I can't do that. What happens if we try to be more than friends and then it doesn't work out? Are we just going to go back to being friends again?"

"I didn't think about it, I guess," I say quietly. I feel like I'm being chastised.

"I never said you were *too much*." He throws up the most sarcastic air quotes I've ever seen. "I said, *it's* too much. What I feel for you is too much." He presses his fist to his chest. "What's going to happen to me if you decide to leave? Or if you just get tired of me."

"I wouldn't do that," I yell. "You're acting as if I'm a flight risk."

"Yeah, well, you're acting as if I'm just like everybody else who's made you feel bad about yourself. I'm not Brad or Brent or whoever the fuck."

"Brian," I whisper.

"I know his name," he snaps. I had no idea Jesse had this level of hurt inside him. "I'm just refusing to say it. I'm not Nora, either," he says, calmer.

"I'm… I…didn't realize." A fresh wave of tears starts and I dash at them, suddenly embarrassed to be crying in front of Jesse.

"No, you wouldn't. You spend so much time trying to get all these other people to like you, Audrey and Miranda and everyone in the study. You can't see me standing right in front of you."

Much like the last time we stood in this doorway, facing off,

Jesse has said the wrong thing, but I'm pretty sure there was still nothing he could have said to make this better.

"I can't *see* you? Jesse, you're all I see. But maybe that's the problem."

He frowns. "What do you mean?"

I shrug, trying to fake flippancy. I'm not even sure that I mean what I'm saying. I'm just sad and mad. "We joined this stupid study to make friends and we just have sex with each other instead."

"Fine," he says, and there's something resolute about him. He's calm while I'm a storm; he's safe. "That settles it, then. We end this. So we can make friends." He says the last words through his teeth.

My arms ache to wrap around him, to go to him. I want to go back to this morning when I was asleep in his bed, start this day over. But he's blank again. He's the Jesse I first met, a man who would only give the bare minimum.

Even though it's a terrible idea, even though I know—I *know*—what the answer will be, I pick this scab. I ask, my voice high, "Can we still be friends?"

He shakes his head once. In the dark, the only light from the security lamp overhead, his eyes are glassy. "No."

I slam the door. Slam it in the hopes that the sound will act like a Band-Aid, a momentary distraction from the pain in my heart. The pain that registers distantly as the loss of him, all of him. His friendship, his love. Everything.

The door shudders in the frame, like he's pressed his weight against it. His voice is closer now, as if he's speaking right into the seam where the door meets the wall.

"I'm sorry," he says. He sounds it.

"I'm not." I gasp the words that are more fiction than truth. But I can't see past the anger, the pain, the embarrassment of being hurt by him and loving him all the same. "Just go, Jesse," I say, taking a deep breath. "Please."

The door shudders again under one, singular knock; the gravel under his feet clatters gently as he steps away from the door. I press myself against the wood, trying to hear more of him, hating myself for it.

The moment he's gone, I wish he was here. I wish he never left.

I cry against the wood until my legs can't hold me up anymore.

Chapter Twenty-Three

Jesse

"What the fuck is wrong with you?" George doesn't even bother to knock. The door slams against the wall and he lets it hang open, bringing the drone of a neighbor's lawn mower in with him. "What the hell, Jesse?"

Betty ran from her perch on top of my chest at his intrusion but my heart rate hasn't slowed yet. "You scared the crap out of me." I sit up, facing him on the couch.

He stands in the doorway, judging the mess that is my house with the same distaste he had the last time he showed up unannounced and stared down at my sweaty chest.

"It's been forty-eight hours. Why are you not on her doorstep groveling?"

I flop back down on the couch. "I tried that," I mutter. "I fucked that up."

He makes a disgusted sound. "Figures."

"What the hell, George."

The door closes and I follow the sound of his footsteps to me. His face comes into view over the back of the couch, looming and grumpy-looking.

"Grump Face," I say.

"What?"

I sigh. "Nothing."

"What are you doing tomorrow?"

I shrug. "Why?"

He taps hard on his phone. "Just scheduling the intervention."

"No more meddling, George. You promised." I feel punch drunk, except the person who punched me is me.

He launches himself over the back of my couch, plops down beside me. "That was before you…" He leans over, sticking his nose directly into the armpit of my favorite T-shirt. "Smelled like that. When was the last time you showered?"

With Lulu. "My stomach hurts," I say.

He grumbles in a way that sounds like "serves you right." My stomach hurts, my skin feels too tight. I've had a tension headache for the last two days and I called in sick to work last night. "This was supposed to help," I say.

"What was?" George looks at me like I'm very much the dumbass that I feel like right now.

I shrug again, leaning on my old crutch: silence.

"Indulge me for a moment," he says. "I'm getting this PhD and all. When confronted with the reality of *more* with Lulu, something real and not just some secret from your other friends, all you could think about was being alone." I rub at my chest, leaning more of my weight against him. "And you decided not to risk losing her."

I open my mouth to argue but he holds up his finger to silence me. "You decided not to risk losing more of yourself." He looks at me, with far more compassion than I probably deserve right now. "You were so scared of being lonely, you tried to protect yourself. But now…"

"I'm alone." The words catch in my throat.

"Oh, Jesse." George opens his arms and I fall into them, my head on his chest, his heart beating in my ear.

"I don't want to be alone again, George. I can't be alone."

He pets my hair, pressing his mouth to the top of my head in a prolonged kiss, benevolent and protective. "Oh, Jess," he says again. His voice is soft, tender. I miss her, madly, but in this moment, between this breath and the next, I don't feel so alone.

"You won't be alone, Jess. You're only as alone as you force yourself to be."

"I don't." I sniffle. "I don't really know what that means."

My head rises and falls on his chest, from his deep sigh. "Shhhhhh." He pets me. "It sounded poetic."

The sun filtering through green leaves casts an off-color shadow on the tiled floor. The therapist, in her chair across from me, shifts. The leather squeaks. George texted me last night after he left, reminding me that I had this appointment this morning. If I could have canceled it, I would have, but I'm pretty sure George would have revoked my participation in the study. And then what would all of this have been for?

The therapist is doing that waiting tactic. The one where they don't speak until you do. She probably thinks I'm doing this on purpose, that I'm one of those toxic men who think the only good thing talking about feelings does is justify the use of a slur.

I want to talk to her. She seems nice. Safe. It's just happening again. It keeps happening. The choking, the blankness, the numbness. I don't trust myself to say the right thing, so I say nothing at all.

I wonder if Lulu is having a therapy session today. If she's in the building. If she's talking about me.

I shut that thought down. It's both arrogant and wishful thinking. But now I'm thinking about Lulu and I can't stop. Her hair was on my pillow when I went to bed last night. I found a tampon and an earring on my bedspread. I put them in a dish beside my bed. I guess I can give them to George to give back to her.

George wouldn't tell me what Lulu said, only that he made sure she got home alright. Voices drift through the closed door of this office and I strain to hear the sound of her voice. What would I even say if I saw her in the hall? Probably nothing. That's what I always do.

Lulu, though. Lulu would have a lot to say. What would Lulu say? That's a fun game. It's an almost impossible game to win because like everything else with Lulu, the reality of her is always better than anything my mind can conjure up.

The therapist—Leigh—shifts again. She doesn't seem annoyed or angry. She's patient. She seems kind. If I were Lulu I'd probably say something about the art on her walls or the books on her shelf. If I were Lulu…

"I'm in love with one of the other study participants," I say.

So much for that money.

Leigh writes something on her notepad. "You don't participate much in the group therapy sessions," she says. "Why is that?"

"Aren't you going to kick me out?"

"For what?" She seems genuinely curious.

"I just…" Might as well go for broke. "I'm in love with her. Lulu Banks. That's against the rules, isn't it?"

Leigh shakes her head slowly. "None of us were operating under the assumption that participants' feelings would or even could stay completely platonic. Many lovers are friends first."

I'm tempted to fully out us, to admit that things have gone way past feelings. We "touched butts," as Lulu would say. But then I'd be outing Lulu and that's the last thing I want to do.

"I don't know what to say," I admit. "When we're in the group sessions everyone seems to know themselves so well. I don't feel that way. I never do."

"Have you always felt like that?" she asks. "Like you don't know yourself?"

I shrug and she raises an eyebrow that very much states she will not let me get away with that non-answer. Now that I'm talking I'll have to keep doing so.

"Not always. There were certain parts of myself that I kept hidden from certain people, but I knew who I was. I knew what I was capable of. I... I trusted myself more."

She leans forward. "What changed?"

My face feels hot, my throat tight.

"I was in an accident a few years ago."

She nods, turning to her desk to pull a file folder onto her lap. She flips through it. "Right. Your medical history mentioned a car accident. What happened?" she asks without any of the sympathetic curiosity that often clouds people's tones. People who are hungry for the gory details.

"It was late. Or early. I was driving home after a shift at the station. I was a firefighter. I probably shouldn't have been on the road, honestly. I was tired. Too tired. I should have just slept it off in my bunk. But I was anxious to get home. My grandfather had just entered a new care facility and I had some grandiose ideas about meeting him for breakfast. I'm lucky that it was only me who was hurt."

A clock on the wall ticks quietly. Leigh sits back in her chair like she's giving me the space to speak when I'm ready, and it works. The cork that usually bottles up my throat has popped now. "After the accident, I couldn't go back to work. My grandfather had been a firefighter. So had my dad. And now I was..."

"Not."

I nod. "I was nothing." My voice catches and she slides the box of tissues across the square gray ottoman she's using as a coffee table. I take a few. "I wasn't able to visit my grandpa for a pretty long time after that. I recovered in the hospital and then an in-patient facility. It took a while before I could drive again. I totaled my new truck so I had to fix up my grandpa's old one and use his."

"There were a lot of changes," she says. "Because of one moment."

"It was my fault. Like I said, I'm just so grateful I didn't hurt anyone."

"What was your reunion with your grandfather like?"

I check the clock hoping that suddenly time is up. Turns out all that time I spent not talking only amounted to about five minutes of our session, though.

"His doctors said it's common for patients with Alzheimer's or dementia to confuse the people in their lives. There's this woman at Pop's facility who thinks I'm her dead husband. I guess we look alike. Or in her mind, she's my age again and sees me and her mind fills in the rest of the blanks."

"Sounds like stage six," she says. "Severe cognitive decline."

"The first time I went back to see him after the accident, Pop called me Joey. My dad's name was Joey. Joseph. I haven't been Jesse since then."

The room is quiet again except for me, blowing my nose.

"That must have been devastating," she says.

"It was my fault," I say. "I was gone for so long and when I came back, he didn't know me anymore. The man who raised me couldn't recognize me."

"If it was someone else who had driven their car tired and they'd hit your car, would you blame that person for the natural effects of your grandfather's disease?"

I don't answer. Maybe? Maybe I'd be angry enough that their mistake made me miss out on time with him.

Dr. Ali leans forward, her elbows on her knees, one hand cupped in the palm of the other. "Alzheimer's is a degenerative disease. There is no cure, Jesse," she says gently.

"I know."

"This would have happened. Whether or not you were in that accident."

I want to say *I know* again but I can't. My face is sore from crying. My cheeks ache.

"How many times had you driven home from a shift tired? How many times have we all done that? It was an accident, a mistake. One that took your profession, your livelihood, and your identity. And you blame yourself for it. That's a heavy load for anyone to carry."

"Yeah," I say, my voice gravel. "I guess."

"No wonder you don't want to talk in group."

We both laugh.

"If I had to hazard a guess, I'd say that Lulu doesn't know about your feelings for her."

"She does," I say quickly. Except...did I ever actually say to her: *I* and *love* and *you* all strung together as a complete sentence? "Or well...maybe not."

"What do you think she would say? If you told her? Is that the reason why you haven't? Are you afraid she won't reciprocate?"

I wince. "Not exactly." I don't want to reveal too much about the relationship and get Lulu in trouble.

"I think Lulu would want to be more than friends and I'm not sure that I'm right for her," I admit. "I'm not enough for her." It's embarrassing, revealing to someone, even someone trained to deal with revelations like this, how very little I think of myself.

She sighs. "It makes me sad to hear you say that about yourself, Jesse, but I'm not surprised."

"Oh. Thanks?"

"Hear me out," Dr. Ali says. "You knew who you were and after a tragic accident, a mistake, everything changed. You lost yourself, your identity. Literally. The most important person in your life forgot who you were. It's not just that you don't know yourself. You don't *trust* yourself, not to speak in group, not to be enough for someone you love. All because of one mistake."

This time I don't know what to say. I feel knocked on my ass.

"And so, you stay silent. You don't speak up. You do nothing."

I see it like a map of my life.

"You don't tell people how you feel."

"How do I start?" I ask. "Speaking up again."

"You give yourself permission to make mistakes, Jesse. Trust that you will make mistakes again and that when you do, you'll be able to come back from them. You deserve to come back from them."

"That easy, huh?"

She laughs. "Well, I wouldn't say that."

After Grandma died, Pop started spending more time in the garden. He'd never cared for flowers much until the woman who'd spent her life growing them stopped. Then he became an amateur botanist. He smiles at the bees buzzing around the flowers in the gardens around his care facility. He complains via faint muttering if I start to push the wheelchair too quickly. I slow as we come alongside a bed of happy, pink peonies. The stems seem to bend under the weight of the heavy blossom, but they never buckle.

He reaches out, so I stop. Pop cradles a thick blossom in his hand. "Your mom loves these," he says. His voice is coarse from disuse. "We should get her some."

I pat his shoulder. "Sure."

He frowns, like he can't quite place me. I smile but it doesn't do much good. My face feels like plastic, the hard kind that's brittle and easily cracks. I'm exhausted despite the nap I took after my night shift.

The doctors say to treat him like normal. To speak to him of the things I always would. "I'm going to start school in the fall," I say as I push him toward a bench underneath a maple tree. I park his chair next to the bench and grunt as I take a seat beside him. I pass him the juice box one of the nurses sent us out with along with instructions not to litter.

"I just got a late acceptance as a mature student. Nursing. Like Grandma."

Pop slurps as he finishes the juice box. "Trudy is the smart one," he says. "I've only ever been good as a ladderman and on the farm."

Pop grew up on a farm. He used to tell me all the usual tall tales. That he walked miles to school, uphill both ways. He had cereal boxes for shoes. He went to school in a one-room schoolhouse. They locked the teacher inside once and had an hours-long recess. I never knew which stories were real or fake, just that something, somewhere in each story was an embellishment. My grandparents were high school sweethearts, but she never saw him as just a farmer, just a ladderman. He was a hero to her, not because of his profession but because he'd go out late at night to get her favorite tub of ice cream when she had a bad day, or he rubbed her feet after a double shift at the hospital.

I might have let my silence ruin things with Lulu. But I'm not going to let it ruin things with him.

"I miss her," I say and I mean my grandmother and Lulu. "I was mad at you for something you had no control over. I was mad at myself, too. Mostly at myself."

The grass is still wet from rainfall early this morning. The building sits between this garden and the road, blocking the sound of traffic and the road construction. We're in the shade here under the tree, but soon we won't be.

"I kept something from you. It wasn't for no reason. I was scared of what you'd say, what you'd think. But I'm ready now. I know who I am, and you deserve to know, too. I wish you could know."

It takes saying it out loud to know that it's true. I *do* know who I am. "Pop." I take his hand. "I'm your grandson, Jesse, and even if you never know me by name again, I'm always going to be here. I'm a bisexual man in love with a woman and I hurt her because I'm scared. I wish you could tell me how to fix it. I'm not a firefighter anymore but I trust myself enough to make a new path."

He pats my hand.

"I think you'd be proud of me."

Pop smiles placidly, like "OK, strange boy." We stroll down the path again on the way back to the facility for lunch. I stop to punch in the key code to open the doors.

"I wish you could have seen him," Pop says, not to me; to himself, I think. His eyes are closed, his head tipped back. He reminds me of Betty, basking with the sun on his face. I should take him out more. He clearly enjoys it. "I think he was the first member of the Logan family to ever win a spelling bee."

It takes a moment to register the memory that has gripped his mind. My fourth-grade spelling bee. "Recommend," I say. "That was the word I won with. I can't believe you remember that."

Of all the things in the world—rugby matches, championships, shaking his hand at my probationary firefighter graduation—he remembers that. A nine-year-old kid who for the first and only time in his life remembered that there was only one C in "recommend." "You and Grandma took me out for ice cream."

"He's so smart, Joey." His moods change fast now and he's lost his formerly white-knuckled control on his emotions. It's a side effect of the disease, but seeing tears in my grandfather's eyes will always create tears in mine.

"Thanks, Pop." I kick up the brake on his chair to hug him, awkwardly hovering over him, trying not to use too much strength on his brittle body. He slaps my back, his palms still big, no matter what.

"I love you, son," he says.

And now I can't help but hug him harder. I get down on my knees and hold him to me. This whole time I've needed acknowledgment from him, understanding of who I am. I forgot the most important thing that I am to him. I am his son. In all the ways that matter, I'm his boy.

The shoulder of his sweater is wet with my tears. "I love you, too."

Chapter Twenty-Four

Lulu

Audrey shares an office with a professor emeritus who is hardly ever on campus. He teaches one class a week, a comprehensive history of China. He doesn't read from his notes, just spouts the knowledge from his brain, and he doesn't assign essays or tests. Student grades hinge entirely on the end-of-the-semester exam, since he doesn't want to waste what's left of his precious time on grading.

The man is a legend.

Audrey opens the door when I knock, nodding to the chair on his side of the office.

"Ready to go?" I sink into it, the orthopedic backrest doing strange things to my posture.

She spends a lot of time unplugging her laptop, rearranging books on the shelf above her desk.

Three paintings, Mondrian-esque with geometric shapes and blocks in primary colors, lean against the brick outer wall. A stylized fruit bowl sits on her desk, spared of any clutter, filled with pomegranates. A faux sheepskin runner hangs effortlessly over the decades-old wooden rolling office chair provided by the university. Some of Audrey's things creep into Professor Yi's space, her modernity at odds with the dynastic maps of China.

"I, uh, I don't think I'm gonna come." She crosses her arms over her chest.

I breathe deeply through my nose and hope my nostrils don't flare. "You're canceling on dinner with Miranda and me half an hour before we're supposed to meet her?" I state the obvious but she looks embarrassed.

"Yeah. Well. Sorry, I guess."

I want to mirror her, cross my arms over my chest, scowl, but all I can do is snort at her absolutely abysmal apology.

Audrey looks up at me through her fringe as I laugh and slowly she smiles; slower, she laughs, too. Once we pull ourselves together, Audrey pulls a book off her shelf. "I was reading this and I thought…well, I wasn't going to show it to you but I do think you'd like it. If you haven't read it yet."

She passes it over and I take it. I don't even bother to check the title to see if I've read it before. "Thank you. I'll read it," I say.

I scan the other books on her shelves. She has a lot of the same books I do, a lot of the same authors. There's so much that's similar about our work that if we weren't competitors, we could be contemporaries. We *should* be contemporaries.

"Hey, so…" Jesse's inkling of an idea burns in my mind. There are so many reasons for her to say no, and hearing another no will hurt. No is scary, but I owe it to myself to try. Jesse's voice, positing that maybe the people here are different, echoes in my mind. And he was half-right, but mostly I think *I* am different. Despite the fact that I, quite recently, climbed a tree to avoid confrontation, I think I might be…braver?

"Listen, I know you have no reason to trust me. Or to want to work with me but…what if we worked together?"

She frowns. "We do work together."

"No. What if we worked *together*. We're both untenured,

early modernist contract instructors in a history department that prioritizes American history. What if we cultivated a space for ourselves in this department," I say. "Remember that course idea I was telling you and Miranda about? What if we combined our courses and came at the history of witchcraft and magic and gender from different directions, but ended up in the same place."

Now that I've gotten going, I'm on a roll. "I mean, we share a department with *the* Dr. Miranda Jackson, one of the greatest early modernists…ever? What if one day students and academics alike came *here* to work with the three of us?"

Audrey looks suspicious, and I don't blame her.

"You'd stay and teach here rather than go to Lancaster?"

I weigh whether or not I'm willing to tell Audrey about all the reasons I do not want to go back there. I am willing, but just not ready yet. "There are a lot of reasons why I don't want to go back there but mostly, I don't want to rest on my father's laurels."

She snorts. "Can I?"

"Audrey, Lancaster would be lucky to have you," I say.

She frowns. "I thought you wanted to work together?"

"No. I mean, I do, I just…" I flounder for the right words. "I just want you to know that you can do either. You can do anything. We're colleagues and I want to help you."

"So, we'd combine our specialties? The history of magic and the history of how we perceived magic."

I nod. "It's a good idea, right?" I want her to say it is, and on the heels of that, I want to be able to tell Jesse he was right. I shove that feeling down.

She leans back in her chair, tipping her head to gaze up at the ceiling. It's her thinking pose, I think, and she holds it for a long time until slowly she turns to me, and she smiles. "It is."

I lean forward, the chair squeaking under me. "Well, see. Now you have to come to dinner."

"How do you figure?"

"We have to pitch this idea to Miranda. Why don't you want to come?"

She shrugs but I've had enough experience with no-talkers recently. I clamp my mouth shut, and let her come to me. Like how I'd hold my hand out to Betty until she slowly got close enough to reach out her nose.

"I'm nervous, OK?" she says, much faster than I expected. "Sophisticated," "socially competent," "poised." All are words I'd use to describe Audrey and Miranda. They're a matched set. I thought I was the only one who was going to be nervous.

"Don't laugh," she says, but she's laughing a little, too.

"I'm not laughing at you," I promise. "I'm just surprised."

"I have a lot of respect for Miranda. I've never hung out with her outside of work before."

"Me neither."

"Yeah, but you've probably been to a lot of dinners with a lot of lecturers here."

"I mean, when I was a kid, yeah. My parents dragged me along to dinners with professors who either work elsewhere or are retired now. And they spent most of their time strategizing about the newest collective bargaining agreement or critiquing each other's work. They'd usually let me watch my ancient VHS of *Sister Act 2* in the living room."

Audrey pulls a face, the one she gives me when I've gone off on a tangent.

"So, you have to come," I say, making myself ignore her arched brow. "I don't think Miranda has a VCR. *Don't*," I say, as she huffs again.

"Don't what?"

"Roll your eyes."

When Miranda first chose The Pump I was excited. Good memories, good food. But as I walk in behind Audrey, smile at the same hostess who greeted me the night I met Jesse, run through the same list of acceptable and unacceptable conversation topics, I have a tummy ache with a side of nervous sweating.

Miranda waves at us from the booth she's snagged. I wave back. I don't look at the bar. I don't. I do not.

Damn. I look at the bar. Stupidly, I think maybe he'll be there, his shoulders broad and back straight. His knit sweater new. And then, when he's not there—because *why* would he be there, Lulu?—I'm disappointed.

"I'm so glad we're doing this," Miranda says as we slide into the booth. Audrey takes the spot beside her and I have the other side all to myself.

Miranda orders a glass of red wine, so Audrey and I do, too. She suggests we share the burrata as a starter and I don't know how to tell them that the texture of a tomato makes me gag without sounding like a child so I agree. I slice off the smallest slices of tomato and wash it down with water.

Nora knew I hated tomatoes, and mushrooms. That I'd rather wear shoes or commit fashion suicide traipsing around in socks and sandals than let my feet get dirty. Jesse knows the sound of a knife buttering dry toast makes me cringe and that I use my hands too much when I talk when I'm nervous. One of the worst parts of making new friends is having to admit all of these idiosyncrasies, hoping against hope they'll like me enough to see past them. The Pump is well-known for its steaks but I order the cheeseburger—no tomatoes—and by the time the server places our entrées in front of us, we've run out of historical small talk.

"So, Audrey and I had an idea," I say, then promptly shove a bite of cheeseburger into my mouth. Audrey pauses with a forkful of double baked potato halfway to her mouth, her eyes open wide like "wtf dude." I look back at her like "didn't we agree to pitch this now?" except now that I'm thinking about it maybe we didn't exactly agree to that.

Miranda glances between us, her diamond studs glinting in her ears. "Oh. Do I get to hear more about it?"

Audrey shoves potato into her mouth. I swallow quickly and almost choke on sesame seed bun. "We were thinking about working together."

"On a paper or…?"

"A new course offering." Audrey wipes her mouth with the linen napkin. "The history of magic and the history of how we perceive it."

The more we explain, the faster Audrey speaks, clearly excited. Miranda sets her knife and fork down, like she needs her hands free to understand us better. I grip my empty wineglass as tightly as I can without snapping the stem to avoid extravagant hand gestures. Miranda hums when we're finished, staring across the restaurant, and I wonder if she can see it as clearly as I can; that we can create an island of early modernists here in this little Pennsylvania college town.

"It's an exciting idea, Doctors," she says and she looks impressed.

Audrey makes a soft sound, grinning down at her plate. "It was Lulu's."

"It wasn't really," I insist. "It was…a friend's. And he suggested it because I wouldn't shut up about how cool your History of Magic class is."

For the first time in my living memory, Audrey beams at me.

"When he first suggested it I said you'd probably rather beat yourself with your own arm than work with me." I laugh, but they look at me like I'm slightly deranged. "I mean, I was joking. It was a joke. I'm sorry." My laugh dies on my lips. "That was too much."

After a moment, Audrey slowly smiles. She shrugs. "You weren't totally wrong," she says, and this time I cackle.

★ ★ ★

It's muggy when we get outside. The sky is pink and purple bleeding into dark blue. We gather underneath it in the parking lot, a scalene triangle of colleagues, maybe friends, being pulled toward our cars. We say all the usual things, that we had a good time and we should do this again soon. I get the feeling that Audrey is still on the fence about me. There's an urge, giving the same energy as a chittering squirrel insisting you stay away from his nuts, that I do something about that. That I fix it. That I *make* her like me. But the thing is, that's so damn exhausting. Especially when there are people out there who do like me without having to try at all.

People like Jesse. Even if he said no to us, I don't think he was saying no to me, to liking me, to loving me. Instead of turning left on Main Street, I turn right. If anyone asks I'll blame it on distraction, that thinking of him made me do it. I make two more turns before I reach his street. As I approach his house, I slump lower in my seat, easing my foot off the gas for a slow roll. The lights are bright on the front porch and a soft glow comes from the side window in his kitchen, but his truck isn't in the driveway. Which is probably for the best. The last thing I need is for him to see me staking out his house like the world's worst spy.

As I pull out of his small neighborhood, I *think* I see the Bronco, but it's fully dark now and the headlights leave me momentarily blinded before the large truck is gone.

By the time I get home, my happy buzz is gone. My tiny flat is dark and a bit humid, and even with the window open the air is too still. I want to tell Jesse about tonight. About how I might have made some friends, work friends, but that even if I didn't, that was OK. Mostly, I want to tell him that I'm sorry. That I was too quick to react, too ready to believe that just because I'd been hurt in the past, I was going to be hurt now. Jesse has lost control over a lot of things in his life: his career, his body, his identity to his grandfather. He's allowed some time to think, but I was too scared to give him that.

I get ready for bed in the dark, like I did the night after our date, climb into bed in my underwear. But before I put on a reality TV show that provides ample evidence in favor of eating the rich, I open my email.

After the last one, I created a filter that sends all of Nora's emails to their own folder. When they were appearing unannounced in my inbox it seemed like there were a lot of them, but there's only twelve. I click reply on the last one.

Nor,
Thank you for your letters. I am well and I hope you are well, too.

I tell her a bit about my parents, whom she met once when they came to visit me three years ago, and what it's like teaching at a different school.

I'm sorry to hear about you and Brian. That's not sarcasm. I am. It's sad when something ends, and I have to assume that he meant a lot to you. The truth is, I do miss you. I miss you more than Lancaster, or Brian. I miss us and what it meant to be your friend.

But you should know that I'm happy here. I wasn't for a while. I was sad and I didn't feel like I fit in at all. Things were hard. But I'm happy. I'm making new friends and I feel like I belong here.

And yes, I do forgive you. I've never been able to hold on to a grudge for long. But as much as I miss us, I'm ready to leave us in the past. And I hope you are, too.

All my best,
Lu x

I know I should wait to send this. The light of morning or a good night's sleep might reveal a typo, or give me more time to revise, or it might reveal that I don't need to send this at all. I don't owe her anything. But it feels good to hit Send, like ending a complete sentence with a full stop. Plus, I've never been good with impulse control. I press Send and put my laptop away and when I fall asleep, I sleep the best I have all week.

Chapter Twenty-Five

Jesse

The firehouse gym smells exactly as I remember: musty, sweaty, metallic. I love it. The music, a combination of classic rock and country, is barely audible over the familiar noise: the hum of the row of treadmills and accompanying pounding feet, the constant, continuous clank of barbells on weight racks, the thump of dumbbells on the rubber floors.

I started working out in my last year of high school. I signed up for a weight-lifting class run by my rugby coach. I thought it would be an easy A, but I was never that interested in the mechanics of lifting. To this day, I despise the cutting and bulking diets that lifters deem necessary to maximize growth. I'll never have a flat stomach or the abs some of my younger colleagues sported. I just love the challenge. I love loading the bar with weight, and then more weight, and then more. The act of it is so simple: pick it up, put it down. But in those seconds between when I wrap my hands around the bar and lift, the only thoughts running through my head are *breathe, breathe, breathe*.

My home gym was a necessity, to recover my leg muscle and strength after the accident, but especially to rehab my head. I wish I'd known that the best rehab was here all along, working out with my friends again.

"Let's go, Jess," Marcus says, his voice low. I settle the bar on my shoulders for my last set. I think, technically, I'm not allowed to be here, working out in the station's gym. But when Marcus mentioned he was going to work out today I took a chance and asked if I could join him. I forgot what it's like to work out with this bunch of meatheads. I haven't hit numbers like this since my accident. The weight on the bar now isn't my pre-accident PR or anything, but it's fucking heavy.

"You got this, Jesse," Buck says. April pauses her lat pull-downs to watch me. I take a deep breath and drop into a squat and as I push out of the bottom, the gym erupts in my old colleagues' shouts and cheers.

My heart is bursting but only partly because I just back-squatted the weight of a whole other man. I don't think I could have done that without them.

Marcus is bouncing on the balls of his feet as I rerack the bar, and he launches his arms around me when I get out from under it. "Dude, that was so sick."

"Thanks," I say, quietly. But my smile is really fucking loud. "For letting me come."

He squeezes my shoulders in his big hands. "Anytime, OK? I mean it. We miss you around here."

Buck makes me a protein shake before I leave and we toast to the good luck of not getting a single call while we exercised.

The fire station still smells the same, like coffee. The side door slams behind me and the second I'm not smelling it anymore, I miss it. It rained at some point while I was inside. The asphalt is dark and the air smells sweet and sticky and warm. My sneakers soak into puddles on the way to the Bronco.

"Jesse," Marcus calls as the door slams behind him; the metal stairs shake and clang as he runs down them. Crickets chirrup in the field of scrub grass behind the station and he rubs the back of his neck. He's showered, changed in the few minutes I took to say goodbye to everyone. When Marcus wears the uniform he *wears* it, and even though I'm in civvies, I don't feel the wave of regret and loss I've gotten so used to. Once upon a time, I knew how to wear the shit out of that uniform, too.

"I just wanted to let you know," he says. "That I meant what I said in the gym. Come back anytime and we miss you and…"

"I know," I say. I feel proud, but also sad. The two people I want to tell most about these accomplishments, the squats and the socializing, are Pop and Lulu. OK, and George, too. He'd want to be included in this. But still. I used to work out with Pop when I was a kid. I'd do endless biceps curls with his smallest weights while he bench-pressed in our garage.

Weightlifting isn't the most attractive pastime. People make weird faces when they're lifting weight heavier than they are. Lulu would love it. She would approach it the same way she does everything: with a willingness to try, her eyes open and bright and smiling, a laugh ready on her lips, and questions, questions, questions.

"You know, if you've got your strength back, you could…" He shrugs. "Maybe you could come back to work. Especially if you're thinking about playing rugby again."

"Yeah. I was thinking." I swallow down my nerves at making this admission out loud. "Of going to school for nursing."

He leans back, brows raised. He looks me up and down and with a slow smile says, "Nurse Jesse. I like the sound of that."

"Me, too." And it's true. Even though it might be hard, it feels right to say it. Much like it feels right when I have Lulu in my house, my bed. My life.

Our conversation is cut short by the sharp sound of the alarm in the station. "Shit." He starts jogging back. "Let's have dinner this weekend," he says over his shoulder. "I want to hear more about it."

Chapter Twenty-Six

Lulu

The unread email taunts me, highlighted at the top of my inbox. "Just open it," I whisper. "You already know what it's going to say."

Jay rolls his chair toward my desk. "Did you say something?"

"No." *Not to you, at least.*

"Ready for this meeting?" he asks.

"Also no."

He laughs, big and booming, like "oh Lulu, you're so silly," and I cringe at the volume.

"I'll meet you there," I say. "Stop stalling," I mutter as Jay leaves. Even if they offer me the job, I don't have to take it. I don't *want* to take it. But it's still hard to ignore the draw of getting my gloved hands on the archives in Lancaster. Maybe I should set up a shrine to Clio so that the muse of history can guide me. I make a mental note to touch base with the professors in Classical Civilizations. They tend to be about as old as their field of study, and one of them has to have a shrine starter kit. But even Clio can't change the fact that if I don't get it,

Audrey likely did, and that leaves my dreams of co-teaching dead in the water.

Closing my eyes, taking a deep breath like I'm about to take a polar bear dive into Lake Erie, I open the email.

It's about what I expected. Cecelia thanks me for the referral and promises to keep me apprised of any new opportunities in the future. She invites me to a conference in Lancaster at the end of the summer. Something that normally I'd feel excited about but now just feels like a consolation prize. With a sigh, I make my way to the meeting. The room falls silent when I walk in. "Sorry I'm late," I say, my voice thin and reedy at the sudden attention. For a moment, I stall, like the weight of every history professor's combined stare is too heavy to walk out from under. I wave, and even though I tell myself not to, I cross my eyes, stick out my tongue. "Just got stuck in my inbox again," I say with forced laughter.

Someone clears their throat. Miranda smiles at the front of the room. Dad is reading and has not registered my entrance in the least. Audrey stares, mouth agape. Of course, the only chair available is beside her, so I slink into it and discussion resumes. These meetings are like most meetings in that they're a bit dull and much of it could be an email, but today we're reviewing our course offerings for the upcoming year, which is usually exciting at least.

"In the winter semester we're going to continue offering the History of Magic class in the early modern era but I'd like to discuss the possibility of Dr. Banks leading the course and including more content on the intersection of gender politics and witchcraft."

I look up from the spirals I'd been doodling into my notebook to gape at Miranda.

"Oh," I say with all of the accumulated intelligence of my decades' worth of schooling. "Cool."

"I really enjoyed the idea you pitched, Lulu," Miranda says, her voice warm and imbued with Miranda-level respect, the kind she doesn't pass out easily. The kind you must earn.

Frank and Jeff erupt in a flurry of whispers, but they're easy to ignore. I blink and blink and blink at Audrey. "Lancaster?" I mouth.

She nods once. Looks down. Then, "Sorry."

"No." I shake my head. I'm the last person she should be apologizing to.

At the sound of our shared name, Dad finally pried his attention away from his book. He looks at me with the same pride that he had on the day I graduated, and defended my thesis, and my chest feels warm, like my heart is wrapped in a cozy itch-less sweater, and it's an awkward juxtaposition of all these *feelings*: excitement at this new opportunity; sadness that the super-cool idea I had won't be possible.

"I...can pull together a draft syllabus," I say, jotting the note down next to the spirals in the notebook.

And disappointment, of course. If I'm not disappointed in myself can I really call myself an academic? The perfectionist academic overachiever in me feels like a failure that I was passed over for a job that I didn't even want. But also I'm proud; maybe I don't need that shrine to Clio after all. I'm choosing where I belong. And it's here.

"Lulu." Audrey catches up to me after the meeting. I stop, waiting for her just outside the door as the rest of the faculty file out. Her black turtleneck and the black cigarette pants are too hot for the middle of the summer. Every time I try to wear a turtleneck, I start gagging, the feeling of the fabric constricting. Meanwhile, Audrey is poised and elegant, like her Hepburn namesake. But she stares down at her feet, shifting her weight nervously. "Listen, I know things between us are weird. Or whatever. But... I just wanted you to know that I'm really disappointed we won't have the opportunity to teach that class together."

"That's OK." I shrug. And it is. It really is. "Maybe we'll get another chance in the future."

Without warning, Audrey leaps forward and hugs me, quick and hard. "I'd like that," she says. "You're a good friend, Lulu."

I smile. "Thanks," I say. "You are, too."

She leans back. "You should come present at the Lancaster Conference. Cecelia said she was going to mention it to you."

"Yeah, maybe."

"We could co-present." She arches a perfect eyebrow. "Test the waters for our future course."

And OK. That lights the fire inside me, a little bit. "I'll think about it."

Jay is gone when I get back to the office. I close the door behind me, sit in my old rolling chair, and inexplicably cry. Something feels like it's ending even though this is all just the beginning. This is the beginning of my research on witchcraft and gender in early modern New England, and carving out a space for myself in the department separate from my dad. It's the beginning even, maybe, of a friendship with Audrey. "So why are you so sad, you dummy," I say to myself. Outside, my tree sways gently in the breeze, the green leaves waving a warm hello. I'm surrounded by books, tomes that have been my oldest friends, my only friends, but right now my hands ache to tear into them. Screw the sanctity of books. I want to throw the shreds of them and my dignity on the floor, rip them apart with my teeth. My throat is tight, but when my sobs escape all my tears are gone and all that's left is an angry, painful sound. I look up at the quiet knock on my door—expecting my dad, hoping ridiculously for Jesse of all people even though he doesn't know where I work on campus, let alone that I'm upset, and probably thinks I still want nothing to do with him—but getting Miranda.

"Lulu," she says, quietly.

It's entirely too embarrassing for my professional hero to find me crying in my office. Her heels cross the threshold, the door shutting quietly. She leans her hip against my desk.

"I'm sorry." My voice is scratchy.

"Normally, I'd say there's no crying in academia," she says.

Of course, that's not true. There is a ton of crying in academia. What she means is academics—especially women—do not cry in the presence of others, lest we give the old men who run the department the impression we can't handle their *very valuable opinions.*

"But let's just pretend this isn't academia."

I sniffle. "Then what is it?"

She drums her lime green nails on my desk, sighing. "Well, at the very least, it's not the history department. It's the psych department. That's a junk science anyway."

I laugh and she looks pleased. "Are you sad you didn't get the Lancaster position?"

"How did you know about that?" I ask.

"Audrey told me."

"That's the thing," I say. "I'm not. I'm really, really happy for her. I want to stay here. Maybe I'm just scared? I don't know."

"It's OK to be scared." Miranda pats my hand where it's clenched around a tissue. "You have me, your dad, you have a whole community of people who are here to help you."

A few months ago, I wouldn't have believed that was true. My community consisted of my mom and my dad and a tree. But she's right. That's not what I've got now. I've got so much more. Except for one thing, one friend. And maybe that's where these tears are coming from.

I miss my best friend. I miss my person.

Chapter Twenty-Seven

Lulu

I scrape my palm along the trunk of my tree. The leaves are full and green and turned toward the sun. I'm stalling. Our last group session is today and I'll most definitely see Jesse. My palms sweat as I walk across campus, strolling along the quad's tree-lined pathways. I try to remember my list of things I can and can't talk about in group: I can talk about cultivating belonging at work, my tentative détente with Audrey that's turned into the potential for friendship. I can't talk about Jesse, how he makes me feel, how much I miss him. I can't talk about how now I see blue Broncos all over town, when before I saw none. Or, how much I appreciate silence since spending so much time within it when I was with him. I can't talk about how obtuse I was with Audrey because if I do, I'll start thinking about the ways I have been obtuse with him, too.

I loiter outside the building until the very last minute, finally making my way up when I get a text from George with just a series of clock face emojis. "You're late," he singsongs as I step off the elevator.

I cringe. "I might be avoidant."

"Well, that didn't work out for you, unfortunately," he says. "Cuz I think I know who you were avoiding and you're in his group therapy sesh."

"You did that on purpose." I point my finger in accusation.

He wears a face of absolute innocence, which is how I know I'm right.

"I'd never." He crisscrosses his finger over his heart.

"Which room are we in?" I ask, rolling my eyes, but on the inside butterflies start a migration to South America. George gives me the room number and I trudge down the hall.

Jesse is the first person I see when I walk in the room. The chairs are set up in a circle like every support group I've seen in movies. Brooke, who's sitting beside him, waves me over when she sees me and gets up.

"You can sit here," she says.

"That's OK," I say quickly. But she's already up, sliding into the spot next to Trey. I search for another chair, but I'd have to pull one down from the stack and then wedge it in between other people and it would become terribly obvious that I don't want to sit next to Jesse and then I'd have to explain why because Brooke would undoubtedly ask and then what would I say?

That Jesse and I did the one thing the study specifically asked us *not* to do and got caught and when we were given the chance to choose between the study or each other I chose him and he chose the study, which was the mortifying icing on top of the cake of embarrassment that is my life, but when he tried to make it better I sent him away, to be alone again.

Except as I lower myself into the plastic chair that ergonomics forgot, he moves his knee to give me more space, and the reality of sitting next to him isn't even half as horrible and exactly as familiar as I thought it would be. There are no flashbacks to his rejection, but when his hand grips his thigh, the one that I know has a scar down the middle, there are other flashbacks.

The way he touched me, held me, tasted.

"Hi," I say to him.

"Hi," he says after a moment. He looks surprised.

Even now, either I'm on hallucinogens or there's *chemistry* between us. Sometimes he feels magnetized, like I am drawn to wherever he is in the room, a compass, a lodestone. Or maybe it's less scientific than that. Maybe he's just the person in this room that knows me better than anyone else. That even after he hurt me, he's still my friend. My best friend.

"I know you said," he whispers in a rush. "Not to talk to you anymore but… Can I please talk to you?" he asks. "After?"

"I didn't get the job," I say. "In Lancaster."

His face falls. "Oh." Jesse scratches the back of his neck. "I'm…sorry?" He seems to register how entirely lackluster he sounds and physically shakes himself. "I mean it. That sucks. They would have been lucky to have you. Or have you back. Or whatever."

"It's not a bad thing—"

"Welcome, everyone, to our last group session," Leigh says, walking into the room with an extra-large afternoon coffee and a big smile.

"I'll tell you after," I whisper and he nods.

Leigh covers some admin stuff, like how we'll all have to go back to the med school to have our blood pressure and blood tests done again. I don't hear much of what she says; my body is primed like a tuning fork next to Jesse but now the tune is off. Am I letting him off the hook? Being too nice? He hurt me. I'm still hurt. We haven't spoken in days and I just roll over and show him my belly like one of the dogs on our first friend date?

This is the constant turmoil of being me. I question everything, which is silly. I know what I want.

"Does anyone have anything to share this week?" Leigh asks.

"I do," I say before I've even fully registered what I'm about to do.

She nods and I stand. Do we stand in group sessions when it's our turn to speak? Now I can't remember. Suddenly, every memory of a person speaking in group and whether or not they were seated or standing leaves my Swiss cheese brain. I might as well commit to the bit. I stay standing.

"As a lot of you know, I recently moved back here to work at the university. I didn't really know anyone and I was having trouble making friends, which is why I joined this study. Duh."

Someone gives a mandatory laugh, which is generous.

My throat gets tight because I suddenly feel like crying and I am about to admit something very embarrassing.

"I had no friends, really. I had broken up with a boyfriend who was frankly cruel, and my best friend who was unfortunately even crueler, and came back here and I thought I'd be able to find kinship with the people I worked with, again, at the very least. I mean, we spend so much time with those people, it should be easy. But they didn't trust me for valid reasons and I ended up feeling really alone for a lot of the time. I... I spent so much time trying to fit myself into whatever mold I thought other people needed from me and I kept failing at it and it was exhausting. And then I fell out of a tree and...but I won't get into that..." I take a deep breath.

Someone wraps their hand around my fist, clenched at my side. I look down at Jesse and give him a subtle shake of my head. I need to do this myself. He pulls his hand away, sitting on it.

"I felt really alone," I admit. "And ashamed. And embarrassed. I didn't know what I was doing wrong or why I couldn't fit in and I felt like a child reliving their first day at a new school day after day after day except it was worse this time because this time I'm an adult and I'm supposed to know what I'm doing. Sometimes it felt like even my parents didn't seem to want me here, which I know isn't true. It's just you know how sometimes your brain repeats your worst fears back to you and convinces you they're real? I felt like I didn't belong. Anywhere. And I just wished for someone to tell me they were happy I was here. I was desperate to hear it."

The room is silent and my mind wants to run away with me, to do that exact thing, and claim they're too embarrassed by my overshare to say anything, to even move. That these people who I hope are now my friends are really just cringing at everything I say. But I don't listen.

"One of things I learned through all this is that if we want to belong somewhere, we need to seek it out. Belonging. In other words, I like me. I am happy here. I get to decide where I belong and this is where I belong. And I'm happy you're all here. You can belong with me, if you want."

The room is so deathly silent, so still, I think I've done it again. Shared too much, said too much. Been *too much*. But Brooke stands up, cuts through the circle of chairs, and wraps her arms around me in a hug tight enough to make my eyeballs bulge out if I were a cartoon character or maybe like a cat or something.

"I'm so happy you are here, Lulu," she says quietly. I can't remember if I was crying before but I'm crying now, though I try to hide it. Until Trey is there next, hugging me, telling me how happy he is to have met me, how happy he is that I'm here. And then more people, the rest of my new friends are squeezing my shoulder and cupping my elbows and smiling and finally affirming the thing I've hoped to hear this whole time but now know I never needed.

They are happy I am here.

I don't know what to say back other than "I'm happy you're here, too," which is awkward but not as bad as the time that I wished someone a happy birthday after they wished me happy birthday but it was not, in fact, their birthday.

I sit back down and Leigh thanks me for my candor and asks if anyone else has anything they'd like to share. She looks very pointedly at Jesse and I don't have to turn to him to see his blush. He shifts in his seat beside me and it takes a moment for me to realize he's leaning closer to me. I look at him out of the corner of my eye. The others are starting to stare, too.

"I'm sorry, Lulu," Jesse says quietly.

"It's OK," I say quickly, a reflex. And then, "What are you sorry for?"

"I'll share," he says to Leigh, letting my question hang. Jesse sits forward, planting his feet on the floor, his legs wide, his hands on his knees. He does *not* stand up but then he doesn't really need to. Jesse has barely spoken through our group sessions so if he's offering to speak now, he has all of our attention.

He's sorry for hurting me, maybe. Or for not being able to stand in front of everyone and say he was happy I was here. The part of me that loves to hurt my own feelings whispers that maybe he's sorry that he *can't* say it because it's not true. He's not happy I'm here. But as I study his profile, I know that's a lie I'm telling to protect myself. His hair is starting to grow in and he's cleaner shaven, but he's the same as the first time I met him. Quiet, nervous, eyelashes for days, and kind. Mostly kind.

Jesse opens his mouth, closes it. Takes a deep breath, and another. I sit on my hands so I don't put one on his back.

"A friend told me that I shouldn't wait for the perfect time to tell someone important, something important. They said that I should tell them as many times as possible and I, uh, didn't take that advice and I ended up hurting them."

Jesse turns to me.

Oh no.

"I don't know if I learned how to make friends," he says. His hands grip his knees like if he lets go, he might fall over. "No offense to Leigh." He cringes in her direction. "All I think I learned is that I love you."

Brooke gasps.

"I waited to tell you because I was scared of being alone

again. Like if I didn't say it to you then that would make it hurt less or something if you didn't love me back. But I should have told you every minute since the first moment I knew it. I'm sorry I took so long."

Leigh is remarkably placid. She gives good Therapist Face. Brooke's hand is over her mouth, her cheeks are red, and tears shine in her eyes. Trey grins like he knew all along and people whisper, trying to catch up with the drama unfolding before them.

"What—what are you saying?" I want to be sure this time.

"I'm saying I want to be more than friends with you, Lu. You talked about belonging." He shakes his head, shrugs. "I belong to you, if you want me."

I should be embarrassed. There is a room full of people staring at me and that has been, without a doubt, a generally terrible experience for me in the past but I'm just too happy to care.

"Yeah?" I ask.

"Yeah."

"I want you."

That little personal sun, the one that brightened his face on my doorstep what feels like months ago but was really only weeks, rises again and I get the profound sense of joy that comes with making Jesse Logan smile. Joy that makes my belly warm, makes me want to laugh like a maniac. The kind of joy that makes me want to kiss him.

So, I do. I kiss him in front of Leigh and Trey and Brooke and all our friends. I kiss him in front of George, who stands in the doorway. I kiss him until I have to stop because I'm smiling too much, and he's kissing my teeth. His eyes are warm, his personal sun shining out from behind them, warming me in golden light.

"I didn't get the Lancaster job," I whisper against his lips. "And it's not because of you and it's not something I'm going to hold against you in the future," I tell him quickly, what I was trying to tell him before. "I belong here. I want to be here."

"Just so you know, though," he says, quiet but sure of himself, of us. "If you did get the job, or you get one next month, or next year, we'll figure it out. Together."

"I love you," I say.

"I love you, too."

Chapter Twenty-Eight

Jesse

Her hand in mine is the only reason mine isn't shaking. "You have to sign in." My tone is apologetic and I don't know why. Lulu doesn't care.

She picks up the pen on the end of a metal chain, filling in her name and phone number. When she gets to the column where she has to fill in the name of the resident she's here to visit she turns to me. "Jack," I say. "Logan."

"All the J names."

"They almost named me Journey."

"Like the band? Really?"

"No. Not really."

Her tongue peeks from between her teeth as she finishes filling in the sign-in sheet, and it calms me. The curve of her mouth and the way her hair falls over her forehead, in her eyes, the few tendrils that have come loose from her ponytail and curl at the back of her neck. These pieces of her that have become a part of my everyday view, so much so that not knowing if or when I'd see them again was a loss I felt in my gut, in my bones. I'm grateful for the chance to see every piece of her again.

Fred, a nurse, gives Lulu a visitor's pass and buzzes us into Pop's residence. "He's in the day room," Fred says, so I lead her there. The day room has a day care vibe to it, which I find infantilizing, but fortunately the residents like it for the most part. It's bright, decorated in pastel colors, with a lot of textured fabrics. The TV is almost always on but there's also art, music, games. Pop likes to sit by the window.

He leans close to the pane, interested in something I can't see. "Hey, Pop."

He doesn't respond but I don't expect him to. I prepped Lulu on all of this on the drive over, but I still feel the urge to explain, to make excuses for behaviors that he has no control over. Lulu sits in the chair beside his.

"This is Lulu," I say.

"Hi, Jack."

Pop doesn't quite smile but he was never much of a smiler. We're similar that way. He quirks his lips and she beams back at him.

"Do you want a coffee, Pop?" I ask. There's a coffee machine in the hallway.

He pats the pockets of his sweatpants. "I—I don't have my wallet." He sounds puzzled by this fact.

"I've got it." I pat his shoulder and suppress my grin when his mouth twists, proud of himself for pulling off one of his oldest tricks. He'd "forget" his wallet when we'd go out for dinner or hit the concession stand at the movies and make me pay for both of us. He'd always get me back. I'd find bills stuffed into my sock drawer, my coat pockets, the drink cup in my SUV.

"You want one, too?"

"Sure," she says. "Decaf?"

Clarice tries to dance with me as the machine spits out the coffees. She's already dressed for the evening in a green dress and kitten heels. I let her take my hands. She hums a tune that sounds vaguely familiar and spins under my arm before winking and drifting away.

I walk slowly back to the day room, trying to balance three paper cups filled with hot coffee. I stop in the doorway. Lulu and Pop sit closer together now, leaning toward each other. She talks mostly, her hands punctuating her words, and Pop nods.

"And basically, that's how I got into studying history."

"Hmmmm," he mutters as I set the cups down on the table beside him. "Yes." He nods.

"Thanks, Jesse," Lulu says, holding one of the coffee cups in her hands like she's cold.

Pop makes observations about the birds perched on the power lines and calls Lulu my grandmother's name, Rose. By the time we're ready to go, his voice is scratchy from disuse. I don't think he's spoken this much in months, but if anyone can get him talking, it's Lulu.

We walk him back to his room and I get him situated in the chair by his window. He's fixated on his television, one of those fishing shows, something he never watched before he was sick. I kiss the top of his head anyway.

"It was nice to meet you, Jack." Lulu holds his hand. He watches the television.

As we leave, Lulu dropping her visitor badge off at the desk, I take her hand in mine.

"Did you end up telling him?" she asks. The glass doors open with a loud swoosh, the humidity covering us in a heavy blanket. "About you?"

"Yeah."

"Do you think he heard you?"

"Honestly, no."

She stops, pulling me back to her when I keep walking. "How does that feel?" She links her hands behind my back.

When I take deep breaths standing with her like this, my

chest touches hers. I take a lot of deep breaths. "I feel…like Pop would love me no matter what. And not everyone gets to say that."

Lulu traces my jaw with her fingers. She trails her thumbs over my cheekbones and her index fingers over my brows. "I think he would, too. He loves you, Jesse. To the moon."

"Yeah? How do you know?" I ask, blatantly fishing.

"The way he looks at you. He might not know you, but he knows who you are. I know that doesn't make any sense—" She shakes her head.

"No. I… I get it."

"He knows you're safe, he knows you love him. And he loves you back."

I kiss her palm.

"Ready to go?" I ask. "George expects both of us to be stretched and warm for the first pitch at five o'clock."

She pounds her fist into her open palm, like she's working in a leather mitt. "Let's do it."

Chapter Twenty-Nine

Lulu

Two Months Later

With the windows down and the road poured out before us, the sun warm on my cheeks, today is evergreen. It's every end-of-summer day I've ever had, complete with my hand out the window, flying along beside us. I think Jesse might even be going a bit over the speed limit.

"You excited?"

I turn to him. "About what?"

It's a trick question. There's too much to be excited—and scared—about.

"The barbecue."

"My father is more British than the Queen and my mother is a vegetarian," I say, deadpan. "But I'm excited for when Trey takes over grilling from my dad so he can go back to pretending it's a garden party."

"They're going to miss you," he says, his voice a soft rumble.

I stare out the window at the farmers' fields around us. If I focus on the trees or the farmhouses beyond them it feels more like the fields race past us than the other way around.

"Yeah." My tummy hurts at how much I'll miss them. And him. It didn't feel this way when I left years ago to finish my graduate degree. And I'm only going to be gone for a month. Not years.

His hand slides across the leather, warm from the sun; his palm on my thigh reminds me that he belongs to me as much as I belong to him. The only thing I am tethered to is his pulse at the base of his wrist, and it will go with me wherever I need. Down this stretch of road flanked by golden fields or up the green foothills of Lancashire and everywhere in between.

He blinks away from the road to smile back at me. His forearm lies against the open window frame, golden skin and wisps of light hair traveling from elbow to wrist, his red Coca-Cola T-shirt, softer and older than Betty, that I've tried to steal more times than I can count. The sun shines like it's only for him. He's sunshine, his hair starting to curl on the top, the summer sun turning it the color of wheat.

"What?" he asks. His dimple presses at the side of his mouth in a self-conscious purse, so kissable I could scream.

"You're beautiful."

He squeezes my thigh, probably meant to be a sweet gesture of thanks, but the image of his hand, big and spread across my thigh, is porn, produced simply for pleasure and a little bit obscene.

"I'm in love with you," he says back. I don't think he knows how good he is at one-upmanship. I tell him he's strong, he tells me I'm a genius. I take him out for dinner, he takes me away for the weekend. I compliment him, he lays me bare with five words.

"*Blergh.*" Sometimes it's hard to put into words how he makes me feel. He squeezes again, the gentlest scold, and he might as well put his hands down my cutoffs. I close my eyes, resting my head against the seat, spread my own hand out on the leather.

"The first time I got in this truck," I say.

"You wondered how many people I'd fucked in this truck. You told me."

"When are you going to fuck me in this truck?"

He huffs a laugh, barely audible over the sound of the tires on asphalt. "Sorry to disappoint you."

At the click of my unbuckled seat belt, he looks over again, his foot easing off the gas. "What's wrong?"

"Nothing." I slide over the seat, the small rips and tears in the leather biting at the back of my thighs. The truck slows more. "Keep driving," I whisper.

"Lulu, what are you…*oh*," he says when my hand lands on the bulge in his faded jeans, as my palm travels down his leg and back up, as he hardens beneath my touch. "Oh," he says again, his voice decidedly neutral.

"Keep driving, Jesse." I pop the button at the top of his jeans. He blinks down at my hand then back at the road, his cheeks flushed like he's spent the whole day in the sun.

"What about the barbecue?" The steering wheel cracks beneath his palms. His chest rises and falls heavily, his stomach quivers against my wrist. "Everyone will be there."

"You just drove past the turn," I remind him and he jerks in the driver's seat to check his blind spot as the road to my parents' farmhouse shrinks in the rearview.

I take my hand away. "We can turn around if…" I offer, even if all I want is to feel him come apart against my tongue, while the wind from the road tickles the back of my neck and my knees stick to the leather seat. But Jesse flips on his signal light, slowing even more and turning onto another road that eventually leads to summer cottages and hunting camps, which don't get a lot of traffic as the end of summer nears.

"OK." I sit back.

"Oh no." He puts the truck in park as he comes skidding to a stop on the gravel shoulder, whips off his seat belt with a click and a *whirr*, and reaches for me. "I just didn't want the car to be moving with your seat belt off."

He kisses my smile, holding my face in his hands. He kisses my teeth more than he kisses my lips but there's nothing I can do about that. It's his fault I'm so happy.

"Is that a yes, then?" I ask, my hands already moving down his body, pulling the zipper on his jeans.

"To road head? Hell yes."

He lifts his hips, pushing his jeans and boxers down his legs, his cock hard, bouncing against his stomach. I kick off my shoes onto the floor of the cab so I can kneel on the seat. "Technically, it's only road head if you're *on* the road." I wrap my hand around him. I hope I never get over the thrill I get from being allowed to touch him.

"I'm not going to drive while we…" He blinks like he lost his train of thought as I pump him in my fist. "It's not safe," he grits out, when I spit into my palm and pump him again. "And illegal."

He's so handsome and rumpled. Distressed at the possibility of danger. I pull away just to frame him between my fingers, naked from the waist to the knees, lecturing me on road safety, golden, handsome, beautiful.

"What are you doing?" He gives Grump Face.

"Remembering this."

I take him in both hands and into my mouth.

His body melts into the seat. He is heat on the tip of my tongue. The wind blows through the trees outside the car window, the cicadas drone in the late Saturday afternoon heat. Inside the cab of this truck, though, there's only the sound of his breath caught between his teeth, my name whispered under his breath, the squeak of leather beneath my knees, my lips stretched around the head of his cock.

He presses his hand to the back of my neck and every point of contact, his hand, my mouth, my knees on his bench seat, my name in his mouth, they all burn inside me until I'm on fire for him, pulling at him, dragging my teeth, consumed by him and consuming him, and he's coming in my mouth with his fist in my hair, the other on his thigh, and he says, "Lulu, Lulu, Lu."

As I sit up, a car speeds by on the highway behind us. Too fast to have even noticed us parked akimbo on the side of the road. Jesse looks asleep, except for his chest, which pumps like he's squatted a new personal best, and his hand squeezing mine.

"Your turn," he says, his voice deep.

"You don't have to—" I say as he moves across the bench, pulling me on top of him, his cock soft against his bare thigh.

"But I want to," he says. "Can I anyway?"

"Absolutely you can."

Jesse pulls aside only what he needs to, pushing up my shirt and shoving the waistband of my jeans down as far as my thighs will allow. Ever since we got rid of the rules, he touches with me with abandon, reveling in the feeling of his skin against mine; he's denied himself for so long.

His fingers are thick inside me, his tongue warm against my nipple. I could keep my eyes open, keep an eye out for cars or an errant hiker, but I don't. What's the point of fucking on the bench seat of his truck if there isn't a little risk involved. I close my eyes and let myself float away on his soft exhales against my collarbone. I drown myself on the smell of his fabric softener, the truck's faded leather cleaner scent, and of him, made acute by the humidity and our sweat and his skin.

I come on his hand and he holds me against him, holds me up. He keeps his fingers inside me until I climb off him, and then cleans himself off with his mouth. My panties will be wet for the rest of the day and when I tell him so he's obnoxiously proud of that fact.

"Ready to go?" he asks. And I nod, but he doesn't start the truck until I've righted my clothes and buckled myself back in. We pull into my parents' driveway almost thirty minutes late for the barbecue. The front of the house is already banked with cars parked three deep. We walk around the back, past my apartment, toward the sound of music and Trey's laughter and Miranda's happy voice. Jay said he'll stop by with his wife and kids later. Cally and her husband and little baby. Brooke and George and Marcus and April and Buck and more of Jesse's friends, all of my people, everyone I could possibly love in one place. Audrey, too. I'll accompany her to Lancaster, her to teach and me to attend the conference and do some research on a woman who emigrated from the area to New England in the seventeenth century. I'll be back in time for the first week of the fall semester.

My chest feels too full for tonight, as if my love for them all, for this life, has increased the volume of love in my body and it pools in my chest waiting to spill out.

I stop before we turn the corner, lean against the vinyl siding, and pull Jesse with me. "Do we look OK?" I straighten his T-shirt, stuck suspiciously to his chest like he's been sweating, and run my hands through his hair in a way that makes it look like I haven't already had my hands in it.

"Yes," he says, even as he rubs at what I think might be beard rash on my neck. "You look…"

I blink up at him. "I'm in love with you, too."

"I know," he says.

"It's just that you said it to me and I didn't say it back."

He tucks my hair behind my ear, a useless gesture, presses his lips to my cheek, a gentle kiss. "You say it in other ways."

As my heart rate finally slows I understand the urgency, the need I felt to touch him before, to show him exactly how much I love him. "I won't be able to say it in those ways soon and I'll… I just…" I touch his chest, press my fingertips to his jaw, lean into the gentle wall of man in front of me. "I don't want you to be alone while I'm gone."

The last thing Jesse deserves is for another person who loves him to leave him.

He blinks, his mouth stays in its neutral line, and I kiss his lips because I can and because I think he needs me to. He looks down and away, taking a deep breath. I give him the time and space to talk when he's ready. "I won't be alone. And you're coming back, Lulu. I love you and you're coming back." He sighs. "But even if you didn't, I'd be OK. And so would you. Besides, now is as good a time as any for you to leave. I don't need any distractions the first month of my first semester back at school in a decade."

"Are you calling me a distraction?" I practically screech.

"Yes," he says solemnly.

"But I can help, you know," I insist. This is a conversation we've had more than once. "I can read your essays. I can be your tutor."

His dimple appears. "I don't think there's a lot of overlap between the history of witchcraft and practical nursing. I'd be distracted by how much I want to kiss my tutor."

I press my fist to his chest. "I'm really proud of you, you know," I say softly. "You're changing everything, your whole life, all over again."

He tips my chin up with his thumbs at my jaw. "I'm proud of you, too," he says. "For choosing to belong here. I'm so glad you're here, with me, Lulu."

"Thank you."

He presses me against the wall behind us, his hands move down my neck, my back, coming around me. His lips move soft and seeking against my neck. "We should…" He gestures to the backyard, his words pressed into my skin.

"Right." I take a deep breath, shake out my hands. "Are you sure I don't look like you just fingered me in your truck?"

He pats my hair down. "You're beautiful."

I'm scared to leave, even if it's just for a few weeks. And, of course, I'm scared I won't be good enough for the Lancaster conference, for my old colleagues. And old friends. Fears that are almost comforting in their familiarity but ones I won't entertain anymore. Well, I'll try not to.

Jesse pauses. "We're going to be OK." He puts his hand to his chest and then to mine, the touch saying more than he can.

I wrap my hands around his, keeping his palm on my chest. The one thing I've learned is to trust myself. To know that I am enough.

"Good," he says with a quiet nod and a small smile. With my hand in his, Jesse pulls me into the backyard to be with the people we love.

Epilogue

Jesse

Six Months Later

Lulu teaches late on Tuesdays. Normally, I wait for her, since my last class ends at six. I get in some study time at the library or grab a coffee with George at one of the coffee shops around campus.

Tonight, Lulu drove her own car to work and I came home early. I tidy. Wipe down the mirrors in my little home gym, pick up the hair elastics and socks she's left there. Feed the cat and freshen her water and clean her litter. I change the sheets on the bed, shower. Open the chest at the end of the bed and find the things I need. When she moved in before she left for Lancaster, she brought everything.

"Are you sure?" she'd asked. "My parents won't mind if I leave stuff in the apartment. We can do this slowly."

"I'm sure," I'd said. I wanted this place to be home when I picked her up from the airport. I wanted to bring her home and have all of her comforts at the ready. Clothes, books, a small DVD collection of rom-coms, her mugs, her favorite spoon.

The plastic bin of sex toys that we rehomed to the chest at the end of my bed to combine our collection.

"It's fast," George had said, after she'd left, but I was still hanging some of her photos and prints on the walls.

I don't know if I can explain it to him or anyone else, even myself, but both of us feel it. Even if we haven't known each other that long, we *know* each other. I know that she can't have more than one cup of coffee in the morning or her hands start to shake, that she reads her students' essays out loud under her breath, and she will only use one brand of tampon. I know that she still can't view that movie we sat down to watch together without putting her hands down my pants. Or hers. I know she still questions herself, how to deal with people at work, if she's talking too much. She knows me, too. That I listen to country music when I work out and I won't drive more than five miles above the speed limit. She knows when to give me a gentle push and say yes to time with my former coworkers from the fire department and when to let me stay home, my head in her lap, her fingers in my growing hair.

And anything we don't know, we'll learn. We're always ready to learn each other.

"Jess?" she calls from the front door. Her keys clink in the plate by the door. I center the toys on the clean bedspread. Water still clings to my back from the shower. I stand, then sit on the edge of the bed again. She knew, she agreed. She was the one who asked, for fuck's sake, but I'm still nervous.

No. Not nervous. I'm excited, horny. Vulnerable. This will be a first for us. And after, I have plans to ensure it won't be a last.

She finds me there on the end of our bed. My elbows on my knees, staring at the reason why I should have said yes to her offer to paint my toenails last night. Lulu walks quietly into the room. She sets her bag down by the door. Her feet are bare as they stop in front of me, her polish red and shining in the dim bedroom light.

"How was class?" I ask. She's in the process of taking her hair out of the high bun on top of her head. She pulls her T-shirt dress off without preamble, standing in front of me in a pair of plain white panties and a blue bra with small white flowers.

"Hold, please." She unhooks her bra and drops it on the floor on top of the dress. "Thank god." She sighs. "Sorry, what were you saying?"

My hands migrate to her hips, like they're called there, rub up and down her rib cage. "Nothing," I say to her boobs. She palms my face, laughing. Bends over me to kiss me. She tastes like the strawberry candies she has on her desk at work. "Have you eaten yet?" I ask.

"Yes," she says too quickly. She grimaces when it's clear I don't believe her. "I snacked."

"Do you want to eat first?"

"Later." She cups my face. It's her touch that calms me, the anxious energy bleeding out by my fingers, my toes curling into the rug beneath the bed. She kisses me again, quick, light. Without thought. It's one of my favorite kinds of kisses. It means I know she'll do it again. I savor each one.

"How do you want to do it?" she asks.

We got very good at FaceTime and phone sex the four weeks she was in Lancaster. Sexting and selfies each put in a hidden folder in our phones. Sometimes we'd pretend it was like before. We were touching ourselves wishing it was the other, not because we were thousands of miles apart but because it was forbidden. It made the short time apart a little more bearable. We still do it now that she's home. Touch ourselves on the couch, the bed, get each other off in the kitchen, in the truck, but never kiss. Use toys, or breath, or friction to fuck and it's wild, a little messy, crude. I love it. But it's not for tonight.

"I want to touch you," I say. "Everywhere. I want to kiss you."

She goes to shower and I crawl to the top of the bed, grabbing the lube as I go. My dick is already half-hard and I push the waistband of my briefs down. The faucet squeaks behind the closed door of the bathroom, the water splashes against the porcelain tub. I cup my balls as I imagine Lulu wiggling out of her underwear, the way her breasts sway and bounce as she moves. The metal ring of the shower curtain being pulled back sends a zip up my spine. I can see in my mind the way her skin turns pink under the water. The paths the water will take as it works its way down her body. I've watched the rivulets as they fall over her collarbone, as the path forks around her breasts, drips over her belly and into her pubic hair. I picture the suds, can smell her lavender soap, see the lather she makes between her hands with the bar of handmade soap that she brought back in bulk from England.

By the time she turns the water off, my cock is hard in my hand, slick from the pre-come beading at the tip. She steps out of the bathroom a few moments later. Her hair is back up in a bun to keep it dry, short wisps around her ears and at the back of her neck curling from the heat of the shower. Steam follows her out, moody and dramatic as she steps onto the rug, leans one knee onto the bed. She's flushed, just like I imagined. She pulls her hair down and it brushes her pebbled nipples. Even though she's wearing far fewer clothes, she reminds me of the first time I saw her. The smile on her face is the same, open and unwavering.

"You started without me."

"I'm prepping," I counter.

She crawls up the bed, pausing to press her lips to my knee, my thigh. She drags her fingers through my leg hair, nuzzles her nose through the hair on my stomach and chest, but avoids my cock, which only makes me squeeze myself harder. I move lower on the bed, letting my legs fall open as she straddles me. Lulu wraps her hands around me, one at my base, one at the head. She leans over me, spitting. We don't need the lube. The bottle is full and my dick is slick with it. But it gets me hot.

That's what friends with benefits, then phone sex, gifted us: learning exactly what the other person liked, and didn't. We got to communicate in ways we never would have when being friends was more important than anything else. It's what makes it so easy for me to say now, "I want to do it like this."

Lulu was nervous when I first asked her. "I want it to be good for you," she'd said, wringing her hands together. "What if I hurt you? What if I'm not good? I've never done it before."

But I have. And we're good at figuring things out together.

I brush the backs of my fingers over her nipples, watching as her body responds. She rubs herself against my cock, her hips moving over me. She's stunning as she tips her head back, getting herself off. I urge her with my hands on her thighs. Tell her she's beautiful, so beautiful. Beg her not to look at me like that or else this will be over long before we get a chance to start. She's hot and wet around me, the pleasure rushing from my thighs, up my back. I try to reach around the tangle of our legs and hips to prep myself, but this angle isn't working.

Lulu rises up on her knees while I shove a pillow under my hips, and the change in position lines the head of my cock with her pussy. She makes a noise, a desperate whine.

"Do it," I whisper. She doesn't need any more urging from me. Lulu sinks down on me and it's a bit awkward, but I can reach now. I play with myself, the space behind my sac, drawing my finger around my rim before pushing in. Even this shallow penetration feels like too much combined with the slow drag of her pussy along my cock.

"I think," she says. She keeps her eyes closed and I want her to open them but I'm glad she doesn't. Her breasts bounce gently, her stomach shivers with every breath. I slip my other hand between us and pet her. I have her body, and now her sounds. If I had her eyes, too, I might do something wild, something too big, too much, too soon.

Maybe ask her to marry me.

"What do you think, baby?" I ask, my voice gravel.

"I think I'm gonna come soon," she says, her voice dripping with lust, sweet like honey.

"Yeah?"

She nods and I pet her faster. She comes off my dick, knee-crawls up my body as I reach for her with my tongue and lips. It's a mercy, the taste of her in my mouth, her come on my chin. A mercy that my focus on her pleasure is the only thing keeping me from coming. She pulses against me, her hand splayed out on the wall behind the headboard, fingernails scratching at the paint. Leave a mark, I want to say. On this house. On me.

Eventually she leaves my chest. I'm cold everywhere she isn't touching me anymore. My heart pounds against my rib cage as I register the sounds of her fiddling with the harness. Slowly, I sit up. I feel dizzy, sluggish, as if I'm the one that just had the orgasm. I help her with the harness and attaching the dildo, the condom and lube. She shakes her head when I offer the bullet vibe that slots into a spot near her clit. "I want to focus on you." She grips the dildo.

"How do I look?" she whispers.

The harness itself is basic. Utilitarian, black, nylon fabric. The dildo that came with it is thin and curved.

"You look like a dream," I say. I don't pinch myself, but I want to. She glows.

We kiss, slowly. Lie back, slowly. Where we were frenzied before, now we're glacial. I take her hand in mine and we explore together. Lulu fingers me with the same studious intensity that she does everything she cares about, watching my face, listening. She asks questions, "like this?" and "more?" and "do you like that, baby?"

"I'm ready," I give as my answer.

She pours lube, on herself, on me, repositions me on the pillows, adds even more lube.

"Hey." I touch her wrist. "C'mere," I say, so I can kiss her. "I love you," I say into her warm mouth, the soft skin of her shoulder as she relaxes and guides the phallus to my entrance.

She bites her lip as she presses in, a little frown that I want to smooth with my thumb. Her first thrusts are shallow and tentative. The flush spreads over me immediately, like our skin bleeds into each other. It runs down her chest, up my stomach, into my neck.

The stretch is hot, it always is. Discomfort, more than pain, that requires a moment to adjust but once I do I ask for more, stroking myself. As she hits my prostate, I grunt. She freezes, watching me.

"It was good," I say. "It's good."

So, she tries again, and I feel it everywhere, in the bottom of my feet, my scalp. "Yes." I gasp. "Like that."

She gets physical, lifting one leg onto her shoulder, then the other, and the angle makes me say, "Oh fuck."

She's new to thrusting and Lulu sweats, the hair at her temples turning dark. She bats my hands away from my own dick and takes over. My heart beats there, in her fist. My body is both melted into the mattress and strung tight.

I want to come now.

I want this to last forever.

"I didn't know it could be like this," she says, steadying herself with one hand on the pillow beneath my head, looking down at me like I'm her most prized possession, a new-to-her old book, the T-shirt she's always trying to steal.

"What could be like this, baby?"

"I didn't know love could feel like this."

"What—" I gasp as she squeezes the head of my cock.

Arousal, sharp and sudden, stabs through me. My whole body contracts. My eyes roll back. "What does it feel like?"

Instead of answering, she thrusts deeper, a little harder. Her wrist twists as she jerks me. I hear her say, "Oh!" as I come, pulsing and pulsing in her hand. It splashes on my chest and neck. Moves through my whole body and I can't see straight, can't think. I reach blindly for her, just to hold her hand, and we find each other sticky and warm.

She kisses me wherever she can reach, my arms and my chest. She sucks at the come on my skin. I curl up and pull her mouth to mine, taste her and me and finally my body stops convulsing. Lulu pulls out slowly. She walks like a newborn foal to the bathroom. I drift on the bed, on a cloud. I even fall asleep but wake up immediately when she comes back with a warm cloth. Once we're somewhat clean, Lulu notches herself into my side, pulling my arm over her shoulders, resting her head on my chest. She rubs up and down my body, kisses me softly. We should probably shower. She should probably eat. So should I. But for now, I'm happy to bask in the afterglow.

"What does it feel like?" I ask again.

"What does what feel like?" She sounds sleepy.

"This. Us. Love."

She hums. "I'm so used to feeling things intensely. Like, too intensely. I don't laugh, I cackle. I don't get mad, I rage. I'm not sad. I'm devastated. I thought love felt like that, you know? Something that burned really hot and then..." She holds up a fist and watches it explode with a quiet *poof*. "Gone. Loving you feels like...like...not too hot. Not like I'll burn myself. It feels warm, like a sunbeam, and it feels hazy. And full. Your love feels safe."

"Yeah," I say. "So does yours." My voice feels gruff. Lulu will always be better at words than me. Which is why, instead of saying something eloquent, I ask, "Do you want to do this, like, forever?"

"What?" She flips onto her stomach.

I roll us together toward the bedside table and open the drawer. One of the reasons I decided to move the sex toys to the chest was so I could hide things in here. I rummage, one-handed, for the velvet box, and roll us back.

"Jesse?" she says, as I place the box on my stomach.

"It's not… I don't want you to think it's one of *those* rings. We haven't spoken about…marriage." I get caught up on the word. "And we haven't been together for long. I know we're doing everything out of order. And I'm not in any rush. But I just wanted you to know that you're it for me and this feels like the best way to do that. And if later on you want to make it more official, we can."

She sits up, naked, glowing in the dim light. With a quiet creak, she opens the box. And smiles.

"It's not much," I say, quickly, even though when I saw it I thought of her immediately.

"Shut up," she says. "I love it." Lulu holds the ring up and the knot in the simple gold band catches the light.

"Knots are supposed to represent romance and friendship," I say. I sit up on the bed, too, finally in charge of my body again. "I was going to do this later. On the weekend. I had more things I was going to say." I rub my hands down my thighs as my palms sweat. "I wanted to explain this better."

She shakes her head. "Just say what you feel."

"I love you," I say simply. "You're my best friend. I know I won't always say the right thing. Or speak at all, but I'm learning. And I belong to you."

Her eyes shine with tears. I think mine do, too. She slips the ring on her finger, but it's too big, sliding around. "Shit. I'm sorry. I'll—"

"Yes," she says. She beams. "I want to do this forever with you, too."

"Yeah?"

Lulu kisses me, our skin pressed together, still a little sweaty, sticky. I follow the curves of her body with my hands, learn them, memorize them, before I realize. I'll get to do this forever.

"Yeah."

★ ★ ★ ★ ★

Author Note

I wrote much of *The Friendship Study* while going through the process of getting a diagnosis for ADHD; something that I only realized I had after my daughter was diagnosed. Lulu, in many ways, experiences the world like I do. While she does not have an official diagnosis in the book, canonically, Lulu is neurodivergent. Many adult women, like Lulu and like myself, are neurodivergent without knowing it or are receiving their diagnoses later in life; this is often because the way we socialize femme-identifying folks means that their symptoms present differently than traditionally recognized symptoms, which are usually exhibited in folks who are socialized as masc-identifying. If you are also neurodivergent but you don't see yourself and your experiences in Lulu, or if you are neurotypical but don't feel like Lulu represents what you have observed as neurodivergent behaviors, that is OK. The thing that I love most about neurodivergence is that there is no one universal experience. Every single neurodiverse brain is, exactly that, diverse.

Jesse uses a mobility aid in some parts of the book to assist him with a previous injury. While I have not had to use a mobility aid like Jesse's before, it was important to me to portray an authentic experience. I conducted research about the use of mobility aids and also relied on the experiences of people in my life who have used them, either temporarily or for a prolonged period of time, after experiencing an accident, like Jesse.

Acknowledgments

In certain ways, writing books gets easier every time I do it. I take the lessons I learned in the last book and apply them to the new one. I learn new lessons, of course, but each time I do this the pressure I put on myself changes. However, writing acknowledgments does not get any easier; if anything it just gets more emotional.

The support I receive as I embark on this dream of mine continues to astound me. *The Friendship Study* started as a very different book, (what feels like) a very long time ago. Thank you, Lyssa Mia Smith, for reading that early version and for loving it. You made me believe in this book again. Esther and Saniya, thank you for taking the time to read this book, for your unhinged text messages, and for your enthusiasm for these characters. I can never fully describe what it means to me to know that I have found complete strangers who always seem to get what I'm doing as an author, and who have become such wonderful friends. Thank you to the Ottawa Fire Service, especially rookie Kyle, who invited me into your world and let me ask weird, probing, or silly questions. I appreciate the work you do for our community. Thank you, Matthieu Desloges, for blasting the same few country songs throughout your CrossFit Open and Quarter Final tests. You helped me appreciate the genre and better connect with Jesse. Thank you, Alexis Shotwell, for always having the smartest solutions to my writing problems. Thank you, Karine Shrum, for allowing me to use my personal training time to discuss the merits of specific sex toys (and for fixing my squat).

None of this would be possible without the fantastic team at Carina Adores/Harlequin. You put your all into our books and I am so grateful for you. A special thank-you to my editor, Stephanie Doig (and Birdie); I continue to count myself as the luckiest girl in publishing, that you picked my first book out of the pile and thought, *yes, this is the one.* There is no one I trust more with my books.

Kiki, as I write this, we are approaching our four-year anniversary as agent and client! Happy anniversary! The traditional gift of four-year anniversaries is fruit, and well, we're fruity enough already, I think. Thank you for taking the time to call me whenever you can sense my panic spirals, for explaining things to me like I am a four-year-old because my anxiety requires it, for continuing to allow me to terrorize you with anecdotes about my very lucrative adolescent horse penis cleaning business, and for your advocacy for my work, and your belief in my ideas. I hope I make you feel as proud of me as I am to collaborate with you.

So much of this book was written on video calls with Rosie Danan. So much of my life is spent on video calls with Rosie Danan, to be honest. I would not have it any other way. Rosie, whether you are across the ocean, improving the entire Western Hemisphere with your presence in it, or by my side, I am so thankful for you. Thank you for being my best friend, dearest one. I'll see you in horny jail.

My family continues to be my biggest supporters. Thank you, Mom and Steve, Susan, and Meaghan, for giving me two of the most invaluable gifts: your time and support. I couldn't do any of this without you.

I have a habit of writing my acknowledgments section like I'd give an Oscars acceptance speech, except there's no music to play me out and no one can figure out how to shut off my mic. All this to say, I'm almost finished.

A quick thank-you to Taylor Swift, specifically for "Daylight," and Twin Atlantic for "Crash Land"; large sections of this book wouldn't have been possible without your songs.

Writing is often a selfish pursuit. It causes me to forget important dates, to not see the mess in the kitchen, to be unavailable for play. To the two people who bear the brunt of this selfishness: oh gosh, do I love you. Karou, my daughter/werewolf (that's a secret)/cheetah/astronaut. You are astounding. You are terrifying. Please never change. If you ever read this, I hope you see in Lulu what a gift your neurodivergence is.

As a writer, I always feel inadequate when I try to describe with words how I feel about you, Michael, or what your love means to me. I think this book is the closest I've ever been able to get. *The Friendship Study* is very much an ode to you, to us, to falling in love with your best friend. What an incredible gift, that I get to write our romance with you.